SOCIAL
LIVES

ALSO BY WENDY WALKER

Four Wives

SOCIAL LIVES

WENDY WALKER

ST. MARTIN'S GRIFFIN

NEW YORK

SOCIAL LIVES. Copyright © 2009 by Wendy Walker. All rights reserved. Printed in the United States of America. For information, address St. Martin's Press, 175 Fifth Avenue, New York, N.Y. 10010.

www.stmartins.com

THE LIBRARY OF CONGRESS HAS CATALOGED THE HARDCOVER EDITION AS FOLLOWS:

Walker, Wendy, 1967–
    Social lives / Wendy Walker.—1st ed.
        p.   cm.
    ISBN 978-0-312-37816-5
    1. Rich people—Fiction.   2. Housewives—Fiction.   3. Married women—Fiction.   4. Suburban life—Fiction.   5. Wilshire (Conn. Town)—Fiction.
I. Title.

PS3623.A35959 S63   2009
813'.6—dc22

                                                                    2009016492

ISBN 978-0-312-37817-2 (trade paperback)

First St. Martin's Griffin Edition: December 2010

10   9   8   7   6   5   4   3   2   1

As always, for my beautiful boys

ACKNOWLEDGMENTS

WRITING CONTINUES TO BE an incredible journey, and I am thankful for the many people who are filling my tank, fixing my flat tires, and traveling alongside me: agent Matt Bialer; editor Jennifer Weis and the team at St. Martin's Press; publicist Tolly Moseley at Phenix & Phenix Literary Publicists; and my other employer, Amy Newmark at Chicken Soup for the Soul.

My deep gratitude also goes out to Terri Walker for cheering me on; Estel Kempf and Charlie Biamonte for their wisdom; Grant Walker for being a fabulous uncle; Jennifer Walker for always making me laugh; Becky McNulty for being my big sister; Sharon Cohen for two decades of friendship; Caroline, Rhys, and Sam Scheibe for being the best cousins in the world; Cheryl Walker for her courage in life; Kris and Steve Pecheone for their open door; my incredible friends who are always there; and the three wonderful boys who inspire me daily.

SOCIAL LIVES

ONE

THE HALSTEADS

JACQUELINE HALSTEAD RUSHED OUT of the bedroom to the study in the adjoining suite. The briefcase was on her husband's desk, closed, and as had been his practice over the past several weeks, locked. That had been the first piece of hard evidence, this practice of securing his briefcase at home, though it had taken her far too long to see it for what it was. *Evidence.* The moodiness, the weight loss, the late nights had finally brought the picture into focus.

Her movements were carefully devised and practiced. She positioned herself around the briefcase, then made a note of the numbers on the lock: 70412. He was changing the combination daily now, though she knew from his demeanor that the distrust was not meant for her. She had a finely tuned sense for these things, for detecting the truth within an embrace, a look. *No.* He trusted her, she was certain. It was not the fear of being discovered that had him twisted in so many knots, but instead the guilt of a caring man. His wife, their children, and all that was at stake were the worries that were eating at him from the inside. And still the lock was changing.

Thinking back over the past months, she realized how tightly she had closed her eyes, not wanting to see, not wanting to believe that the life that had lifted her out of darkness could itself be in peril. She had become complacent over the years, trusting and as close to carefree as her history would allow. She had come to think of her past as something she had shed, like a snail outgrowing its shell and slipping into a new one. Her stupidity was maddening.

There was a saving grace. Her proficiency at seeing into the hidden corners of a life, especially her own, had not completely vanished. Not even with seventeen years of being Mrs. Daniel Halstead. The wires of suspicion were still there inside her head, the ones set in place by a childhood of fear. And now thoughts moved across them freely, the consequences of different scenarios weighed. Plans of escape devised.

She took a long breath and listened for the shower. With her children and nanny at a movie, and their dog, Chester, locked outside, the house was unusually quiet. The shower, with its oversized head and powerful jets, was still pounding against the marble tiles, broken only by the body of her husband as he moved about, unaware that his wife was breaching his trust for the third time in the course of a week. With nothing but a towel wrapped around her slender body, her long dark hair dripping wet on her face, she turned the knobs with shaky hands. One after the other, she entered the digits of the fail-safe code that had come with the briefcase. She finished the code sequence and popped open the lock. Her movements quicker now that she was committed to the treason, she flipped through the papers, sorting out the work documents from those related to the U.S. Attorney's investigation. The letter was still there, tucked deep within a back compartment. RE: INVESTIGATION OF HALSTEAD, WHITTIER, ET AL. Daniel's firm. The government had not filed any charges, satisfied at the moment to make inquiries about the location of certain funds. Nothing had made it to the public eye. Not yet. And as far as she could tell, only a handful of the investors in David's hedge fund suspected that their money might have been mishandled. None of this concerned her as profoundly as the name on that letter. She looked at it again, as though seeing it there in the bold black ink one more time would make her believe it any more or less than she did. DAVID HALSTEAD.

Working quickly, she found what she'd been looking for—a new letter. It was the first one in eight days, and it was not from the government. This one was from a law firm, one she'd heard of because of its reputation for high-profile criminal defense work. Dirty cops. Public corruption. And now her husband. She reached for a pencil, wrote down the name of the lawyer who'd signed the letter. She jotted down the numbers of federal statutes that were being threatened. There would be little time now, so she worked furiously, trying to analyze what she could, writing down the rest. She felt her stomach tighten, but she forced herself to continue as though she were not reading the blueprint for her own life's destruction.

Finishing the last paragraph, she tucked the letter back where she'd found it, then made a quick study of the briefcase contents. She pulled some papers up, others down, until she was as certain as she could be that they were laid out the way she'd found them moments before. The sound of the shower dying to a drizzle made her stop by reflex, but there was no time. She willed herself to move faster now, to concentrate as she pulled down the lid of the case, clicked the clasps into place, then spun the number dials back to 70412.

Outside the study, she felt it again, the wave of panic as she held the door. Had it been open or closed, the study door? A small detail, but one more detail that would have to be explained. And it was just that very thing, the slow disintegration of explanations, that had given David away and could easily work toward her own exposure.

"Jacks?" He was calling for her. She'd left the bathroom the moment he'd stepped into the shower, and by any accounting, she should now be in her closet dressing for the nursery school benefit.

She didn't answer—if she could hear him, she would have no excuse for her absence other than being in a place she had no business to be.

Think! But her mind was on the letter, the notes in her hand, and the work that needed to be done. She would scan their bank statements, the weblike array of the family's personal investments, their 401(k)—their only nest egg after all this family-raising was said and done and they were put out to pasture by a world that favors the young. There was little equity in the house after the loan for the new wing they'd put on last year, and the severe drop in the housing market. Nothing remained in the checking account beyond what was needed to pay the bills. Where could it be, the money that was missing from the fund? And why, *good God, why*, would David take it?

Closed. She felt the air reach her lungs. *The study door had been closed.* She turned off the light then pulled the door shut, turning the knob to slide it into place without a sound.

The hallway was quiet again. With light steps, she returned to the bedroom where David was standing inside his closet, dry and partially clothed in boxers and a fresh undershirt. He was visibly distracted, and Jacks knew in that instant that she had not been discovered.

"Aren't you going to get dressed?" he said to her without turning around. He was so thin now, she could see his ribs protruding through the cotton undershirt.

"I won't be long." Sitting on the bed so she could slide the notes under the mattress, she kept her eyes glued to his back. She felt the sickness in her gut, the same restlessness of an insurgent that she'd had for days now. That was what she had become, an insurgent in her own life, a spy embedded within her own family. In every room it followed her—the bright, sun-filled kitchen, the cozy family room, the delicate pink enclaves of her three daughters. The places that had been her haven, that had held her in the embrace of comfort and safety, were now the places where she had to hide what she knew, what she felt. And with every breath her husband took, she waited for him to drop the bomb.

David was humming as he moved about his closet, surely out of nerves. He was a good man, no matter what he'd done. He loved their children as much as she did, and it would be killing him to know that their fate might be sealed by whatever crimes he had committed. Their reliance on him had been the unwritten contract between them, the standard agreement between men and women in places like Wilshire. Husband works. Wife tends to the house, children, and the husband's needs. And she had done that, produced three children, overseen their care, managed the house. She had cultivated one of the most envied social lives in Wilshire. They were close friends with the most coveted family in this town, the Barlows, and that had been her doing. Hours of lunches, exercise classes, reading groups, and school benefits. From the book fairs to the nail salon, she had done the social research and placed herself wherever she needed to be. Getting to this position had been her job, and she had done it well.

That they would lose all of that was a given, and she didn't care. Everything she'd done for them socially had been calculated to keep David happy so he could do his job—the one that brought home the money. And it was the money that paid for the rooms, the schools, the happily-ever-after. That was the end goal of the professional's wife. They had nothing without the job, which was the very thing David had placed in jeopardy. Even if he avoided prison, no one would ever trust him again. And for Jacks, the working world was as far gone as her own childhood. It had been more than seventeen years since she'd earned a paycheck as a waitress. What would she put on her résumé now? Still attractive after bearing three children? What about her perfectly decorated house? Her trendsetting taste? Her honed sense of timing that made it possible for her to get so close to the Barlows? No. None of that would be worth a damned thing. After seventeen years, she would return to the workforce exactly where she'd left it. If they really lost everything, if David went to jail, how could she raise three children on the salary of a middle-aged waitress?

She was in her closet now, moving robotically from section to section as she chose the various items. Undergarments, skirt, blouse, shoes. She could smell David's cologne drifting in from the bathroom, and it brought back, for the smallest moment, the feeling of him—David the man, beyond the provider, the father. There had been times when he'd held her and she'd felt herself lost in his strength, his certainty, when he'd been able to reach behind the curtains where she kept her true self, the one with the memories and the pain. And in those instances, she had believed that the struggle could finally end, that her life might actually be what it appeared from the outside. Good. Happy. Normal. She inhaled deeper and pulled back the tears that were starting to come. No matter what he meant to her outside all of this, she could not leave her life, and the lives of her girls, in his hands. She would not lay herself down in the arms of faith. That was not the way of a survivor.

She'd been through it in her head and kept coming back to the same conclusion. Seventeen years ago, she'd let go of her raft, the one that had kept her afloat but could never fight the tide, and climbed onto David's cruise liner. If what she believed now was true—if that ship was about to go down, taking her and the kids along with it—then it was time to find a lifeboat.

TWO

THE BARLOWS

"Do it, Daddy! Do it!"

Melanie Barlow screamed with excitement, her four-year-old body jumping up and down at the edge of the pool.

"Should I do it?" her father teased. He was standing at the end of the high diving board, dripping wet, and smiling at his audience.

Two more small voices joined in. "Do it, Daddy! Now!"

Seated in a lounge chair a bit farther back from Mellie and her twin brothers, Caitlin Barlow pretended not to care, her ear glued to a cell phone. At fourteen, she was old enough to see all this for what it was, and had recently grown tired of her father's juvenile efforts to endear himself to his children. Then, of course, there was the deep trouble in which she now found herself, and the way it had trapped her inside a vault constructed from defiance and shame.

"I'm gonna do it!" Ernest Barlow threatened one last time before leaping spread-eagle from the diving board. As he sailed through the air, the shrieks of his children filled his ears until he hit the water with a loud smack and sank beneath its surface.

Nine-year-old Matthew was impressed. "Aw, man, that's *gotta* hurt!"

The smaller of the twins, John, had suddenly taken to repeating every word Matthew spoke, and now agreed wholeheartedly. "That's *gotta* hurt!"

"Shut up!" Caitlin yelled from the lounge chair, shaking her head at the escalation of her father's immaturity, and her own annoyance at his attempt to balance the scale against years of absence.

Ignoring their sister, as was common practice, the three young ones gathered near the deep-end ladder, staring into nine feet of dark blue-gray water that, to their eyes, was as mysterious as the depths of the ocean. Mellie moved closer, leaning over to get a better view of the bottom. Her brothers followed, and Matthew grabbed the straps of his sister's suit to keep her from tumbling in. It was then, and only then, that their champion appeared, popping out with a loud roar from the edge where they were standing, scaring them into hysterical laughter.

They parted as their father climbed out, making room for him to pass through their ranks and find a towel. It was late fall and the air was crisp, sneaking in through the glass walls that enclosed the pool complex.

Barlow (as he liked to be called—partly because the alternative was Ernie, and mostly because he could get away with it) dried his face, then wrapped the towel around his broad shoulders.

"Well?"

Matthew and John offered their hands for high fives. "Awesome!" Matthew said.

His echo followed in short order. "Awesome!" John was smiling, his eyes wide.

"Check out this belly!" Barlow opened the towel to reveal streaks of red against golden flesh from forehead to knees. He tousled Mellie's hair. "Pretty gruesome, huh?"

Mellie nodded as she took it in, not sure what she thought of their glee at watching their father hurt himself, and his willingness to do it. Then there was the inevitable influence of Caitlin, whose response, though unwelcome, seemed inherently more appropriate.

After a moment, her father's need, which was innately felt by the four-year-old, rushed in, forcing a smile to gather around her plump cheeks and eventually overwhelming her. She fell into his arms and gave him a hug. "Good, Daddy."

Barlow kissed her forehead, his eyes glancing first through the glass walls to the stone mansion in the distance, and then to his oldest daughter.

"Want to better that, Cait?" His tone was sarcastic, drawing a carefully perfected look of disgust that was as brief as it was cutting.

Caitlin Barlow rolled her eyes, then looked away as she dialed up the volume of her own voice on the phone call.

"I can't tonight," she said into the phone. "I have to help babysit." Again, the disgust resounded in the early evening air, a silent predator circling around Barlow and the younger three. She couldn't stop her father from employing his tactics, but she could infiltrate each maneuver, dispensing a subtle sense of doubt that would stand between Barlow and his children's love like an invisible bullshit shield. And given the suddenness of the change in his daughter's overall disposition, Barlow was at a loss as to how to dismantle it.

A soft monotone voice seeped from a small post built into the stone tile floor. It was Rosalyn Barlow, the mother, whose interruption of their fun had become a daily occurrence.

"It's seven o'clock. Time to come up."

Letting go of little Mellie, Barlow seized the moment. "Darnit! And I was just about to try one on my back."

Matthew's eyes were still on the post, as though his mother might somehow appear, catching up to her voice like thunder to a lightning bolt. "You have time! Do it, Daddy!" he said.

"Yeah, do it, Daddy!" John was at his side, tugging at his suit and looking at him with pleading eyes.

Barlow shook his head, feigning regret. "No, no. Mommy's the boss. Grab your towels, and let's go."

His answer came as no surprise to any of them, least of all Mellie, who was already walking outside to the golf cart that would deliver them back to the house. Not one of them needed reminding that Mommy was the boss, and enforcing her rules to the disappointment of his children was as much a part of Barlow's self-amusement as was breaking them.

Barlow gathered kids, towels, goggles, and shoes, then loaded everyone into the golf cart.

"You coming?" he said to Caitlin.

She took a long second to excuse herself from the call, then placed her hand over the receiver. "I'll walk."

"Suit yourself. The boss and I are leaving at eight. It's your behind if you're not ready."

Caitlin waved him off. "Whatever."

As he climbed beside the driver, Barlow sized up the battle. There'd been points on both sides, but overall, he felt victorious. The young ones were happy, and he would now leave this new war with the girl who'd become a "teenstranger" to the more capable adversary waiting inside the house.

"Move over, Roger, and watch how it's done," he said, smiling now. In a few minutes there would be dinner, baths, homework for the boys, then bed. He listened to his children giggling behind him, and he knew. The fun was over, but at the end of this day, the fun was all they would remember.

From the window in her dressing suite, Rosalyn Barlow watched the cart bump up and down across the sprawling lawn as it made the long journey from the pool. Having pushed aside the driver, Barlow was at the wheel and moving fast to impress the kids as they shivered through their wet towels. With nothing on himself but a suit and towel, his dark overgrown hair blowing wildly against his tanned, unshaven face, he looked like a child himself. And at forty-five years of age, looking like a child meant looking like an idiot. Still, it suited him, Rosalyn supposed as she moved to her vanity table to finish her makeup. *My brilliant billionaire idiot husband.* She leaned forward to study her eyes, holding them perfectly still to apply a light brown liner. They were, she liked to believe, the eyes of her mother—almond shaped, pale green. Calm. Steady. Even with Barlow's hooting and hollering coming within earshot and the image it provoked of him swerving about, tearing up the grass and endangering the lives of her children, she could hold their expression. Their *absence* of expression.

She finished the liner, replaced the plastic top to the pencil, and gave the mascara a slight shake. He was a complete child now, wasn't he? It was more an acknowledgment than a judgment, and was perfectly justified. The one-time workaholic entrepreneur was now a very wealthy, but retired, little boy. Every purposeless day brought with it further regression toward infantile behavior. Then there was the alcohol. Cocktails at five. Cocktails at six. Cocktails all night until he passed out in a pool of sweat and drool on her fine upholstery.

She brushed on the mascara, then dabbed her lashes with a tissue to remove the small pearls of liquid that had failed to spread evenly. Leaning back, she placed the cap on the mascara and twisted it between her long manicured fingers.

Late nights playing poker. Driving around in that ridiculous Creamsicle-orange Corvette. Golf and tennis all summer. Paddle tennis and skiing all winter. The hockey league. *Hockey*, of all the blessed things. A long sigh sneaked out of her body before she could catch it, and she felt herself shudder, as though she could shake off the source of its inception. She leaned into the mirror again and checked the stillness in her eyes. *Good*, she thought. *We're just fine*. She studied her skin tone, pale ivory, before selecting the lipstick.

Caitlin hadn't been in the cart. Of course not. Her oldest daughter had remained behind in an effort to avoid her father. She would stay there, Rosalyn imagined, just long enough to cause them to worry about being late to the benefit. Yes, she would appear just in the nick of time for babysitting duty, which was, in fact, little more than a contrived punishment. Their two nannies could easily handle the children. Still, there had to be some consequences after what had transpired.

A soft red, just a few shades beyond her natural lip color. It would go with the neutral silk blouse and beige suit. It had been two days. Everyone would know, and even if they didn't, Rosalyn had to make that assumption, and the decisions that followed. They would not decline the benefit. Regardless of the humiliation—which was appropriate and which she would have to display (within reason, of course)—they would attend and hold their heads high. And, of course, support Mellie's school. The Barlows were dignified survivors of this little tragedy. That was what they would leave behind when they politely excused themselves before the dancing began. Dressed conservatively in her neutrals, discreet makeup, pinned-back blond hair, and nothing to adorn her lovely hands but a simple gold wedding band, Rosalyn Barlow would let them all have their moment of glee. If she didn't do it now, her first real outing since the tragedy, they would hunger for it like savages. No—she had to throw them a bone. Then she could get on with the work of rising above it all.

She heard the cart pulling around the side of the house. She listened as the team of young Polish nannies bounded down the steps from the servants' quarters to meet the children. Then the outside door closing, and those heavy accents. "Give to me towel. . . . Upstairs wid you, Miss Mellie. . . . Out of wets suits."

She pressed a tissue to her lips, peeled it off, and checked her face one last time. She practiced a smile, went over in her head her carefully concocted responses to any comments she might have to endure. *Are you all right? How's Caitlin? How's Barlow handling it?* Rosalyn adjusted her face slightly. Pleased with the expression, she committed it to her memory, then rose from the table. She was ready when her husband entered the room, out of breath and dripping wet. His face was flushed with the thrill of childish antics and the cool evening air.

"We're leaving at seven thirty, darling," Rosalyn said sweetly.

Barlow pulled off his swimsuit, dropped it on the antique oriental, then used his towel to dry his hair. Naked in the middle of their room, he answered his wife. "I thought it started at eight."

Rosalyn stood before him, seemingly indifferent to the exposed genitalia that were jiggling about as he toweled off the mop on his head.

"We should get there early tonight."

Barlow looked up, puzzled. "Early?"

"We should be the first ones there."

"Aren't we always the *last* ones there?" The question was rhetorical. Still, Barlow couldn't imagine what the hell she was up to now.

"Yes, darling, you're right. We usually are. But tonight, we will be the first ones. And we're taking my car, if you don't mind."

Suddenly aware of his wife's eyes upon him, Barlow stopped drying his hair and wrapped the towel around his waist. He studied her as she stood there before him, arms draped delicately beside her petite frame in a demure pose, bland outfit, flat shoes. Her hair was unusually casual, her face colorless. And where were the jewels he'd bought her? It was calculated, he knew. Everything his wife did was carefully planned to achieve some end result, though it was rarely apparent to him until the plan bore its fruit. He thought about this night. Nursery school benefit. They'd been to a dozen of them over the years. With the oldest boy away at prep school, it hardly seemed possible they still had to massage the preschool system. It was so very contrived. Parents got to meet one another—though this was a joke, since you had to know everyone to get into the damned place. And Rosalyn practically owned this school. She chaired the board. She donated half the operating budget. She hired, she fired, and hers was the final stamp of approval, or rejection, for the wee little applicants dying for a spot at Wilshire's finest learning institution for the under-five crowd. This was her show, and if he was remembering correctly, this was usually her night to shock and awe.

Then it hit him.

"Holy shit." He rubbed his face, now in a state of genuine disbelief.

"What?" Rosalyn asked coyly, though she'd enabled the battle that was coming and was fully prepared to wage it.

"Is this what I think it is?"

"What?" she asked, more fervently this time.

"Is this about Cait . . . ?"

Rosalyn waved him off as though she were surprised at the accusation. "Oh, don't even—"

"Don't even what? This is all about Cait, isn't it? The clothes and hair. Taking your car. Arriving early."

"And what if it is?"

Barlow was stunned. How was it possible he kept overestimating his wife?

"I thought this was over. She had her day of suspension. She met with the counselor. For Christ's sake, how long is this going to be an issue?"

Rosalyn crossed her arms now, though her face remained calm. Barlow, who kept his head conveniently buried in the sand, would never understand the subtleties of their world. "This is our first night out after—"

"After what? You think anybody cares about this? She's a *teenager*. . . ."

"Uhh . . ." Rosalyn was on the verge of being disgusted by her husband's ignorance. She took a breath to retrieve her composure. Then she struck.

"Our lovely *teenager* was caught in a hallway with a boy's dick in her mouth. She's *our* daughter. Believe me, Barlow, *everyone* cares!"

Barlow stood before his wife as the vulgarity of her words encircled his head. This was her best move, the one he usually forgot in the face of her perfect breeding and skilled aloofness. Just when one was expecting a delicate pearl of wisdom, she could drop something like this, something so dreadful and ugly, yet delivered with a silky tone. It was downright eerie.

"You're right about one thing: She's our *daughter*. And I don't want this whole twisted, morally corrupt town to think we're ashamed of her."

"That's not what I'm doing."

Barlow's face was red with the heat of anger. "Of course it is, Rosalyn. You're showing contrition. Why don't you put on a red dress with a neckline to your navel, and we'll dance on the tables! I mean, fuck 'em if they think they're better than us just because our daughter was the one who got caught!"

Rosalyn let out a long sigh and unfolded her arms. "I'm not ashamed of our daughter. But if we don't do this my way, it won't be over. If you want it to be over, shave, shower, put on a blue blazer, and get in my car by seven thirty." Her voice was calm, her face steady. She was right, and somewhere inside him, Barlow knew it. Whether or not he liked it was another matter altogether, and not one with which Rosalyn was overly concerned at the moment.

She walked past him, leaving him naked, standing on the wet carpet. When she was gone, her footsteps no longer heard against the wooden staircase, Barlow shook his head and accepted the defeat. He walked to the table in the corner, where he kept a decanter of scotch, and poured himself a large glass. As he let the alcohol settle his nerves, he peered out the window onto his estate. Good fortune had brought them significant wealth. They were the wealthiest family in Wilshire, the wealthiest town in the country. In the whole goddamn country. There was no way this was what life should look like after all that accomplishment. A wife he couldn't understand. Boredom. Loneliness. And now a daughter whose teen years were slipping away from them like a wet bar of soap.

Right out of their grasp, Caitlin was sliding—into *what*, Barlow could hardly fathom. What would posses a young woman who would never have to rely on a man for anything to perform sexual favors in a school hallway? What world was she living in? Their oldest had sailed through these years—sports, schoolwork, PlayStation. His world had been straightforward, and Barlow had believed this to be evidence of the invincibility his wealth provided.

He closed his eyes as he swallowed more scotch. With his gift to focus, he chased from his lids the image of her on her knees and instead played across them her broad smile, the one she used to get when playing with Mellie. He let his ears remember her infectious laugh, more like a child's silly giggle, and he thought now how he would sometimes think the sound was coming from Mellie and not Caitlin at all. Those days were months gone, but he would not believe they were over. This was a problem. A glitch. And though he recognized the arrogance his conclusion implied, it came nonetheless. He had accumulated over a billion dollars in wealth by the age of forty-five. This problem had a solution, and he was hell-bent on finding it.

THREE

THE LIVINGSTONS

IT WAS A FULL closet. That was not the problem. Actually, it was *more* than a closet, at eight feet by fifteen. With plush cream carpeting, adjustable track lighting, and its own temperature control, it was an actual *room* by any reasonable measure outside of Wilshire, Connecticut. Standing at its epicenter, surrounded by an absurd amount of clothing and footwear, and now overwhelmed by her own indecision, Sara Livingston wondered where else a room such as this would be demeaned to closet status. Only in Wilshire, Connecticut, it seemed. And it *was* keeping to scale with the six-thousand-square-foot house, the same one that had turned out to be unlivable after all and was now under construction. That was a whole *other* story. Closet? Room? What did it matter? That this closet-room was occupying her thoughts to such a degree was, she knew, one last (and entirely futile) attempt to distract herself from the task at hand.

She should have had it down after four months, the wardrobe choices for a Wilshire mom. Neat slacks, button-down shirt for school pickup. Black stretch pants with a T-back sports shirt for exercise classes (if she ever found time for them). And for the present occasion, the nursery school benefit, that evasive sexy formal. The trick here was the "sexy" part. She had the body for it—long legs, moderate height, a cute light brown bob, and healthy C-cup breasts (all hers)—but that did not help with the choices. Short skirt? Low neckline? Bare shoulders? Stiletto heels with lots of straps, shoes that cried out for attention, first to the ankle, and then, of course, to the leg? For once— *Christ, is it too much to ask?*—she wanted to fade into the backdrop, go unnoticed.

But for Sara, sexy formal was more complicated than it seemed. It was one thing to be sexy, and quite another to be slutty. To be slutty, or not, was currently the domain of a small clique of Wilshire women who had snatched it up as the latest fashion trend when they'd grown tired of seventies-retro. It was their trademark, a stake inside some invisible hierarchy that Sara did not fully understand. But it seemed to indicate that they had risen above the discretion of others in this town. If they wanted to wear thigh-high leather boots and thick black eyeliner to pick up their preschoolers, then by God, they were going to do just that.

This was her conclusion, after much analysis (and analyzing her new environment had risen to the point of obsession), that there was, in fact, an invisible hierarchy. It was not strictly based on wealth, though wealth was a prerequisite. Social connections seemed to be of equal importance, and getting them required a certain level of wealth. It was confounding to Sara, who had a degree in journalism from Columbia and, until moving to Connecticut, had thought herself a capable analyst of the world around her. Her pedigree aside, there was an art to rising through the ranks in Wilshire that still eluded her after months of astute and careful observation. She had stormed into this town with high expectations. This was a place of educated people, where even the stay-home moms were former professionals, well traveled, and in many cases, transplants from Manhattan like herself. They were just like her, and yet no matter what she did, she could not manage to be just like them. Every decision she'd made from day one had been wrong. First, it was the car she'd chosen. A red minivan. Minivans were, apparently, out. In were monstrous three-row SUVs: Lexus, Mercedes, Cadillac.

After the car, it was the choice of decorator, then the choice of everything the decorator had shown her. She'd gone with French country when old European was in, chunky white dishes when delicate china was back in favor. And the deer that roamed as freely as New York pigeons had devoured every flower she had planted. Now she had bare stems when everyone else managed to keep flowers.

She had adjusted her goals within the first month. Her new aim was modest. She had no need to be Rosalyn Barlow—Wilshire's reigning queen—or even to befriend her, for that matter. What she now wanted was *not* to be noticed. And at the moment, that meant choosing something on the sexy scale that wouldn't cross the line.

She loosened the sash of her silk robe as she walked to the built-in drawers containing her undergarments. She pulled open the drawer with the panties and thongs, and made the first decision of the night. Panties, no question. After fighting with her contractor over the price of crown molding, then driving two hours to pick out antique light fixtures for the new living room, and ending her day by spending more than sixty dollars on gas, she just didn't have it in her to tolerate a string up her ass.

The bra would be more difficult. Low-cut padded, low-cut push-up, strapless, crisscross, lace, cotton, nylon. Going braless was not an option, though she imagined one day after she'd mastered this universe and risen sufficiently among the ranks, it would be, and would go nicely with the fuck-me boots and black eyeliner. *Ugh!*

She was hanging up the robe when she heard the voice through the open door.

"What time is this thi—?"

Nick Livingston was in midsentence when he noticed his wife, nearly naked under the bright lights.

"Oooh laalaa."

Sara managed a smile as her husband entered the closet, his hands reaching out for her, and a look on his face that belonged to a teenage boy seeing his first pair of tits. He was almost in a full-on grope when she gently pushed him away.

"We don't have time, honey," she said in a playful way, the way she might if she actually had an ounce of energy to be interested in his advances.

"Come on, Sara. We could christen the closet." He reached in with his head and kissed her neck, then ran his hand along the inside of her thigh.

Sara studied his face for the signs of kind deception. Could he really feel this way after three years and one demanding toddler? But what she saw instead was a handsome forty-one-year-old man who was turned on at the sight of his wife. Bright blue eyes, dark hair, the deadly combination that had lured her from her life into marriage and motherhood, and an easy way that was as foreign to her as it was seductive. He pulled her to him with a soft hand against her bare back, and she closed her eyes, hoping to be transformed, transported from this place to another she could hardly remember. Wrapping her arms around his neck, she let out a sigh.

"It's a closet-*room*," she muttered into the fold of his collar, and he laughed out loud, making her believe that he was still her comrade though he had been raised in Wilshire and had returned to it like a fish back to water. "It's a little early for a christening. Did you see all the work they didn't do today?" Sara started to pull away, her mind turning to Roy the Contractor and his piss-poor construction crew that was taking them for a ride and prolonging her daily misery of living in dust and chaos.

She waited for him to respond, to tell her that he saw it, too—that it was horrible, and of course, how could a person think of anything else when there was such trouble underfoot? She had her list of complaints, which she wanted to unleash into the space between them, and she waited for him to extend the invitation.

But none was forthcoming. Instead, Nick released his arms from around her waist and said nothing, though his disappointment and bewilderment stopped her from saying more. She felt her shoulders drop.

"I'm sorry," she whispered, holding him again, and he squeezed her tighter. The feel of his cool starched shirt against her bare skin made her feel exposed beyond her apparent nudity, and it was surprisingly sexy. She reached for his belt and released the clasp. "Let's christen the closet."

Nick hesitated, confused by the third mood shift in the scope of mere seconds, but she only kissed him harder, forcing out of the room the worries over the house, her clothing, and dishes and other nonsense. They fell to the floor, her bare body under his against the soft carpet.

He reached for the buttons on his shirt, but she pulled his hands away. "Leave it on," she whispered. "Leave everything on." She reached down and unzipped his pants, then pulled him inside her as her legs wrapped around the small of his back. With the lights glaring down upon them, Sara kept her eyes open, finding their image in the mirror that covered the length of the inner door. Nick in his suit, her beneath him on the floor in a moment of unexpected abandon was like a bolt of electricity short-circuiting the wires in her head. She could almost imagine that they weren't in Wilshire at all.

Reaching her hands around her husband, she grabbed hold of him. "I love your ass," she said, losing herself in a kind of passionate irreverence that felt forbidden in her new life. She wet his ear with her tongue and smiled as he moaned.

"Oh, Christ! Say that again. . . ."

"I love your ass . . . your rock-hard, massive ass. . . ."

"Christ!"

He was gone, and she was quick to follow, an unusual occurrence of late. Something about her private defiance, even for a few stolen moments, had lent a heightened sense of excitement, like screwing in the backseat of a car. It was a strange rush. *Good*, she thought, though she was equally disconcerted because it had nothing to do with her husband. Her mind felt as foreign to her as the thongs that rode up her butt all day long.

Nick was happily oblivious as he rested on top of her, catching his breath. "I love this closet-room," he said.

Sara smiled, then kissed his neck as he nuzzled into hers. She fought to make conversation from thoughts that were spinning recklessly in her head. "Is this another suburban secret? Having big closets for doing the deed?"

Nick laughed, relaxed. Contented. "After that, I think it will be from now on. Let's just burn that bed. I mean, who needs it?"

They stayed there for a while, and as the time passed, Sara grew increasingly unnerved. Beyond her altered state and the abduction of her entire being by alien forces, she felt the question coming.

"Do you think we did it? Did we make a baby?"

He was so careful to hide his anticipation, his growing worry that they might be joining so many of their peers who couldn't have a second child, and the fact that he was being considerate felt like a giant knife of guilt plunging into her.

"We'll see." Her tone was encouraging but also dismissive, and Nick quickly changed the subject.

"I'd better get my rock-hard ass in the shower so we can be on time." He kissed her and got up from the floor.

"Thanks." Sara smiled as she stood up, pulling the robe around her. She watched him turn the corner, heard the shower come on. Still, she couldn't move from where she stood. Her head was swimming—drowning, really—in a dull, unrelenting anxiety. Finally, she ran her hands briskly across her cheeks and turned toward the enemy she had been so terrified to face. Embracing the sense of defeat fully now, she pulled on clothing, shoes, jewelry.

"I'm going down," she yelled into the bathroom as she walked past their bed, ignoring the blue-and-green flowered spread, the one that matched the pale yellow walls and plaid draperies. *Shit*. She didn't even like French country.

Walking quickly to outpace the thoughts that were following close behind, Sara made her way to Annie's bedroom across the hall and peeked her head inside.

"She's asleep." Their Brazilian nanny, who went by the name Nanna, was standing by Annie's bed, looking over the small child.

"I was going to kiss her good night," Sara said.

"Oh," Nanna answered, her face taking on a hint of pity. "You're too late."

Sara felt a vise around her temples as she nodded and forced a smile. "We won't be late."

Nanna smiled back and nodded but did not leave the room. And as Sara hurried down the hall to the back stairs, she closed her ears to Nanna's soft humming. She focused instead on gathering her belongings and fitting them into her clutch purse—keys, phone, lipstick from her other bag. She reached the kitchen and caught a heel in the plastic that covered the floor. Pulling off her shoes, Sara passed through the room to the back hall, where she set the shoes on top of more plastic, this time covering the antique pine benches that no one ever sat on and were, of course, very last year. The powder room door was closed, though this did little to keep out the dust and other debris from the tearing down of walls and floors in the neighboring rooms, and she fought not to notice as she went inside, closing herself in. She flipped the toilet lid closed and sat down, hanging her head between her knees, face in hands. She wanted to cry then, for so many things, but she held it back. There was nothing to be done tonight. Not about her marriage, her child, her ripped-apart, poorly decorated house, or her red van. Or the fact that she could not find one moment of happiness in a life with a two-million-dollar-a-year price tag, the life her husband slaved to give her.

Tonight, she would go to the party, an important party. She would make nice, safe conversation and look for the cheapest auction item to help a school that needed no help. She would drive home with her husband, force herself to say nothing about the people who silently judged her, then pray for sleep. And in the morning, when her head was clear, she would think about what was wrong with her life. And if she found nothing, she would think about what might be wrong with her.

She took a breath and opened her purse. There was a hidden compartment with a zipper, which she opened slowly, methodically. She pulled out the contents—a round case with the multicolored pills that were keeping her body from becoming pregnant, fooling her husband. She flipped it open and checked the ones already taken. Then she popped out the one scheduled for this day. It was a tiny little pill, but the lie that it implicitly held was undeniable, and as she dropped it on her tongue and began to swallow it down, she could feel it sticking in her throat.

FOUR

UNFINISHED BUSINESS

"Are you still there?"

Amanda Jamison was on the line waiting for her answer, but Caitlin was busy making the adjustments. They were gone, out of sight. The golf cart with her father and younger siblings had pulled into the garage, and she was, mercifully, alone in the yard. In an instant, the taps were turned back on and the stream of new feelings was again flowing inside her, washing away the anger, guilt, and shame. All at once, the wicked girl, the ungrateful daughter, the poor role model, receded with the sound of the garage door closing, and of her friend's voice.

"Yeah. I'm here."

And she was, fully. Caitlin Barlow was back from her alternate personality, the rude, cynical, unfeeling monster that lived inside the mansion she was now gazing at from the swing that hung from a giant oak. It was cold. But she didn't care. With a bare foot dangling from the wooden seat, she breathed in the smell of the decaying leaves and settled back into herself.

"So . . . you didn't answer me. Did you . . . you know . . . *finish the business?*" The anticipation oozed from Amanda's voice, and it made Caitlin smile. In spite of the trouble she'd had to weather, this confirmed it. She was now firmly entrenched within their elite circle of friends.

"It was so close, I swear. I mean, if Mr. Carter hadn't come in, it was *over*."

"*Really?*" Amanda said, begging for details. "How could you tell?"

"You know—from the stuff you told me."

"Hard, harder, then . . ."

"The grand finale . . ."

"Exactly. Only no finale for Kyle. Went home with a boner. Poor baby." Amanda's tone was mocking, though they both knew Kyle Conrad was immune to their ridicule.

Caitlin smiled again, her mind now filled with the contours of the boy's face, his broad shoulders, and the smell of his cologne, which she had managed to capture on her not-so-subtle descent to her knees. Thinking of how awkward she'd been, how unsure—downright terrified, if she were being honest—made her shiver deep inside her body.

"Yeah, poor baby," she managed to say through the devastating embarrassment she was now reliving.

"Well . . . don't worry about it. I'm sure you'll get another chance, and he's usually really quick. So how long are you grounded?"

There was a pause, a long hesitation as Caitlin connected the dots. *Of course, idiot,* she thought to herself. *You're not the only one.*

"Two weekends, including this one."

"Fuck."

"I know." Caitlin managed a response, though her mind was stuck somewhere between Kyle's smile as he stroked her hair, and the image of her new best friend getting him off in some hidden corner of their world.

"Sucks for you. Listen, I gotta get ready. . . ."

"Yeah. No problem. Text me when you get back?"

"Course I will. Love ya," Amanda said. Then she was gone.

When Caitlin flipped the phone shut and saw the time, a heavy weight filled her body, and with it came the churning. It was a part of her now, as much as anything. As much as the exhaustion that crept in after lunch hour. As much as the hunger that she tolerated day in and day out, and sometimes in the night as she tried to sleep. It was the churning of the new. Her new friendship with Amanda and the informal club she was now a part of. Her new discovery of Kyle Conrad, and the feelings he stirred up. And at moments like this one, when she teetered between this new world and her life inside that house, it was driven by the impossibility of living in both.

She could see it in their eyes, each and every one of them. Her mother was more pissed off than worried. Cait was now interfering with her plan—the plan that had worked so well with her older brother, who was now a jock at Choate. Keep them busy, keep them on a schedule, and they will grow like structures off an architect's drawings. Cait's refusal to try out for varsity squash, her inability, which was taken as unwillingness, to get A's at the Wilshire Academy meant mommy dearest would need a different plan. Different drawings. Such a bother with all her charity work and luncheons and, of course, the incessant baby-making.

Her father, on the other hand, was more worried than pissed off. The vertical lines between his bushy eyebrows were becoming deep caverns drawn into his face. Nothing a little Botox couldn't fix, but Daddy was hardly the type for that, and even if he was, this thought did little to alleviate the guilt that was thrown into the brew that had infected Caitlin's blood. She was Daddy's little girl, his first girl, and the only one until Mellie was born. After her brother left, she'd been Daddy's best buddy, then an occasional buddy. Once upon a time, she'd loved board games, cards in particular, and he had taught her to play blackjack. Once upon a time, that had made her feel edgy and grown-up, listening to him talk about Las Vegas, how he would take her there when she was older. He'd taught her to drive, let her peel around on the grass in his coveted Creamsicle Corvette.

It wasn't fair that he expected this never to change. She was fourteen. Card games were the equivalent of a merry-go-round to the Amanda-Kyle roller coaster. The first time she'd broken a plan, he looked like a child who'd discovered the cruel farce of Santa Claus. Fuck him anyway. He'd canceled on her for business meetings before his retirement. And what? Now that he was bored out of his mind, she was supposed to provide entertainment, like his cars and scotch and arm-fart contests with her little brothers? This was her *life*, her defining moment that would dictate everything for the next four years. She had been a social nobody since before she could remember, the blanks having been filled in by her older brother. *Remember when we had to beg kids to come to Caitie's birthday party? Remember when Caitie puked in kindergarten and no one would talk to her?* Even the Barlow name hadn't saved her from herself all those years, and those were the years that had set the stage.

It was cruel how this was sorted out in towns like this one. Preschool, lower school, middle, and upper. They had grown up side by side, the Amandas of Wilshire and the Caitlins—the ones who lacked that something, the secret ingredient that was necessary to be in and not out, though what that ingredient was, Cait still had no clue. At first blush, she had the obvious things, some of them in spades. Enormous estate. Private plane. Servants. World-renowned father, socially connected mother. As for her appearance, even in a place like Wilshire where you'd have to search the maid's quarters to find a fat chick, Caitlin Barlow was attractive. Petite like her mother. Skinny legs. Blond hair, long and straight. Blue eyes. Straight teeth. Adequate tits for a fourteen-year-old. Clearly showing potential. Not too smart, not a retard either. By all accounts, Cait should have been popular.

And yet, she had not been surprised by her fate. There was, she had observed over the course of her school years, a kind of calling that was felt within before it could be outwardly displayed. It was a calling that she had always lacked, though she had tried in so many different ways to fake it, to pretend that she was born to be admired, to be coveted. Amanda Jamison had possessed it since their first days in pre-K. Long, curly brown hair, pretty sundresses, she had carried herself like a princess from the start. And her admirers had fallen into place and never left her side. It was, Caitlin knew, something expected of the Barlow children, and her brother had pulled it off with his usual effortless brilliance. It showed on his face, in his gait and smile. Even with defeat, rejection, momentary failure, it never left him. One look, and you knew he had it, that he felt it inside.

What Cait felt inside, she was certain, could not be anything like that. Confusion, insecurity, and doubt, a deadly potion that ran through her blood and invaded every cell. When she looked at her life—at any piece of it—she saw a senseless jumble of tasks and imaginary hoops, of distraction and blindness, and it left her with a giant pit that was filled alternately with anxiety and resignation. Not exactly the makeup of a born leader. No one made sense to her. Not her older brother, who filled his time with sports and video games. Not her mother, whose eyes drew her in but left her with a greater mystery each time. Barlow was a child himself, brilliant they said, but now somehow happy rolling around on the floor with the babies. He said there was joy in a hard day's work, in achieving great things. Even little things. And yet, when the money rolled in, he had retired.

There was a chance for her now. He should be proud. All of them should. Weren't they the ones who scowled at her old friends? Weren't they the ones who pushed her to "expand her social circle"? She had done it, found a way in, and now they were disappointed because they didn't like what she'd had to do. How could they not have known the price of admission?

The anger was powerful as it poured from a well inside her, a place she had never known existed. She let out a moan and closed her eyes. The anger was surpassed only by the agony—the sum of all these loose and scattered pieces. Pure agony, churning and churning. Standing on the brink of a social breakthrough. Soaring with possibilities. The thoughts she allowed herself at night in her bed. *Kyle*. His hand sweeping through her hair. Was it really possible to want to crawl inside another person and be lost forever? Had he stroked Amanda's hair? Would he ever notice her again? Then there was the dismissive way her mother looked at her, the look that had once been laced with pride, narcissistic as it might have been. It had felt good at the time. And her father—was that the worst piece? Or was it Mellie, who sulked incessantly because Cait refused to play? But how could she, really? How could she sit on the floor and pretend to be the purple Pretty Pony when she wanted to scream until it all stopped? And how could she ever enjoy the turn her life had taken when she had to go back inside that house—right now, as a matter of fact, and every day after this one—and feel the weight of their disappointment? What would they do if she were dead? Somehow the family would go on, mourning their dear saint Caitlin and accepting visitors with plates of food (prepared by chefs, of course—Wilshire didn't *do* homemade), like at her grandmother's funeral. After it was said and done, they would carry on, filling in whatever gap was left. Why couldn't they just do that now? Pretend she didn't exist and let her get on with her life?

"Cait!" The boss sounded pissed as she screamed from the kitchen sliders. Now she would have to pretend to babysit while the nannies supervised her every move. At least it was past seven. All that was left was TV and bed. She could survive that. She shoved it down, the new Cait, and brought out her shield. Sarcastic Caitlin. Indifferent Caitlin. Typical teen Caitlin. The teen-stranger, as her father now called her. She willed herself off the swing. The ground was getting cold, the grass starting to stiffen from it. With frozen toes, she began her journey back to her family, screaming as she walked.

"I'm coming!"

FIVE

SURF'S UP

"Wait—was she just *looking* at it, or was she actually . . . you know . . . ?"

"I think so."

"But she's *fourteen!*"

"I know. It's tragic. Scary. How's Rosalyn doing?"

As Jacks Halstead stood in line for a drink at the Wee Ones benefit, she was surrounded by chatter that had now morphed into an annoying buzz. At five-nine, she towered over the others, but this proved to be no match for the gossip. And yet her mind was far too saturated with worry to absorb any more talk about the Barlow family. Was it really that interesting? Tuning in again, she thought about the words that had been spoken over and over throughout an evening that was still unbearably young. *Fourteen. Blow job. Barlow.* The last held the greatest significance. Rosalyn Barlow was Wilshire's version of royalty, which meant that this dark incident would not go away on its own. It would have to be managed, finessed, and despite Jacks's own brewing troubles, her friendship with Rosalyn necessitated her involvement. She was resigned to this and fully prepared to perform her duties. Still, at the moment, the investigation into her husband seemed more than enough to have to bear, and she felt an intense desire to scream, though she swallowed it down, concerning herself instead with the scene that surrounded her.

Staying true to form, the special-events committee for the nursery school had outdone itself. The theme was "back to summer," though the early chill in the air was lending itself more to cashmere wraps than to sleeveless silk. Despite the fashion dilemma that the theme had inadvertently created, the small uninteresting space had been transformed into an exquisite beachside resort. With giant heat lamps shining a soft orange glow onto a sand-covered floor, a wall-to-wall mural of ocean surf, and canvas beach umbrellas sheltering the auction tables, the mood had certainly been achieved. Swarms of peroxide-white smiles, hoisted breasts, and jewels drifted effortlessly around her as she waited for the only thing in the room that she truly cared about at the moment.

"Gin and tonic," she said after seizing the bartender's attention.

But she was not off the hook.

"Jacks?" It was Eva Ridley, official town gossip and, ironically, one of her closest friends.

Watching with anticipation as the young bartender poured the gin, Jacks reluctantly entered the conversation. "I'm sorry—what did you ask?"

"*How* is Rosalyn?" Eva repeated herself, her eyes shifting between Jacks and the other women. Eva was teeing her up for the perfect response, which Jacks was now forcing herself to consider. Too much information, and she would betray their friend to the small group of women that now surrounded them. Too little, and this conversation (and that was a generous description) would never end. Either way, she supposed, it would eventually get done. Rosalyn Barlow was fully capable of defusing the situation and maintaining her position as Wilshire's most envied woman. Still, there was an unprecedented glee in the air over what had happened in that stark gray hallway of the Wilshire Academy. With music from the dance playing in the background and nothing but cold metal and fluorescent lights surrounding them, the blond-haired, doe-eyed Barlow beauty had dropped to her knees as a "favor to a friend." It was salacious and humiliating and worst (or best) of all, evidence that the Barlows' perfect life might not be so perfect as it seemed. That it took a hallway blow job for them to arrive at this most obvious conclusion was in itself perplexing to Jacks.

"Rosalyn is concerned, of course, for Caitlin," she said finally. "She's concerned for *all* the girls at the Academy."

As her words took flight on the winds of the gossip storm, Jacks felt a hint of relief. *One hurdle cleared*. Three of the four women flittering about her had girls at the Academy, and their minds were now racing with fear.

"Has it happened before?" one of the women asked.

Jacks shrugged with the nonchalance of feigned ignorance. "All I know is that the school is planning a *big* investigation."

Silence. And just in time. Jacks grabbed her drink from the bartender and smiled at Eva, who gave her a discreet wink.

"Enjoy the evening, ladies." Wiggling her way back through the line, Jacks held the gin firmly in hand. When she was safely out of the fray, she exhaled deeply. Then she took a long sip and watched her husband, who was casually socializing in the far corner by the auction items. He was with the new family, the Livingstons. David knew Nick from college, and Jacks had orders to make nice with his much younger wife. *Susan? Sandy?* She couldn't keep a damn thing in her head anymore. Nor could she imagine enduring the small talk that would be required of her.

She'd known the people in this room for years. The club. The Wilshire Academy. Young Women's League. Her library of knowledge was seventeen years deep, stacked to the ceiling with files upon files of information. Someone's breast cancer, another's autistic son. An affair with the tennis pro. A plot to steal a nanny. Sexual preferences, disease, plastic surgery. She knew what each woman was feeling as she stood beside her husband at this very moment, what passed through her thoughts while his hand brushed the side of her breast or the flesh of her ass. Hope—*he still wants me*. Hatred—*I'm not his whore*. Either way, the woman would smile. These were the things she had always noticed, the subtle exchanges that were so benign to the untrained eye. They were the hidden codes that were embedded within each social interaction, and she dissected them with the internal tools inherited from her childhood—tools that had been necessary to adjust to the madness. Perception. Analysis. Understanding. Everything said to her, whether in passing or the deepest confidence, was fed into the processor, brushed onto the canvas that revealed their darkest thoughts and fears, their very humanity. They were, at their core, just that. Human.

And yet, if she squinted her eyes, the giant pool of deception morphed into a different picture altogether. A lovely cocktail party with rich, carefree people. She felt her face quiver as she forced a pleasant smile. Was she as transparent to them as they were to her? Would they notice the change in her

demeanor? There was only so much of the panic she would be able to sub-
due, even with the gin.

A voice came from behind her, pulling her out of the spiraling anxiety.

"Here." It was Barlow with two drinks in his hand. Keeping the scotch
for himself, he handed the gin and tonic to her. "You look like you could use
another."

Jacks smiled and glanced into her glass, which was now bare down to
the ice.

"Thanks."

She took the fresh drink and clicked it against his. "Cheers," she said,
raising an eyebrow. No one could lift a person's spirits like Ernest Barlow.
Handsome, rich, funny, and, most of all, intent on having a good time under
even the worst of circumstances.

Barlow took a step back and conspicuously scrutinized Mrs. Halstead.
"Mmmm. *Nice!*"

Nearly his height, Jacks looked him dead in the eye and swatted him
playfully on the arm. "I think you're in enough trouble already. Now be a
good boy and drink your scotch."

Barlow raised his glass, then took a drink. "Yes, ma'am."

They stood there for a moment, silently watching, drinking, and enjoying the comfort of each other's company. Within the boundaries of married
couples, they were as close to being friends as was possible for men and women
in such a tight-knit community. Their daughters were in the same grade at
the Academy. The Barlows and Halsteads had for years been thrown together at school functions, playdates, birthday parties, and the like. Then
came the formal dinner invitations to the Barlow estate, swim parties, long
weekends on the yacht. Despite their vastly divergent personalities, they
worked well as a foursome and after fifteen years were far beyond the for-
malities of the other acquaintances they had cultivated.

"What's with all the sundresses?" Barlow asked after a while.

"It's a summer theme: Surf's Up. Didn't you read the invitation?"

Barlow looked himself over. Dark blue suit. Red tie. Standard business
attire. "Clearly not."

Jacks smiled and shrugged. "Only you, my dear Barlow, could get away
with it."

"Not according to my wife."

Jacks took another sip of gin and nodded silently as she turned her eyes to Rosalyn, who was stationed across the room. Also dismissing festive attire, Rosalyn was incredibly subdued. And it wasn't just her beige suit, subtle hair, and restrained makeup. It was everything about her, the way she nursed a glass of white wine, holding her other hand around her stomach as though she were protecting the injury this incident had caused. It was in her facial expressions, the slight cheerless smile and exaggerated interest in the conversation of others. As Jacks watched the woman work the audience, she found herself surprisingly impressed. She was a tiny thing, but every inch of her was fully engaged tonight. This was a command performance, even for Rosalyn.

"Wow," Jacks said.

"Yes. Incredible, isn't she?" Barlow's tone was sarcastic. "But tell me, Jacks. Honestly. Do you think all of this is really necessary? Do people really care that much?"

Jacks shrugged, thinking that this was precisely why she and Barlow were such good friends. They were both, in their own vastly divergent ways, former outsiders.

"Some of it is. Some of it is probably just . . ."

Barlow watched her face as she struggled for the right way to say what they both were thinking.

"Just my wife's imagination?"

"No," Jacks muttered, turning her eyes back to Rosalyn. "Not imagination so much as anticipation. She's been burned before, and she has the scars to prove it."

Barlow drank some scotch. "Ah, but her most fearsome foe is dead and buried. It's been almost two years."

"And sometimes a ghost can be more powerful than anything that walks among us. Especially the ghost of one's own mother."

Barlow looked at Jacks carefully as he took in this bit of wisdom.

Smiling warmly now, Jacks changed the subject. "So, all of this bullshit aside, how is Cait doing?"

Barlow shook his head. "Honestly, I don't have a clue. She won't talk about it. Not that I really want to—*believe me*. But I know she's talking to her new friends and I'm afraid they're the ones who dragged her into all this."

"At least it's not just Cait. Hailey said there's a lot of talk about it."

Barlow turned to face her. "Is Hailey doing it?"

Jacks thought about her oldest daughter. She was overweight for her age, and a bit of a geek. Two things Jacks was grateful for. "No—though I guess I should say I don't know, because we don't ever. Do we?"

"That's the damned truth of it. I just never thought my little Caitie would be vulnerable. And now her mother is making it into a national crisis. Global warming, the shitty economy, and hallway blow jobs. Somehow I don't think that's exactly what Caitie needs right now, to be the poster child for teenagers gone wild."

Even in the midst of his deepest worries, Barlow managed to find humor. It was his way, his defense against the pain that was floating through his body, looking for a place to anchor.

"I don't know. I doubt she'll even notice it. It's really for *them*, isn't it?" Jacks said, drawing her arm across the room.

As Barlow peered out into the crowd, Jacks studied his face. They should be nothing to him now. He no longer needed them, having made his fortune, and his contempt for the very world he still envied in spite of his every effort to stop was now crawling beneath his skin.

"Does it help to know that most of the women here performed similar favors before leaving high school?"

Barlow laughed. "And look how well they turned out."

"Oh, come now. These are some of the finest ladies in Wilshire."

"And not exactly the life plan I had in mind for my daughters."

Jacks looked at him wryly. "And yet, here you are."

"Here *we* are." He turned then, to meet her eyes. The irony had never occurred to him, but it struck him now, hard and cold. He drained the glass of scotch, then did what he always did when too many adult thoughts entered his brain. "So getting back to hallway blow jobs . . ."

Jacks laughed out loud and shook her head, though she was far from being embarrassed. "Oh, no. Not a chance. You'll just have to use your imagination."

Barlow grinned flirtatiously, lowering his eyes then raising them again to meet hers. It was the look that came as close as any ever did to crossing the invisible line, and it was now, at the line, that one of them always stepped away in search of a spouse. Or another drink.

"I think I'll need more scotch to do that."

"Actually, it looks like we need to sit for dinner."

Barlow slid his arm around her waist as she moved in front of him. "After you, Mrs. Halstead."

Their table was in the front of the room, of course, the unofficial head table that was always reserved for the school's chairwoman at these events. And what a lovely table it was, with white linens, bright colorful peonies and roses in a round vase, and little menus shaped like surfboards. Cheery, cute. Perfect.

Jacks found Rosalyn standing by her chair, engaged in conversation with the school director.

"Lovely party," she said casually.

Oblivious of, or perhaps merely indifferent to, her husband, who had dashed off to the bar, Rosalyn reached out and kissed Jacks on the cheek. "Hello, there. Where have you been hiding?"

Jacks smiled. "Nowhere. What a fabulous setup!"

The director smiled. "Thank you. I hope you enjoy it. And don't forget to bid—the tables close at ten."

Rosalyn and Jacks nodded in agreement. "Of course!"

"Well, I'd better mingle. Nice to see you both."

The two women smiled as they watched the director move on to the next potential deep pocket. Then they turned to face each other.

"So," Jacks said, her expression one of genuine concern.

Rosalyn continued to smile, though Jacks detected the traces of weariness she knew must be lurking inside the woman. This just wasn't in Rosalyn, this contrite, apologetic tour de force. It was effective, to be sure. And necessary in Rosalyn's mind. But there was no doubt Wilshire's reigning matriarch was growing tired of it in a hurry.

"So," Rosalyn replied.

Jacks smiled reassuringly. "This won't be just about Caitlin much longer."

Rosalyn was slightly relieved. "The natives are worried, are they? Now I have to follow through."

Jacks touched her arm. "You will. I know you will."

"I had other plans for the fall. And the winter, and the spring." Her voice sounded irritated, as though that was all this was to her, an annoyance. An inconvenience. Jacks played along, though she knew her friend was using her social concerns as a distraction from what was really eating at her from the inside out. Cait would always be her little girl.

"Well, who knows? Maybe it really is an epidemic and you'll be doing all of us a favor."

Rosalyn waved her hand in the air as though she could somehow magically erase the whole incident. "Let's sit down. Do we know who else is at the table? I'm hardly in the mood for surprises."

"Just us, the Ridleys, and the new family."

"New family?"

"They're friends of David's. And they're *new*."

Jacks studied Rosalyn as she pulled out her chair and gracefully placed herself in it, obviously contemplating the situation. *Yes*, she was most definitely thinking. *New could be good.* They wouldn't know a thing about anything, and the rest of the room would see how generous Rosalyn Barlow could be. Inviting the new family to her table would go beautifully with her theme for the evening. She had that look, the intensity of obsession, that Jacks understood well. The ghost of Rosalyn's mother might as well be sitting right there beside her.

"What are their names?" Rosalyn asked, now fully committed to the idea.

Jacks sat down, leaving one chair between herself and Rosalyn. Boy-girl-boy-girl. That was the rule.

"Nick Livingston and his wife. Susan, I think."

Rosalyn was not satisfied. "Is it Susan?"

Jacks shook her head. The gin had calmed her nerves but had done nothing to improve her memory. "I have no clue, to be honest. But she's *young*. Late twenties. Princeton, then Columbia for some journalism degree. Met Nick at a bar in New York."

"Christ. You know all that but not her name?"

Jacks shrugged. "What's more important?"

Barlow appeared with a fresh drink in hand. He pulled out the chair next to his wife, but was stopped when she grabbed his arm, nearly causing him to spill the scotch.

"Shit," Barlow said under his breath, steadying the drink. "What now?"

"You can't sit there." Rosalyn looked at him incredulously. How drunk was he? Spouses never sat beside one another. That was also the rule.

"Oh, fuck it." Barlow walked around the table and planted himself next to Jacks, who patted his knee—briefly—beneath the table.

They sat in silence, Jacks and the Barlows, sipping their drinks and waiting for David Halstead and the Livingstons to make their way through the crowd. And as they sat there, pleasant expressions pasted on their faces from a powerful force of habit, their sheer beauty cast an invisible shield against a reality that was discernible solely in the air that surrounded them, air that was thick with worry. When the others appeared, still engaged in the amusement of shared stories from years past, they were stopped in their tracks by the unsettling sense of contradiction they had stumbled into.

"Hello, David," Barlow said first, standing to greet his friend.

"Barlow." David reached out and shook his hand. "Good to see you, man."

"And you."

Then, turning to the table where the ladies had remained seated, David made the introductions. The Barlows to the Livingstons. The Livingstons to Jacks and the Barlows. And after this seemingly harmless interaction, they all took their places at the table.

—————

SIX

THE EVA FACTOR

"MEET NICK AND SARA Livingston."

Eva Ridley and her husband, Marcus, both smiled warmly as they joined the table moments later. "It's a pleasure!"

And no one doubted this was true. Eva Ridley loved to meet new people. Moving fluidly through the details of others' lives, she was the woman who eventually came to know everyone in this town. At first glance, she was a walking suburban stereotype. Long red hair, chiseled cheekbones, and a size 2 frame (accessorized, of course, by designer D-cup breasts). A confoundingly solid marriage. Five well-behaved children. She was funny, pleasant, and made it her business to know everyone else's. But contrary to the practices of other accomplished gossips, Eva collected knowledge not to malign, but to befriend. She remembered people's birthdays and anniversaries. She knew their favorite restaurants and which drink they would order at any given occasion. She sent small thoughtful gifts, planned surprise luncheons. And as a result of her tireless efforts, her collection of friends was vast and, like Jacks, her encyclopedia of facts about nearly everyone in Wilshire accurate to a T. She had become, simply, the refined oil that kept the Wilshire social machine running.

She glanced at Jacks, then at Rosalyn, then back to Sara Livingston, who smiled as she shook Eva's hand.

"So . . . ," Eva said, settling into her chair. "What's with this theme? I'm freezing my ass off." She pretended to shiver in her strapless mini-sundress. "And what's with the two of you?"

Eva was looking back and forth between the Barlows.

Rosalyn gave her a wry smile. Her friend had been at the table for less than a minute, and already the mood was lighter. This was, as Rosalyn had come to think of it, the Eva Factor. No one was better at pointing out the elephants and chasing them from a room.

"What? It's a suit!" Barlow, who was sitting between Sara and Jacks, looked himself up and down, then studied Mrs. Livingston longer than he would have had he not been drunk.

"I see you fucked up the clothes, too," he said, turning to face her, his breath heavy with the smell of alcohol.

Sara smiled nervously. What could she say to *that*? Having worn what *should* have been a perfectly acceptable ensemble at a school benefit, she had overlooked the line on the invitation that read ATTIRE: BACK TO SUMMER. Now she was completely out of place in a gray skirt and long-sleeved black top.

"What will they do to us?" was her response, and it drew a chuckle from Barlow.

Then, in a very serious voice, he told her, "After they serve us the finest of meals, we'll be hauled outside to be drawn and quartered. Everyone will watch, of course, so they have one last go at making fun of us."

Sara didn't hesitate. She'd grown up on witty sarcasm. "I see. Well, in that case, it was nice meeting you."

Ernest Barlow smiled, and Nick gave her a wink. Even surrounded by a billionaire, his influential wife, and the renowned Eva Ridley, Sara was managing to be herself. And the relief swept through the young woman like an enormous sigh.

Eva took a long sip of her white wine. "Sara's from New York, Barlow. They wear black all year long. What's your excuse? And don't even try to garner sympathy with some preposterous story about teenagers and hallways and—"

"Eva!" Jacks was trying not to laugh, and that was the problem. Laughter seemed entirely inappropriate, and yet somehow Eva had managed to bring it to the table.

Eva shrugged. "It's not like someone's *died*."

Nick and Sara were the only ones who were completely confused. "Did I miss something here?" Nick threw the question into the air between them, and the others seemed to be staring at it as they waited for someone to answer.

"Time for the men to smoke a cigar." David Halstead came to the rescue, and his wife sent him a warm, almost nostalgic smile. David had always been the designated mediator, providing outs like the one he'd just given the Barlows.

"We haven't even eaten yet." Eva gave the obligatory female objection, though it was less than half hearted.

"Yes! Cigars!" Ernest Barlow was already up from his seat. "Madam— please excuse me," he said, now standing over Sara and propping himself up with the back of her chair.

"Of course," she answered. Though Ernest Barlow was drunk and inappropriate, Sara was already sure she liked the man in spite of it. Maybe even because of it.

"We won't be long." Nick circled around and gave his wife a peck on the cheek. Marcus Ridley did the same. Then they were gone.

"Ahhh," Eva purred, leaning back in her chair. "Finally."

Rosalyn Barlow spoke, her face taking on an entirely different tone. "Yes, indeed. *Finally*."

Taken by surprise, Sara glanced inconspicuously at the three women. With the men gone and the other partygoers busy with their drinking and eating and chatting, it was as though a partition had been instantly erected around their table. It was as though they could now, and only now, be themselves. Or perhaps be their *other* selves, the selves they could be only with each other. And the fact that Sara could see this, that she could feel it within herself as well, was unsettling. It felt like the schoolyard in eighth grade again—boys throwing balls, girls gossiping by the swings—only without the anticipation of what it would be like when the two gender factions began to intermingle. They'd been through all that, and now that they had followed that tumultuous path to its inevitable conclusion of marriage, they were simply relieved to be alone by the swings.

"So," Eva said after a long moment, "a blow job."

Sara froze, drink in hand, eyes wide.

Jacks leaned into her slightly. "Rosalyn's daughter. School hallway."

Sara looked at Rosalyn, then back to Jacks.

"Don't worry. Everyone knows about it," Rosalyn said, draining her wineglass.

Eva nodded. "That's why she's wearing beige." She said the word as though it were the Antichrist. *Beige*, of all blessed things.

Rosalyn tried, but having had it thrown out there now in spite of her efforts to avoid it, in spite of the beige, she was overwhelmed. She felt the laughter in her gut, the kind of laughter that emanates from sorrow and the wisdom that can put sorrow in its place. It was the laughter that has to come before the sorrow takes over everything. She felt the air rush in, and then the wine, which had just passed her lips.

"Oh, shit!" Jacks said, handing Rosalyn a napkin.

The dignified woman was choking gracefully and somehow laughing without a sound, without even a smile, as she grabbed the napkin and covered her face.

Eva held a hand to her own mouth, and Jacks just smiled and shook her head.

"Is she all right?" Sara asked. What was visible of Rosalyn Barlow's face was now red, and she didn't seem to be breathing.

"She's fine." Eva and Jacks looked at each other, then to Sara. Then they started to laugh out loud. Jacks felt the tears roll down her cheek, felt the mascara running through the small crow's-feet that had taken shape at the corners of her eyes. She hadn't laughed in weeks, hadn't even come close. It was almost desperate, this need to laugh, and to let the tears fall.

Sara smiled by reflex, though she felt almost invisible, erased by the bond of a long friendship that was exposed in everything that was now being left unsaid between the three women. There was nothing funny about what had happened between Caitlin Barlow and that boy. It was, they all knew, the beginning of a ride that no one could predict, that none of them could help her navigate. And though they would talk solely of the social consequences Caitlin Barlow's *incident* had provoked, through the laughter, they now let out their fears for their daughters, and the pain from their own memories, some of which they had never shared with another soul. It was within these

memories, from the most blissful to the most blistering, that a silent understanding flowed among them—simply because they were women, and because they had seen the pieces of life that only women experience.

Rosalyn let the picture of Caitlin in that hallway, the one that had been
constructed from her imagination, flash before her eyes. When she caught
her breath, she pulled the napkin from her face, then gently dabbed her lips.
She shook her head briskly, regaining her composure, and looked nonchalantly around the room. The change she managed to quickly facilitate within
her own being was impressive.

"Damn you, Eva Ridley," she said, the hint of sarcasm barely discernible.

Eva took a deep breath and looked across the table. She smiled warmly,
seriously this time. "It'll be all right."

"I know it will." Rosalyn nodded.

"So—now that we've had our little *moment*," Eva said, back to her playful demeanor, "why don't we stop being so rude and ask Sara about herself?"

"Yes," Jacks agreed. "Tell us how you met Nick?" Knowing the answer
was beside the point.

"Oh." Sara was taken aback at the sudden acknowledgment of her presence and was now blushing. "We met at a bar. Typical New York story," she
answered dismissively. From everything she had learned in her few hours at
the Surf's Up party, and from being seated at this particular table, she had no
intention of revealing anything more. No one needed to know how quickly
after that night she and Nick were married—or why, for that matter.

"And you were a reporter?" Rosalyn chimed in.

"There wasn't time," she began to explain. "I was just finishing at Columbia when we got married. Then there was the apartment to set up. I don't
know, actually, what happened to that year before Annie was born. Nick was
so busy at work. . . ."

The women looked at each other, smiling slightly. Had they not all been
there? Done that? Once the honeymoon was over, the roles were already
waiting for them. It was as if the universe stepped in and carved them into
stone while they were away making love on beaches and dining on French
cuisine.

"Well," Rosalyn said, getting up from her chair. "Screw the men. Let's
eat." She was hungry. Laughing was more work for her than a Pilates class.

Besides, in spite of this little tidbit of pleasure she had shared with her friends, she was ready to get this thing over with.

Lifting their invisible partition, the women took a moment to gather themselves. Smiling, chatting, sucking in their guts, and making nice, they stood among the others in the buffet line. And Sara stood with them, mistakenly thinking she had begun to figure them out, and hoping she had not given too much of herself away.

SEVEN

THE BOY NEXT DOOR

CAITLIN BARLOW WAS THIRTEEN when she first kissed a boy, and as was true of most first kisses, the memory still lingered at the core of her body. Billy Pike, fellow eighth-grader. Behind his pool house. It was early spring, and he'd invited some friends over. Thinking back on it now, it might as well have been a lifetime ago. So much had changed, and in so little time.

They'd been a small group of friends, social outcasts who stuck together by default because no one else would have them. Watching the others make their plans, seeing them out in town and wanting with every fiber to be with them instead of with the ones by her side. Every day at school, banding together out of necessity, swallowing the explicit rejection from the likes of Amanda Jamison, and the implicit rejection from one another.

Still, they had been as content a group of misfits as was possible—Cait, Billy, and the three others—flying under the radar at school, making their own fun on the weekends, watching movies, sneaking beer. And when she pretended there were no Amandas, no perfect others doing something better, something bigger, their mundane amusements were actually satisfying. When the kiss came, finally, after months of flirting and talk within their circle about the attraction everyone could sense, this almost seemed possible, this feat of closing Amanda Jamison from her thoughts.

They'd gone to look for beer in the pool house fridge, but before they could get there, Billy had pulled her to the back. He'd given no explanation, and she hadn't needed one. They had both known from the outset that this would be the moment. He'd steadied her face with his hands, as though he might somehow miss her lips. They had closed their eyes, shutting out their surroundings, traveling instead to that magical place where fantasy becomes reality, even for a split second. Of course, reality is never quite as good. His breath smelled of chips, his tongue lay inside her mouth like a giant anchovy, and his shaking body wasn't exactly the manly figure she had so needed to hold her, to keep her from falling further and further from any vision of life that was worth the effort. But it was tender and warm, and Cait had felt a different kind of pleasure than she had expected. It was, at its core, genuine and sweet.

They kissed many times after that first time, stolen moments in private corners of the large estates that were their playground. Billy's performance improved, the shaking disappeared, and they fell into the comfortable rhythm of a first relationship. His family's property abutted hers on one side, and it was there that they would meet, sometimes in the middle of the night, to talk and roll around in the cool grass, kissing and holding each other, wondering where it would lead and how soon. They talked about their families, the teachers they hated at the Academy, and the stories they heard about their peers. It was as close to peaceful as Cait had ever felt, which was, she imagined, the reason she'd had to kill it.

Everything had a place and time, and it was here and now, in the ninth grade, that her life was finally turning around. She'd been accepted, and no one in her right mind would turn down that invitation. That it came at Billy's expense was the price she'd been willing to pay, even though it haunted her, the guilt, at moments like this one, when they were sitting in the same room eating lunch two tables apart. She did her best to avoid catching his wounded gaze, and she could feel today the scornful eyes of her former friends upon her. Everyone knew about the hallway, the incident with Kyle Conrad. She could hardly think the words without wanting to crawl under the table, but yes, the *blow job*. What must he be thinking? For six months, all they did was kiss and wonder, kiss and fantasize. Every time he'd reached his hand under her shirt, she had pulled away. How desperate he now seemed, looking back. Lying on top of her, his hard dick pressing into her leg, and that puppy dog look in his eye like she was the love of his life and wouldn't she please give him just a little more? It was all so after-school special.

"Cait?" Amanda was watching her as well, wondering where she'd gone.

"Is he staring again?" Cait asked, looking up to meet her friend's eyes.

Amanda leaned back nonchalantly and did a wide perusal of the cafeteria. "He was, but not now. He's getting up with his tray."

Cait nodded and took another sip of her diet soda. "And the others?"

Amanda gave her a disapproving look, then leaned forward to accentuate the point. "Screw the others, okay? They used to be your friends, and now they're gonna judge you? What—just because it wasn't Billy in the hallway?" She leaned back and shook her head with disgust. "Hypocrites. I mean, come on! *As if*."

"You're right. Sorry. It's just a little weird being back."

"It'll pass. Besides, you're kinda famous now."

She was kidding, of course, but it still made Cait nearly gag on her soda. Popular had been good. Popular had felt like someone had stopped throwing dirt on her coffin and instead lifted it from the ground, pried it open, and let her out. She'd been washed in sunlight, finally noticed by the world. But today was more like a laser beam cutting her in two. If only she hadn't been caught.

Amanda's face changed suddenly, and Cait turned to follow where her eyes had gone. Kyle Conrad was walking to their table.

Cait felt her cheeks flush as she looked back to the table. It was a high, as good as any she could ever imagine. She could feel him standing behind her, and it took all her will not to turn around and acknowledge him.

"Hello, girls," he said. At sixteen, he had a deep, commanding voice that carried just enough indifference to make any audience stop and take notice.

Cait felt his hand resting on her shoulder, and she could tell from her friend's expression that he was also looking down at her.

"Hello," Amanda said, failing miserably to hide her jealousy.

With his hand still upon her, Kyle sat down beside Cait. It was then that she allowed herself to look at him. Her mind—no, her entire being—was rapt with a bittersweet longing that left room for nothing else.

"Hi," she managed to say along with a smile.

Kyle smiled back, then looked down at the BlackBerry he held in his hands. "So, listen. I'm sorry about all the trouble. Has it totally sucked?"

"Not too bad. I can deal," Cait answered, though Kyle's concern was somewhat undermined by the fact that he was now checking his messages. And that he had missed entirely the irony of the word he'd used to describe her situation.

With his fingers clicking at the speed of light, he nodded and said "Good" before finishing his texting.

Amanda and Cait waited in silence.

Finally, he looked up again. "So, I'll see you both this weekend?"

"Absolutely," Amanda answered.

Cait nodded as well, though she had no idea what he was talking about, or how she would manage to be anywhere when she was still grounded.

"Good." He got up then to leave, and Cait prepared herself for the pain that was coming. Could this be the most dreadful misery known to mankind? She was nerve-racked when he was near her. Despairing when he was gone. All that saved her was the hope that one day, she might finally have him. It was sheer insanity, and she was powerless to cure it.

"See ya." His parting words were delivered with a smile, then a slight brush of Cait's hair the way he'd done in the hallway that night. It was a small gesture, but there was no doubt she would spend the rest of the day (week?) analyzing it, reliving it, and breathing into it more significance than it could ever deserve. Each morning, she would trace the path of his day—the classrooms and hallways and lunch breaks. She had memorized his schedule, knew when he would pass certain places within the school or on the grounds, and she would be sure to be there, watching, waiting. Hoping. The blissful misery of infatuation.

"Cait . . ." It was Amanda, again breaking her train of thought. "Why did you tell Kyle you'd be there this weekend?"

Cait shook her head. "I don't know. I didn't even know what he was talking about."

Amanda let out an exasperated gasp. "He's having a party at his house— while *your* parents are having their big party! Your house will be swarming with help. You can't possibly go!" Her voice was deadly serious, as though Cait had done something unthinkable.

Inside, Cait felt like dying. "Who's gonna be there?"

"Only a few of us. And now Kyle's expecting *you*." She raised an eyebrow, as if Cait couldn't connect the dots on her own. As if she didn't know that if she failed to finish what she'd started, he would find someone who would. The thought of it made her nauseated.

"Maybe I can get out in the middle of the party. Can I get a ride?"

Amanda gave this serious thought as she rubbed her chin. "I guess. I can ask my brother."

"Really?" Cait said, her voice replete with desperation.

And though it was completely contrary to her own self-interest, Amanda found herself making the promise. "Really. Text me when you get to the end of your driveway."

Relief set in as Cait muttered the words, "I will!".

Suddenly, life became about one thing—getting to the end of that driveway Saturday night. As she got up from the table with her empty can of soda, her back to the small group of friends from her recent past, she felt lifted by the emergence of this new purpose, and the rescue of hope it afforded her.

EIGHT

APPLES FROM A TREE

NINE FIFTEEN. ASSUMING NO traffic, which was assuming a lot, Jacks was still counting on an hour's drive. Sitting behind a school bus trying to make a left-hand turn on the most traveled street in Wilshire, she could feel the steady flow of adrenaline like a perfectly calibrated IV drip. She wasn't panicked—not yet. But the blood was flowing. The bus turned and she sped past it, along South Avenue to the Parkway ramp. The cars were moving. *Thank God.* She pressed her foot to the floor and felt her Mercedes take flight.

The night had been long, restless, maybe even entirely sleepless, though she couldn't recall one way or another. She had been in the bed, heart pounding, mind racing, and there had certainly been moments of delusion. None of this mattered. She'd copied everything she could think of. The mortgage papers, the 401(k) reports, credit card bills, bank statements. She'd downloaded their budget and investment schedule from the Excel file on the family computer, then printed it out. For hours, she'd gone over it all—the financial landscape of the Halstead family—and the numbers were still playing before her eyes.

As she passed the last exit for Wilshire, the stream of traffic thinned, leaving only those on the road who were heading north toward the grayer parts of Connecticut. With her Starbucks cup in one hand and her eyes glued to the road, she put the pedal to the metal again.

Where had it all gone? David had told her the equity in the house was down because of the money they'd spent on the addition. He'd complained about the drop in the housing market, and Jacks had bought it. What did she know about these things? Now, nothing he'd told her made sense. They had borrowed nearly two million dollars with the home equity loan, yet the contractor's bills Jacks dug up totaled less than one million. They were covering that loan with a mortgage payment that had jumped from $50,000 a year to $170,000. And the checkbook for the account was missing. It was the same everywhere she looked. The 401(k) had been divested in large chunks over the past several months, their private equity investments sold, all at a loss.

She had their budget down cold in her head, partly because it had shocked her, and mostly because she was moving that much closer to believing the life they had was ending. They would never make it with what was left. Home maintenance, yard, pool—that alone topped fifty thousand. The maid was another fifty. The nanny was seventy. Car payments, sixty. Private clubs, another sixty. Private school for three girls, eighty-five. Donations to the same schools, another hundred. Dance, piano, squash, riding: thirty thousand. Then there were the gifts, parties, clothes, trips. Another eighty. Now add in the utilities, gas, oil, cable, and phones: sixty thousand. They had a seven-thousand-square-foot house to heat and cool. The list went on. Medical expenses, therapists. The Christmas season, with the endless array of presents and gatherings. And, last but not least, taxes.

They could pare down. Of course they could. Jacks had a mental checklist of all the things that would go first. But at the end of the night, after the mind-bending analysis of their financial reality had taken her into the little cracks and crevasses of their existence, the larger picture emerged. Living on a smaller income didn't alarm her. Nor did the vanishing equity and 401(k). Those things could be rebuilt over time. It was what they said together that had Jacks racing north for the slums of Connecticut.

It took forty minutes to reach the exit. She turned off the Parkway and drove to the end of the ramp. As she waited for the light to change, she exhaled for what felt like the first time all morning. With the car stopped, she allowed herself to take in the dismal surroundings. Dull, gray concrete littered with debris, cracked sidewalks, dilapidated brick town houses with rusty metal railings and clothes hanging from lines out back. The only foliage was the occasional weed that no one bothered to pull or spray, as though it would make a difference. The accumulated neglect lent itself to more neglect. What could one person possibly do to hold back the tide that swept through cities like this one? It was a plight Jacks knew well, having grown up in places so similar, she felt a wave of remembrance every time she came here. They had their own feel, their own smell—gas fumes, garbage. It was the smell of rot. The feel of hopelessness, the acute kind that makes a person want to flee, and if that proved impossible, then to find another avenue of escape. Alcohol. Drugs. And, if one were lucky, a man like David Halstead.

The light turned, and she went through it, one hand on the wheel and the other curled up over her mouth as though she could hold back the air that was trying to get inside her. She had made it out, for seventeen years she'd been on a kind of parole, a furlough, and the thought of returning for good was as impossible as anything she could imagine for herself, let alone the children. She drove two blocks, made a turn. Another three blocks, another turn, her mind seeing documents and numbers as she drove. She knew the way by heart. By feel. She'd been going there for over twenty years.

As she pulled up to the house, she felt strangely relieved. Even with the state of things, the peeling paint, the unruly patch of grass littered with plastic balls that were faded from the sun and blackened with mildew after a rainy month. Nothing had been done to this house for years, nothing could. Her sister was so damned stubborn.

She drove around back and parked next to an old Ford station wagon. She gathered the papers from the front seat, grabbed her purse, and headed for the back door.

"Kel?" she called in through the screened window, pressing her face closer to see inside. The kitchen was dark, even through the morning hours, shaded by the other units that crowded around.

She heard the footsteps, then the familiar voice. "Coming, Jacks—hold on a sec. . . ."

When Kelly Moore finally appeared through the doorway, she was in her usual state of controlled chaos. Still dressed in a beige Holiday Inn uniform, her name tag slightly askew as it hung from her chest, she was pulling a long drag from a cigarette with one hand and steadying a cup of coffee with the other. A broad smile came across her face as she opened the door and saw her sister.

"Hey, baby girl," she said, throwing her arms around Jacks. "You okay?"

Jacks squeezed her back as the competing forces of her own need and profound guilt tugged at her emotions. With everything that she had, it seemed entirely wrong to have turned here—of all places—for help. Still, it was the only family she had left, and she found herself letting go.

"Shhh . . . it's okay," Kelly said as her sister cried in her arms.

"Come sit down. Did you bring the papers?"

That had always been her sister's way, to focus on the task at hand, worry about one thing at a time. It was how she had survived their childhood, and the many mistakes she'd made since then, including the reckless behavior that had produced two children over the years.

"I have them." Jacks wiped her face and followed Kelly to the metal table set up next to the window in the small family room. Having only two rooms on the first floor, Kelly had struggled to transform the space to serve as a dining room as well, and a place for her kids to do their homework. There were crates with school supplies set up against one wall, and a large bulletin board with a chore wheel. Tirelessly, she had done her best to make the home tolerable—torn out the old carpet and wallpaper, sanded the floors, painted the walls and sewn window treatments. It was tidy, orderly. She ran a tight ship for those kids. All that with two jobs—hotel clerk for the benefits, nanny in a neighboring, more affluent town for money. There wasn't a moment in her life that Kelly Moore didn't devote to her children. Still, the problems came, which was exactly what had Jacks sitting here now.

"I only have an hour. Mrs. Linder took the baby to the doctor, but she wants to get her hair done." Kelly dropped the cigarette into the coffee mug, then turned on a fan to push the smoke out the window. "Goddamned cigarettes."

Jacks reached out and touched her hand. "It's okay. You do what you can do."

Kelly smiled and nodded, but the sadness on her face was unwavering. Nothing she did would ever be enough. Not now. Not ever. Her face turned deadly serious. "This can't happen. Not after all these years . . . after everything."

"I know."

They looked at each other then, and in a way that took them both back in time. It had been years, decades since they'd shared this look. Not that anything had been forgotten, or ever could be. But there had been a sense of calm, a reordering of priorities. Urgency had been replaced with long-term planning, parochial school for Kelly's children, a college fund. They were close to teenagers now. They were almost there. She had refused to take a dime for anything else, not a piece of clothing or furniture or food. It was more than just her pride, though her pride was not insignificant. Kelly understood people, even people like David Halstead. It was how she had gotten by for so many years. Giving the poor relations money for school made him feel good. Wondering what might be next—loans for the phone bill, a new car, the list could be endless—would make him feel used. Kelly knew the difference, and so she remained disciplined, even in the face of deprivation. She accepted the school tuition and, at Christmas, a small trip somewhere, a time when the two families could be together on equal footing. The cousins had grown close because of it, and in spite of the vast disparities in wealth. Kelly had dreamed of their futures, the things that college could give them. The things she had never had. It was the light at the end of this long, miserable tunnel, the reason she tolerated one boss who grabbed her ass and another who belittled her. It couldn't be for nothing.

There was a knock at the front door, and Kelly jumped to get it. From her seat at the table, Jacks watched as a chubby middle-aged man passed through the entry and into the house. She could smell the stale alcohol from across the room.

They spoke quietly for a moment, this odd little man and her sister, and it soon became clear from Kelly's demeanor that she was uncomfortable around him. He was standing close, too close even for a hushed conversation, and though Kelly hid it, Jacks could see the repulsion spreading across her face. A pasty, bloated hand reached out for Kelly's waist, accompanied by a seedy grin, and that was, apparently, the last straw. Kelly pushed him away and turned toward the table, where Jacks was waiting. The man followed, somehow amused by this most recent interaction.

"This is Red," Kelly announced, her eyes avoiding the man. "My neighbor."

Red extended his hand, and Jacks felt obliged to take it. "Red?" she asked, observing the waxy white pool ball of a head that seemed to be resting on the man's sternum. Not a neck in sight.

He chuckled and rubbed his scalp, clearly unaware of just how unattractive he truly was. "Yeah. Used to have a full mop. You have to get to know me a lot better to see the evidence." He winked then, eyebrows raised, provoking a loud sigh from Kelly.

"Christ, Red, give it a rest."

Jacks smiled politely and changed the subject. "So . . . Kelly said you were an accountant?"

Red sat down, nodding with pride. "*Am* an accountant. Just between firms at the moment. I think I'm gonna open my own . . . you know, get some clients, hang a shingle. Everybody's got taxes, right? I'm what you'd call a necessary evil."

"You should pass out some business cards at the Pink Panty," Kelly said, stifling her disgust. Red had moved in next door three months ago following his release from prison on a vehicular homicide. He'd plowed down an old man after a night of heavy drinking. Now he spent his days and nights at a sleazy strip club, drinking away what was left of his savings, and his conscience.

"I might just do that. Those girls make a lot of dough. I keep telling your sister . . . she could work half the hours—"

"Well, thanks for agreeing to meet with me," Jacks said, interrupting his train of thought before Kelly took a bat to his bald little head.

"Oh, yeah. No problem. I know it doesn't look that way, but I handled a lot of corporate investment reports. I know my way around the paperwork."

Jacks could see he was serious, though Kelly was now rolling her eyes. No matter—even if he was merely half the man he seemed to think himself, he was free and far from Wilshire. She cleared her throat, then reached for the papers she'd copied through the night. "I brought what I could. I know there's over seven million dollars missing from all of our assets."

Red took the papers, his interest now piqued. "Seven million, you said?" Still, his tone was nonchalant. "And you said there were letters from the government?"

Jacks nodded. "They're in there—at the back. They haven't charged him with anything. That's good, right? Wouldn't they charge him if he'd done something wrong?"

"Depends," he said, reading over the letters from the U.S. Attorney's office. "They're still asking for explanations."

"For what?"

He looked up then, his face solemn. "This statute—the one they've cited here. It's . . . well, it's basically embezzlement."

The words tore through her. She knew what David did for a living—gathering other people's money, pooling it all, and investing it in large-scale deals that none of them could afford on their own. There were no stocks or bonds, no securities regulations he had to worry about. The hedge fund business had been the Wild West of Wall Street. Private money. Private investments. And just enough rope for David to hang himself with.

Kelly reached out and took her sister's hand. "Red, what does this mean? What has her husband done with the money?"

"That's what the government wants to know. It looks like he and his partner raised two funds. It's the second group of investors that have lodged the complaint. They're probably gearing up for a civil suit—the criminal complaint is the first step."

"But what would he have done with their money!" Kelly was growing impatient. They needed answers, and they needed them soon.

"Look—there could be tens of millions that disappeared here. And that would be a small fund for this business. Could be in the hundreds."

"Hundreds of millions?" Jacks hadn't imagined it could be that much. "What would he have done with hundreds of millions of dollars? And why would he need our seven?"

Red shrugged as he dug through the pile of papers. "Just give me a minute—let me see if there's anything here—"

"This can't be happening. . . ." Jacks got up from the table, her face flushed with panic. "Why is this happening?"

Kelly left Red at the table and joined her sister. It was incredible, impossible. David Halstead was as steady as they came. Duke undergrad. Harvard Business School. Five years at a top firm, then many more years of success on his own. His two lovely parents had retired to a farm in Vermont. His sister was a nurse. They were good people. Solid people. How could Jacks have been so wrong?

Standing behind Jacks now, Kelly wrapped her arms around her little sister and rested her chin on her shoulder. Cheek to cheek, she whispered into

Jacks's ear, "It's okay . . . we'll be okay," and Jacks was taken back to that dark night three decades gone, when Kelly had left for good, left her alone to wait and hope and fear what might be coming. It was months before she'd returned for Jacks. The familiar desperation was in her now, the feeling that all was lost. How easily it came back, after so many years—years that had been filled with contentment, even joy at times. They had made it out. Kelly had saved them back then, but things were different now. They couldn't scrap it out day by day, sleep in the subway, clean up in a public bathroom somewhere. They had five children between them.

A moment passed before the two women let go of each other. Their connection was like a force field, their minds running along the same track. They were apples from the same tree, and even now, living lives at polar extremes, they moved in unison.

"Maybe he's tucked it away somewhere—the Caymans . . . ," Kelly said, releasing Jacks from her arms.

Jacks shook her head, smiling sadly. They both knew that wasn't the case. It just didn't fit.

"Yeah." Kelly nodded. "Wishful thinking."

"What if I just tell him? At least then we'd know what's going on."

Kelly's face tightened. She took a step toward her sister and grabbed hold of her arms. "You can't. Tell me—promise me you won't!"

Jacks was puzzled by the intensity of her sister's reaction. "He's my *husband*, Kel. He'll tell me the truth."

"Really? Is that why he's been hiding it all these weeks?"

"He's just afraid. And ashamed."

Kelly walked away then, past Red, who was pretending not to listen, and into the kitchen, where she lit another cigarette. Jacks followed.

"It's not the same," Jacks said. This was not the first time they had covered this ground.

Kelly took a long drag, then let it out. "No, it's not the same. This time there are other lives at stake."

"Oh, Kel. You think I don't know that?"

Kelly turned then to face Jacks. "It's too late now."

"Too late for what?"

"Too late to trust him," Kelly said, her words pleading. "He's lied to you for weeks, maybe years. He's taken every asset he could get his hands on.

Can't you see? He's already done it! This isn't something that's happened *to* him. He did it to himself—and now it's on you, the lives of these children." Her eyes grew wide as she made her case. "We have to rethink everything we've ever believed about him. People don't just up and do something like this. Are you really willing to bet your life on a man who's stolen your future?"

Jacks felt the shift inside her, the same shift she'd been having for weeks, back and forth, back and forth between two versions of the same reality. David Halstead, loving father and husband. David Halstead, thief. And who was she, the comfortable housewife or the woman on the brink of ruin?

"I'm sorry," Red said loudly from his seat in the other room. "I need more time to look through this. Can I have a day or so?"

Jacks started to turn for the doorway, but Kelly took hold of her arm one last time. "Promise me," she said.

In spite of everything Jacks had come to know, the safety of being one in a couple, a wife to a wealthy man, she could feel herself residing now in the past lived not with David, but with the woman whose blood she shared. Telling David was a one-way street. There would be no turning back. She couldn't afford to lose any option that came her way.

Jacks nodded then, and Kelly slowly released her hold. Pulling themselves together, the sisters returned to the living room and stood beside Red.

"Please—just give me your gut reaction," Jacks said, ready to get down to business.

Red sighed, his face almost apologetic for what he was about to say. "I think he lost it."

"Lost it? How can you lose that much money?" Kelly asked.

"Bad investments. I think he lost most of the first fund, then raised a second fund to cover the first, hoping to buy some time."

"To do what?" Jacks was confused. "Why wouldn't he just tell the investors the deals went bad?"

"He probably thought he could hit a big payoff with whatever money he had left. Then he could show a decent return on the second fund—not great, but nothing to raise eyebrows—and he'd be saved. His firm, his reputation. All of it would be saved."

Kelly got it. "It's a pyramid scheme. Isn't that what you've just described?"

"Basically. And it's illegal. He could face jail time. And all of your assets—"

"What's left of them—"

"What's left of them. They could be seized as well."

Jacks nodded with resignation. It was all just speculation, but something about it struck her as real. She just couldn't put her finger on it. Maybe it was the humiliation of choosing the wrong deals or stocks or whatever he'd sunk his investors' money into that had driven him to this point. He was Harvard. He was Wall Street. He was a winner. Still, this was far more than unwise investing. He'd spiraled out of control, and she could not stop the image of her father from transposing with that of her husband. But all this wondering, this bone-deep confusion about who her husband really was or was not—that was beside the point. Kelly's words resounded inside her. This was on her now.

She looked at her sister and drew a long breath. "Call me when you know something."

"We will. Red can stay all day. Can't you, Red?"

It would be a long day crunching through these papers, not so much as a beer in sight. But there was something in the room, a profound need—and with it a sense of purpose—that had taken hold. He nodded. "I'll stay."

NINE

DECONSTRUCTION

"I'M HOME!" SARA YELLED as she stumbled through the mudroom door, arms loaded with grocery bags. There was no answer, only the smell of dust and primer. Mentally exhausted and desperate to see her baby girl, she walked across the plastic sheeting to the kitchen island, where she heaved the bags, her purse, and car keys.

She'd been gone just four hours, though it had felt like an interminable odyssey in some bizarre faraway land. Alone in her journey, weaving through a maze of home-goods and decorating stores and the pompous ladies who worked in them simply to kill time, her mind was now altered. Four hours were now lost, and she would never get them back. A bit dramatic, but true. Everything and everyone she'd encountered had been nothing short of intolerable roadblocks to spending time with Annie, whom she hadn't seen since breakfast.

"Hello?" she yelled again, turning toward the kitchen door. This time, someone came.

"Oh—hey, there, Mrs. Livingston." Standing in the doorway, Roy the Contractor smelled of cigarettes, which meant he'd just come from her yard, where he'd indulged in another break. From what, she couldn't tell. The house looked exactly the same as it had when she'd left to run her errands.

"Hi, Roy," Sara managed, though Roy was the last person she wanted to see at the moment. He was the real reason her day had completely sucked. "How's it coming along?" The question was rhetorical. Comical, actually, though the humor was lost on her today.

"Just fine. We're waiting on the electrician. Kinda stuck for a while till he gets here."

Sara didn't let the words sink in at first. Her mind was fixated on wrapping her arms around her daughter, if only to make sure she still existed. "Nanna? Annie?" she called out.

The silence annoyed her. She would have to go looking now, and Roy was in her path. She let his words enter her consciousness.

Then she let out an audible sigh. "And why is that?" she asked, her tone infused with sarcasm. The niceties had long since left their relationship.

"Well, it's like I told you yesterday. The wiring in the walls we took down was old—"

Sara waved her hand to silence him. "Yeah—I remember. The whole house needs to be rewired or we're all gonna burn up in an electrical fire. Never mind the house has survived for thirty years."

Roy scowled. Then he shrugged, and Sara couldn't decide which was more infuriating as she began to shove groceries into the few cupboards that were still functional. *It's your family*, he was saying. *If they burn, it's on you, lady.* And yet she couldn't help feeling that it was part of a scheme, a gigantic con that had started with a reasonable bid on a small renovation and was now a do-or-die deconstruction of the entire dwelling with no end in sight.

"Isn't there anything you can do in the meantime? No flooring? No plumbing? No tile work?" She opened the fridge and stared at shelves caked with dust. It was everywhere. A plague of dust. She placed the milk inside and closed the door.

Roy shrugged again in that *sorry* way of his. "Not really." Shrug.

It kept coming. An all-out assault on her senses. She scoured over this man standing before her, so calm, so matter-of-fact. They both knew he was putting a gun to her head. That's all this was. Good old-fashioned armed robbery. And yet, there wasn't a damned thing she could do about it.

Except cry—which is exactly what she did. It came from her gut and burst into the dusty kitchen air all the way up through the torn-apart walls to the second floor and back down again in one giant echo that only served to humiliate her further. Not only was she getting screwed royally, but she'd now lost control of her very self in front of Roy as well. She would be, from here on out, the hysterical housewife, the one he'd planned on turning her into all along.

Roy seemed to be smiling. Somewhere behind his serious face, crossed arms, and filthy, cigarette-stinky T-shirt, he was definitely smiling.

Eyes fully pooled with tears, Sara held a hand over her mouth. *Who are you?* she thought. Never had she been so consumed by her external circumstances. Even in the roach-infested apartment at Columbia that Nick had saved her from. She used to thrive on hardship. But this was entirely different for her. She had no idea how to manage this life. It was a life she had never planned on having.

She placed her hands around her face and let the tears fall. "I just want to see my daughter." Her voice was desperate, but she didn't care. "Can you please . . . just leave me alone so I can see my child?"

Roy was not fazed. Of course he wasn't. "Sure, Mrs. Livingston."

"Just find Annie," she whispered to herself. She turned toward the door and yelled again. "Hello?"

It was well past three. Nanna should have had Annie home from school two hours ago.

She moved closer to the stairs, the tears still falling uncontrollably. "Hello?" she called out, her voice riddled with frustration.

Roy walked past her silently, an unlit cigarette hanging from between his fingers. As he neared the door to the yard, he turned back to her. "They're not home."

Sara drew another long breath, but it did nothing to ease the pounding in her head that was now a constant, unrelenting stress ball ready to explode. This was the third time in a month that Nanna had disregarded her instructions to bring Annie home after school. And she was having to hear this news from Roy, of all people.

She raced upstairs to her bedroom and closed the door, but in every corner, something was staring her down. The plaid valances, a small dust ball in a corner missed by the cleaners who had just been here yesterday, the sunlight placidly sifting through her picture window—all of it was pushing her right over the edge. She rushed to her closet and locked herself inside, as though somehow she could keep it at bay, these forces that were spinning out of control. Destroying her home. Eating her flowers. Stealing her time, and erasing her from her daughter's life. She sat on the floor, knees to chest, and stared at her tear-stricken face in the mirror.

She forced herself to exhale as she considered the facts that were tangled in her head. A torn-apart house that they couldn't afford to walk away from. An irreverent nanny who was necessary *because* of the torn-apart house and the demands it placed on her time. The impossibility of breaking into a circle of friends because, again, she had no time to invest in understanding their world. She was Alice down the rabbit hole, a pawn who'd been sucked into the vortex of a giant suburban storm and was now being tossed and turned and twisted. Could she just scream? *Stop!* Send Roy packing. Fire Nanna. Stop caring about the women of Wilshire. Could she do all that and start again? She could hardly remember what it was like before Annie came, being twenty-three with nothing to do but explore the world.

That was it. She raced out of her room and called down the stairs. "Roy!"

Then she grabbed the phone and called Nanna's cell. It went straight to voice mail. *The nerve!* Never mind—she would deal with Nanna the moment the woman walked through the door. Feeling a burst of empowerment, she called out again from the open hallway window—louder this time.

"Roy!"

She heard the door open from outside. Almost giddy now, she formed the words in her head. *You're fired!* His steps were approaching the bottom of the stairs, and she moved toward them.

"Mrs. Livingston?" It was Roy. She could smell the stale smoke. She started her descent.

Then the phone rang.

"Hold on—don't go anywhere!" she called down to him. Then she ran back for the cordless, which she'd thrown on the bed.

"Hello?"

"Sara?"

"Yes?"

"It's Rosalyn Barlow."

Sara froze. It had been only three days since the nursery school benefit, and she had been quite certain that Rosalyn Barlow would never give her the time of day again. They had figured out how young she was, revealed enough of their secrets to be embarrassed, if they were even capable of that, and otherwise excluded her from the conversation. Yet here she was—calling?

Sara tried to sound pleasantly surprised and not shocked, which she was. Completely.

"Oh, hi! How are you?" She wiped the wetness from her face with the back of her hand.

"Fine, thank you. Listen, I apologize for the short notice, but I have a proposition for you."

With Roy waiting at the bottom of the stairs, Sara listened. And as she listened, her new plan, the one where she took back the reins of her runaway life, was deconstructed the way her house had been—one piece at a time. The reasoning she had used, the inputs and assumptions, were suddenly open to question, and she was left with nothing but a head full of whirring uncertainty. Rosalyn Barlow wanted her to join an intimate committee to solve the social problems of teenage girls, to prevent other girls from the plight of the hallway blow job. She wanted Sara to write an article about it for the local newspaper. (*Wouldn't that be a great way to restart your career?*) And if Sara accepted, she would somehow, miraculously, be cast into the circle of Rosalyn Barlow and her most trusted friends.

Why this mattered to her was as puzzling as the phone call, but somehow it did. Maybe for Nick, who so wanted to rebuild his life here. Maybe for her, to make Nick happy? If she were honest, no. She had never failed at anything before moving to Wilshire. She had never been on the bottom rung. Valedictorian of her high school class. Magna cum laude at Princeton. The master's degree from Columbia.

She hung up the phone and sat down on her bed. Maybe she'd been right. Impatient, but right. Rosalyn Barlow wanted her on this committee because of all she had been and maybe still was, and with the innocence of her own youth, she let herself believe that her two worlds might actually be able to meld together after all. She wiped her face again, removing the last traces of the tears. She felt the charges begin to settle inside her.

"Mrs. Livingston?" Roy was still waiting.

She thought about what to do. Surprisingly, it wasn't hard. Everything had changed. The house would get done. She could spend the entire evening with Annie. All was not lost. This was not the time for rash decisions.

She walked to the stairs and yelled down, "Nothing, Roy. Nothing."

TEN

THE BRILLIANT PLAN

IT WAS A BRILLIANT plan. Now that she had made her first public appearance since the *incident*, Rosalyn Barlow was ready to tackle the larger problem, the social problem that was making its way across the country, and doing so indiscriminately. Wealthy or poor, the scourge of teenage promiscuity and this latest twist, this "friends with benefits" phenomenon, were infiltrating the lives of children everywhere. That her daughter had become a victim in its powerful path had opened her eyes, and she would not turn her back on the other girls who were potential prey. Like Al Gore and climate change, Rosalyn Barlow was about to become the poster woman for this important social cause. When she was finished playing spin doctor, this problem would be viewed through her eyes, and the town would believe it was virtually breeding inside the walls of the school. Whether or not that was actually true was of little concern.

And that was why, seated around her at Asi (Wilshire's answer to Nobu) and eyeing a platter of designer sushi were the people essential to the plan. First, of course, was Wilshire Academy headmistress, Marcia Preston. With wavy but neat chestnut hair and a serious, angular face, she was just what the situation called for: an intellectual. That she was here solely out of obligation to the Barlow family, and the large donation they had recently made, was silently and mutually understood.

Eva Ridley was seated to the right of Ms. Preston, and Rosalyn was counting on her love of storytelling to broadcast everything that went on at these meetings through the underground sound system she had installed into the far corners of this town. *Rosalyn Barlow, hero. Caitlin Barlow, victim. Who would be next?* The scandal at the Wilshire Academy would fit nicely on her playlist.

Elbow to elbow with Rosalyn was Sara Livingston, who was not only perspiring under her wool suit jacket and silk blouse, but was actually soaked with sweat. Rosalyn still wasn't quite sure what she made of this young woman. Middle-class breeding and only twenty-seven years old with one three-year-old, Sara Livingston was a suburban virgin. But Princeton and Columbia—nothing to smirk at. Besides, it was there, on her face. The unmistakable desire to be one of them, to fit in, and Rosalyn was betting Sara would give this agenda the attention it deserved. The local paper would print her articles, providing instant credibility to the cause.

Finally, there was Jacks, the perfect example of the reinvention of oneself. No one really knew about Jacks's past. She told people she went to a small college "upstate" somewhere, that her parents died when she was little. She had one sister who also lived "upstate," though Jacks never committed to a specific town. She was a crafty one, dodging questions with more questions—the kind of questions people in Wilshire loved to answer. Questions about themselves. *Where did you say your sister lived? Oh—upstate . . . That reminds me, didn't you rent a cottage in Groton last year?* Brilliant. And Rosalyn admired that. No one could read a person better than Jacks, and now Rosalyn was counting on her to be the psychic along the way.

With the team assembled, Rosalyn tapped her spoon against a glass of water. "Ladies . . . ," she said, interrupting the chatter. "Should we get down to business? Let me first thank all of you for coming. I am—" Rosalyn paused then to be momentarily choked up. "—so grateful for your support."

There was a collective sigh and a gentle shoulder-pat from the headmistress.

Rosalyn shuddered as though shaking off her emotions. Of course, her emotions had been placed in a vault and locked away earlier that morning.

How else would she survive this meeting? The sincerity, the angst, the endless talk of girls and self-esteem and the gender politics of horny teenagers. At the end of it all, it would still be there, sitting on the table in front of them among the vibrant pink salmon rolls and milky white toro—the truth of the matter. Her daughter had been branded a loser somewhere along the way, and the hallway blow job was nothing more than a down payment on a ticket out. Wasn't that the way of the world? The exploitation of the weak? The scratching and clawing up ladders—social, economic, political?

In any other town, the Barlows' money would have guaranteed Cait's ranking among the bloodthirsty teenage girls. But in Wilshire, everyone had money. Owning property here was the great equalizer. It took work, hard work above and beyond her husband's money, to achieve the kind of status Rosalyn had cultivated. Her mother hadn't come close to it. Had it been anything else, anything but sex, Rosalyn Barlow would have been relieved that Cait had found an angle to move up the social ranks. God help her, she would have seen it as a welcomed sign that the weakest of her five children would actually survive in a world that was, despite the appearance of civility, ruthless. Rosalyn knew this firsthand.

Taking a breath, she continued. "I need to thank the school, Marcia, for the gracious way everyone handled things. Really—it was the perfect balance of discipline and support. We will never forget it."

Marcia blushed. She wasn't used to flattery, and in fact, had developed the skin of an elephant to keep out the shit storms she usually received from the parent body.

"Thank you, Rosalyn," Marcia said. "She's a good kid. We all know that."

"Yes, which brings me to the purpose of this meeting. There are a lot of good kids who are losing their way when it comes to their sexuality," she began, though the words were sticky as they emerged from her carefully lined lips. "They've lost the true joy of first love, first kisses. They don't have relationships anymore."

Rosalyn looked at Sara, eyebrows raised in an unspoken invitation for her thoughts.

When the request finally registered, Sara opened her mouth. "Um" was all that came out. Then a pause. Then, finally, something articulable. "It's a national problem, actually." Her words held confidence, though her voice was a bit shaky, mirroring the unsteady ground beneath her that shifted between her old life and her seat at this table.

Still, what she said next pleased Rosalyn.

"Although teenagers aren't engaging in sexual activity any earlier, the circumstances under which they do have changed. Sex has been separated from emotional intimacy. I did some research on it last night. There's been a lot of discourse lately."

"Ha!" Eva Ridley was chuckling to herself as she took a gulp of wine. "That sounds like most of the marriages in this town."

"Oh, Eva," Jacks said.

Eva shrugged. "Well? Am I wrong?" She knew what she knew.

"Anyway," Rosalyn interrupted, "I would be very indebted if each of you could come up with a few names. Maybe we can do a little research. Sara, weren't you a feminist in college? There must be some feminists who specialize in this area."

Sara had a mind-boggled expression. "Um . . . I can look into it."

Again, the subtle smile from the hostess.

"Thanks—I really appreciate it. Can I e-mail everyone to stay in touch? And Marcia, can you get me some dates to work with? Just after the holidays, maybe?"

Marcia nodded. "Sure. A winter event seems appropriate for such a somber issue."

Rosalyn raised her wineglass. "To our girls," she said.

They all took a sip. Then Marcia Preston gathered her things. "I really should be getting back. Thank you for the lovely lunch," she said, now rushing to get the hell out of there.

"We'll be in touch." Rosalyn stood to give her a mini-hug at the shoulders.

Eva watched the educator walk away, then set down her wineglass before giving Rosalyn a disapproving look. "*Weren't you a feminist in college?* Did you really say that?"

Jacks forced a smile. "She really said it."

"What? Sara—*weren't* you a feminist in college?" Rosalyn asked, pretending to be indignant.

Sara thought about that for a moment. Then she decided to answer the question the way she might were she not so damned intimidated. "I don't think you can actually *be* a feminist anymore. Feminism is really a way of life."

"Exactly!" Eva said, though she had, on numerous occasions, boasted about being one. "It's not like being a *communist*. Any woman who believes she has a right to choose her own destiny is a feminist. End of story. In fact, Rosalyn Barlow, you are a feminist."

"A feminist who shaves her legs," Jacks said. Eva laughed hard. Rosalyn smiled.

"I mean, look at all of us." Eva eyed her friends, old and new. "Every woman here went to college, had a job, then chose to stay home with her children. We are living the legacy of choice that the feminists laid down."

"Huh," Rosalyn said, her eyes narrow as she pretended to think about this seriously. *Choice* was an interesting word to describe the gender politics of Wilshire. It was an interesting word to describe what had happened between her daughter and Kyle Conrad in that hallway.

"All I know is that the world looks very much the same as it did when I was a child. Maybe it's a sad state of affairs that the feminists worked so hard to give us all these choices, and we chose to stay put."

Eva gave Rosalyn a sad smile. "Well, anyway, I think we can all agree that keeping dicks out of girls' mouths is a worthy cause—feminists or not."

Jacks raised her glass. "Well put, Eva. Tactful, as always."

Eva smiled. "Thank you. I guess we can now adopt a name for our cause. The blow job committee. Oh, and speaking of prurient things, how is the Halloween party coming along?"

Rosalyn paused for a moment to glance at Sara. The Barlows' annual Halloween party was Wilshire's most prominent and infamous event, and Rosalyn had not invited the Livingstons. Not yet.

"Sara, I completely forgot!" Rosalyn lied, covering herself. "The invitations went out before we met and I just didn't think—"

Sara brushed it off. "Don't worry about it, really. . . ."

"No, you must come. Call my assistant for the details. Here—" Rosalyn pulled a business card from her purse and handed it to Sara. "—it has all my numbers."

Then, with the plastic smile returning, Rosalyn raised her glass for the second time. "One final toast. To our girls."

ELEVEN

TOTALLYFKD

INSIDE HER ROOM, CAITLIN buried her face in a pillow and let out a scream. There was so much to sort out, so many things swimming around in her head, drowning her. She needed to focus, stay afloat. First on the agenda was this incessant daydreaming about Kyle Conrad and the evidence that it would never be anything more than that. He had touched her hair, but then seemed indifferent to her. He had smiled at her, but then winked at Amanda. He'd asked her into that hallway, but how many others had there been before her? All of this needed sorting. She needed time, and space, to relive each moment, to comb through each event in her head and somehow come to a conclusion so she wouldn't go mad. Then there was the problem of Amanda Jamison and how easily she could take away the surprising social elevation she'd bestowed upon Caitlin. Would it last? Could she make it last, or would she piss it all away with another move like puking in kindergarten?

Plopped on her bed in a heap of nerves and a wrenching stomach that would not be placated, she clung to the pillow and closed her eyes, letting it take her to the only escape she had. Kyle Conrad, towering over her, broad shoulders, tanned skin, blue eyes. He walked like he would never have a worry in this world. Not ever—over a job, a girl, or whatever it was a person like Kyle could afford to desire. Kyle was a mystery, but that did not concern her so much as the burning desire to attach herself to him, hitch a ride on the golden road he was surely headed for. He had been a vehicle, a task she needed to perform to adhere herself to Amanda and the new life the girl had given Cait. But something shifted in that hallway, something had been ignited, and now Kyle Conrad *was* that life.

She sighed hard, breathing in deep the anguish that filled her room, and wondered how long she could take any of this.

There, she said to herself, entering the imaginary world that was all about him and nothing else. *There he is. There I am. The world is frozen around us.* He kisses her hard, then pulls back, sending a message through his eyes. This is what he wants, and he will have it. And her doubts, the ones that kept sneaking in like thieves to loot her deepest desires, are suddenly irrelevant. *The world is frozen.* He removes her clothing, calmly and with clear intention. He is not subjected to the mortal failings of emotions. There is something calculated. His control is absolute as he lays her down.

It was sweet, the abandon she felt in her most secret fantasy, running across her shattered nerves like a soothing balm. That it was often followed by disgust and self-loathing was no longer an impediment, as she could hardly feel any worse than she already did. Could she not have, at the very least, these few minutes of peace?

She heard the blip on her screen and pulled herself from the bed, the pillow, and the other world she had let herself run to. There was a message from one of the many Web sites she had found. It was a new entry from someone she didn't recognize. Totallyfkd was the screen name, and it had her instantly intrigued. She clicked on the link to pull up the entry, and the words dragged her in like a tornado's vortex.

Totallyfkd: Help! Need advice! I'm so fucked. Anyone there?

Caitlin paused for the briefest of moments before responding.

Cbow: I'm here. What happened?
Totallyfkd: Thank God! Who are you?
Cbow: Cbow.
Totallyfkd: Right. Duh. I mean who are you—girl, boy, old, young?

Cbow: Girl. Seventeen.

Totallyfkd: Not sure I want to tell a stranger.

Cbow: Maybe that'll be easier. Nothing you tell me will ever get back to you.

Totallyfkd: OK. Totally anonymous then. Here goes. I lost it last weekend with this guy I really liked and he hasn't called. Prick. I feel like I wanna die. Maybe kill him first (ha). Why would he do that? Why fuck me at all? He can have anyone he wants and I'm a nobody—really I am.

Cbow: Maybe he will still call. Why do you think you're a nobody?

Totallyfkd: I am. Trust me. I'm so stressed this year my ass is as big as Texas. All I do is eat. Senior year is supposed to be the greatest. And my parents suck more than ever.

Cbow: I can relate. And I'm sure your ass isn't the size of Texas.

Totallyfkd: Maybe Rhode Island. I hate my parents. It's like I'm a little tro-phy and they can't wait to get me into Smith so they can hang my head on their wall, all stuffed and puffed like the last thing I saw was their gun pointed between my eyes. Fuck. And I thought this guy really cared about me.

Cbow: Maybe he does. How long have you gone out?

Totallyfkd: What planet are you from? We never went out. We just fucked. And I waited til senior year for the right guy. He's amazing. Do you think there's a chance he'll still call? Is there some three day rule on fuck-ing and calling? I swear to God, if he doesn't, I don't know. . . .

Cbow: I don't know either. Haven't been there yet. Maybe you just have to wait till you see him again? Like a party or something . . .

Totallyfkd: Wait. . . . Can't wait! I feel like I'm drowning. Life feels like a big fucking nothing. Sorry to keep saying fuck all the time. I hope I haven't upset you. It makes me feel better. I'm probably on some terrorist watch list now—kids trying to destroy the world with the f word.

Cbow: You're funny. I think he'll call you. And if not, at least you got it over with. Now the next time won't be such a big fucking deal. I like saying fuck too . . .

Totallyfkd: Just don't know how to stop feeling this way . . . like I can't even breathe without him . . . like I won't survive if he never touches me again . . .

Cbow: But you did survive before he touched you, so you must be able to.
You are lucky to be a senior. College could be a whole new world and
this guy a distant memory.

Totallyfkd: Do you really believe that?

Caitlin read the last entry again and again. It provoked her from the inside out, this girl's story. *Yes*, she thought, *that's what it feels like—drowning slowly in the quicksand of your own life.* Could she survive if she never felt Kyle's hand against her skin again?

Cbow: I don't know. But it feels better to talk about it. Wanna hear about my
guy?

Totallyfkd: Yeah, I do.

TWELVE

CRIES IN THE NIGHT

FOR ALL INTENTS AND purposes, life had returned to normal. David left for work every morning at the same time, on the same train. He came home after work at the same time, on the same train. They had dinner together, he and Jacks, after the kids were in bed or settled in their rooms. The menu was leftovers from the meal prepared for the kids, usually by the maid, sometimes by Jacks if she was feeling inspired, which hadn't been much lately. Consumed with worry and a biting anxiety, she'd spent every spare moment hounding Red for answers and concocting an escape plan.

It had taken him over a week to figure things out, but he had done it. That little bald man who was most certainly motivated by the faint hope that her sister might warm to him, as well as a primal sort of curiosity about a world he had never experienced, had managed to sort out what he could.

The words from that conversation were still playing over and over in her head: *Embezzlement. Fraud. Bankruptcy.* Everything Red had surmised that day at her sister's house had been right. It had not been easy to track down the information. Now that Red was a criminal, the vile and repulsive sort who had taken a life for nothing more than a night of debauchery, he had few contacts to work with. Some had turned him away, indignant, and wary that his stink might rub off on them. Some had felt a shred of sympathy. He'd sought out public filings. And he'd called in a favor with a local lawyer who had worked at the U.S. Attorney's office in Hartford. It was more of an exchange than a favor, really. Red had promised to forget the man's presence at the Pink Panty Lounge, and the man had made a call to some government lawyers he still knew in New York.

All told, there had been over two hundred million dollars lost, most of it on a hotel complex in Vegas that hadn't been properly insured when it burned to the ground. David's fund had been the primary source of capital—capital that was now gone. All that remained was the land, but there was no money to rebuild. He'd raised the second fund under false pretenses, presenting the investors with bogus deals that didn't actually exist, thinking he could save the firm and himself if he could pay off the first investors, then get the hotel up and running before people started asking questions. But his race against the clock had ultimately failed. Desperate to hold off the investors, he'd bought time with his family's assets, the equity and 401(k), but it hadn't been enough. Now the investors wanted an accounting, and they had the weight of the government behind them.

Something had made him careless, and now he, and they, were close to losing everything. This was the thought that ran through Jacks's head as she watched him toy with a filet mignon across the table from her. He wouldn't eat it. The hollow spaces around his neck were proof of that. Maybe a few bites, swallowed down with glasses and glasses of cabernet. She knew this because his worry was now hers. Burning inside her like acid, it left no room for food, for rest. It was not the worry of having to make a decision. Or find a solution. Or even to come clean. It was the worry that rides on the back of tidal waves, hurricanes. The kind of worry that comes with the certainty that disaster will strike and that it will be devastating, leaving as a prelude nothing less than the torture of waiting. It was the kind that cannot be settled.

David was quiet now that the kids were gone. The show was over, the feigned enthusiasm as he listened to their stories, their tales of days spent in ignorance of what was about to occur. It was now, sitting alone with his wife, that he appeared capable of being absorbed into the silence. Jacks had seen him like this before, tired, things on his mind. And had she been another woman, a woman not so observant, it might all have gotten past her, as he seemed to believe it had. Still, in this moment, as she watched his face staring down into the full plate of food, aged beyond his years from the past several months, she could almost believe that he knew—that he could feel it lurking from under her skin.

But then he looked up and smiled. "How was the field trip?"

Jacks heard his voice, but the words went right past her. "What did you say?"

"How was the field trip? Beth's trip to the fire station? She told me you drove."

"It was good. This is my third time going, so I've got it down pretty well."

David smiled. Jacks had been mothering their girls for fourteen years. "I guess this is the last one."

"Is it awful to say that I'm not even a little sad about it?"

This drew a smile from her husband. He reached over and touched her hand, giving it a squeeze. "No. I'm ready to move on, too."

"I've been thinking," Jacks said, pulling her hand out from under his.

"What's that?"

Jacks sharpened her focus on his face, hoping to catch him flinching as she gave him the test. "I've been thinking that maybe it would be nice to bring the girls to France for spring break. They've never been to Europe." It was a cruel test—surely the thought of an expensive trip four months away would be nothing less than a wrecking ball, plunging into his already weakened frame. But she was at her limit. This charade had come between them, a barricade that held her from the primary source of comfort she had in her life, her love for her husband. And his love for her. In spite of her promise to her sister, she needed them to share this secret together.

Nothing.

"That sounds great. Maybe I can get some time off and join you for the second week. Will you start in Paris?"

He was almost carefree now, back in the role he played when the kids were underfoot. His face had even lifted a bit, making her wonder if she was wrong about everything. Maybe it was all a mistake—the letter from the government, the information from that drunken little man. Could she believe all that over her husband? And more important, could she believe her husband would deceive her so completely?

"Really? It's not too much?" Her voice was shaky, and she could barely look at him. *Please*, she thought. *Let me in.*

"It's fine. You'd better start planning it before the flights are gone."

"I will. I'll start tomorrow. But let's not tell the girls until I have it all set."

"Good idea. Maybe we can make it part of Christmas."

"That would be fun."

David took another sip of wine, slipping back into his silence. Jacks stared into the same silence, her eyes replaying scenes from a past she had thought was gone forever. The promises, the highs that would elevate her to the heavens. *This is the year, girls.* Promise after promise would come, at times for something as little as a new pair of shoes. Sometimes there were dreams of Disney World, or a house by the shore. None of it ever came, and it did no good at all to understand now, as an adult, what had driven their father from the heights of optimism to the depths of despair. Jobs came and went, and with them their only means of survival. The evidence had been there, but what is evidence to a little girl? Empty cupboards, eviction notices, the hushed conversations between teachers and social workers when she came to school dirty and hungry. In spite of it all, she had always believed. He was their father. He loved them. And they were promises.

"You look tired. Why don't you go up to bed?"

David nodded and stood from the table, taking his plate.

"Leave it. I'll get it later."

"Are you sure?" The maid was off at six.

Jacks smiled at her husband. "I'm sure."

She watched him leave, then cleared the table. She rinsed the plates, put them in the dishwasher, scrubbed the pots, and put them away. Reality was a strange thing, always shifting and turning with the light. It had taken her years to grasp this—far longer than her sister. *He's lied to you.* That's what Kelly had said. She was older, but more than that, she was simply built differently. Or maybe it was because they had suffered differently, Kelly having had to carry within her the memories of their mother's love, and the agony of her departure soon after Jacks was born. It was Kelly who had always been wiser, more perceptive, and inherently distrustful. It was Kelly who had taught Jacks what to look for, how to excavate the truth from the layers upon layers of earth that were used to keep it buried. In the grips of agony brought on by their mother's abandonment, Kelly had been programmed to trust nothing and no one but herself, not even the men she had been so careless with, the ones who had given her two perfect children. But no matter how well she had tried to teach her sister, Jacks still, miraculously, harbored the hope of trust—trust she had placed in her husband.

She heard the words as she climbed the stairs. *He's lying, stupid.* Of course he is. But it had been seventeen years, and Jacks was not ready to crawl back into the dark hole where her sister lived.

He was in bed when she entered the room. His sighs were heavy as he tried to will himself to sleep. Standing in the darkness, staring at the body that lay beneath the covers, she thought back to the man she knew. He had been predictable in so many ways, the clean-cut Wall Street banker with the nice family and impressive education. And yet he had somehow known, even before she told him, that there were many walls he would have to break down to get to her. The first night she spent with him, he had held her in his arms until she felt something real, and he had been that man ever since. Now he was lying. But there were reasons. Nothing was black or white. Everyone Jacks had ever known lived within the complex shades of gray that were formed from the passing of time, the mistakes and reinventions of oneself that were inevitable. He was a good man.

She brushed her teeth and washed her face. Changed into a nightgown. She turned out the closet light and pulled back the covers on her side. The need was powerful as she reached for him in the darkness, enveloping him in her arms.

"I love you," she said, and she felt the air rush out of his body, his heart pounding beneath his ribs. It was in these primal reflexes that she heard his silent confession.

She kissed him then, not to say good night, but to draw him back into her soul, to tell him she knew, that she could forgive him if he would only let her. She felt his arms reach back for her, pulling away her nightgown, drawing her into him. Surrounded by their deceptions, they made love, and through the desperation that pulled their bodies together, Jacks could feel the pleas of a drowning man.

She held his face, which was wet with tears, kissing him again and again. Whatever price she had paid along the way, she had survived her past, and now, as her body let go, she could feel the strength inside her, convincing herself that she would do the impossible. That she could do now as a grown woman what she had been unable to do as a child. Feeling the rush, she told herself she could save this man. She told herself she could save them all.

THIRTEEN

CHILD'S PLAY

AFTER SLIPPING IN A quick pedicure, Rosalyn returned home from a day
of errands and other tedious nonsense made necessary by the party that was
quickly approaching. There was the trip to the costume designer, the test run
with the makeup artist, and a stop at the caterer to approve the hors d'oeuvres.
Of course, all this busyness did serve the purpose of distracting her from
the other contents of her head, and she tried to remind herself of this as
she walked through the kitchen and into the playroom, where she found Mellie
and Barlow. Their four-year-old should have been down for her afternoon
nap. Of course, nothing was ever as it should be since Barlow's retirement,
and today was no exception. Barlow, who should have been doing something
productive for the party, was instead wearing a pink Indian-princess head-
dress as he sat cross-legged in the family room. He had apparently whirred
Mellie into a little tornado, and she was now dirty from head to toe and in the
pajamas from the night before. Her hair was matted into a giant brown tangled
mess, and she was wired from sweet snacks and no sleep. Nothing about this
was endearing to Rosalyn—not the crazed look of glee on her daughter's
face as she ran circles around her father, not the enthusiasm with which her
middle-aged husband sang a made-up Indian song and shook maracas.
None of it.

This was the new world according to Ernest Barlow. No rules. No schedules. No parenting of any kind, in fact. Just play. Child's play.

Rosalyn walked silently through the room to the kitchen, where the chef was doing the prep for the dinner. He offered her a cappuccino, which she politely refused; then she unloaded her bag by the computer kiosk on the other side of the room. Logging on to her Mac, she tried to block the sound of her husband's voice as it rang through the house. The high pitch, the inane lyrics about bringing a rainstorm. Did he really think this was what a child needed from a father? It certainly wasn't what she wanted from a husband.

She had thirty-eight messages—social callings and pleas for help from around the world. Friends in Monaco and London. Others in L.A. Wilshire Republicans. They had donated more than ten million dollars to charities last year alone. She sat on four boards. Wellesley College. Miss Porter's School for Girls. Save the Children and the local chapter of the American Red Cross. Her duties included writing checks, writing checks, and writing more checks. Then there was the overseeing of their many properties. The houses in Florida and Telluride. The estate in Nantucket. The Montana horse farm. The villa in Antibes. Some had to be opened, others closed for the winter. There were groundskeepers, chefs, maids, and nannies at all these places, some who rotated with the family's needs, some who worked seasonally.

She answered the queries that couldn't wait, the ones concerning last-minute details for the party. *Yes, the valets had to be in costume. No, they could not have the ice sculpture arrive early. Where would they keep it?* It was aggravating at best, the managing of their lives, and her husband was still singing. She logged out, leaving the rest to be handled later by her personal assistant.

Pushing away from her desk and out of her chair, she stormed back through the kitchen and out to the adjoining family room. It was enough already. Without a word to her husband and ignoring his look of astonishment, she scooped up her daughter and carried her kicking and screaming up the stairs to the nannies' study. It was there that she found Marta.

The young woman froze when she saw Rosalyn and the now very angry Mellie Barlow.

"Mr. Barlow said I should let her play," she muttered, obviously unnerved having been caught taking personal time during work hours.

But Rosalyn had no hard feelings toward Marta. Those had all been assigned to her husband.

"I know, Marta. But she needs a bath and some quiet time. No nap—it's too late. She'll never go to bed tonight. Maybe some books."

"Yes, of course." Marta reached out to take the child, but as she did, Mellie nuzzled her sticky wet face into Rosalyn's neck.

Rosalyn was taken aback. It had been a long time, weeks perhaps, since she'd felt those little arms clutching her back, squeezing with all their might, since she'd smelled the smell of juice and dirty hair that was somehow intoxicating. It had been far too long since she'd felt the warm breath against her cheek.

"You, Mama, you!" Mellie yelled.

"Come on, love. Mommy has things to do." And she did, didn't she? Endless things.

But Mellie only tightened her grip. Rosalyn shut her eyes against the emotions that had escaped the vault and were now staging a surprise attack.

"Please, Mellie, go with Marta."

This was her job now, to make the decisions and delegate. It was still mothering, different perhaps from what it had been years before, but still mothering in spite of the guilt she now felt from her four-year-old. She had one boy in prep school, a daughter giving sexual favors, two more boys in grade school, and at the present moment, this little girl draped around her like a rag doll. It was more than anyone could manage alone, and in the decades of Barlow's absence as he built his fortune, she had been forced to choose which roles to take on and which ones to dole out. Giving baths and reading books were things a young nanny could easily handle. Managing teachers, classes, grades, activities, and now Caitlin's problem, required a kind of expertise that she alone possessed within this house.

Life in Wilshire was complicated. The establishments that held the fate of her children needed constant tending. The Wilshire Academy, the country club, the exclusive and very private sports complex. No matter how well her children performed, the ones who rose to the top, who got the best teachers, the shiny medals and trophies and placement on the most coveted teams, depended on her and how deeply she could plug herself in. Through donations and constant face-to-face involvement, she had become the mother to please, and as a result, her children were never overlooked. Not once. This profound understanding was embedded within Rosalyn, at her very core.

She had learned how to manage her world from the greatest puppeteer Wilshire had ever known—the late great Mrs. Eddings.

"Just go," she said to Marta, dismissing the nanny. "Clean up the family room, please. I don't want the boys to get into Mellie's things."

She waited for the nanny to leave before squeezing her daughter back.

"Okay. You want Mommy to give you a bath?"

"Uh-huh."

"Come, then."

Rosalyn carried her child to the bathroom and filled the tub. Silently, she pulled off Mellie's dirty pajamas and helped her step into the water. Rosalyn sat on the closed toilet seat, still dressed in her silk slacks and heels, and watched as her daughter covered her favorite doll with soap. Inadvertently, Rosalyn drew a long breath and let it out as a sigh. She was tired and sitting still. And the sound of rushing water was beginning to slow her down.

Mellie looked up then, her face covered with a beard of bubbles. "Do I look like Santa?" she asked.

Rosalyn pretended to study her from different angles. Then she nodded. "Yes, I think so."

"So what do you want for Christmas, Mommy?"

Looking around at the carefully organized toy bins that hung from the wall behind the tub, Rosalyn spotted something on top. Then she closed her eyes. "I would like a Dora the Explorer doll, please."

"Okay . . . now close your eyes. . . ."

"They're closed."

There was splashing, then the sound of toys dropping into the water one after another. More splashing, then silence.

"Okay . . . now open your eyes. . . ."

Rosalyn opened her eyes and, with feigned surprise, lifted the wet, soapy doll from the side of the tub and held it in the air. "Just what I wanted! Thank you, Santa!"

Mellie smiled as she wiped the beard from her chin and returned to her own doll, who was floating facedown beside her. Rosalyn held a hand to her mouth as she studied her daughter. Long brown hair sticking up every which way in a parade of curls, those little arms and legs, the potbelly stomach and droopy brown eyes. Her skin was like fine china—pristine and unblemished. If Rosalyn closed her eyes and erased a decade, she could be sitting here right now, in this same bathroom, with Caitlin playing in the tub. They were so different, her two girls. Mellie had inherited her father's eyes and hair. Caitlin had her mother's. Still, the faces were the same, the little bodies. The innocence. And like a switch being turned, provocative memories of those early, simple years when life had been about two little children and nothing else were pulled from the shadows of her mind.

She wrapped her arms around herself, trying to hold at bay the rush that was taking her over. But they were unstoppable now, the warm memories from those years, running side by side with the burning fear of losing control. She was under assault by the love a mother has for her little girl, the dreams and hopes and worries. Little Mellie playing with her doll . . . Caitlin in that hallway. The images flooded in, immersing her in the reality of their life, the prurient things her daughter had done and the memories they provoked within her. She pulled from her conscience the relief she'd felt when Caitlin made these new friends, friends who had degraded her, and she could find no way to reconcile these thoughts with the little naked girl, covered in bubbles, who was right before her eyes.

She bent down and stroked Mellie's cheek with a washcloth. The child looked up at her, ready to protest, but instead just studied her mother's face.

"Mommy, do you have a boo-boo?"

Rosalyn shook her head and smiled, letting the tears roll off her chin and into the warm water that held her daughter. "No, Mellie. Mommy's just a little sad today."

Mellie pondered the situation for moment. "Do you want some ice cream?"

Her mother smiled again, but the tears kept falling. "Why don't we both have some after the bath?"

Mellie's eyes lit up then, and she gave a huge grin, even as her mother scrubbed the juice from her face.

This was not something a warm bath and a bowl of ice cream could fix. With all their money, all the status the Barlows had achieved, they had not been able to contain it, this corruption of innocence.

Mellie stood up, and Rosalyn wrapped her in a towel. She pulled her close as she bundled the little body, shaking off the remaining sadness. Then she pressed her lips to her daughter's cheek and kissed her one more time.

FOURTEEN

DEVILS AND VAMPIRES

"I just think we should get it checked out."

The moment had finally arrived. Nick Livingston was asking questions about their apparent infertility, and pleading with his wife to go to a specialist. Sara thought about the birth control pills in the hidden compartment of her purse, biting her nails as they drove through the dark, winding streets of Wilshire's backcountry.

"How about next month? I'm so crazy with the house."

A month should do it. One month off the pills would get the hormones out of her system, giving her clean test results. She'd pop one in the second they left the office, and no one would be the wiser.

"Okay. Next month." Watching the road with its twists and turns, Nick did not sound at all satisfied. "It's just . . . I'd like to have them while I'm still lucid. And Annie's not getting any younger. They say it gets harder the more space there is between them."

"They say a lot of things. Annie's not going to like a baby no matter how old she is."

Nick sighed, and Sara heard it loud and clear as she pondered the recent turn of events—her admission onto the now-famous blow job committee, the invitation to this party—and asked herself why, in light of those events, she couldn't stop herself from taking those pills. Then there was Nick, the way-too-tall Napoleon sitting beside her. He had taken her face in his hands that night four years ago, a face drowning in tears and anguish. The face of a stranger. And he had opened his heart to her without reservation. She would give him anything she had to repay him for that night and every day and night since. Except this one thing. Another baby. She had already traveled farther down this road than she had ever imagined. She was a housewife at twenty-seven who didn't know her own mind. And she needed desperately to stop and catch her breath.

"How far out are they?" Nick's voice was curious, and duly impressed. Having grown up in this town, he knew as well as anyone that the estates grew in size the farther along this path you ventured. Nick had lived only two miles from the downtown. Not an awful address, not great either. Now they lived four miles out, but in an older house. It was a crazy system as far as Sara was concerned. Crazy and inconvenient. But that was the way of the Connecticut suburbs.

"There," Sara said, pointing into the darkness at a pool of bright light that was unfolding through the tree cover up ahead.

In a moment, the woods disappeared, revealing a brilliant, star-studded sky that was interrupted solely by a stone homestead. Built along the reservoir in 1812 by one of Wilshire's founding families, the mansion had been inhabited only by the wealthiest residents and found its integrity well preserved. Though nearly doubled in square footage, the architecture had been meticulously duplicated, giving the resulting structure a seamless, and timeless, appearance. And even in the darkness, the backdrop of the water against the magnificent stone pillars that flanked the house on either side was breathtaking.

"God," she said, taking in the view. It was, to Sara, something out of a Jane Austen novel.

"This has gotta be worth thirty million." Nick's eyes were glued to the house as he pulled into the driveway through the wrought-iron gates.

"Thirty million?"

"Look at the *land*."

Nick was right. Land was gold in this town, and the Barlow estate looked like it held at least two dozen acres—something unheard of in Wilshire.

Slowly, they wound around toward the front, where white-gloved valets waited for them. Sara could feel Nick's excitement. Or was it her own? Judging from the number of cars already parked on the lower lawn, there were easily five hundred guests at this party, which implied, of course, that five hundred people could fit inside the Barlow home. How many square feet was this house? Sara couldn't imagine. How many times bigger was it than their house? Ten? Fifteen? And she couldn't even see around the back. There were gazebos and other random structures, perhaps a guest cottage, maid's quarters. The landscaping was glorious, with weeping juniper trees spaced evenly along the front lawn, and what looked like a small apple orchard to the right side.

"I can't believe we're going to this party," Nick said, almost giddy. Almost like a little forty-one-year-old boy at an amusement park. These were the homes, the parties, the world within a world that his family had been excluded from. They'd had a nice house, a three-thousand-square-foot colonial, in a prime part of town. They'd been members of the country club, and his mom had sat on the town council. Nick had felt privileged. But like most of the area, Wilshire had been plowed over by Wall Street money. Houses like his were leveled and replaced with enormous McMansions. And people like his parents became the hangers-on, the guests who didn't have enough sense to know that the party was over.

Nick had always talked about his parents' move to Florida dispassionately. But now that they lived here themselves, Sara could feel what was growing inside him, mostly because a trace of it was now growing inside her as well. *Can we make it? Are we good enough?* It was creepy, this intense awareness of the invisible exclusion that had been resurrected from Nick's past and was now driving them to covet things they didn't need, or even want. A huge house, friendships with people they barely knew. It was as though they were both playing catch-up. She for being too young and he for being too old.

They got to the front of the house, where they were ushered by one of the valets. Upon closer examination, Sara noticed the white fangs, the pointed collar on his black tuxedo jacket, and the streak of blood down the middle of his white shirt. They were in costume, these valets, each and every one of them. Devils and vampires.

The Livingstons were unfashionably late. Contrary to the Wilshire etiquette handbook, which required a delay of at least forty minutes from the time stated on the invitation, the rules were apparently suspended for this one annual occasion. As they were escorted through the foyer to a room the size of an auditorium, Sara was instantly consumed by the feeling that they had missed something.

A young attractive woman dressed like a turn-of-the-century French tart, down to her fishnet stockings and up to her protruding cleavage, met them at the entrance. "Good evening. My name is Heather, and I will be your party guide this evening. May I offer you a glass of Cristal?"

Sara gave Nick a puzzled look and shrugged. *Party guide?*

"Thank you," Nick responded, accepting the chilled glass of bubbly and listening as Heather the tart explained the myriad events planned for them this evening. He was smooth, as though he always attended parties with guides who were tarts.

"Look at you!" Sara said, poking him playfully in the ribs.

"What?"

"Nothing, honey." Her voice was sarcastic, but Nick was too preoccupied to notice.

Staring into the room filled with costumed guests—all of whom were dressed as French royalty—Sara hardly felt the glass as it was slipped into her hand, then barely noticed that it was half gone within a split second. Her mind played back the conversation with the assistant handling the party. *French historical figures.* That was what she had said, and Sara remembered it because it was such an odd theme. The word *royalty* had not been mentioned. And now here she was in her clever costume that was not only all wrong, but also unflattering.

Still, she listened as Heather continued with the long list of party goings-on.

"Shall I direct you somewhere in our main ballroom?" Heather asked, but Nick and Sara could barely take it all in. Scattered among the five hundred or so guests were dozens of other tarts and manservants, the latter wearing authentic reproductions of the long coats and breeches from the period. They carried elaborate silver trays of champagne and martinis in real crystal glasses, gourmet appetizers, and oyster shots. Along the sides of the room were gorgeous food stations with mounds of meat, fine imported cheeses, sushi, shrimp—it went on and on. The room itself was exquisite, easily two thousand square feet, lined with white pillars and accented with elaborate cornicing that covered the entire ceiling. The floor was interlaid wood tile that formed a symmetrical pattern from the center to the corners, and the walls were adorned with magnificent paintings, many of which were originals. It was impossible to remember that they were in a home when this room was most certainly built for parties of this nature, remaining idle for the vast majority of the year, and that somewhere in this same dwelling were bathrooms and bedrooms and a kitchen where the Barlows lived like the rest of them. They were, after all, human.

At the far end, there was dancing to live music from a twenty-piece band. The acoustics were incredible, giving life to the horns and strings that bellowed out baroque chords.

"I'm afraid you missed the vocal performance by the renowned Madame Somande. But you still have the band to enjoy," Heather said with the same smile that hadn't left her face. Not for a split second.

Sara nodded. "Yes. Then the beer-chugging competition, the best-costume award—guess we can skip that—the carving of the suckling pig, the raffling off of the ten-foot Versailles ice sculpture—where is there an ice sculpture?"

"There," Nick said, pointing to the back right corner.

"Oh. Yes, very nice. After that are vodka shots, chocolate-covered strawberries, and the haunted house. At midnight, of course." Her voice was laced with sarcasm.

"This is incredible." Nick was lost in the extravagance, but Sara was making rough calculations.

"Two-fifty?" she whispered to Nick, betting he had already done the math.

"At least—and that's without the haunted house. Heather?" Nick turned to the tart guide.

"Yes?"

"You mentioned a haunted house."

"It's outside, through the rear door. The line will form at midnight."

"And do we just walk through it?"

"Oh, no!" she answered, coming out of her professional persona to display her own amazement at the party she'd been sent to work. "It's a ride, like at an amusement park. I hear they rent it every year. Takes them three days to set it up."

"Thank you," Nick said cheerfully.

"Will that be all for now?"

Nick and Sara nodded.

"I'll check back with you in a little while, then!" The woman actually curtsied before dashing off to another beckoning guest.

"Okay. Now I put it at three-fifty. Can you imagine the insurance they must have had to get? Come on—let's go have fun. Are you hungry?"

"No."

Nick looked at her, really looked at her this time, and saw her the way he had always been able to. "What's wrong? Is it the costume?"

"You noticed?"

"Sorry. Is that what has you in such a funk?"

Yes. No. She didn't really know, though she was grateful he had even asked with all that was distracting him. "I don't want to spoil it for you."

He leaned down and kissed her on the mouth, then caught her eyes. "You're not. Just tell me what's up."

There he was—thank God—there was her husband. Her confidant. The man who had come to her rescue that night in New York and made her fall in love with him.

"It's just . . . *three hundred and fifty thousand dollars.* On one party!"

Nick smiled at her lovingly.

"I don't know. I don't know what it's about. I just feel like . . ." She paused then, not even sure what she was feeling.

"What?"

"Nothing. I see David Halstead over there. The King Something-or-other by the carving station. Why don't you go say hello while I find a bathroom. Maybe I can cover my face with makeup, shove some tissues in my bra, and pass as a tart."

Nick kissed her again. "I like the sound of that!"

Sara gave him a playful nudge. "I'll find you in a little while."

As she watched him walk away, she felt a wave of relief. Three hundred and fifty thousand dollars, and she wasn't even going to enjoy herself. At least she could save Nick from the same absurdity.

FIFTEEN

ROYALTY

THEY WERE STANDING TOGETHER, the three women, as Sara walked through the crowd. She didn't see them, or at least didn't recognize them in their ornate costumes.

"Rosalyn Barlow!" Eva said, scolding her friend. "Was that really necessary?"

Rosalyn smiled, her red lips pulling up against the white powder that covered her face. "What?"

"You know what. You should have made the theme a bit more clear, don't you think?"

They watched the newcomer walk out of the room in her strange getup, dodging in between the partygoers, food stations, and general merriment that filled the enormous space.

"What is she supposed to be anyway?" Jacks was tending to the conversation, though with great difficulty. She was on edge, nervous, and most of all in an acute state of concentration.

"She's actually very sweet. And I thought you wanted her to like you so she'd write a good article?" Eva was now scanning the room for the indiscretions that would inevitably be added to her file cabinet of information.

Again Rosalyn smiled. How could she possibly explain it? There had to

be a certain level of discomfort to keep the woman off balance, to feed the
desire to finally get it right. It was the source of the respect she commanded
and, more important, the reverence. She looked at her friends who stood beside her. They had been let in completely, as completely as anyone ever was,
and now they were at ease in her company. They took things for granted, and
that was what she loved most about them. Everyone needed people like that
in their lives or they would certainly go mad. But Sara Livingston could not
be one of them or she would never be believed. Her tone had to reflect a hint
of scrutiny, though in the end, she would write the truth that Rosalyn
created—not because she was being loyal to a new friend, but because she
was led to it by her own unsuppressable need to please.

Still, she *was* a sweet girl.

"Am I a complete bitch?" Rosalyn asked. "I just thought . . ."

Eva looked now at Rosalyn, her head tilted slightly. "No, Your Majesty.
You're just a little obsessed at the moment. Sara will write a nice article. She
would never cast Cait in a bad light. Not everyone is out to destroy you."

Rosalyn listened as she watched her guests. That was exactly how she felt
at the moment, as if every person in this room hated her as much as they
adored her. And now they had her daughter to use as ammunition. That was
what had her head so muddled, so incapable of reining in the paranoia. Sara
Livingston was a young girl. What agenda could she possibly have after living among them for under a year? She looked more carefully at the people
occupying her home. *Yes*, she thought. *You know who they are.*

"You're right. Not everyone . . ."

"Exactly. But at the moment, I happen to be one of them. My wig is fucking
killing me. Could you have picked a worse theme this year? French royalty?
There must be two hundred Marie Antoinettes in this room. Honestly." Eva
drained her champagne glass, then turned to Jacks. "No offense, Jacks—you're
the best one here, of course."

Jacks smiled as though she had heard every word, but her attention was
elsewhere, scouring the party for Ernest Barlow.

"Maybe you can help her out?" Rosalyn suggested, and Eva read her
mind. She needed to repent for her little sin.

"I'm on it."

Eva gave Rosalyn a hug, then left to catch up with Sara.

Feeling a sense of atonement, Rosalyn drank in the divine satisfaction from the spectacular accomplishment that now surrounded her. The band, the dancing. The flow of the crowd. All of it was working. There was a mood in the room that she hadn't felt for several years—a genuine frenzy of consumption at everything she had dished out. They were, in short, eating it up, and that was the secret ingredient that one could never count on. She had tried in the past to force it, to map out what had worked in other years at her own parties and those of her peers in New York. But there was no map for this kind of magic, and being in its presence, having made the magic herself, was as unexpected this year as it was delightful. And it was just what she needed on the anniversary of her mother's death.

She looked at Jacks, hoping to soak up more of the mood from someone else who would appreciate it, but Jacks was visibly distracted.

"Are you all right?" she asked, more out of curiosity than concern.

"I'm fine," Jacks answered her, smiling with forced enthusiasm. "Just looking for David."

"He'll turn up."

"And the Conrads?"

Rosalyn's face turned hard at the thought of that family. How could they have raised a boy like that, and why hadn't they called to apologize for his behavior with her daughter? "They had the good sense not to show. I heard they went to the Hamptons."

"I should hope so." Jacks was coming alive now. She had to. There was work to be done tonight, whether or not she had the nerve for it.

"Have you heard something? Did they say something about Caitlin?"

"No." Jacks turned her attention back to the crowd. Where the hell was Barlow? "They really should have called you. Don't they know you're on the membership committee?"

"What would that have to do with anything?"

Jacks looked surprised. It seemed impossible for Rosalyn not to know, and this made Jacks wonder if her friend's ignorance was genuine. "They're applying to the club. The Dawsons are sponsoring them."

Over the red lips and white face, a delicate manicured hand was drawn, and in that subtle action Jacks caught a rare glimpse of actual unfiltered emotion from Rosalyn Barlow. She hadn't known, and the implications were numerous. The Conrads trying to join *her* club. The club that had been in her family for four generations.

"Rosalyn, I'm sorry," Jacks said. And she was, truly. "I can't believe I'm the one breaking the news—and tonight of all nights."

But Rosalyn was gone now, to that bunker deep within herself where she prepared for battle. It had been short-lived, her reprieve from the paranoia, the bliss that the party had inspired. She'd foolishly let her guard down, allowed herself to be in the moment, a good moment that was light and easy. *Stupid*, she thought. *You know better.*

"I have to go," she said, and Jacks could see a plot already brewing to undo the damage that had been done.

Jacks grabbed her arm gently and caught her eye. "I really am sorry."

"Don't be. I'm grateful for you tonight."

Rosalyn started to turn her back, but Jacks stopped her one last time. "Have you seen your husband? Maybe David is with him."

Rosalyn shook her head. "I doubt it. My dear husband is punishing me by hiding in the wine cellar with a cigar."

"Oh, Ros . . . it's his loss. The party is fabulous."

She nodded then in complete agreement. "That's something, I guess."

SIXTEEN

SIMONE DE BEAUVOIR

She heard them outside before the door opened, their voices growing louder and louder from down the hall until their words became intelligible.

"I'm just not going to make it with this wig," Eva Ridley complained as she pushed through the hidden door to the ladies' room with Jacks, who had rushed to catch up with her.

It was more of a lounge, really, than a bathroom. Easily the size of Sara's dining room, it had two enclosed stalls with high-end toilets (the ones with the flusher on the top), gilded toilet paper holders, and walls lined with soft red toile. In the back was a double sink vanity skirted with the same fabric, linen cloths stacked in a hand-carved wooden box, and luxuriously scented soap that somehow managed to fill the air throughout the room. Or maybe they were piping the scent in from some hidden vent. Either way, the smell made you want to stay, linger, and, Sara imagined, gossip. Sitting on the toilet, listening, Sara was suddenly panicked by the choice the situation presented—make her presence known, or remain a fly on the wall.

"Well, that's Rosalyn for you. How's the back?" Jacks asked Eva, turning so her friend could inspect the other side of her costume.

"Fully intact. And mine?"

Jacks peeked her head around Eva. "Good."

As they proceeded to the vanity to check their makeup, a look passed between them. Then, as if they had read each other's minds, they simultaneously bent over at the waist to peek beneath the stall where Sara was hiding. The black shoes and white stockings gave her away instantly.

"Uh!" Eva said, standing straight again and pulling hairpins from her wig. "I have to take this sucker off."

"Go ahead. We have plenty of time before the contest."

"Did you see those manservants? Right out of Chippendale's."

Spreading her lipstick across her mouth, Jacks let out a sarcastic laugh. "And young enough to be your sons."

"You are the devil. Pure evil, Jacks Halstead!"

They heard the flush of the toilet, quiet and somehow elegant, then heard the latch pull open. Sara emerged, looking as though she was surprised to find them standing a few yards away.

"Sara Livingston," Eva exclaimed, turning to face her with a friendly smile. "I'm so glad you made it!"

"Are you having a good time?" Jacks asked, knowing the answer full well from the look on Sara's face.

As for Sara, she decided she was too damned tired to keep up appearances, even assuming she would be able to figure out what appearances a situation like this one called for.

"Actually, I think I screwed up on the costume."

Both women turned then to fully inspect her clothing. The dress was drab gray, the stockings white, and the shoes—very rounded mary-janes. She wore black-rimmed glasses and had her hair pinned back. Adding to the catastrophe, there was far too little makeup on her face, giving her a pale, gaunt appearance. Overall, she was a party disaster.

Eva sighed. "Well, you have the right country."

Sara looked surprised. "You know who I am?"

"Of course. Simone de Beauvoir, right?"

"Yes! You really got it, wow, I'm . . ."

"Surprised?"

Sara shrugged, growing slightly embarrassed at her assumption that she possessed superior knowledge.

Returning to her makeup, Jacks smiled slightly. "Eva has a master's in French literature. Summa cum laude, no less, from Yale."

"Really? That's impressive." Fully embarrassed now, Sara tried to cover her blunder with compliments.

"Like it does me any good as a housewife," Eva said dismissively. Still, despite its general uselessness, her degree did make moments like this one just a little bit tasty. "Anyway, it happens every year to somebody. Usually the last-minute invitees who don't get the engraved invitation. Rosalyn's staff can be a bit preoccupied."

Of course, none of the women really believed this, Eva and Jacks from experience, and Sara from her innate skepticism at all things coincidental.

Eva returned to pulling off her wig, making a little pile of hairpins on the vanity counter. Sara walked to the space between the women and set her handbag down. *Now what?* she thought. She washed her hands with the lovely soap, dried them with a linen cloth, all the while thinking of what to say.

When Eva's wig was done, she shook out her long red hair and ran her hands through it. Then, with her face suddenly flush with excitement, she looked at Sara. "I know," she said, pulling Sara's arm to turn her sideways.

"Jacks, what do you think—Marie Antoinette just before the guillotine?"

"Oh, good God! That's a dreadful idea. So morbid!"

"We could make it funny. Sara would be the talk of the party!"

That had Sara in a cold sweat. "I don't know. . . ."

"Look," Eva said, her eyes meeting Sara's dead on. "You can either be an embarrassed feminist intellectual, or a proud queen who laughs in the face of *death*!"

Tilting her eyes as she examined Sara's costume, Jacks shrugged. "Maybe. It *would* be funny."

"But will Rosalyn think it's funny? I don't want her to think I'm mocking her theme." In truth, this was the least of her worries. Being the center of attention at this party, of all places, was not something she was prepared to manage.

"Can't be worse than a feminist intellectual."

Eva was right. Sara would be a screwup tonight whatever she did, and it occurred to her that at the very least, she could please the only two women who seemed willing to be her friends.

"Okay. But how?"

With her hand to her chin in deep contemplation, Eva looked over all three of their costumes.

"Jacks, can we have your shoes? Your dress is to the floor anyway."

Jacks pulled off her high-heeled Manolos. "They're size nine."

"I'm a seven," Sara said.

"We'll stuff some tissues in the toes. Next, you can have my wig. Standard-issue French royalty."

"Wait—but Jacks will be barefoot, and your hair—"

"Sara, in another hour, everyone will be so shit-faced that half of them will have no shoes, and the other half will have lost their wigs. And believe me, things will go on that will make you think you're back in college at an out-of-control frat party."

Sara looked at Eva, curious and a bit uneasy. "Even the Barlows?" she asked, trying to picture Rosalyn falling-down drunk.

As they went to work on Sara's new costume, Eva and Jacks both started to laugh.

"Remember the year she convinced Linda Griggs to ride a horse around the room dressed in nothing but a sheet?" Eva was almost howling as she recalled the night.

"And then the horse just stopped in the middle of the room and let out a huge load of shit? How could anyone forget that night?" Jacks was smiling. The real story was, and Eva knew this herself, that Rosalyn had ordered the horse to be brought up from the stables. She'd planned on riding it herself, but before she could stop her, Linda Griggs insisted on being Lady Godiva. And anyone who's ever tried to ride bareback while holding a sheet around their body could fill in the pieces that were missing from Eva's rendition. It was actually a stroke of luck for Linda that the horse had relieved himself on the floor, because that ended up being the punch line that would be retold for years.

"The thing about Rosalyn," Jacks said, changing the tone of the conversation, "is that she has an uncanny knack for creating the fray while avoiding it herself. It's what makes her parties so exceptional. It's one of the many bricks she's used to build her kingdom, if you know what I mean."

Sara stood still in front of the mirror as the two women worked on her, thinking about what had been said and not said, but heard just the same. She was beginning to understand, though so much was missing.

"Did her mother throw parties here?"

"God, no. This is all Barlow," Jacks said. "The Eddings lived a bit closer to town. They were the fourth generation of Eddings to live in Wilshire, but never really struck oil the way Barlow did. When Rosalyn's mother died, her father remarried instantly and moved to West Palm Beach. The house was sold, the estate settled. Mr. Eddings took it all, though I suppose Rosalyn will get her share when he goes."

Sara was becoming engrossed in the story, almost to the point of forgetting what the two women were doing to her clothes.

"And this was hardly Mrs. Eddings's style," Eva continued. "She was old money. Stodgy to the core."

Jacks was nodding as she remembered the woman. "She was. Never even came to one of Rosalyn's parties. And she rarely broke a smile. I always got the feeling from her that if she ever actually had a real emotion, it would break her into tiny little pieces."

"That's horrible," Sara said, her own emotions doing a 180. Poor Rosalyn Barlow.

"And Rosalyn could never get it right when she was alive. If she planted pear trees, they should be apple. If she bought Valentino, it should be Givenchy. Her mother almost had a stroke when Rosalyn married Barlow, in spite of his obvious brilliance and the big job he'd landed. The family breeding just wasn't there. Nearly killed her when he hit the jackpot. The irony of it all."

Hearing Barlow's name, Jacks felt her face go pale, her hands begin to perspire. She had been distracted, but it was all rushing back to her—the plan she was determined to follow at all costs.

She looked Sara over. "I think it's good," Jacks said. The panic was full-on. She had to get out of there.

Taking her time, Eva examined their little pet project. With the elegant wig, the shoes, costume jewelry, and makeup, she did indeed look like a queen in peasant's clothing.

"Good, right?" Jacks was gathering her belongings back into her purse.

"Just one last thing." Reaching now into her bra, Eva pulled out two kidney-shaped gel pads. "Here—put these under your tits."

Sara could not hide the horror on her face as Eva placed the fake breast inserts into her hands. In the first instance, Eva Ridley had perfect tits, thanks to a very skilled New York City surgeon. And in the second instance—*yuck!*

Sensing her hesitation, Eva reached into Sara's dress and put them in herself. "We can all use a little more—especially tonight," she said, stepping back to examine her handiwork. "There!" she said. And she was right—the added cleavage did complete the outfit.

"Wow." Sara was dumbstruck. The fake tits made her look downright glamorous. "I should hate it, but it does look good."

Eva waved her off. "Why should you hate it?"

Sara shook her head. She hardly had the energy for her own thoughts. "What does this say? What if my daughter has small ones?"

"Then you'll buy her a boob job. Now stop it! You are no longer French feminist Simone de Beauvoir. You are a young, gorgeous, sex-starved queen who's about to face her own beheading."

"Lovely," Sara said sarcastically. "To the guillotine, then."

"We should really get going. I don't hear the music, which means they're probably setting up for the dance exhibition." Jacks was desperate to get them out of that room.

"Let's go, then!" Eva said, leading the way.

Jacks felt the pressure give a little, but only a little. "You two go ahead. I have to pee."

"We can wait . . . ," Sara offered.

But Jacks was definite. "No, really. Go," she said.

Slowly—so very slowly—they moved through the hidden door, down the hall, and into the ballroom. Peeking her head out, Jacks did not move until she saw them disappear into the crowd. She gathered her things, a handbag and the glass of champagne that was now too warm to drink, then she pushed through the door herself and turned the other way, toward the back stairs off the old kitchen. The stairs that led to the wine cellar—and Ernest Barlow.

SEVENTEEN

EAST COAST OC

SHE WAITED UNTIL THE last second, hedging her risk. With every passing moment, the chances they would even remember they had a teenage daughter diminished, and this would facilitate her escape.

Dressed in black and taking the back way around the pool house, through the woods, and out to the street over the stone wall, Caitlin made it to the end of her driveway just after ten. She pulled out her cell and rechecked the text message from Amanda. *Just be there by ten and wait.* She sat in the grass, knees bent to her chest, compressed into as small an object as she could manage, in case someone drove past. Her mind was racing, as it had been all day, a day that had seemed endless. With her parents busy overseeing the party arrangements and the nanny watching her like the dutiful employee that she was, Caitlin had been forced to amuse herself within the confines of her room, battling the torturous anticipation that was, mercifully, about to end.

There had been one saving grace over the past twelve hours. Another exchange with her new friend, the mysterious TF.

Totallyfkd: Hey Cbow. I'm in! Smith took pity on me. Mother leaving me the
hell alone now. Like it's over. I should be happy, right? I'm in to college. All this work and stress. Fucking SAT's and grades and joining

worthless committees and sports. I don't even know who I am anymore. I guess I'm a Smith girl, whatever that is.

Cbow: That is awesome. Congrats. Is Smith far from home?

Totallyfkd: Not too far. I guess it's a relief. But what if I just become my mother? Maybe that's the whole point. Do you ever feel like the whole system is just one giant meat grinder, turning us all into little patties?

Cbow: You should see the meat grinder that is my family! Generations of ground meat—top quality, of course.

Totallyfkd: Of course.

Cbow: All I do is play sports I hate and fuck up my homework. Is there really a future in squash? What about field hockey? Know any rich and famous field hockey players?

Totallyfkd: Exactly. It's all bullshit to put on a resume to get into college which then goes on a resume . . . ugh . . . but fuck, I can't even think about that now. Need advice about the guy. Here's an update. The prick never called—never. And now he barely says hi to me at school. OK, and I guess I have to admit it—he's a junior. It really couldn't be more humiliating. Not even if I tried. For the first time in my wretched life I'm glad I'm a nobody, cause now nobody knows.

Cbow: Sorry. Sucks! Still think it must help having "it" be over.

Totallyfkd: Maybe a little. Not sure yet. Heart still broken.

Cbow: Sometimes I feel like screwing the next guy I see so I can stop thinking about it all the time. Then I think about this one guy . . .

Totallyfkd: Dick Head?

Cbow: Do you have to call him that?

Totallyfkd: Guilty until proven innocent. How about I just call him DH?

Cbow: Whatever. I think about him and I want it to be with him. But then it feels like it'll be this huge thing. Why can't it just be like kissing? No one cares if a girl has kissed someone. No one marks the age when they first had a kiss.

Totallyfkd: Mountain climbing, Cbow.

Cbow: Mountain climbing?

Totallyfkd: Yeah. It's all about the fucking conquest. Pun intended.

Cbow: I don't know.

Totallyfkd: I do. There should be a class in high school. Fucking 101. Everybody has to fuck whoever they're assigned. It would be the great equalizer.

Cbow: That's fucked!

Totallyfkd: And what happened to me isn't? Listen—got to go.

Cbow: OK. XO.

Totallyfkd: XO.

The conversation and the thoughts it had provoked were still spinning in Caitlin's head when she saw the car. It was moving slowly, crawling down the winding road with the brights piercing the black winter sky. She held her hand to her forehead and squinted into the glare. She couldn't tell the make, but there was only one shadow moving inside. Caitlin stood as it approached, holding out her arm so he would see her. Amanda had said she might send her brother. Her heart was in her throat. If she didn't make it to this party, there was no telling what punishment her body would inflict upon her.

It was slowing, *thank God*, coming to a stop. And as it did, she could make out the shape and color. She knew this car—Christ how she'd studied this car, searched for it in the parking lot at school, on the streets in town. She ran up to the passenger door and peered inside, pressing her nose against the glass. She could barely see the driver, but she knew just from the outline of his face, the shape his hair made against the filtering light, that it was Kyle.

She opened the door, too quickly she would later decide as she processed every second that would occur from this moment on. She tried to stay calm, seem indifferent, but it was impossible to slow the rush of blood that flooded her brain, clouding her thoughts.

He was watching the road, even though the car was at a stop, maybe to make sure no one had spotted them. Maybe because he was indifferent to her. This, too, would be mulled over for hours when the evening had come and gone. For now, in the present, there was still a shred of possibility, and it washed away the day's torment like a giant crashing wave.

"Hey," he said, turning briefly to greet her. Was he smiling? Maybe a slight grin.

"Hey," Caitlin said back. "Thanks for getting me."

He didn't answer as he pulled the car back into the road and sped off. Was he pissed that he'd been forced to come get her? Then why bother? Surely he wouldn't do it just because Amanda had made a promise. Was he high and trying to concentrate? Would she ever, in this lifetime, be able to figure him out?

"We have to make a stop," he said as they neared an intersection, and turned in the opposite direction of his house.

Caitlin shrugged. "Sure. No problem. It's early."

They drove for ten minutes, music blaring from Kyle's iPod, longing seeping from Caitlin's skin. He was even more beautiful tonight, if that was possible. Faded jeans, a loose-fitting white linen shirt falling from his perfect shoulders. He hadn't shaved what little facial hair he possessed at sixteen, but smelled of aftershave somehow, clean and sweet. With one hand on the wheel and the other hanging out the open window with a cigarette, there was no doubt in Caitlin's mind that he knew her every thought and, having already decided what to do with her—if anything—was simply charging down the road. That he seemed to hold this kind of power over her was nothing short of intoxicating.

The car slowed as they approached a driveway. Kyle pulled past it before stopping completely. He turned then to Caitlin, smiling warmly for the first time since she'd climbed into the car. And she smiled back, a bit wary. Was this it? Were they about to finish what they'd started weeks earlier? Maybe he'd chosen to pick her up so they could be alone, pull over on a deserted street, and be together. She was, in equal parts, excited and terrified. What if he wanted more than a blow job? What if this was the moment she'd gone over again and again in her mind? She thought about what had happened to TF. She had in her head a catalog of information that had been shoved down their throats by the school: STDs. Pregnancy. Condoms. Pills. And the most irrelevant in the end, abstinence counseling. She felt the surge inside her, and in an instant, everything she'd read, heard, studied, and memorized melded together into a wall of resistance that crumbled as quickly as it had come together. There was no question in that moment, she would do whatever he asked. Though, in the end, what he asked was devastating.

There was a knock on the passenger-side window, startling Caitlin, but then sending her into a tailspin of utter confusion. Standing outside the car, the way she had minutes earlier, was Victoria Lawson, a very buxom and flirtatious tenth-grader who, it was rumored, had lost her virginity with a senior only to dump him a month later. True or not, it was all believed, and now the sexy, available nonvirgin was standing on the other side of a thin pane of glass.

"Do you mind hopping in back?"

Caitlin heard the words and felt her head turn around to Kyle. *Yes*. He was talking to her, not Victoria. He was asking *her* to climb in back.

She didn't think. She couldn't think. How could she, possibly? The surge was still flowing through her, though her mind was short-circuiting from the shock of it all. She had given in to the abandon, and even if she alone knew this to be the case, it was no less humiliating. Like a scavenger collecting things from a littered street, she quickly gathered the contents of her head and shoved them back into their proper places. The hope, the wonder, the belief that she had her answer about Kyle. Her pride, her self-esteem. All of it was again tucked away.

The girl climbed in and closed the door. Perky, happy, gorgeous. She kissed Kyle on the cheek and said something incredibly cool, like "Hello, handsome." Then she turned her head to face the backseat, where Caitlin was now seated.

She reached out her hand. "Hi. I'm Victoria. Are you Kyle's little sister?"

Kyle reached his hand over and flipped Victoria's hair in a playful, excruciating way. "I don't even have a sister." He was different suddenly, goofy and flirtatious.

Victoria laughed and straightened out her long blond hair. "Oops."

"That's Caitie. She's a ninth-grader."

Victoria's face changed then as she put the pieces together. *Yes*, she seemed to be thinking. *You're the one from the hallway.* She let out another giggle then, and turned back around. Kyle hit the volume on the iPod, and the three were silent the rest of the way.

They arrived at his house not one moment too soon. Never had she suffered so. Never had she had to fight this long to contain herself, to stifle the tears that would cement her fate if they came inside that car. They pulled into the driveway. The house seemed empty, lights dim, silent.

"I thought you were having a party?" Victoria said, still cool and seemingly unfazed by the absence of others.

Kyle just smiled as he opened his door. "I am."

He walked to the side entrance without waiting for either of his passengers, and Caitlin allowed herself every horrid thought that offered itself to her. He had no manners, no sense of chivalry. And his house was puny—a little colonial compared with hers. Not even seven thousand square feet. *Yes*, she thought. *I am so much better than you.* The anger felt good and righteous.

Still, she excused herself immediately and found a small bathroom near the laundry machines. The tears came like water from a busted dam, pushing against the back of her eyes. She cried so hard it was actually painful, leaving her with a pounding head and a red face. She looked at herself in the mirror. *Shit*. This was all wrong. They would be waiting for her inside, whoever they turned out to be. Amanda, for one. Kyle. Victoria. How would she explain this? The bloodshot eyes, the flushed cheeks. She filled the sink with cold water and dropped her entire face inside the pool. She opened her bag and found the Visine. She squeezed it into her eyes and felt her pupils contract.

Having done all that she could, she cautiously opened the door and followed the soft buzz of music and voices down the hall. They were in the family room, which was lit only by a few candles burning on the square pine coffee table, and the moonlight that fell in through the skylights above. There were eight of them, maybe ten, and she made mental notes of the guests. Amanda was there, sitting on the floor around the table, smiling at her as though she could read her mind. *Poor thing*, she seemed to say. *Did you really think he was interested?* Or maybe it was just her imagination. Either way, it didn't feel right. The others—Kyle, Victoria, and a handful of upperschoolers from the Academy—didn't notice her at all as she approached them and found a place to sit.

They were talking about music, some new underground band that could be heard only online, some video on YouTube that was so outrageous it was removed and relegated to personal sites that made the band all the more popular. A bottle of Grey Goose, still icy from the freezer, was being passed around, along with three prescription bottles.

Amanda leaned over to her—into her, really—and, smiling, whispered, "Take the OC."

Caitlin whispered back, "What?" But it was followed only by a *shhhh*. She was high. They all were. High and happy. The conversation was easy, relaxed, and the room was filled with a kind of calm that was almost disturbing.

"Who's ready to play?" a tenth-grade boy asked as he set one of the prescription bottles down on its side in the center of the table.

"Let's give everyone a chance to catch up." Kyle grabbed the bottle and opened it. He took out a white pill and handed one to Victoria.

"Thanks," she said. Then she reached for the vodka. "Something to wash it down, if you don't mind."

The vodka was passed, and everyone was smiling, except for Caitlin, who knew she was next.

EIGHTEEN

TRICK OR TREAT

LIKE MOST OF THE homes in Wilshire, the house had an old part and a new. At the Barlow estate, the old part was toward the back and was rarely used. The rooms were tight, the ceilings low—nothing that resembled functional. It was a stone structure, not easily changed, and it held a sense of history that no one really wanted to alter anyhow. Staking claim to its 1812 birth was part of its charm, and its value—and besides, after several renovations it was no longer a bother. There was a small formal living room, which the Barlows used for intimate gatherings, and the kids had spent their early childhoods hiding in the small crevices that could be found behind the wood-paneled walls.

But it was the basement that held the real mystique. Once nothing more than the bare guts of the house, the underground of the Barlow's estate was an intricate maze of stone-lined passageways, and it was in this part of the house that Ernest Barlow had insisted on building his wine cellar.

Jacks was no longer thinking when she pushed through the small wooden door that led to the underground. Ducking her head to clear the opening, she gathered her skirt and the massive ruffle that gave it volume, and began her descent. The smell of cigar smoke filled the narrow stairwell, growing stronger as she proceeded through the hallways that led to the wine cellar. That led to Ernest Barlow.

Though it was in the old part of the house, Barlow had spared no expense in building the room. It was state of the art—the shelving, the cooling system, and ventilation for his cigar smoke. Reds were kept at forty-five degrees. Whites at fifty-five. The hard liquor remained in the wet bar at room temperature, and it was there that Jacks found him, laid out across a red velvet couch.

She took him by surprise. "Hi," she said, nearly out of breath from the journey. From the anticipation.

Barlow sat up, cigar in mouth, glass of scotch in hand. "Christ, you scared me!"

Jacks smiled casually, though she could feel her lips trembling. "Sorry. Didn't think I'd find anyone here. What on earth are you doing?"

Barlow took a long pull on the cigar and let the smoke drift out of his mouth. "I could ask the same thing of you."

Jacks walked to the door that enclosed the wine. "I came for a bottle of Romanée-Conti. One of the guests wanted a glass."

Barlow looked perplexed. "What—the Cristal isn't good enough?"

"Guess not," Jacks said, smiling again.

"Who is this finicky guest?"

"Me," she answered, her smile narrowing, along with her eyes.

Barlow smiled back as he stood, placing his cigar in a silver ashtray. "Well, then. Allow me."

He walked past her and into the cooler. When he returned, he held a dusty bottle of the Romanée-Conti, vintage 1978. He placed it on the bar.

"Barlow—not the 1978!" Jacks said, feeling a rush of guilt. Barlow had paid nearly $24,000 for it at an auction.

But Barlow insisted. He was in one of his moods—tired of his wife, these parties, and the human race in general.

He opened the bottle as though it were nothing and poured it into a carafe. "It'll need to breathe. Better sit down."

Grabbing his cigar and his glass of scotch, he placed himself back on the couch, legs crossed in a gentlemanly fashion, and patted the space next to him.

Moving slowly, gracefully, Jacks gathered her gown and sat down. Then she turned herself to face him. "So—the party isn't doing it for you to-night?" she asked in a playful tone.

"I'm waiting for the strippers to show up."

"Ahh. I see. Only the nice tart upstairs said nothing about strippers."

"Well, then, I guess I'll have to wait until the guests get drunk enough. Someone will take their clothes off by the end of the night. I'll bet my good name on it." He was being his usual sarcastic self, only tonight his tone had taken a sharper edge. "Assuming my name is still good."

"Oh, Barlow . . . ," Jacks said, looking at him now with sympathy. "Is it Cait? How is she?"

Barlow shrugged. "I wish I knew. I'm just trying to get used to the idea that I have precious little control over anything."

Jacks felt a knot in her throat. *No*, she thought. *No control at all*.

"That's a hard thing."

"You say that like you know something about it."

Jacks looked at the beads on her skirt and nodded.

"From your childhood?"

"Barlow—I don't . . ."

He waved his hand in the air then, as though erasing his last question from the conversation. "I know—you don't like to talk about it."

"Right."

It was then that she knew, from the change in his look, the softening around his eyes. Ernest Barlow was a suffering man. Of course, Rosalyn paid no notice to it, and it was because of her indifference that Jacks had come to see them as individuals rather than as a married unit. They lived separate lives, Barlow and Rosalyn, and they missed each other completely. Barlow missed the ghost of Mrs. Eddings that lived in the house with them and that followed on his wife's heels everywhere she went. And Rosalyn missed the side of Barlow's brilliance that made him see the irrelevance of their world, that made their world intolerable to him. And yet he couldn't help himself from coveting everything it held. At his core, he was the geeky outsider who would always have something to prove. Jacks knew them both, and in her own way, loved them both as well.

But tonight was not about that. Her life was under siege, and every friendship, no matter how dear, was expendable.

"I understand because I understand. It's that simple, Barlow," she said, getting up from the sofa. She walked to the carafe holding the precious wine. Taking it gently in her hands like she might a newborn infant, she rocked it back and forth, then held her nose to its rim. "Do you think it's ready?"

But Barlow was silent. He was staring at her now, feeling a connection between them, beyond the flirtation that had been so innocent it had been practiced in the open for many years. This was something new, born of the secrecy of this underground place. She could sense the vulnerability of a man close to breaking and felt the shift that it provoked, the chemical change of her blood that came on like a sudden charge that had been latent within her for decades. It had been years since she'd felt it. Life had been steady as a rock. There had been no reason for such a response. And now, with her world coming apart, her own children at risk, she recognized the feeling. In spite of the shame it dragged along with it, the instinct for survival had resurfaced.

"What should I do, Jacks? Tell me what to do." His eyes were filled with yearning.

She turned to face him. "I don't know, Barlow. Just keep loving her. She's so lucky to have you."

A long silence passed as Jacks struggled with the internal conflict. This was the chance, the last chance, to leave this room, to find another way. Years of self-re-creation stood in the face of the instinct that was embedded deep inside her. Barlow was a good man, but a man with everything. In the end, she didn't move.

"You're a sweet soul, Jacqueline Halstead." Barlow got up from the sofa and walked to her. He took the carafe from her hands and smelled the wine, all the while making his own calculations.

She could see his mind spinning as hers was, deciding how badly he needed to feel the comfort of another person.

He set the wine back down and turned to her. "What happened to you?" he asked.

Jacks turned her eyes away. He needed to be let in by someone, but it could not be her. Not like this. She struggled to find a clever reply, but none was at hand. She said nothing.

"Where did you come from?"

His hands reached out for her face, holding her gently at first, then with conviction.

This was what she had wanted, was it not? To pull him close, make him want her and in that wanting render him vulnerable? Still, she couldn't answer. Her past had no part to play in this life, her Wilshire life, though the two had been coming closer and closer to a disastrous collision.

She looked at him then and shook her head slowly. "I can't," she said.

But he was not turning back. "Tell me. . . ."

With his hands embracing her face, his eyes searching for the pieces of her only David had known, she could feel his frustration. He was shut out now, from everything in his life. His company, his daughter. His own wife. His need was powerful as he stood beside her.

"Tell me!"

But Jacks couldn't. She looked away as she placed her hands on top of his.

The feel of her skin against his was the final blow to whatever resistance he had garnered, and in an instant, his mouth was on hers, his arms wrapped now around her back. It was shocking, the feel of another man against her body, and it took a moment before she was able to respond, before she could kiss him back. But when she did, it was with the force of abandon.

They stumbled onto the sofa, mouths locked together in a kiss that was laced with need and the hunger to survive. He lifted her skirt and ripped out the ruffle that was keeping his body from feeling hers beneath him.

"What are we doing?" he whispered. "What the hell are we doing?"

He pulled away from her for a second, searching her eyes. And in his she saw a sadness that made her sick at her core. They both knew his marriage to Rosalyn had grown cold over the years. Still, that was no reason to end it. Not for people like them. He had accepted his fate like so many others. He had beaten down his desire to love, and now this—a chance to feel again. How could she be the one to do this? How could she be the one to break him?

She didn't answer him. Instead, she reached under her skirt, pulling off the black-laced thong, then the garter belt and hose. He buried his face into the soft fold of her neck as he unbuckled his belt. His face was wet with tears, the consequence of imprisoned emotions finally set free. His heart felt like it would explode against her.

Together, they slid off his pants, lifted her dress over her head. Barlow stroked her hair, kissed her cheek as he lay down beneath her. And as Jacks felt him inside her, she kissed him hard, thinking of the words she needed to say. *I'm sorry* filled her head over and over as his body moved with hers. But when she whispered into his ear, other words left her mouth. The words she had rehearsed, knowing they would not come easily.

"I love you, Ernest Barlow."

NINETEEN

SPIN THE BOTTLE

IT TOOK TWENTY MINUTES. One tablet of oxycodone and a shot of Grey Goose, and Caitlin had forgotten nearly everything that was wrong with her, with her life. Unlike anything she'd felt before—drunk (a few beers), stoned (once with her brother)—this was a high that surpassed all others. It was euphoric.

Doug Paulson had been in charge of the party favors, and he'd come through. His mother had been through not one, not two, not five, but six surgeries to become the beauty she was today. And with each surgery came a bottle of pills. Lucky for them, she was a hearty woman who recovered easily and, in spite of her addiction to being cut and pasted, did not even indulge in alcohol, save a few times each holiday season. The bottles were kept, because that's what people do, though so forgotten, they had accumulated dust in the back of the medicine cabinet.

"Wow," Caitlin said, pressing her hands against her warm, flushed cheeks.

Amanda smiled knowingly and took another sip of vodka.

"Are we ready *now*?" Doug asked again, growing impatient.

Kyle nodded and called everyone to order. "Time for spin—the—bottle!" he said with a wide grin and the intonation of a talk show host.

Caitlin giggled. Honestly, wasn't that game for prepubescent middle-schoolers?

Kyle took the first turn. The pill bottle turned an awkward circle, then stopped with the cap facing Amanda.

"Amanda Jamison—you are the lucky winner of the first spin," Kyle said, smiling from his own high, which had so changed his appearance that Caitlin couldn't stop staring. It was eerie. Gone completely was the smug, cool expression.

With a seductive look on her face, Amanda stood up. But instead of kissing Kyle, she pulled off one of her sandals to the cheers and clapping of her small audience. Again the bottle turned, and again a piece of clothing was removed.

It wasn't hard to do the math. Through the haze of the painkillers and vodka, Caitlin could still feel a functioning alarm system, and it was going off. The only problem was that she was too high to do anything about it.

How many minutes had passed, she wondered, sitting now with nothing on but her white cotton panties. Even through the relative darkness, and perhaps because of it, the sexuality in the room was stifling. The four girls were topless, with breasts of all sizes and shapes standing at full attention from the narcotics and general sense of anxiety that was not as easily hidden as they imagined. As for the boys, hiding was a bit easier, as they sat on the floor around the table, though Caitlin could see Doug's erection as he sat beside her. He was watching her now, in that seedy, porn-movie kind of way, and she fought against the impulse to cross her arms over her chest. Never had she felt this uncomfortable, this exposed. The air against her breasts was different somehow from the air she felt in her room as she dressed, or in the bathroom just before a shower. It was cold, and not even the oxycodone could mask the humiliation it brought to bear.

"Well, I think we're at the end of the road," Kyle said. "We have a winner—Cait Barlow, congratulations!" He was at it again with the talk show thing, but all Caitlin heard was the dreadful sound of her name reminding her that she really was here, sitting around a table of naked teenagers.

She had won. Being the last one to keep her underpants, she imagined herself to be lucky. But lucky was not how she saw herself at that moment.

Watching one another and pretending not to be affected in the least, as though they were so beyond the failings of human nature that their sexual feelings were under their total control, they began to dress. Caitlin was the first to finish, and she rushed out of the room with as much poise as she could muster, finding the same bathroom as before. She did not look in the mirror. She did not wash her hands or face, or even pee, for that matter. Instead, she paced back and forth and around in little circles, trying to outrun the sense of dread that was bearing down upon her. Dread at having exposed herself to strangers. Dread at feeling excited, then disgusted by her excitement. She felt like an animal, a dirty, filthy animal who had rolled in the mud and would never be clean again.

"Cait—hurry up if you want a ride." She heard Amanda through the door and scurried to gather her things, to gather herself.

Suddenly, a burst of light. *Home—just get home!* To her house, her room, even her dreadful parents. The thought of Mellie's little face, the innocent pudgy cheeks, nearly brought her to tears.

She rushed into the hallway, but the house was empty. She saw the lights in the driveway, heard the cars pulling out from the back of the house where they had been hidden from the road.

"Wait!" she yelled, running outside. Then she heard the voice from inside the last car.

"Come on." It was Doug, the budding pharmacist.

Caitlin approached the car and looked inside. He was alone. "Where's Amanda?" she asked.

"I don't know—she left. If you want a ride, you'd better get in."

She scoured her brain for the choices. None came forward.

"Get in!" he said again, revving the engine.

Her body was moving before her mind could try to reason. And, in the end, Caitlin got in the car.

TWENTY

TRICK OR TREAT, PART TWO

THE PARTY CARRIED ON. And on, and on. Through the alcohol fog, they danced and ate, then danced again. They watched the show, drank some more, laughed and talked of outlandish things—things that were said only after reaching a certain threshold of inebriation. Places they'd done it, their most embarrassing moments, which celebrities they'd screw if given the chance. They were things they would regret tomorrow, things that would make them look at each other differently, until time passed and they slipped back in their roles of respectable, elite members of the upper class.

Rosalyn mingled effortlessly through her crowd of admirers, though her mind was in another place altogether.

"I think we're good," Eva said, coming upon her from the back of the room.

Rosalyn nodded, though her mood remained unchanged, hovering somewhere between angry and vengeful.

"The costume looks good, right? I mean, we did the best we could under the circumstances."

"It's fine. Thank you."

Eva studied her friend's face as she dangled her fifth drink from her hand like a permanent accessory. "I think she feels better."

Rosalyn nodded, her eyes now scouring the room for signs of Barlow. What was keeping him? The awards ceremony could not go on without the host, and it had already been put off for more than an hour.

Eva gave her friend a curious look. Rosalyn's world had taken an unusually dark turn, which Eva could not, at the moment, understand.

"Can you do one last thing for me while I get the staff ready?"

Eva took a long sip of her champagne. "Why not?"

"Can you please find my husband? He went to the wine cellar hours ago."

"I'm on it."

Eva scurried off, somehow managing to steady her glass and maneuver her full skirt through the drunken crowd. Forging a path this way and that, she dodged champagne and martinis as they spilled from glasses, avoided acquaintances who tried to pull her into conversations, and finally stepped right over a woman who had fallen to the floor. Eva looked back to take in the spectacle, catching a glimpse of the woman, who was laughing so hard it was silent, as two men tried to get her to her feet. When Eva reached the edge of the room, she hurried through the double doors, past the bathroom where she and Jacks had transformed the young Sara Livingston, then toward the old section of the house. As she reached the kitchen, which now served as nothing more than storage for china, crystal stemware, and canned food that Eva could not imagine would ever be consumed by a Barlow, she heard the hushed voices coming from the basement stairs. Stepping to the back of the room, she pulled her drink to her chest and folded in behind an antique breakfront.

It was almost whispering, and she could not make out a single word. Still, sometimes words were immaterial. It was in the tone, the intonations, the long pauses between the words that came only when people were studying one another's faces, or perhaps embracing. It was the conversation of lovers. She smiled for a second, instinctively, at having finally encountered something at this party that was remotely interesting. Then it occurred to her. Barlow was in the basement—who else could it be? Who else even knew about the wine cellar? And whatever glee she had begun to feel vanished. *Not the Barlows*, she thought. *It can't be.*

The door opened slowly, and a foot stepped out and into the kitchen. It was dark, but Eva could see. The foot was bare. The woman turned the corner too quickly to reveal her face. Still, there was only one person at this party without shoes. It was Jacks. Barlow followed close behind, though with enough distance to give Jacks a head start. He walked to the sink and ran the water, taking some in his hands and splashing it onto his face. His sighs were deep, and Eva wondered if they would ever stop. She wondered what they said. Then she saw it—as he turned around and leaned against the sink's edge, his face appeared to her, at first despairing, then transforming with a quizzical expression and, finally, a broad smile. Whatever regret he had, it was subdued by bliss. The only kind of bliss that could bring that kind of smile.

Another moment passed before she watched him leave. She let out the breath she'd been holding and sat down at a small wooden table, which was piled high with crates from the rental company. *Barlow and Jacks.* How long? she wondered. How could she not have known? She had come to believe that nothing in this town could surprise her—flings with personal trainers (as common as white bread), drug addiction, vaginal reconstructions. The extreme behavior of her peers was no longer extreme; it was ordinary. But this, something about this, was all wrong. They were close friends, Jacks and Eva, Eva and the Barlows. And Ernest Barlow was hardly a playboy.

She chugged the remains of her drink and set the glass down on the table. It was done. She was now the holder of their secret, and all that remained was the dreadful decision of what to do with it.

Rosalyn and Barlow were standing together on the band platform in front of a mic. From the smiles on their faces, and the way Barlow draped his arm around his wife's waist, how could anyone doubt their unified front? They were the Barlows.

"Good evening. Thanks for coming!" Barlow was speaking, as was customary. His money. His house. His speech. "How about a hand for my wife for putting it all together!"

They were playing their roles to perfection. Rosalyn smiled lovingly and with great humility at her husband's words, as though somehow embarrassed by the attention. And Barlow gleamed with sincerity, as though his wife's hard work behind the scenes of their lives filled him with pride. The great woman behind the great man, and all that.

Barlow held up his hand to quiet the roaring crowd. "And now, without further ado, the nominees for best costume. Rosalyn . . ."

His wife smiled and took the mic. "As you all know from years past, the nominees are based on an informal poll of the guests. I would like to ask all these wonderful people to please come up on the stage."

Sara was in midsip of her fourth glass of champagne as she listened to the names. She swallowed half of it down her windpipe when she heard her own.

Nick grabbed her, his face beaming. "Look at that! Go on!"

She had pulled herself together, gotten drunker than she'd been since college, and danced with her husband. She'd eaten pulled pork with her fingers, downed vodka shots, and listened to story after story of debauchery and bad behavior. But this?

"No . . . ," she managed to get out between the violent coughs.

"What do you mean! You have to go." Nick was also drunk, as much from his wife's seeming engagement in the night's pleasures as from the expensive alcohol.

Sara looked at him and gave one last cough as she weighed the consequences. To go or not to go? It wasn't really a question. Of course, she had no choice.

Walking gingerly in the size 9 shoes, Marie Antoinette just-before-beheading dragged herself to the stage, forcing a smile. She joined three other guests—two men and one woman—as they stood behind Rosalyn and Ernest Barlow. Rosalyn gave Sara a sweet smile and a wink when she turned back to acknowledge the contestants. *Christ*, Sara thought. Rosalyn Barlow winking at her could not be a sign that this would end quietly.

"Now, as the nominees step forward, please cast your vote with applause. The loudest applause will determine the winner. Ready?"

The crowd cheered. Rosalyn called the contestants' names, then pretended to gauge the collective volume of her guests. As though anyone was paying attention. Each nominee drew cheers and clapping, hooting, whistling. It was a crazy, inane display of human conduct.

"Okay," Rosalyn said when the last nominee had stepped forward and been humiliated. "Barlow, what do you think? Do we have a winner?"

Rosalyn made a show of conferring with her husband. What she really said through the plastic smile was *Where the hell have you been, you son of a bitch?* But what was the difference? The winner had been decided hours before.

Eva was shaking her head from the back of the room as Rosalyn said the name into the mic. "Sara Livingston!" The young woman stumbled forward in Jacks's shoes to accept the award. It was over in an instant, the crowd eager to get outside for the haunted house.

They started to file out—stumble out, if one were really watching them. Eva stayed behind, waiting, observing. When the crowd had thinned, she was finally able to spot Jacks, hanging on her husband's arm as though nothing had happened. Jacks and David Halstead, just another Wilshire couple. The Barlows, the Halsteads, the Ridleys, the Livingstons. Jacks turned then and waved to her, giving her a thumbs-up in recognition of their costume design that had walked off with the blue ribbon. Eva saw her own husband beckoning her into the line, where he was saving their place. Her husband. Her friends. Her life. And now her decision.

Saddled with this new feeling of bewilderment and disorientation, she got a refill and headed toward them.

TWENTY-ONE

─────────

FIVE THINGS

THERE WERE FIVE THINGS that Rosalyn knew to accompany an affair. First was a change in the cheating spouse's weight. Adrenaline, fear, excitement, and sexual energy could virtually erase an appetite. Second was a change of hairstyle. It might be length, color, perm, or flat-ironing. Somehow, the hair would change. Third was choice of clothing. Infused with newfound sexuality and perhaps feeling attractive for the first time in years, the cheating spouse started to care again about what he or she put on. Fourth was a new hobby. This was required to provide a cover story for the affair. And fifth was a sudden interest in music, a new band or sound that provided an emotional outlet for the charges the affair had inserted into the spouse's life.

Rosalyn knew this from many sources. She had heard it as a child from the corners of her home, where she would observe her mother undetected. *Number three*, the reserved Mrs. Eddings would say to a friend in their kitchen. *Hair*, she would say. Then she would wait. Nothing would be said for weeks, and she would seem to let it go. Then it would start again. *He didn't have dessert! And he loves bread pudding!* As far as Rosalyn knew, nothing ever came of it. Her parents stayed married for forty-two years.

Some of her friends had not been so fortunate. *He's started listening to*

John Mayer. Look at how tight those jeans are! They would discuss the possi-bilities, the probabilities. But it was never a coincidence when all five ap-peared at once.

That Barlow exhibited none of these signs struck her as curious as she stood in the wine cellar holding the two glasses.

They were cleaned and carefully hung by their stems from the mounted rack to the left of the sink. A carafe had also been rinsed and turned upside down on a bar towel to dry. The empty bottle that had contained Barlow's most prized vintage was still wet, still smelling like a divine bouquet as it sat on top of the drying tray. Lifting the bottle, she held it to her nose and breathed in deeply. Then, with her little finger, she pulled a drop of the red liquid from inside its neck and dabbed it onto the tip of her tongue. Within hours, it would smell of rot, taste of vinegar. But at the moment, it was still as precious as it must have been when Barlow and his mystery guest opened it earlier that night.

Idiot. This was the thought she had in her mind as she searched in vain for the cork. It should have been set down on the counter to dry. Barlow al-ways saved the corks. *Yes*, she began to reason with herself. There was the news about the Conrads trying to join her club and the need to redeem her-self with Sara Livingston. But those were not excuses. She had come to the wine cellar to make sure Barlow had not left a cigar burning. That was all. Nothing more sinister had come close to entering her mind. He had been gone a long time, but he had been in a particularly sour mood lately with the Caitlin trouble. And when he had reappeared, he'd been as ornery as ever. Now he was dead drunk, asleep on the chaise in his dressing room, still fully dressed and snoring. There had been no overt signs. But this was a futile de-fense to the case she was building against herself.

The glasses were the thing that first caught her attention. Strange how that could happen so suddenly. She had peeked her head in, turned on the light, and scanned the room for a burning cigar butt. It was a job she would never entrust to the party staff. The wine in their cellar was far too valuable, and if she were being entirely truthful, part of her had hoped to catch Barlow having done something irresponsible, and dangerous. Her anger toward her husband typically exceeded her arsenal of explanations, and she was always in the market for new ones. Now it looked as though she would have all she would ever need.

She had been drawing back toward the door, her hand resting on the light switch to shut it off, when the image ripped across her eyes. They were Riedel crystal, Sommeliers Series. Their bowls had a thirty-seven-ounce capacity; they stood nearly ten inches tall. They were meant to be grasped from beneath the bowl, with the stem drawn between the ring and middle fingers, to ensure as little contact with human flesh as possible. Human flesh warmed the glass and the wine within it, spoiling the taste. But their size also made them difficult to wash properly, and Barlow was hardly a man for details when it came to such things.

To wash a Riedel on the fly, one had to at least use a soft soapy cloth, gently running it around the bowl and down the stem. They were fragile, and Barlow had broken more than a few. He had come over time to rinse them only, then hang them to dry. And that was just the thing about wineglasses—how they could, in fact, appear clean with only a rinsing. The oily imprints from a human finger somehow hid within the film of water, until the water dried and the glasses were left hanging on the rack, the fingerprints still bonded to them.

Two glasses. Both covered with prints. Rosalyn turned them to the light for a closer look, her mind racing but her body somehow calm. The prints on the glasses were different sizes. A small trace of lipstick clung to one of the lips. It was smeared, and she found herself smiling, almost laughing really, as she pictured Barlow running water over the rims, thinking he was erasing the evidence of his transgression. Had she not told him over and over that the glasses needed more than a rinsing?

Rosalyn sat on the red velvet sofa where her husband had been just hours before. With a steady expression, she let her eyes fall upon it, let her hand run slowly along the center of the cushion next to her. It was five o'clock in the morning. Her head was spinning from exhaustion, from the alcohol, and from the scenes at the party that had just ended moments ago. On and on they had danced, drunk her champagne, and made complete asses of themselves, long after the haunted house was shut down, long after the band had packed up. She could hear the sound of the workers above her, shuffling about to remove the debris. They had used nearly two thousand glasses. Over seven hundred plates had been soiled. There were twenty-eight food tables to be taken down, an ice sculpture to salvage. Bags upon bags of garbage would be collected, napkins and half-eaten appetizers, fruit garnishes from the drinks, and mixing straws. All of this had to be racked or bagged and packed onto the trucks that waited outside.

She narrowed her eyes as though she might be able to see back through time. Who had been here with her husband? She had told dozens of people where the host of the party was hiding, because they had asked her and because she had found it somewhat cathartic to tell them. *Why is he down there?* Exactly. Why, indeed. The party had been extraordinary and there was no reason for him to be hiding from it that did not make him seem a complete ass. She had shrugged. *You know my husband.* And they had given her sympathetic smiles and gentle pats on the puffy shoulder of her costume. *What a trooper, that Rosalyn Barlow. So much to deal with these days, and still she managed to throw a fabulous party.*

They would never really see her, she had come to realize over the years. Her strength and resilience masked the turmoil that was just beneath the surface. How could there not be turmoil? Should she break down, fall to her knees, and plead for their help? Is that what it would take for them to believe she was human? That these things did not break her was no more her fault than any trait a person came to possess. That she didn't curl up into a ball and weep like a little girl didn't mean she was immune to pain. Her mother was dead. She had five children and six estates to manage. Her life was now under a microscope, and even the people she considered her friends—Jacks and Eva aside— were hoping for something good to chew on. If Cait wasn't enough for them, this would certainly do it. Barlow's *affair*.

She let the word enter her mind, and she did not chase it away. Instead, she pulled it in and let it grow until it stopped growing. Then she held it, felt it, and, finally, fenced it into a corner. It was real. Barlow had brought another woman to this underground place. He'd given her his greatest wine. Twenty-four thousand dollars' worth of wine. Then he'd rinsed the glasses and hung them on the rack. He'd taken the cork as a memento.

Yes, this is real.

Gathering herself from the red couch, she straightened her costume. They were coming now; the reinforcements were marching in like the good soldiers they were. She turned on the water in the sink and pulled a cloth from one of the drawers beneath it. Using the nonabrasive soap, she made a thick lather and gently ran the cloth around the soiled glasses, removing the fingerprints, the lipstick. All traces of her husband and his new lover. Then she hung them back to dry properly, rinsed the cloth, and tossed it in the small bin for used rags that the maid would collect on Monday.

It was one more thing, this affair, piled on top of an already heavy load. But this was what separated the strong from the weak, the ones who made it to the summit and the ones who froze to death along the way. She turned off the light and shut the door. Something could be done. Something could always be done. She passed through the long hallways and up the narrow stairs, emerging into the old kitchen fully intact.

"Everything okay down there, Mrs. Barlow?" The manager of the crew was weary, but motivated by the exorbitant amount of money she was about to give him.

Rosalyn sat at the table, pushing aside the assortment of glassware to make room. "Fine," she answered as she wrote the check. And when she was done, she handed it to the man, thanked him with a warm smile, and walked through her house to the spiral staircase.

Once safely inside her dressing room, she closed the door, noticing right away a barrage of light pouring in from the small oval window. She turned instinctively to see which lights had been left on, which ones she would now have to turn off before they were forgotten in the morning. She held her face closer to the window and looked outside. It was at that moment she felt the floor give way beneath her feet. It was just a shadow at first, the figure that grew nearer as it darted across the lawn, scantily dressed and in a hurry. *Should have remembered the floodlights, darling*, Rosalyn thought as she watched her daughter's desperate attempt to return to the house undetected. That was where it ended, the train of thought the image had provoked. She did not wonder where her daughter had been, what she was returning from, because she didn't need to. She knew all that was needed to understand.

Rosalyn pulled the draperies shut and began to undress. In a neat pile, she laid the pieces of the costume that would have to be returned on Monday, and she busied her mind with similar details and arrangements and other nonsense. Anything to keep her head above ground. She grabbed a pair of jeans from the neatly folded stack of pants lined up within a shelf. Next was an oxford shirt, then a pair of leather loafers. In the bathroom, she ran a brush through her blond hair and quickly rinsed the makeup from her skin. She applied some cream, first under her eyes, then to the rest of her face and neck.

When she was through, she walked to the edge of the master suite and listened for the footsteps that she knew would be coming, having just turned off her bedroom lights. Soft against the stair runner, an antique she'd purchased in Hong Kong just last year, were the bare feet of her daughter. When they had disappeared, she waited a few seconds more, giving Caitlin time to finish the plan that, Rosalyn imagined, had been carefully constructed over the course of several days. Then she followed her own plan, the one that had been devised in mere seconds, and out of sheer instinct.

Downstairs, she ignored the questions of the various staff, some who were winding down and others who were just getting started, then grabbed her purse and her keys and headed for the door.

TWENTY-TWO

CBOW

THE TEARS STUNG HER cheeks as they streamed down her face. She had held them at bay across seven miles of winding roads, then through the thick brush that surrounded their property. Standing in the center of her room, surrounded by the flowered wallpaper, the unmade bed, the clothing draped over chairs, she was overwhelmed with relief. She covered her face with her hands to hold some of it back, but it was futile. Everything about this room, the intense familiarity of all that it held, of its smell and feel, was washing over her, washing away the mask that concealed the night.

She was sobbing as she removed her clothing, the cropped black tank and the bra beneath it, then the miniskirt and underwear. She kicked off her wedge heels, pulled from her wrists the thick band of bracelets. With her mind spinning, her emotions fully exposed, bare and raw from her core to her skin, she stepped into the shower. It had all happened so quickly.

The events played before her as water ran through her hair and down her back. Sitting in Kyle's car, the night so full of hope and anticipation, she could barely contain herself. Then the ousting to the backseat as Victoria Lawson took her place, looked at her like she was a barely tolerable distraction. That was when she should have known. Could there have been a clearer sign? And still she had plowed ahead, determined to ride the wave to the end, where maybe, just maybe, the shreds of evidence she carried in her head would actually prove themselves to be more than pieces of an illusion she had willed together against all sense of reason. His hand on her shoulder in the cafeteria. The invitation to the party, and the ride that had brought him so far out of his way.

Her arms and legs were stinging from scratches she could only now feel. The drugs, the sheer adrenaline that had enabled her to make it home, had rendered her numb as she pushed through the wild blackberry bushes. They were dormant now from the cold, and were impossible to see in the darkness until they cut into you like barbed wire. She reached for the soap and rubbed it into her skin. The pain felt good as she flashed back to that square coffee table, the bottle of vodka, the pills. The slow return of sobriety had brought with it a disturbing sense in her gut. What had they done, all of them? Slowly, turn after turn, exposing themselves to one another in a depraved, perverted way. The creepy silence as they watched a bra come off, gaped at breasts falling on bare skin.

She scrubbed every inch of her body, washed her hair twice, then stayed beneath the water until the exhaustion overtook her. She turned off the faucet and reached for a towel, drying her face, her mouth.

She never should have gotten into that car.

But that was not the only thought that came as she wrapped herself up in long cotton pajamas and combed her hair. Kyle had driven off without her, but he had not been alone. She played back the final moments, the sound of Amanda's voice, Victoria's laughter. Had they both gone with him? And which one would he have dropped first? Amanda was farther out, almost as far as Caitlin. Would he have made excuses to take Amanda anyway so he could be alone with Victoria? Or would he not have given the matter so much as a passing thought? It had all seemed so random, how they had ended up in the cars. Like no one cared. Like it didn't really matter.

Then again, Doug had seemed pissed when she turned out to be his only passenger. Perhaps he'd had his hopes on Victoria, the only confirmed non-virgin at the party. Either way, she had known when her hand touched the door handle, when he looked out at her with a mixture of annoyance and resignation, that she should not have gotten in that car.

She sat at her desk and waited for the screen to come to life. Her nerves were shot, her eyes heavy, and it felt good, or maybe just better than the panic she had endured for the better part of the night. She logged on to the site and started to write.

Cbow: Totallyfkd—are you there? SOS. Something has happened.

TWENTY-THREE

WAKING THE DEAD

"HELLO, MOTHER."

Rosalyn Barlow sat on a cold stone bench in the center of the Eddings family mausoleum. It was six thirty, and the sky was still dark as she looked up through the glass dome ceiling.

"How has it been for you, this second year of being dead?"

It had gone so quickly, these past two years, that Rosalyn had hardly felt them at all. In fact, it might as well have been mere moments since she received that call from her father.

Rosalyn let out a sigh as she stared at her mother's portrait. It was, of course, the portrait the woman had specified in her carefully drafted instructions for burial. The cremation. The urn. The placement within the mausoleum, which she had commissioned as a present to herself on her sixtieth birthday. The picture, and the words beneath it—a full-page eulogy that she had written herself. The memorial service, the caterer to use, the guests to invite. The list of mourners permitted to speak. It wasn't that she was a morbid person. Far from it. Mrs. Eddings had not planned on dying. What she had planned on was immortality, one way or another.

"My year has sucked, if you're at all interested."

It was the smile that always got to her, the way it seemed to respond to whatever it was Rosalyn said. Sometimes it seemed cheery. Other times sour and laced with cynicism. Today, it seemed more of a smirk as it stared back at her from the canvas.

Oh, for Christ's sake, it was saying. *Get over yourself and move on.*

"Yes, Mother. Of course. I'm not a complete imbecile."

Still, she had come here to think, to regroup before leaving behind events that by all rights should have devastated her. She'd come on the heels of those events, and in the face of exhaustion, to reflect before coming up with yet another brilliant plan, this time to control the impending damage from her husband's affair, and to save her daughter who was digging herself a mighty large hole.

It was a strange place to do this, to think. In the center of a cemetery, surrounded by the dead, whose bones lay beneath the ground, and her mother's ashes, which were carefully sealed in the sterling silver urn she was now holding in her hands. But it was precisely that—the presence of the dead—that opened the gate to the thoughts that were, on every other day, unavailable to her. Death was inevitable. Death would come. And when it did, even the most carefully laid plans would not be enough to stop the waves of indifference from rolling in, slowly erasing the lives that were lived. It had been a mere two years, and already the famous Mrs. Eddings was little more than a blip on the memories of those she had known. Rosalyn's father was remarried. Her brother in London. It was Rosalyn and Rosalyn alone who carried the woman in her soul. And this was not by conscious choice.

She might have escaped this fate of carrying around a woman who was not only dead but also wholly unworthy of such a favor. But she had been branded years ago with her mother's imprint after making choices that could not be undone.

It was the knowledge of this fact that was now consuming her as she held her dead mother in her hands. Ashes. That was all that was left of the force that had stood in her path like a fallen tree, the path she sometimes believed she should have taken. And whether or not that was so, there was no doubt she would long for it until she, too, was nothing but ash. In this room, among the dead, she closed her eyes and allowed herself to look down that path to a vision of a young man. It was a vision of love that she could hardly recall. Still, it had been there. She saw his face—the olive skin, the dark wavy hair, and the wonder he held in his eyes at sights he had never seen.

Paris had grown old for her. At seventeen, she had been there nearly a dozen times. For him, a middle-class kid from Maine, it was magical.

The regret of following her mother's orders to return home had not come for years. Wasn't that always how it was with the young? There is nothing that can't be fixed. Nothing that can't be salvaged. And so she had plowed forward, numb from the profound loss of her first real love. She passed every test, met every expectation that was laid out for her. And when she did, new ones were put in place, like the little jumps and tunnels at a dog show. Over this one. Under that one. To the finish line.

Only there was no finish line. Her mother was dead, and she was still jumping and crawling.

Not that she disliked her life. Her husband lately, perhaps. Her friends, some. And the moment she left this room, she would again feel the invisible girders of a social structure that were stronger than steel. Her place in the community, the schools, the country club, the charity work and social engagements. She was raising five children who would never want for anything, who would be exposed to every corner of the world through travel and education. It was as meaningful a life as any other, as far as meaning went. After all, meaning was hardly intrinsic.

And that was precisely what made crossroads so tricky. She could blame her mother all day long for losing the life she might have had. It wouldn't change a damned thing—not the fact that she had not chosen that path, or the impossibility of knowing how her life would have otherwise turned out. The journey had been her own, and it had taken incredible restraint for her not to tell Caitlin just how similar they were. There was nothing her daughter could do that would shock her, nothing she couldn't understand from a place, not of empathy, but of familiarity.

"Yes, Mother. I know what you would do." Her hands were gripped tightly around the handles of the urn, her knuckles white. "Should I accept the Conrads into the club as well? Would that make them grateful? Would it make them indebted enough?"

There had been a Kyle Conrad in Rosalyn's life years before. Handsome, popular. Every mother's dream for her daughter. And Rosalyn had delivered, doing things that had to be done to keep him by her side all through junior year. Until the trip to Paris. And upon her return, there had been a price to pay to win him back.

"Should I send him an invitation to my daughter's bedroom?"

Her mother was still smirking at her. Nothing and no one could ever loosen the woman's grip on her own righteousness, and Rosalyn felt it even now.

"There are things you don't know, Mother. Things that would wipe that smile right off your face."

But she knew that wasn't true. Her mother had been immune to feelings of guilt, shame, or even mild regret. She would never stop smiling, never stop believing that everything she had done had been for the best. And Rosalyn's perfect life gave her more than enough ammunition.

"I won't be coming next year," she said softly as she placed the urn back on the white marble pedestal built to hold it into eternity. "But don't worry. I'll have someone polish you."

Her mother had been clever, but she hadn't been intelligent. Had she been intelligent, she would have opened her mind to the possibility of her own failings, her severe miscalculations. It would have been pointless to tell the woman about the happiness Rosalyn had felt in Paris that summer, how her eyes had been opened to a new version of herself. A version she liked. Had Mrs. Eddings even allowed herself to believe it, it still would have done nothing to weaken the woman's resolve, or change the course of events that had come to pass.

As Rosalyn stood to leave, she felt the presence of another person in the cold stone building. She turned toward the door and found Eva standing just inside its borders.

"You look like hell," Eva said. Wearing a tight Juicy sweatsuit and no makeup, Eva wasn't exactly looking herself either.

"I could say the same." Rosalyn had planned on fleeing this place, on pushing her mother's smile from her thoughts and letting her mind find comfort within the plans that still had to be formulated. Now the keeper of her memories was blocking the door.

"I told you I wasn't coming this year," she said.

Eva shrugged her shoulders and took a step toward her friend. "And I knew you still would."

Rosalyn nodded. Of course Eva knew. Eva always knew, but even so, she seemed oddly sure of herself. This was their secret, Rosalyn's homage to her mother's crypt after the Halloween party. She had come alone the first year, after the party was over and her husband was dead drunk and asleep. But she had not left alone. Eva had made a point of it.

Silently, the two women sat on the stone bench facing Mrs. Eddings. They looked between the urn and the portrait, Rosalyn feeling what she was feeling, and Eva holding whatever part of those feelings Rosalyn couldn't bear. Eva had been there that summer, the study-abroad trip to Paris their junior year. It was one of the many programs that made the Wilshire Academy so prestigious. The students who were chosen studied at the Sorbonne, living in university dormitories that were chaperoned by a handful of teachers. Of course, with Paris at their doorstep, *supervision* was a generous term, and the summer had become as much about becoming fluent in promiscuity as in learning the French language. Eva knew the joy that had found the young Rosalyn Eddings that summer, and the damage that followed upon her return. The weight of all this was particularly heavy on this early morning after seeing Barlow with Jacks hours before.

"I really am not coming next year," Rosalyn said flatly.

Eva draped her arm around Rosalyn's shoulders. She would come; they both would. "Okay," she said, "okay."

TWENTY-FOUR

NO TIME FOR REPENTING

SLEEP HAD COME QUICKLY for Jacks. After arriving home at 4 A.M., her head swimming in a cloudy pool of wine and vodka, she had barely managed to change into a nightgown and wash the thick makeup from her face before crawling into her bed and passing out. And everything else that had been lurking inside her had been beaten back by exhaustion.

But morning hadn't been far off. Curled up beneath the covers, she felt her body awaken. It was slow; her muscles were stiff, her temples throbbing. She opened her eyes to light that was already full, the light of midmorning, and from the rooms beneath her, she could hear the living that was well under way within the house. She was alone in the bed, which meant that David had heard the kids and let her sleep. Or perhaps he hadn't slept at all, tossing and turning beside her until he finally gave up and went someplace else to tend to his worries. His secrets.

She took a deep breath and lifted her head to see the clock. It was nine thirty. She began to think about the day. Kelly would be here with the kids at noon, their monthly get-together that Jacks's girls always awaited with persistent impatience. It would be a good day for them, and knowing this was the sole trace of peace against the dread that crawled up from the corners of her subconscious.

She placed her hand on her stomach and pressed down hard, but the waves continued as the picture emerged. Ernest Barlow, his hands on the flesh of her thighs, his tongue brushing hers. She could feel him, smell him. She could even taste his precious wine swirling against her palate, which was close to unbearable with such a raging hangover. It was the kind of regret that cuts deep, that twists and carves with each visceral reflection. She knew things about Barlow now that she hadn't before—the intimate things reserved for spouses in their insular world. The sound of his sighs, his moans. The intense look of desire and release. She had taken these things from him and given nothing back because nothing about her had been genuine. It had all been staged, and the fact that she knew just how to perform the act was equally disturbing. What would she do with this? He would never leave Rosalyn, and Jacks could never live with herself if he did. Still, he would be obligated to her in a different way now, and that could be the very thing that could save her.

She curled up into a tight ball and closed her eyes hard, forcing herself to remember what was going on in this house. The lies. The investigation. And the crimes. The laughter that was now seeping through from the rooms below could not erase any of that. A lazy Sunday morning, David making breakfast for the girls, tickling Beth into a fit of giggles. It would be so easy to forget. Or maybe to pretend. People did that, didn't they? Ignored the things that were right in front of them but too ugly to face? Reality could be woven from whatever fabric one chose. And what Jacks wanted to choose was the scene that was playing out on this crisp fall day in Wilshire.

But that was impossible. The sickness from her own actions was in her now, and it would not be suppressed. Whatever capacity she may or may not have had to ignore David's troubles was now irrelevant. Maybe this was a good thing, a necessary thing, because it would remind her. It would wake her from sleep, pull her back from a moment of laughter with her girls, a loving feeling toward her husband. It would never leave her, and in that would be her salvation, and that of the family. This was not going away. David was about to lose everything, and something had to be done. Now she had done it.

She felt the adrenaline kick in. She felt her new self return—the self that was fighting for survival. Within seconds, the headache was gone, her insides steady as though cement had been poured down her throat and then solidified within her. She got up from the bed and headed to the bathroom for a shower.

The leaves were thick in the yard. Jacks had asked the groundskeeper not to blow them into the woods, so the kids could make piles. Sitting on a lawn chair beside her sister, both of them bundled beneath a wool throw, Jacks watched the five children rake and jump, and the significance of seeing them together was not lost on the Moore sisters. Their children's happiness had done nothing less than break the chain of their history and the cycle of fear it had brought to bear.

"Remember doing that?" Jacks said out loud, though mostly to herself. Kelly wasn't one to reminisce, and she didn't answer. But Jacks saw a smile fighting to come out. They did have some memories that were good, pure memories of climbing trees and riding bikes, searching for neighborhood kids to join them in one kind of mischief or another. Of course, what was normal or not back then had no significant relevance to their childhood. Any traces of normalcy, in fact, were the result of sheer coincidence, or happenstance.

Jacks let herself smile as she watched the children in the leaves, their faces light, free of the burdens their mothers carried. Then she scanned the perimeter for her husband. Not finding him in earshot, she leaned in closer to her sister. "Any more news?"

Kelly nodded but kept her eyes on the children, her expression steady. "Some of the investors were paid off. They withdrew their complaint with the government. Red said the others might be forced to do the same."

Jacks steadied herself against the surge of hope that rushed in. "What does that mean? Where did he get the money?"

"Red doesn't know. He either had the money squirreled away somewhere, or found new investors. Either way, he was able to settle with the ones that were making all the noise. Probably not at face value, but enough to make them back off. They must have thought there was nothing more to get out of him."

Jacks exhaled deeply. It didn't make any sense. "Where would he have gotten the money? The hotel burned, there was no insurance. Why would anyone invest with a firm that was under investigation for embezzlement?"

Kelly shook her head.

"Not so rough, Pete!" she screamed into the yard. Peter was tossing Beth in the air onto the pile of leaves.

"She's fine. She likes it." Jacks smiled briefly as she watched her little girl in the leaves, nearly paralyzed with excited laughter. "What does Red *think*?"

Kelly didn't answer. Instead, she stared out at the children and took a sip of her tea.

"Kelly?" Jacks knew her sister. There was something she was not saying.

"Nothing. He doesn't know. He'll keep looking."

Jacks let it go, though it had her unnerved. Still, she moved on because they were nearly out of time. David was fixing a tray of graham crackers, chocolate, and marshmallows to make s'mores. He would be out soon to light the fire pit.

"What should I do now—about Barlow?" That was the question of the hour. She had started the affair, told him she loved him. They had made a plan to meet again.

Kelly looked at her and saw the guilt on her face. "Are you okay?"

Jacks nodded. This was no time for repenting. She would do that later, when this was all over. That's what she told herself, what she forced herself to believe.

Kelly placed a hand on Jacks's shoulder. "I know you've been friends for a long time . . . but a man will do far more for a woman he loves than one who's just a friend."

The sound of the screen door slamming ended their conversation. They turned then, both with a warm smile, as David Halstead walked out with the tray of food.

"Time for s'mores!" he yelled into the yard. Four of the five children came running. Janet, Kelly's oldest, walked with indifference, though she would enjoy the smell of the fire as much as any of them. What could be better on a cool November afternoon?

There he was, the good man. They were both thinking it. Whatever walls they had built around them, David Halstead had made it past them, and it was impossible not to feel that everything that was now happening was some kind of punishment for their abandon. The world was not constructed of good and evil. Their father had been a good man. Their mother had loved them. But there was no comfort in any of this. Only a reminder that life could fall apart at any second.

They started to get up to join the kids, but Jacks grabbed Kelly's arm, pulling her back. Her face was streaked with tears, her eyes suddenly desperate. "Fifteen years. We've been friends for fifteen years, so I have to know. Was all of this for nothing . . . what I've done to David, to Barlow?"

The fire was lit, and she could smell the burning leaves. The children were standing together, pushing sticks through soft marshmallows, their cheeks flushed from the clean, cold air and the raw feeling of being alive. And at the center of it was David, as he had always been. Her husband. Her love. The man who had betrayed her, and the man she had now betrayed.

Kelly wrapped her arms around her sister and held her, taking on the despair that was too heavy for her sister to carry alone. Then she whispered back to her, "I don't know."

Sensing David's eyes upon them, Jacks pulled away and turned her back to him. She busied herself folding the blanket and wiped her face with the palm of her hand. Kelly grabbed her tea and let out a laugh as though they were enjoying a happy moment together.

With her sunglasses in place, hiding her eyes, Jacks turned around, then headed for the fire.

TWENTY-FIVE

REGRETTING

CAITLIN BARLOW PAUSED BEFORE getting out of the car.

"What's wrong?" her father asked, his face replete with far more worry than the situation called for. At least as far as he knew. Cait could feel the worry reaching out from him, wanting to hold her, and the fear that it might just succeed was enough to overcome the sheer dread that was keeping her from leaving his side.

"Nothing." She pulled the handle, grabbed her things, and left, slamming the door behind her. She did not look back, even as she heard the car idle in place. Her father was not yet ready to let her go from his sight.

It was a cold Monday morning. The sky was gray, threatening an early snow. Caitlin had prayed for its arrival in time to keep this very moment from coming, but the ground was dry as a bone. And now the moment was here.

She had not heard from any of them. Not completely unusual, but after the night they'd shared, it was strange for Amanda not to call. *Can you believe what we did?* she might have asked. Or maybe not. Maybe she was unfazed. Maybe it was Cait alone who was in a state of disbelief. Still, it was not like Amanda to forgo the collection of details from every unfinished story, which meant it was entirely likely she knew how Cait's night had ended.

The thought of it crashed inside her like a wrecking ball, squeezing the air right out of her lungs. *Shit*. If Amanda knew, then everyone knew. She'd relived that moment in Doug's car again and again until she no longer had any perspective on how horrific it really was.

She entered the front doors of the Wilshire Academy, then made a quick turn toward the lower school. She could cut through the hallways, up the back stairs, through the cafeteria, then out again to the upper school. That would leave her steps away from her locker and her first-period class. Maybe she wouldn't have to see anyone. Maybe no one would see her. It was a stupid thought, of course. First period would come and go; then she would be back in the hallway and on to second period with Amanda. One look and she would know. One look and her fate would be revealed.

Her stomach was cramping with hunger. Nerves had kept her from eating. It had been nearly twenty hours since she'd had one bite, and even with the acid that was now demanding it, the thought of food was unbearable. She ducked into the nearest bathroom, which was swarming with little girls busying themselves before the start of school. Some were half the size of her, dressed in the same uniform, checking themselves in the mirror. Little mini-me's of the upper-school girls who were acutely aware of Cait's sudden presence among them. But Cait didn't stop to notice them. She went into a stall, sat down, and bent over at the waist until the feeling passed.

Taking a long breath, she leaned back against the wall. How would she ever get through this day? From her backpack she pulled out her iPhone and sent a text.

Cbow: TF, you there?

Totallyfkd: Yeah. What's up? Still feel like shit from the weekend?

Cbow: Yeah. Hiding out in bathroom. Can't face everyone.

Totallyfkd: Yes you can. Didn't you listen to what I said? DH is a total prick. And so is the little weenie who drove you home. Can I tell you something? It wasn't your fault. It was the oc and the booze and maybe it was just him. He won't tell anyone. Watch and see. No one will know. Gotta get to class. You?

Cbow: Yeah, OK.

Totallyfkd: XO, TF.

Let it be true, Cait prayed in the bathroom stall, the chatter of little girls surrounding her. She thought back one last time to those few minutes in his car, willing herself to see the expression on his face, the one she had initially read as embarrassment but then convinced herself was really anger.

The drive had been silent, the car twisting and turning through Wilshire's back roads on the way to her house. She had tried to make conversation, but Doug had been wasted. Holding on to the edges of her seat, Cait had watched the curves, the trees that were grazed when they were cut too close and the open black space as he cut wide and wandered into the middle of the road. There had been nothing left to do then but hold on and watch. Her life had been in his hands, a stoned tenth-grader eager to get rid of her and, maybe, disturbed by the bizarre intimacy they had all shared. There was no question he was wondering the same things she was. What were the others doing on their journeys home? What were they doing with the mix of sexual urges and the implied expectations that, if not met, would have repercussions come Monday morning? She knew what it had done to her that night, the ingredients frothing over like a shaken can of beer. She had wanted to make it home to her bed, safe, alone. She had wanted Doug to drive and drive to the edge of her property and then to want no part of her as she fled the scene. But that had not been the case.

Looking back, she was certain he had not planned it. His driving was almost frenetic, like he could outrun what the night had provoked in him. But in the end, he had made a sudden stop on a dark back road. He'd pulled the car to the side, as far from the road as he could manage, scraping it against the tree cover. He'd turned off the ignition and started to unbuckle his pants. He had not looked at her. He had not spoken. And with the fear pounding in her chest, she might not have heard it anyhow.

The bell rang. The warning. Classes started in five minutes. Cait exhaled hard as she pulled herself together. She was a lit fuse now, burning toward something that might ignite, only it never did. She wanted to ignite, to explode into a quick blast of flames that would burn off this energy and leave nothing but calm ash. Feeling like dead, gray ash would be better than this. Anything would.

The little girls scurried out of the bathroom, and when they were gone, Cait checked her face in the mirror. Her cheeks were bright red, the effects of adrenaline brought on by exhaustion, and her right eye had that subtle twitch, the one that came only when she was facing something that terrified her. She'd felt it that night in the car, and seeing it in the mirror, seeing the evidence on her face, brought her close to tears. Still, she grabbed her things and headed for her locker on the other side of the school.

First period came and went. History. They were covering Europe, memorizing timelines of events that spanned hundreds of years. She wrote down the important points, the things that would surely be on the exam later that month. And she listened to the teacher expound his theory that these events had been links in the chain that eventually brought down an empire, all the while her knee bobbing up and down, then her foot, then a hand. She never stopped moving. All of this was bullshit anyway. Theory and conjecture about the unforgiving nature of human beings. Grudges that perpetuated war. She didn't need to study history to know about those things. Those lessons had been burned inside her from her own family history. And the history she herself was now creating—history that was waiting for her in second period.

The bell rang again. *Shit.* She lingered as long as she could, gathering her things.

"Is everything okay, Caitlin?" her teacher asked, looking up from his desk to find her still in the room.

Cait hurried then. "No. Just a little slow."

"Ahh." The teacher smiled. "Monday morning."

Cait smiled back, then swung her backpack around her shoulder and headed for the door. If only Monday morning was all that was wrong with her.

How would TF know what Doug would or wouldn't do? Were boys that predictable? She, whoever TF was, hadn't been able to predict what the boy in her life had done—slept with her then never spoken to her again. Would that be Cait's fate one day? The irony was that Cait knew Billy would never have done that to her, but she also knew she wouldn't have given Billy a blow job in the school hallway. Maybe not at all. Maybe not ever. He hadn't provoked her the way Kyle had. Or maybe *provoked* wasn't exactly the right word. He hadn't *motivated* her. That's what Kyle had done. Motivated her to do something she didn't want to, that wasn't in the least way enjoyable to her. And even after everything that had happened over the weekend, the way he treated her, the things that went on around that coffee table and in Doug's car, she now found herself longing for a chance to do it again, and for no other reason than to be close to him. How could anyone teach her not to want that?

That was the reason for the anxiety that now returned as she emerged from history class and into the hallway. Seemingly distracted but acutely aware of her surroundings, she went to her locker. She didn't spot Amanda until she turned the corner for second-period math.

"Hey, you," Amanda said, her voice full of insinuation.

Cait fought to remain casual. "Hey!" *Shit. Too cheery.* No one was that cheery on Monday morning.

Amanda sidled up to her and pressed her shoulder into Cait. "Soooo?"

A wave of euphoria swept in. Amanda said *Soooo?* only when she was looking for the story. Which meant she didn't have the story. Which meant Doug hadn't told anyone. TF had been dead-on right.

"Nothing to report. I was lucky to get home alive. He was wasted," Cait lied. "And you? I saw you leaving with Kyle. . . ." She tried to sound as though she was happy about it, as though she had been waiting all weekend for the exciting news of what might have happened between Amanda and the guy she thought about day and night.

Amanda shook her head, pretending not to care. "Victoria lives farther out. Rules of the road. I'm sure we'll hear all about it today. She probably fucked him right there on South Ave. She's such a slut. Anyway, it was an awesome party."

Cait nodded as the words sank in. It was as she had suspected, and dreaded. Kyle and Victoria. It was twisted and wrong, but the need inside her was profound, and it now had her praying that if Kyle had slept with Victoria, he would move on. Back to her.

As the rest of the day unfolded, the relief grew with every confirmation of Doug's discretion. Although *discretion* was a generous word to describe what was holding him back from talking about that night. It was embarrassment that now bred the silence. She could still see his expression when she'd leaned across the cup holders toward his lap. The expression he'd had when he closed his eyes and thought about something else, someone else, porn stars, or Victoria Lawson. Who could know what entered a guy's mind in those moments when his body failed him? His words had been harsh. *Suck harder!* He'd held on to her head by fistfuls of her long, delicate hair, thrusting her onto him, then finally pushing her off. His face was flushed with anger and sexual frustration, his dick limp as an old stalk of celery—all of it melding together into desperation. She was wiping her mouth, settling back into her seat, totally confounded as to what she should say, and far too wasted herself to feel the disgust that would attack her after the long journey home.

"That didn't work," he'd said, rubbing himself. The sight of it had been shocking.

"Sorry." Cait had tried not to watch as she sat beside him, expecting him to zip his pants and start the car. But that was not what he'd had in mind.

Reaching across to her seat, his hands were up her skirt and on her panties before she knew what was happening. There was no explanation given, and none needed. He was climbing over awkwardly, but somehow managing to maneuver himself on top of her and recline the seat as though it was all well rehearsed. As though he had done it a hundred times before. And it was more than apparent that he'd expected her response to fall into line.

She'd felt his dick, hard now, against her thigh, then the weight of him over her as he struggled to get the panties down and off her legs. They were below her knees when she tried to move, and she could feel them like a rope tying her legs down, rendering them useless. But she'd started to struggle then, from a place deep inside her. It came from her body, not her mind, this reaction that had her holding on to the panties with one hand, pushing against his chest with the other. She got them up above her knees, freeing her legs to move. And they had done just that. She thrust one into his gut, crossed the other over her chest to add some muscle to her resistance. *Push!* She could still feel the strength of the reflex that had been so powerful, it sent him flying back to the driver's seat. Then came the door, shoving it against the trees and thick brush that were keeping it closed. She'd squeezed out that door somehow and started to run, through the bushes and into the yard of a stranger. Seven miles from her home. Seven miles she would walk in the cold, her body covered in sweat and blood from the scratches. And her head filled with the sound of his laughter as she ran away.

"Cait?" Amanda's voice pulled her back.

"Yeah?"

"Math? The bell?" *Duh.*

She hadn't heard it, but was quick to catch up. Smiling as though it were any other day, Cait followed her friend into the classroom and felt the wave of adrenaline finally, mercifully, leave her.

TWENTY-SIX

GETTING CAUGHT

IT WAS HARD TO remember.

Wrapped in Barlow's arms, feeling the hot breath from his sighs against her neck, Jacks searched her memory for the feeling. *Bliss. Lust. Abandon.* After seventeen years of marriage to the same man, the memories of new love were hard to come by.

Sighing seemed right, less from the sexual pleasure than from the deep bewilderment at needing another person in the midst of a marriage, and the risk they were taking with lives that were so carved into stone. *Yes,* she thought. *There should be sighing.* For David, for Rosalyn, and for the children who were being dragged along on this path of deception.

She wrapped her arms tighter around his back, moved with him as though he were her fantasy, her passion. Wasn't that how it had felt? Wasn't that how her body had responded so many years ago, to David and the lovers who'd come before him? It was long gone, and in the face of the profound fear at being discovered, it was hard to remember.

Barlow pulled away and threw himself back onto the pillows. His skin was glistening with sweat as he closed his eyes. When he opened them again, Jacks was there, right on cue, looking over him with a warm smile.

This part wasn't so hard to manufacture. She held genuine affection for

Ernest Barlow, with his long wavy hair and cute rounded face that seemed not to have changed since the day she met him. He was like a mischievous boy, and it was impossible not to be drawn in. Always moving, always joking, his charisma was born of a manic energy, and a neurotic insecurity that his outrageous success had done little to eradicate. She knew him. She saw him. She just didn't feel about him the way she was now pretending to.

He shook his head as he had been doing lately, and ran his hand through her hair. Then came the look, the sad resignation that what they had between them was like a poison that grew stronger with each of these afternoon encounters.

"What are we doing?" he asked, just as he had asked that first time in the wine cellar.

"I don't know," Jacks answered as she lay down upon his chest. But, of course, that was a lie.

"We should get going," she said after a few minutes, her voice filled with regret.

She lifted her head, but he reached for her, pulling her back down for one last kiss. It was soft and honest, and it made her body tense. How could she be this person? She thought about the letters, how they had stopped coming. Red was looking into it, and she couldn't help but hold out hope that it was true. That maybe it was over, maybe David had found a way. Maybe this could be the last time.

"Do you want to go first?" she asked.

Barlow frowned playfully. "If I must." He got up from the bed, gathered his clothing, and headed for the bathroom.

It was a lovely inn, the Lindly, nestled by the shore just at the edge of town. The small, cozy rooms were filled with antique furniture, fine linens, and the softest towels. Too quaint for business travelers, it was used, almost exclusively, for wedding receptions and out-of-town family members who were too unruly to be put up in one's house. Without a spa service in sight and a menu that was a bit too pedestrian to draw attention, it was virtually deserted during the week. Come tomorrow, the Wednesday before Thanksgiving, it would be booked solid. But today, a day of shopping and cleaning and packing, it was as safe as they could get without traveling out of town, and Barlow had decided it was the perfect scene for their crimes.

None of their planning, it turned out, would matter.

Searching the room for her own belongings, Jacks heard the soft buzzing in her purse. The phone had been turned to vibrate and now, it seemed, she had missed a call. Sitting on the bed, she pulled the end of the sheet across her body and called in to her voice mail. There was only one message, which seemed at first blush to be entirely benign. It was Eva Ridley, first going on about some tiff she'd had with a teacher at the Academy, then the meeting for Rosalyn's blow job committee that was scheduled for this afternoon. Jacks had planned on attending, but then Barlow had sent her a text message: *Wouldn't it be perfect to meet today?* He had been right, of course. Knowing where Rosalyn would be, and for how long, made it as perfect a time as they would ever have. Rosalyn had selected Casa Michelle, a pretentious and overpriced French restaurant on the other side of town. And Jacks hadn't told anyone she had changed her plans and would not be joining them. That was a call best left for the very last minute, when they would all be too preoccupied to push her for an explanation.

Sitting on the bed, Jacks felt the breath rush into her body. She stood up, let go of the sheet, and began to gather her clothing—underwear, bra, slacks, blouse. With the phone still pressed to her ear and the water running in the shower, she took in every word at the end of Eva's message. Having been to Casa Michelle the night before, Eva had asked that they change the location of the meeting. And the new destination was the Tavern at the Lindly.

Embedded within a story that was going on and on in the message were the pieces that Jacks was now putting together. *Eva said she knew a woman who knew another woman who was friends with the chef and wouldn't it be fun to try the new menu . . . only they didn't start serving lunch until after noon, so the meeting would be pushed back. . . .*

As she buttoned her blouse, Jacks stood behind one of the draperies by the window and looked outside. Snow had been falling for over an hour and was now blanketing the small parking lot that was behind the inn, hidden from the road. There were seven, maybe eight cars, but only two that had Jacks concerned. Her gold Lexus with the vanity plates that bore her initials, and Barlow's orange Corvette. Flipping the phone shut, she checked her watch. It was five minutes to twelve. When she looked up again, it was just in time to see a red minivan turn the corner.

With her mind reeling, Jacks scrambled to put on her shoes, buckle her belt, comb her hair.

"You're dressed," Barlow said, sounding surprised as he stepped out of the bathroom.

"They're here." It was all that Jacks could manage to get out. Her throat was bone-dry.

Barlow smiled. "What, aliens?" He laughed and reached out for her, his arms wrapping around her waist.

But Jacks pushed him away. Moving as she spoke, she managed to tell him about the phone call, about the red van.

"Fuck!"

"I'll go down first. I think I can duck into the ladies' room. You come down later. After everyone has arrived—after Rosalyn." Saying her name in this room, under these circumstances, was agonizing.

Barlow was shaking his head. He was deep in thought now, thinking through the options. "No—I need to get the car out of here. What reason will I have for being at the Lindly in the middle of the day?"

"Listen to me. There's no time. They'll either see you drive out, or they'll see the car parked here. Which would you rather explain?" She'd dressed and gathered her belongings, and was headed for the door.

"Right. You're right. I'll think of something. I'll stay here until I see them all."

Jacks stopped for a second and looked at Barlow. This was a disaster for both of them, and the recklessness of their actions crashed down in pieces at their feet.

"I'm sorry," she said.

But Barlow took her in his arms and kissed her. "Don't be sorry. Don't ever be sorry for this." How desperate he was in that moment, to have her feel for him what she had made him feel for her.

But Jacks didn't have time to think about that now. "I have to go."

"Go," Barlow said, suddenly drawn back into the urgency of the situation.

Jacks left him in the doorway as she hurried down the service stairs that led to the kitchen. She was barely noticed as she emerged, the nicely dressed customer who'd lost her way. She was nonchalant as she wove through the workers, chopping and washing as they prepared the lunch menu. She pushed through the door used by the waitstaff and into a hallway that led straight to the powder room.

When she got inside, her senses began to return, the thoughts settling into place. *Yes—I have arrived early. I'm freshening up. And I have no idea why Barlow's car is parked outside.* She was covered, as covered as she was going to be, and convincing herself of this made room for the other conclusions that had been forming inside her head. Eva never cared where they ate, as long as they had wine and salad. And why at the last minute? Rosalyn had confirmed the meeting days ago. And, finally, why here? It was almost too perfect, the coincidences that had been woven together and were now threatening to expose her. It was almost as if Eva had known.

The door opened. Jacks finished the stroke through her hair she had started moments before and smiled. "Hi, Sara! How have you been?" She leaned over and kissed Sara Livingston on the cheek.

"I'm good. How are you?"

"Fine. Just fine. Getting ready for Thanksgiving."

Sara took out a lip gloss, though she seemed to have a fresh layer. "I think we're the first ones here," she said, revealing the reason she had come into the ladies' room. Late, early, late, early. Poor Sara Livingston never got it right.

"Did your family come up?"

"They did. They've been here since yesterday."

"How's that going? Do they just *love* the house?" Jacks took out her own lipstick.

Sara sighed as she would with a close friend. "Actually, no. They think it's extravagant. They're pretty modest people."

Jacks managed to look surprised as she rubbed her lips together, then blotted them into a tissue. She would have been surprised were she not so consumed with panic. "Your house? Extravagant?"

Sara nodded. "I know."

"Oh, well. That's family for you."

The conversation stalled as Jacks let her thoughts go where they wanted, to the plan that was forming in her head. *No,* she said to herself. How could she even think it? But it was too late. She had started down this path and was too far gone to turn back.

"I guess I'll see if the others have arrived." Sara was out of excuses to stay now and was putting the gloss back inside her purse. She turned to Jacks and smiled.

Let her go. Jacks looked into her bag and pulled out her concealer. She held back until the last second, until the opportunity was almost lost. The battle being waged inside her now was tearing her in two.

"Wait. . . ."

Sara turned to face her, her hand on the door handle.

Jacks closed her eyes as she jumped off the cliff she'd been standing on since the moment Sara Livingston walked into the room. And the feeling of the free fall nearly took her breath away.

"I think we're meeting on the second floor."

Sara looked at her with gratitude, her voice perky, innocent. So very innocent. "Thanks!" she said.

And Jacks had no words to justify what she was doing, what she had done. She thought about David, how he'd cried in her arms that night. She saw the faces of her girls, felt their happiness within her the way a mother does. *God forgive me.*

Sara was watching her, waiting for some kind of response.

And Jacks, after pulling herself together, managed to give her one. "You're welcome. I'll see you up there."

TWENTY-SEVEN

THE SUSPECT

ROSALYN SAW THE CAR as she pulled into the snow-covered parking lot of the Lindly. But she said nothing of it to Eva, who was sitting beside her. "Honestly. This place is so far out of the way."

Eva studied Rosalyn's expression. There was a hint of annoyance, perhaps. Irritation. And yet it was unmistakable, the Creamsicle Corvette whose tires were nearly covered by the snow that had begun to fall an hour before. The car had been here for a while.

"Sorry. I ate at Casa Michelle last night, and honestly it was terrible. Plus I know the new chef here—"

"So you said. Let's just get inside before we're buried alive." As Rosalyn focused on turning the car in the snow, Eva could see her eyes taking in the other cars in the lot. Jacks's gold Lexus was parked just beyond Barlow's, but the tire tracks were fresh. And beside the Lexus was the unmistakable red minivan. Hard to tell how long it had been here. It was under a tree, which at the moment seemed to be holding the majority of the snowfall. The information swam in both their heads as they circled the lot.

They pulled in as close to the entrance as possible and went inside. An older gentleman met them in the foyer.

"Yes, mesdames. Are you guests of the inn or just dining with us this afternoon?"

Rosalyn was too busy shaking the snow from her brand-new Jimmy Choos to answer.

"Just lunch. I called earlier. We have a party of seven," Eva said. Then she paused and turned to Rosalyn. "It's seven, right? You asked three more?"

"Yes, seven—if everyone can make it. What a day it is out there!" She lifted her head and smiled politely, handing her coat to the man.

"Indeed. Right this way. We have you in the back dining room. It's very warm by the fire."

Rosalyn turned to Eva, looking absolutely delighted. "A fire! How nice."

"Yes, it's lovely. One of your guests has already arrived."

They walked in silence past the small reception desk, the women marching behind with cautious steps as though any move they made might disrupt the evidence that could be hiding around them.

On the second floor, Sara was making her way back toward the stairs. She'd walked down two narrow hallways, each lined with a worn antique runner and floorboards beneath that creaked like her grandmother's house. The inn had actually been a home, someone's mansion nearly two hundred years ago, though it was now modest compared with the estates in Wilshire.

The small meeting room at the end of the first hallway had been empty, and it hardly seemed appropriate for a lunch. With nothing but plush chairs and reading tables, it was clearly intended for just that—late-night reading. The second hallway had proved equally futile, lined solely with the closed doors of the guest rooms, and Sara now found herself perplexed and frustrated. She checked her watch. She was ten minutes late to the meeting, if there even was a meeting, somewhere in this maze of rooms and hallways. Finding an exit door, she pushed through it and started down the stairs. Then she heard the same door open again from just above her, and she stopped.

"Sara?"

Ernest Barlow was shocked, though with his unfailing charm always on standby, he managed to appear only mildly surprised when he came upon her. He'd done as Jacks asked. Waited until she could get to the table, then thought of an excuse for his presence at the inn. Finding Sara Livingston in the back hallway where he was making his escape had not been part of the plan.

"Barlow," Sara said, though it felt strange to call a grown man by his last name. That practice usually didn't make it past freshman year of college. Still, she had felt from the moment of their first introduction that it was his stubborn desire to hold on to the amusements of youth that made him so enjoyable, and she found herself smiling now.

"I see you got the same bad information I did."

Barlow's face lit up as he bounded down the few stairs to where she stood. From the sky had just fallen his escape. Whatever excuse Sara had for being in this hallway would now become his as well.

"Unbelievable, these women. Can't get a damned thing straight!"

"Yeah, yeah . . . ," Sara said, pleasantly unnerved once again by his delightful sarcasm.

"I think they must be in the dining room."

"That would make sense, wouldn't it?"

They walked down the staircase side by side, quiet at first but soon engaged in easy conversation.

"I think it's great you came today. Teenage girls need their dads."

"Unfortunately for us old-timers, you are in a far better position to remember such things. I'll have to take your word for it."

Sara laughed, mostly to herself. She hadn't felt like a teenager in more years than he could possibly know, knowing her so little.

"What is it the old-timers like to say? You're as young as you feel?"

"In Wilshire, my dear, what the old-timers say is you're as young as you *look*."

Of course, Sara thought. And the thought amused her. "I like mine better."

Barlow stopped as they reached the last stair. He smiled then, warmly, as he turned to face her. "Well, then, how about joining me in the sandbox?"

Sara laughed out loud this time, and as she did, Barlow pushed through the fire door that led to the back of the inn, and also to his wife, who had just passed it by.

Hearing the laughter, Rosalyn Barlow turned instantly. She had been waiting these few minutes for a sign of him, a sign of something that would explain his car, which was now fully embedded in the snow. The look on his face when he saw her—fleeting as it was—told her all she needed to know.

Recovering quickly, Barlow paraded without hesitation up to Eva Ridley, the tall gentleman who had paused beside her, and, of course, his wife, giving her a peck on the cheek. "Hi, honey. Hell of a day out there."

Rosalyn smiled curtly. "You could say that."

She didn't ask. It was time for the explanation, and they both knew it.

"I hope you don't mind that I joined you. I want to be more involved . . . *really* get involved. Hands on all the way."

Rosalyn nodded smugly. "Great, honey. That's really great. I'm so glad you got the message about the change of location."

Barlow had nothing. They both knew there had been no such message.

Rosalyn turned then to Sara. "Did you get lost? I'm so sorry . . . this place can be a real maze."

Sara, being the only innocent party among them save the concierge, blushed with honest embarrassment. "I just got a wrong direction. I've never been here before. It's really a nice little hideaway."

Barlow was smiling on the inside. If his wife had come to the wrong conclusion about things, she would certainly be wondering if Sara's comments had been cleverly woven to rub their farcical affair in her face. Either way, his mind quickly tuned in for a way to rebuke this conclusion and save Sara from the wrath of his wife.

But it was Eva who came first to the rescue. "I called Barlow, Ros. When you didn't pick up this morning, I thought I could get the message to you through him, and he pleasantly decided to join us as well. Then I found you on your cell and I forgot to tell you. . . ." Blah, blah, blah. She lied easily, only because the cause was worthy, and because it was her plan that was now getting turned on its head.

She'd had her feelers out—discreetly of course—since watching Barlow and Jacks emerge from the wine cellar that night. After three weeks of no information that had elevated her hopes that the *moment* between Jacks and Barlow had been just that, one moment, the call she'd been dreading had finally arrived. It had come midmorning, from her chef friend at the Lindly, who'd spotted the Corvette. Moving the meeting here, then giving Jacks just enough time to evade detection, was her way of sending a message: *Stop this thing before someone gets hurt.* Whether they would see it for what it was, or as a message instead from some greater power, didn't concern her. She knew in the brief seconds the plan was formulated that it would send their hearts racing and make them face the gravity of their actions.

Only now her plan had gone all wrong. Not only was Rosalyn misguided, but Jacks and Barlow would have even more cover under which to hide their affair. And poor Sara!

She turned to the waiter, who was growing impatient beside them. "I'm so sorry—I forgot we'd had a late addition. Can you reset for eight?"

The man tried to smile. "Not a problem. Shall we go to the table now?"

With an awkward silence surrounding them, Eva, Rosalyn, Sara, and Barlow followed the man to the back room, where they found Jacks sipping a glass of wine at the table by the fire.

She looked first at Eva, then to Rosalyn. "Hello, friends," she said. "Crazy weather, isn't it? Came out of nowhere."

"It certainly did," Eva agreed, taking a seat across from Jacks. She looked damned put together for a woman who'd been upstairs with her friend's husband not ten minutes before.

"Jacks, my dear. Lovely as always. I see you've recovered from our night of debauchery." Barlow said it with his usual flirtatious tone. And, as always, it went unnoticed by everyone except, on this occasion, Eva.

"Barely, but yes. I survived one more year. And you have decided to come and help in the search for a speaker on female sexuality?" The words were not easy to get out, but they were the words she would have said had she not been sleeping with the man, and so she forced them out with a wry smile.

"I have indeed. When Eva called this morning to tell Rosalyn where to meet, I just decided it was the perfect way to spend the afternoon. Of course, I had to come early for a drink or two." Barlow was feeling at ease now. Eva, for whatever reason, had given him his alibi. Sara had been legitimately confused. Jacks had been at the table ahead of them. It didn't occur to him to wonder about Eva Ridley's motives, and, not knowing about the wineglasses, he made the wrong assumption about how easily his wife's suspicions could be assuaged.

Jacks smiled and raised her glass to toast his brilliant plan. What was brilliant was the coded message he'd just sent. Of course Eva had not called him. So why would she have covered for him? And why had she changed the location in the first place?

As they got settled in their seats, Jacks caught Sara's eye then mouthed the word *sorry*. Sara, not wanting to make a fuss, smiled and waved off

Jacks's apology for sending her to the wrong room, the wrong floor. Having found Barlow there, she had no reason to suspect the mistake had not been genuine.

Is it done? Jacks wondered. She could see nothing on Rosalyn's face but the usual relief at being with friends, and a tense back as she sat next to Sara Livingston. The seed was planted there, but what about Eva? She must have suspected Barlow of some indiscretion; she must have known he would be here. The chef, maybe. Would she believe that Sara was his new dance partner? Jacks had managed to move the car just after leaving the ladies' room. The tracks were fresh, while Barlow's were covered. And Sara had parked under that tree.

Regardless of what Eva suspected, what mattered most was that Rosalyn was off course, and anything Barlow did or said that raised her guard would be like drops of water on the little seed that now lay in the ground.

Of course, it was more than a seed. Rosalyn's mind was stirring over the stained wineglasses she'd found that night, and retracing her memory of when and where she'd seen Sara during the party. Had she been gone that long? How long would it have taken? And what would provoke this young woman to want Ernest Barlow when she had the far more handsome, younger version in Nick Livingston? And, finally, why would they be so cruelly indiscreet as to meet right here, where they would surely be at risk of discovery? She could not sort it out now, with two more women just joining the table, smiling, making their introductions. Not now, while she had to find the right words to shape the debate about teenage blow jobs, of all blessed things, to save her daughter from the social vultures that shared the sky with her. But she would later, when she had time to think and piece it all together. The party. The glasses. Barlow's car. Eva's cover story. And, of course, the mysterious Sara Livingston, who was now dead center on her radar screen.

TWENTY-EIGHT

THANKFUL

SARA LET THE WATER run down her back, through her hair, and over her ears, filling them completely and blocking out the world. Her eyes were closed, and she could feel the air trapped inside her lungs as she held her breath, letting the water cover her entire face, her nose and mouth. When she couldn't hold it any longer, she emerged and gasped for air, her blood pumping and her head light.

She had learned this trick as a child, this way of shocking herself back from something she no longer wanted to think or feel. Or both. That she was doing it on the eve of Thanksgiving, the day of being thankful, made her sad beyond words.

She was about to go under again, a second round of shock therapy, when she heard Nick yell out from their bedroom, "Great dinner, babe! Really great."

She turned off the water and opened the door, reaching for a towel. "Thanks."

Then came the next question. "You coming to bed?"

It was totally predictable and dreadful all at the same time. "Just a sec . . ."

The dinner should have been great. It had all the makings of a great dinner. The turkey was made and set to cool. The china was pulled from cupboards, dusted off, and set on the table. Wine was poured, and cartons of mashed potatoes, green beans, and gravy were nuked in the microwave and placed neatly in serving dishes. Sara had removed the plastic from the dining room floor, dusted and vacuumed until the air was clean and the room suitable for food consumption. Still, without draperies or paint, it had felt barren as they all sat down for the feast.

Sara reached for a towel and dried her face, then wrapped the towel around her body. Was it her imagination? No. It was there. As the plates were filled, a strange silence had taken over the room. It was the same silence that used to fill her house when she was a child and her parents were thinking things they didn't want to say. Like the night they met her sister's fiancé, or the morning after Sara blew her curfew. They loved a good heated debate, and they were not ones to shy away from the discussion of personal business. But there were some things that could not be said, some arguments that could not be waged, because once they were, they could never be taken back. And Sara knew exactly what they had not wanted to say earlier that night as they sat around her table.

It had been written on their faces, these lovely people who did not know how to fake it. As they walked through her enormous house that was now being expanded, as they listened to her vent about Roy the Contractor, Nanna, and her litany of other problems, she had seen their expressions morph from genuine excitement at seeing her new life to an almost grave concern. Then Nick had emerged from his man cave in a cashmere sweater, his hair just a little slicker than he used to wear it.

Through the turkey and cranberry sauce, they had learned that their once-intellectual daughter hadn't read the paper in weeks, hadn't even followed the latest Nick Kristoff series in the op-eds. And as they listened to the story of the Barlow Halloween party, the description of extravagance and the way their daughter had been transformed into a spendthrift queen about to be beheaded, their faces had again taken on the look that Sara dreaded. It was as though they had marbles in their mouths that they could neither expel nor swallow.

And she knew now, as she looked at her own face in the bathroom mirror, exactly what they were. Marbles filled with worry, with misgivings, and worst of all, wonderment at what had become of their daughter. It pissed her off and made her sad all at the same time. What had they expected? Had they not been thrilled that for once she brought home a man who was not a self-centered child yearning to roam the world? They knew Nick's age, and hers. And it wasn't hard to do the math when Annie was born seven months after their elopement. None of this had been charted out, and yet they had the nerve to be surprised at her life and where it was taking her.

"Hey." It was Nick, startling her from the doorway.

With the towel wrapped tightly around her body, she turned to face him with a smile.

"You almost done?"

"Yeah. Almost."

She could feel him wanting to come in, come closer. Maybe pull the towel away and feel her next to him. But he didn't. "I'll be in bed."

"I'm coming in a second." She turned back to the mirror and thought about the pills she had removed from her purse and stored in the back of her jewelry box. She hadn't taken one for two weeks, hoping to clear her system before the tests were taken next month. After his prodding and pleading with her, she had finally given in to Nick's request, and they were now headed down the path of the fertility doctors.

It was the dead middle of her cycle, which Nick had memorized, and this was precisely why he was in there, waiting. She had managed to avoid him for the seven days since her period ended. Her parents, the house, headaches, and tiffs with Nanna that she invented in order to explain the bad moods. What did she have left, besides the truth?

She brushed her teeth, flossed, and gargled. She tweezed the stray eyebrow hairs that were growing in around the edges. Then came the moisturizer, one for her body, another for her face. She brushed her hair.

Walking slowly, she turned out the light and headed for her closet. He was lying still beneath the covers. Was he sleeping? There'd been a lot of wine, then an after-dinner scotch with her father in the man cave. She took out her thick flannel pajamas and buttoned them all the way up. She hung the wet towel on the rack. Then she tiptoed to the bed.

As she pulled back the covers on her side and slipped beneath them, she heard him sigh and roll over, reaching for her. "Great dinner," he said again, wrapping his arms around her. "You are amazing."

Shit, she thought. *Flattery*. It was the gold standard of marital foreplay, but it also meant there was no escape. He started kissing her neck, moving his body closer to hers, pressing against her. Under any other circumstances, she would have found all of this a turn-on. His tongue on the outside of her ear, strong hands reaching under the tightly buttoned shirt. But tonight she was just afraid. She wanted the sex, *Christ* did she miss the sex. It was the rest of it that had her wanting to run like hell from this bed, this house—this entire life, if she were honest with herself. Biology was cruel.

"I know you're tired, babe, but if we miss the next few days, we're done for another month."

He was feeling her lack of enthusiasm, being considerate. *Damn him.* Couldn't he just be an insensitive prick once in a while? The guilt was digging in even deeper. How could she not want to have this baby? It wasn't as though she was choosing between motherhood and some dangerous, exciting assignment overseas. Motherhood had already chosen her once, and it was a lifetime gig. Annie deserved a sibling. Nick deserved the family she had promised him when they made the plans and flew to Las Vegas without really knowing each other at all. Years had passed. She should have been used to this life by now, the life she'd accepted on impulse, but which had turned out pretty damn good for a twenty-seven-year-old. Couldn't the rest of it just be noise? Noise that she could turn down?

Sara kissed him back. "I'm not tired. Just a little drunk." She laughed in a naughty way as she peeled off the flannel pajamas.

"Really?" Nick pulled away until she was done, until she was naked with him beneath the covers. "*How* drunk?" he asked playfully.

Sara ripped the covers from the bed and climbed on top of him. "Pretty damn drunk."

Nick was laughing as she held him down, kissing him hard, first on his mouth, then his neck. She moved down his body, licking his inner thigh, making him moan.

"Sar—you know I'm sucker for this, but—"

"Shhh . . ." She interrupted him and kept going, turning her own body around, wrapping her legs around his face. He resisted for about a second. They hadn't done this for years, with the pregnancy, the birth, the breastfeeding, and then the mere presence of their child in the room next door—it had felt far too deviant.

"Sar . . . ," he said again, in between the moans. "Sar . . ."

But she was not listening to his protests.

"Sar . . . oh, *fuck*!"

It wasn't long before she felt his body give in, felt his release, then faked her own. She was far too disgusted with herself to feel any pleasure tonight. She rolled over, kissed his stomach, and headed for the bathroom. When she returned with a towel, the bliss had all but vanished, leaving behind an expression that captured his utter bewilderment.

"What?" she asked innocently. But he didn't answer. Instead, he disappeared to the bathroom himself. Sara found her pajamas tangled up in the covers that lay on the floor. She pulled them on with hands that were shaking. What kind of evil had taken her over? How could she do this to the man who had given her everything and asked for nothing in return but the very thing she had promised to want as well?

She straightened out the bed and got under the covers on her side, the place she had come to dread. If she could take back the last ten minutes . . .

"Why don't you just say it?" Nick was standing in the doorway now, his face flushed.

"Nick . . ."

"Just say it. I mean, Christ. What are you doing?"

She had no answer. She hardly understood it herself.

"Just say it!"

"Say what?"

He walked to the bed, fighting to shed his anger as he sat down beside where she lay. He reached out his hand and wiped the tears from her cheeks. "Just say you don't want to have another baby."

He looked at her then, but she could not meet his eyes. Instead, she held her hands over her face, shaking her head. She should have known this would catch up to her. She was too young, still a child in so many ways, and he was a grown man. A grown man who loved her but would never understand.

"Please," he said as he watched her cry. "I need to know why."

She lifted her hands and managed to look at him. "I don't know," she said. It was the truth.

But Nick was confused. And why shouldn't he be? She had been pretending for over a year, safe behind the birth control pills he would never know about.

"Is it me?" he asked, steadying himself for the answer.

"No—I love you. You know that."

He smiled, but it was sad. "I know you love me. That's not what I meant."

Sara tried to deflect the question. "It's me. . . ."

"Am I not a good enough father to Annie? Do you think I would love her less?" Nick choked on the words as they left his mouth, and Sara reached for him, taking him in her arms.

"No! God, no! Don't ever think that. Not ever. You are the perfect father. It's me. I swear to you. It's *me*."

Nick held on to her, and she could feel him fighting against the realization of the truth as it began to take hold. Their master plan, the one they had forged in spite of convention and their own doubt, had seemed to be working. Their love had lasted, weathering the storm of a quickie marriage, Annie's birth, and the drastic change for Sara. And he had allowed himself to believe it would keep on working, that they were both looking forward to the next step, the second baby that would be the cement around their life together.

But he had not taken in the weight of the change for Sara. How could he possibly, having passed through those youthful years on his own terms, and without obligation? For him, they were frivolous in hindsight. If he could turn back the clock, he would, gladly, and spend his time being more productive. He could have shaved ten years off his retirement clock. She was lucky in his mind, to have jump-started the part of life that was substantive. Meaningful.

Still, for Sara, those years would always be things that were taken from her. And she ached for them, for her ten-speeder that was now a minivan, her radical, chain-smoking friends who had been replaced with older, jaded women whom she never would have chosen for her peers. Another baby felt to her like the last nail in the coffin that held her youth.

Nick pulled away and sat against the headboard. "So what now? What do we do now?"

Sara wiped her eyes one last time. "I don't know."

"Well . . . let's start from the beginning. You don't want another baby. What about the rest of it?"

"What do you mean?"

"The rest of it—the house, the town, staying home with Annie. Staying with me."

She looked at him, shocked by his honesty. It was what they were both thinking, what she had been thinking for months. Still, it took more courage than she had to say it out loud. And it deserved an honest answer.

She reached over and took his hand, holding on to it tightly. Then she swallowed hard. "I don't know," she said. "I just don't know."

TWENTY-NINE

THE BROTHER

CAITLIN BARLOW LAY ON her bed, her stomach feeling like it might burst. But what had she actually eaten? With her headphones blaring the latest Pink single into her ears, she thought about everything that had gone into her mouth. One piece of turkey. Some green beans. A forkful of mashed potatoes. She'd piled the plate high with other things—sweet potato mash, stuffing smothered with gravy and that sickening-sweet cranberry jelly her mother insisted on making every year because it was a family recipe and God forbid they didn't honor the dead by consuming things that should never have been created in the first place. She hadn't touched any of that. Still, what she had eaten was more than what she had come to consume in one sitting lately, and her stomach was simply no longer used to the feeling of fullness.

It was torture, these five days. Thanksgiving was for families, which meant she would be stuck in this house for the duration. Secluded from her friends and, worse, subjected to her perfect brother and worried parents, she really had no idea how she would get through it. Maybe the way she had been. One hour at a time.

The meal had been the worst of it, though it had been perfect as always. It was one of the things her mother seemed to have down, the annual re-creation of family traditions. Every year, the oval table in their formal dining room was decorated with linens, china, silver and crystal, antique figurines and miniature pumpkins, candles burning softly in their silver holders. Then there was the food. From the kitchen came the distinctive smell of roasted turkey with rosemary stuffing, and from the dining room the sweet odor of wine that filled the glasses. Somehow, in the midst of her mother's charity work and manicures, shopping and constant prodding, she had managed to create a lasting tradition. And in spite of everything Caitlin had ever carried with her into that room, the anger and fear and overall unhappiness, it was impossible not to be overwhelmed by the assault on her senses and the feelings that were provoked—good feelings about family, tradition, a sense of belonging to something even if that something was corrupt to its core.

This was the conflict that stirred inside her as she waited for the feeling of food to disappear from her body. The need to belong somewhere, and the sole outlet for this need a family she couldn't understand, and that didn't understand her. Even the comfort of the babies, having known them since their birth and watched their every monument of growth, was muted now as she saw the easy affection they elicited from the others simply by being young. That would change soon enough, the moment their misbehavior—which was now a source of endearment—became an embarrassment. And if not, then later when the expectations began to creep into their carefree lives.

It had started already for the twins. With the third grade came homework and after-school sports. Hockey and squash would begin this winter, baseball and golf in the spring. Summer would be spent on the swim team with tennis clinics thrown in around the four-hour practices and meets. And fall, which was winding down, had been nonstop travel soccer. They had their own nannies this year just to shuttle them around. If Cait bothered to look hard enough, she was sure she would see it in their eyes—the slow mourning of their youth as their time was gobbled up in the name of personal development and growth.

The thought of it made her want to scream. A few years felt like a death sentence. Day after day, working and working. School, homework, squash. Then stuffing herself down this well so she could exist within her family. If she told them the truth, that she hated every minute of her life, what then? Impossible. It was so much easier to be the reluctant teenstranger, bitter and angry, but always doing what she was told.

Lying in her bed, she wrapped her arms around herself and held on as she turned her thoughts from this hypocrisy to the reinvented version of Caitlin Barlow that lived in the world of Kyle Conrad.

There was a loud banging on her door, which she felt more than heard with the iPod still blaring. She gathered herself back from the place that had just begun to make her smile as she lay in her bed with her full stomach. They came in before she could get up.

"What's up?" It was her older brother, Brett, and his buddy Reed, who was a habitual presence at their house. His parents were divorced and living in the far corners of the world. The Barlows had all but adopted him.

Cait removed the earphones. "Nothing."

Brett walked to her desk and pulled out the chair. He turned it around and sat in it backwards, his legs spread-eagle, arms draped over its back.

"Wanna come to a movie?"

Reed walked in now and stood in the corner. "Yeah. Come with us."

"What are you seeing?"

The boys looked at each other and shrugged. "Does it matter? We're getting the hell out of here to smoke a joint. Come on. What else have you got to do?"

Cait studied their faces. It wasn't like them to cajole her into accepting an invitation. It wasn't like them to extend one in the first place. They had each other, and when they went anywhere, it was usually to the arcade, which was about as dreadful a place as Cait could imagine. Even compared to this house.

"Mom told you," she said after a moment.

Brett looked at Reed, who shrugged, and looked back at Cait. "She didn't have to. It was, like, the first thing we heard when we got home."

Cait nodded, her arms crossed now as she sat on the bed. "Great. That's just great."

Brett leaned back, trying to be casual. "Well? What'd you expect? News is news."

"And I'm news all of a sudden? Who told you?"

"Reed heard from Mark, who heard it from his sister. Cbow, it was in the fucking hallway. Everyone knows."

"You guys suck. Did you come here to rub my face in it?"

Reed, the softer of the two, stepped forward and sat on the bed next to Cait. "No. Of course not. We just wanted to see if you'd come to a movie."

Brett echoed the sentiment, though Cait didn't believe them.

"Look. If you wanna talk about it, that's cool. I just wanna say one thing, and that's it."

"So say it."

Raising his eyebrows as though he were digging for the perfect words, Brett told her exactly what she knew he would. "Cbow, you can't do that shit. From a guy, I gotta tell you. That's not how to get a boyfriend. Girls who do . . . you know, that shit. They don't get boyfriends."

Cait felt her entire chest tighten. "How do you know what they get? You don't even live here anymore."

"Cbow—we spent ten years at the Academy. And besides that, you think it's any different at Choate? Reed—tell her. . . ."

Reed was reluctant. He reached out and rested his hand on Cait's shoulder. "He's right, Cbow. I've known Kyle since first grade."

"And what? There's no way he'd actually like me? A lot has changed since you guys left. *A lot*." Cait got up and went to the bathroom, slamming the door. The tears were coming, and she couldn't bear the humiliation.

Reed followed and knocked gently on the door. He glanced back at Brett, who shrugged. How the hell should he know how to talk to a girl?

"Cait?" Reed whispered.

"Leave me alone."

"Cait! That's not what we're saying. It's just that you deserve better than Kyle Conrad. He's . . . I dunno . . . he's like always trying to prove something because his parents have no cash."

Cait was shaking her head on the other side of the door. "What the hell is wrong with you? He has a perfectly nice house on South. He's like the most popular guy in the junior class."

"He's a fucking loser, Cbow." It was Brett this time, not mincing words. "Any guy that would do that . . ."

Brett couldn't finish. Somewhere inside him was anger, rage even, that this punk whose family didn't even belong in Wilshire had done this to his little sister. It made him sick. It made him want to kill Kyle Conrad and his whole fucking family. The testosterone was pumping. He took a breath to keep himself under control.

Then came his sister's voice through the door. "So—you guys never got head from a girl who wasn't your *girlfriend*?" She said the word as though it were the most ridiculous concept to begin with.

There was a collective sigh and then a moment of silence, which revealed the answer, and Cait felt within her a bolt of rage. Fucking guys. They could do whatever they wanted and no one ever judged them. Not ever. There was a fate attached to being a girl, the fate of longing and waiting and seeking— always on the other side of the pursuit, always trying to figure out what had to be done to get a guy, and then doing it without any hesitation. What would those assholes know about *that*?

Ignoring her last comment, Brett decided to press forward. "He's a fucking loser, Cbow. At least pick someone who's a good guy next time."

"Like you two? Are you good guys?"

Reed was feeling defensive now, and for the record, had never gotten head from any girl. But that was something Brett didn't need to know. "We are good guys. Now come to the movie with us."

"No way."

Reed knocked again. "Come on, Cbow. We won't say another word about Kyle. Just come out with us. Get out of this house and get stoned. When was the last time you got stoned?"

Cait thought about the oxycodone. Did that count? "Last time you jerks were home."

"See—you're long overdue. Get your ass out of there, and let's go."

There was a slight pause, but then the sound of the doorknob turning. Reed stepped back, letting Cait emerge at her own pace.

Her eyes were red, her cheeks flushed, and Brett pulled her into his arms. Was there anything worse than watching his sister cry? "Come with us," he whispered as she pulled away.

Cait wiped her eyes with the back of her hand, then looked at her brother. He would never understand her, never see her as anything more than his little pet, his little awkward Cbow. Still, it did beat the hell out of staying home.

"Fine," she said. Then she followed them out the door.

THIRTY

STRANGERS

THE DAY AFTER THANKSGIVING, David went in to work at the normal time. With the maid and nanny off for the weekend, Jacks had her girls to herself, and it felt like the world had been placed on hold just for them.

They were gathered at the kitchen counter, still bundled in pj's at mid-morning, when the first call came. Stuffed from the enormous meal the night before, they had skipped breakfast in favor of hot cocoa and begun a game of Uno. Jacks was smiling when she heard the phone, and she let it go longer than she might have on another day, caught up in this small moment that had made her come close to forgetting. Watching them together, she could feel remnants of the contentment that had settled into her life, that had been her life before the letters started to come, and she didn't want it to end.

It was nothing short of a miracle to Jacks that mothering these girls had become easy for her, that she had come to understand who they were, each so different, yet so wonderful in their own ways. She had worried from the first sonogram how she would raise normal, healthy girls, not knowing how to be one herself. But David had been there to reassure her, and he had been right, though it would be years before she would come to feel it. Somehow, some-way, she had managed to keep from her own children the internal angst that lingered within her, showing them only the parts of herself that were good and honest and loving. Now she wondered if any of those things would be left after waging this war to save them.

The phone was still ringing.

"Hold on . . . and no cheating!" Jacks said, finally moving toward the counter. "It's probably Daddy—who wants to talk first?"

"Me!"

She heard Beth's reply as she was picking up the receiver. "Hello?"

"Is this the home of David Halstead?" The voice was dark, and something in the intonation—something eerie—sent a chill through Jacks.

"Who's calling?" she asked, glancing back at her girls, who had resumed the game. Her blood was picking up speed, her body knowing before she did that something was not right.

"Is this his wife?"

"We don't take any solicitations over the phone, and we're on the no-call list." This is where she would normally hang up, satisfied that she had not been overly rude and at the same time facilitating a quick exit from the annoyance. But not this time. This time she needed to know.

"Is Mr. Halstead at home?"

"No. He's not. You can try his office if you need to reach him." She waited a second to see if the caller would ask for the office number, but he didn't.

"Mrs. Halstead, your husband didn't go to work today. I'll try again later."

The phone was pressed to her ear even after she heard the *click* from the other end. The breath left her body, as she heard the sound of her girls calling to her from across the room.

"Mom! Your turn!"

But she couldn't move or speak or breathe.

"Uh!" Andrea shouted, frustrated by her mother's distraction. She had one card left and was about to win the game. "I'm going for you!"

Hailey screamed in protest. "You can't . . . you'll see her cards!"

Jacks could hear the fight as it erupted, though the volume was muted by the pounding in her ears. She felt the air race back in, a gasp that made her take a step forward and jolted her into action.

"Just skip me and finish, okay? I have to call Daddy. It's important." Their complaining trailed off as she rushed out of the room and down the hall. Leaning against the stair rail in the foyer, she called David on his cell. It went to voice mail. She tried his office next. Got his assistant. Yes—he was there, had been there all morning.

Jacks felt her legs fold beneath her as she slid down to the floor. The relief was overwhelming. Still, there were questions.

Against the backdrop of the battle being waged in the kitchen, Jacks fought to make sense of what had just taken her from her morning with her children to the maze of lies and deception her husband had created and that she now had to decipher.

"Mom!" Hailey was screaming for her now, in that tone that she used only when she was at the end of her rope with her sisters.

"Coming . . . ," she called out as she stood up and rushed back to the small catastrophe of the spoiled card game.

"Okay, what happened?" she asked, forcing herself to keep it together.

Standing beside her three children, she listened to their conflicting versions of events. Then she asked questions to sort out the truth from the untruth, being careful not to pass judgment, though her patience was in short supply. In the end, they decided to make a fire and get out the Christmas card envelopes. Jacks had purchased an embosser for the return addresses, which Hailey could do. Andrea and Beth could put on the stamps, and Jacks would begin to sign the cards. Girls were easy that way.

It was around three when the second call came. And this time, it was far too familiar.

"Hello, Jacks. Is your husband home yet?"

She held on longer than she should have, longer than she had promised herself she would as she'd gone through her day anticipating this very moment. Still, she stuck to the plan and hung up without saying a word. He called again at three thirty, then again at four, only those times she did nothing but listen to the ringing and watch the words UNIDENTIFIED CALLER spread across the caller ID panel. She fought to steady her nerves, which were already frayed from spending the day half in fear, half engaged with her kids. Thoughts raced through her mind. Should they leave? They could go to a movie, go shopping. Then she imagined sitting in a theater, just her and the three girls. Beth would have to use the bathroom, or want more popcorn. Was there ever an outing where one of them didn't leave her sight for a small stretch of time? She had never given it any thought. They lived in

Wilshire—one of the safest towns in the country. But now all of that had changed. The doors were locked, the alarm was on, the dog was in the house.

David came home at six thirty, weary but faking it well when his three little angels jockeyed into position to greet him. He leaned in and kissed his wife. They had dinner and put on a movie. Another fire, popcorn. Then the phone rang.

THIRTY-ONE

FEELING GOOD ABOUT BEING BAD

Cbow: It's cbow, are you there?

Totallyfkd: Hey. What's up?

Cbow: Nothing. Just hangin.

Totallyfkd: How was turkey day?

Cbow: Sucked. But I made it. Five days!

Totallyfkd: I know. Now we have finals. You?

Cbow: Same. Right before break. Are you going away?

Totallyfkd: Yeah—St. Barts. Can't wait to get outa here. My mom's practically having an orgasm over Smith so I'll get to party as much as I want. Ever been?

Cbow: Yeah. We go in March. We go to Florida after xmas. Just wanna sleep. Can I ask you a question?

Totallyfkd: Course.

Cbow: It's personal.

Totallyfkd: OK.

Cbow: I keep thinking about that guy you did it with. I keep thinking about my guy.

Totallyfkd: About DH?

Cbow: Yeah. DH.

Totallyfkd: You wanna know what it was like?

Cbow: I guess.

Totallyfkd: Hard to write about it.

Cbow: Then don't. I shouldn't have asked.

Totallyfkd: No, it's OK. It was kinda like getting high, except it hurt—no way around that. It hurt and it was over so fast I never got to the part where it's supposed to feel good. The worst part was I knew I shouldn't be do-ing it, like I knew the whole time he was going to fuck me over and I'd feel like shit after, but it felt good anyway—in my head it felt good. Does that make sense?

Cbow: Like it feels so good to be bad. I feel like that all the time now. After doing the OC and the whole thing at the party. Totally creepy but I can't stop thinking about it. Can't stop thinking about DH. Am I one of those messed up people who's gonna end up on heroin or cutting myself with little medical tools?

Totallyfkd: I dunno. I mean—NO! No cutting, please. Gross.

Cbow: I can't stop thinking that he'll suddenly start liking me but knowing he won't. But if I don't let myself believe it I feel like killing myself. Like there's nothing without that hope.

Totallyfkd: Be careful Cbow. I knew the guy I lost it with was a shit. I knew it! But I kept thinking maybe I was wrong. And I couldn't help it. Like I was totally addicted to my own self-destruction.

Cbow: That's what it is. Addicted to self-destruction. I really hate myself sometimes.

Totallyfkd: Do you really hate yourself?

Cbow: I must. Why else would I do these things?

Totallyfkd: If it helps at all, I like you.

Cbow: Thanks. It helps a little. I gotta go.

Totallyfkd: OK. Just promise me one thing, as your elder and everything (ha).

Cbow: What's that?

Totallyfkd: Think about what happened to me. I would take back those few minutes to not have the days and days of feeling like this. He's like my love heroin now, now that I've felt his body on mine.

Cbow: Yeah. That sucks. I'll try to think about what happened to you.

Totallyfkd: Promise?

Cbow: Promise.

THIRTY-TWO

THE GREAT DIVIDE

SETTING A CUP OF coffee down on her desk, Rosalyn looked at the letter she was composing on the computer screen.

> *Dear George and Betsy,*
>
> *I am writing about the application of the Conrad family for member-ship to our beloved club. . . .*

It was a delicate matter. She had been left out of the loop this time, un-doubtedly because of the inherent bias she carried toward this family of the boy who, for all intents and purposes, had molested her daughter. Still, she was on the committee. Her family had been members for generations, and she wasn't going to go away.

She was reading it over when Barlow appeared, stomping in and now hovering over her shoulder. "What are you doing?" he asked.

Rosalyn quickly closed the file and turned to face him. "Just some odds and ends. Paperwork."

Christ, it was hard to look at him now, to be cordial, knowing he was hav-ing an affair with Sara Livingston. It was bad enough Sara was a newcomer to their circle of friends, that she was on Rosalyn's blow job committee, *and* was working on an article about the whole mess. But she was so young. *Twenty-seven*. They had friends with kids who were twenty-seven. Barlow was forty-five. It was disgusting, though it would be far easier to explain, to justify as a puerile midlife fantasy, than if he had chosen someone *mature*, for lack of a better description. All middle-aged men wanted to fuck someone young again. Wasn't that what people thought? And that was exactly what they would think about Barlow, even if it was far from the truth.

The truth in this matter was that a great divide stood between her and her husband, one that had been growing for years, and in particular since he sold his business and inserted himself into their lives. And in spite of the social advantages to having his mistress be so young, it cut Rosalyn deeply.

Barlow sighed, his arms crossed as though he had cause to be self-righteous. "Have you checked in on Cait?"

With her eyebrows raised, Rosalyn shot it back at him. "Have you?"

Another sigh. "I just got back from dropping the boys. You've been home all day?"

"Yes, Barlow, I've been home. And I decided to give her some space. In case you didn't notice, she wasn't exactly overjoyed at the quality family time we've all had to endure for the past few days."

Barlow was suddenly incensed. "Why would you say it like that? Brett seemed great, playing with the kids, taking Cait to a movie. I thought it was a nice weekend."

Rosalyn bit her lip. *A nice weekend*. Interesting interpretation. What she had seen were two freewheeling teenage boys who got Caitlin stoned, then came home and roughhoused with the twins *because* they were stoned, then passed out in front of the TV, woke up, and raided the fridge. But Barlow would see only what he needed to.

"Okay, Barlow. It was a nice weekend."

"All I'm saying is that maybe you should spend less time looking for some speaker to talk to us about sex and more time talking to Cait. We aren't the teenagers here, in case you haven't noticed."

Rosalyn felt the blood rush to her face. *No, but maybe that will be next for you . . . scoping out your daughter's friends*. Why had he done this, on top of everything? They hadn't been intimate for months, she would give him that. But there were reasons. And this was marriage.

"Don't tell me how to take care of our daughter. I've been doing it for fourteen years. You've been at it for six months."

She didn't wait for a reply. A fight was not possible today. She was at the breaking point, and if he pushed her into a corner, she wouldn't be able to hold back. Caitlin. The Conrads. Barlow and Sara. Now Brett. And she felt like she hadn't seen the twins and Mellie all weekend.

She shut down the computer with two clicks, then pushed out of the chair and away from Barlow. Her shoulder brushed his as she made her escape, and he did what he always did when she walked away, huffed loudly and watched her with dismay. There would be nothing inside him but a recognition of his own feelings and the self-pity they would evoke. And knowing this disgusted her further.

Rushing upstairs, she closed herself off within the confines of her sitting room and leaned against the wall. Where did a person go from here? She hadn't felt this way for many years, since her return from Paris as a senior at the Academy. She had given in to the crushing wave of Wilshire conformity, and she had not come up from under its swell until she was away from it again. How ironic that even then, away at college, she had found a man who would bring her right back. But now the lives of five children were in her hands. She knew what to do with all of this, every little problem that was before her, and the plans were in place. She could lie down and die, let everything play out on its own, or scrape herself off this mental floor and stay the course. Her plans had never failed her before. Not ever.

She sat at her desk and pulled out the little box of engraved notecards. This was what she had left to do today, write the invitations to the dinner party. She took out her best pen, the one with the smooth black ink that rolled with perfection across the ivory pages.

Dear Sara and Nick . . .

THIRTY-THREE

KEEPING ENEMIES CLOSER

SEVERAL DRINKS INTO THE evening, Sara found herself in the Barlows'
dining room, cutting into a rare veal shank smothered in rich merlot re-
duction. She heard Nick laugh from across the table, and she was reminded
of how they had suffered through the past ten days, speaking but not *really*
speaking. Sleeping next to each other but never touching. Sara had gone to
the fertility clinic. In spite of the ambivalence about the second baby that
she had confessed to him on Thanksgiving, she had done the tests—blood
work, ultrasound, a pelvic exam. He'd whacked off into a cup. It turned
out they were just fine. Only they weren't fine, because Sara didn't want to
get pregnant. How could the impact of *that* be measured? Surely it was
part of the explanation. And now they had stopped trying by virtue of the
distance that had grown between them.

The dinner was fabulous, of course, and the company certainly the reason
for Nick's sudden change in mood. The Barlows, Halsteads, Ridleys, and
Livingstons all enjoying food designed by a world-renowned chef. The first
course was butternut-squash soup with a dollop of sour cream, accompanied
by a large dose of town gossip. Sara had the soup and washed it down with a
glass of white burgundy. The second course consisted of heirloom beet salad
with blue cheese and finely chopped greens, and even more gossip, which

Sara digested with a glass of pinot noir. Now the veal was sitting on her plate as they talked about vacation homes—exclusive this, exclusive that—and she could not put a piece of it in her mouth. She reached for the third wineglass of the evening, a large bowl-shaped thing filled with something red.

"He's hot. I'm telling you. Hot, hot, hot. Hats off to the pool committee this year." Eva Ridley giggled and raised her glass to toast the women who had just made their selection for the club's pool manager. "There are some perks to being on the board."

Smiling at her with affection, Marcus Ridley raised his glass and clinked it against hers. "Thank God. Now I can play golf in peace. Gentlemen—I think we're in store for a great summer." Like his wife, Marcus was lean, well dressed, and generally slick in both appearance and demeanor.

Seated at one end of the table, Rosalyn forced a smile. It was almost cruel how they could do that—pretend they were the stereotype of a dysfunctional suburban couple when they were still deeply in love with each other. Marcus Ridley never played golf, and Eva rushed in and out of the pool solely to deposit and collect her children. They could make Brad Pitt the pool manager, and Eva would still race home for a quickie with Marcus while the kids had diving practice. But the people they pretended to be— the wife who sat poolside in her bikini all day reading novels and watching the lifeguards and the husband who didn't care, because it meant he could play another nine holes without complaint—were all around them. And what they represented could be found in some manifestation right here in this house. That's what was cruel. Unintentional on Eva's part, but cruel nonetheless. And with all that was going on in Rosalyn's life, it hit her particularly hard tonight as she watched her husband converse with Sara Livingston.

Barlow, who had been intentionally seated next to Sara by Rosalyn, was leaning in now to whisper in Sara's ear, "You've gone quiet."

Sara smiled politely. There was no simple answer. This was her tendency when she drank, chatty for the first one, then pensive and dark as the intoxication grew. But it was more than that. Unlike her college days, when all she had to be pensive about were external, geopolitical problems facing mankind, she now had a litany of very personal crises.

"I'm just thinking, that's all."

"Thinking? What are you thinking?"

Sara turned to face him, looking him dead in the eye. "Do you really want to know? I mean *really*?"

Barlow was curious, and his smile was infused with enthusiasm. This was their third encounter, and he once again had the feeling that beneath her awkward attempts to fit in among them, there was something interesting waiting to be found.

"I asked, didn't I?"

Sara shrugged and took a sip of the wine. "Okay. I'll tell you. I'm thinking about little calves chained to wood troughs in stalls so small they can't move. And I'm thinking that I'm a complete hypocrite because if this were a cheeseburger, I'd be all over it."

Barlow's smile widened. "I see. So it's better to let them run free and grow up, then pound a battering ram between their eyes?"

Sara pretended to be indignant. "Jeez—I already admitted to being a hypocrite."

"But you still aren't touching the veal."

She shrugged again.

"Maybe your objection is to what that piece of meat is saying to you."

"Saying to me? You think the meat is sending me a secret message?" Sara was smiling now, fully, as she pulled off a piece of her dinner roll.

"Yes. Shhh . . ." Barlow tilted his head and leaned his ear over Sara's plate. "I hear it!"

"Stop!" Sara was laughing, suddenly self-conscious as she felt her mood lifting.

"It spoke to me, I swear it," Barlow said, sitting straight again. He took a long sip of his wine, then cut off a large chunk of his own veal and put it in his mouth.

"Apparently, it didn't ask you not to eat its friend."

Barlow kept chewing, but nodded to acknowledge the worthy retort. Then he washed down the veal with more wine and pretended to ponder the situation of the meat on Sara's plate. "Here's what I think," he began.

"Okay . . ." Sara watched him carefully, waiting for the next amusement from Ernest Barlow. That he was a billionaire seemed incomprehensible to her, as did his interest in this conversation. Still, it felt genuine.

"Veal is the meat of the wealthy. Hamburger is not. Therein lies your objection to our chef's finest work—not the plight of milk-fed, imprisoned calves."

Sara could feel her mind engaged, even through the alcohol. Even among this crowd, which had so intimidated her before. "Really? You think? 'Cause calves are pretty cute, and their plight is certainly worthy of concern beyond the socioeconomics of meat consumption."

Barlow nodded and leaned back in his chair. "Mrs. Livingston, I think you just might be a socialist."

This made her laugh. She wasn't a socialist, but her views were down-right radical in a town that was this concerned with money. "Maybe by Wilshire standards. Anywhere else, I'm a moderate Democrat."

"Good God, woman! Don't use the D-word around here."

"I know. It's a sacrilege." Sara took a drink of water, now oblivious of the rest of the table that was buzzing away with chatter about ski resorts. "Why is that? I've only been here a few months, but why is it that all these Northeastern, liberally educated people are such staunch Republicans?"

Allowing a servant to remove his plate, Barlow turned his chair slightly to face her, crossed his legs, and perched his elbow on the table, where the veal had been. "Oh, come on. You seem like a smart girl. You must know."

"Taxes. I know. But really? Isn't there enough money?"

Barlow's laughter now filled the room. "All right, let's have it. What's so funny?" Eva asked from across the table, masking the worry that had been growing all night.

Sara looked at Barlow pleadingly. But he was having too much fun to let her off the hook. "We are discussing the quandary of Wilshire politics, and in particular, why we vote Republican despite our liberal social views."

Eva managed to smile at them, but this wasn't good. Barlow loved to talk politics, especially with idealistic people like Sara Livingston, who were still untainted by the corrupting influences of their privileged lives.

"Taxes," Marcus Ridley said matter-of-factly from his seat next to Rosalyn.

Barlow was quick with an answer. "We know that, Marcus. But why don't we ever admit that we have enough and it's time to give back? That is the question on the table."

Sara felt her cheeks flush. "Not exactly—I mean that's not exactly the question."

Barlow reached out and touched the back of her hand with his. "It's okay. It's a good question."

Rosalyn managed a smile, though she was irritated by the complete lack of discretion her husband and his lover were displaying. She had brought Sara here for one reason: to keep her enemy closer. Now she was finding it hard to swallow.

"It's not difficult to understand, Sara." Rosalyn's voice was laced with condescension. "Money buys us out of reliance on the government. Paying taxes is the only way the government touches us."

"Christ, Rosalyn Barlow," Eva replied scornfully. "You make us sound like anarchists!"

"Anarchy! I like it!" Barlow said, fully enjoying himself.

Marcus Ridley moved in with smooth, nonchalant charm. "Maybe we should secede. The Republic of Wilshire. Jacks, what do you think?"

Seated beside Marcus, Jacks tried to care about the unfolding complexities the conversation had taken on. What was actually concerning her at the moment was the ease with which she had displaced Rosalyn's suspicions on this unsuspecting young woman, and the guilt that would not be quelled by the abundance of wine.

She smiled coyly because it seemed appropriate. "What is it they say? Never discuss politics, religion, or pets at a social gathering."

Marcus was shaking his head. "I think it's children. Never discuss politics, religion, or *children*."

"What the hell's the difference?" Eva's remark brought uniform laughter to the table, though little of it was real. Still, it gave Rosalyn the chance she needed to change the subject.

"So enough about all of those things. Let's move on to something totally selfish and indulgent."

"I'll drink to that." David Halstead had been politely quiet for most of the evening, latching on to small chances like this one to say something benign.

Rosalyn allowed her expression to soften. She looked first to Sara, then focused on Nick—ignoring her husband as his face morphed back to a state of misery. She was going to do this, sponsor the Livingstons at the club, and there wasn't a damned thing he could do to stop her. She needed to offer the membership committee an alternative to the Conrads, and the Livingstons were the obvious choice. Their lives would become instantly enmeshed with hers, and Barlow's, making the affair a living hell for all of them.

"Let's talk about frivolous, ostentatious, and offensively exclusive country clubs."

THIRTY-FOUR

BREAKING DOWN

"MERRY CHRISTMAS." BARLOW'S VOICE was sullen, his mood sulky in a childish way as Jacks rushed about the room, gathering her clothing.

"It's still two weeks away," she said, though they both knew they would not see each other until after the holidays. Still, she could not pretend to join him in his displeasure. For her it was a relief, and there had been enough pretending for one afternoon.

"Come over here." He was reaching out for her with a bare arm, the rest of him snuggled beneath the plush bed coverings.

Jacks looked over with a playful smile, though it was close to painful. She could feel Barlow's need for her, his unrelenting desire to love and be loved, which she could not provide. He felt it. *He must.* And yet he kept trying to squeeze it out of the twisted, corrupt thing that their affair had become.

When she was in his arms again, he pecked her lips with a passionless kiss. "I'll miss you. Will you be all right?"

"I'll be fine. And I'll miss you. But the time will fly by. You'll see. It always does." She felt him against her with a strange intensity—the coarse hair of his legs, the sticky sweat that was still on his chest. She was suddenly aware of every inch of him, and it was unbearable. "I really need to go," she said, smiling again as she pulled away.

He didn't stop her. "I guess I should get going, too." Pulling back the covers, he sighed loudly. Then he swung his legs around the side of the bed and plopped his feet on the floor. Another sigh.

Jacks finished buttoning her blouse, which had been strewn across a chair. Then she walked to the bed and stood before him. "You'll be all right. I promise."

He nodded and looked up at her, and it was then that she saw it. Whatever she had made him feel that night in the wine cellar was fading, and it was fading fast. It was inevitable that the truth would appear, she knew. Deception carried a strong odor that even the best practitioners could not mask indefinitely. And she was hardly the best, perhaps not good at all. Maybe there was some comfort in that—in knowing that she still had a soul. But David was in trouble, serious trouble, and the man standing before her in this hotel room was the only way out she could see.

A sick feeling rushed through her. She leaned down and kissed Barlow hard on the mouth. "Will I see you first thing—after Florida?"

Surprised, Barlow smiled at her and stroked the side of her face. "Sure. First thing."

She met his eyes and held them, hoping he would see beyond the disgust she held for both of them. "Okay."

She pulled away, grabbing her coat and purse, then headed for the door. She did not look back again, but instead rushed to her car. Tears streamed down her face as she drove. It was nearly three. The girls would all be home—two on the bus, Beth with the nanny who'd taken her to a friend's house to play. How carefully she had orchestrated this day, thinking through their schedules and plans. And now it was done and she was returning to them, her sweet girls, her house, her life. The insurgent resurfacing from the bottom of a rancid cesspool. How could she see those beautiful faces, the bright blue eyes, the shining hair and chubby cheeks, and not feel totally and completely vile in their presence?

She pulled into the driveway, then stopped abruptly when she saw his car. Parked in the garage with the door left open was David's black BMW. Thoughts flew in and out. *He knows, he's waiting inside to confront me.* She wiped the tears from her face, but her face was still flushed. There was nothing she could do. She'd gone through the gate. It was too late to turn back.

She constructed her response. Surprise would be appropriate. Worry, perhaps, as well, given the phone calls that had started coming again. Once, twice, sometimes three times a night, and each time David had either taken them behind the closed doors of his study or ignored them, stepping outside for a cigar and a glass of whiskey. She had not asked questions, and he had not offered explanations. She had, instead, become acutely aware of her surroundings. Doors were locked when they were home. She followed the school bus in the mornings and turned down playdates for her girls. When they were not at school, they were under her supervision, or that of their trusted nanny. When they were gone, so was Jacks, using the season as an excuse not to ever be home alone.

And now here they were, in the middle of the afternoon, David home from his work and Jacks home from hers.

She walked in the house through the garage, set her purse and coat down in the mudroom. "David?" she called into the kitchen, but there was no answer.

She saw his briefcase open on the counter, its contents strewn about as though he'd been in a hurry. Whatever worry she had that this was somehow about her and Barlow was erased in that instant, and she knew in her gut that this was far worse.

"David!" she called as she bounded up the stairs.

The door to their bedroom was open.

"David!"

The room was empty. The sound of running water seeped beneath the closed bathroom door. Jacks moved cautiously toward it. "David?" she said again, softer this time.

She knocked but there was no answer.

"Honey?" she whispered as she turned the knob and pushed the door open. "Oh, God!"

He was there, though it took a moment for Jacks to see him. He was more like a small child in a man's body, curled up in the bath, hugging his legs, and rocking back and forth. A faucet was running at the sink.

Stepping cautiously, Jacks walked to the sink and wet a cloth under the running water. Then she turned off the open faucet, all the while talking slowly. "It's okay now. You're going to be okay." Returning to his side, she pressed the cold cloth to his forehead and watched him respond, pulling back from the state of shock. His eyes broke their stare and turned to meet hers, briefly and with confusion. "Shhh," she whispered.

She was in another place now, a place so familiar, it had returned without the slightest conscious effort. The transformation was seamless. The fear was gone. She had been here before, in the presence of human unraveling, in the face of total breakdown, and she knew what had to be done.

"You're okay, David. You're safe," Jacks said, running the cloth over his forehead then the side of his face.

He met her eyes again, and this time she saw it. It was exactly the way she remembered it, exactly the same as it had appeared on her father so many years before. Like a medical disease that could be photographed and documented for future students to identify, he had the look of mental departure, the distinct external appearance that was in the eyes—the way they widened softly into hollow holes. The rest of the face was blank, like the face of the dead, lacking the urgency of fear, the uplifting of joy. The message was sent through the eyes alone, a plea for help that screamed silently from the hollow spaces.

She finished wiping his face, helping the blood to flow to arouse his senses. Then she placed the cloth on the side of the tub and climbed inside behind him, wrapping her arms and legs around his body. She rested her chin on his shoulder so he could feel her face against his, so he could hear her whisper over and over, "You're okay."

There was a time when she had been on the other side of this porcelain wall, watching and learning. Kelly had been the one inside, holding their father like she was his mother, or his wife perhaps, but certainly not his daughter. It was far too intimate a procedure to be appropriate for a daughter, and yet boundaries such as those had concerned them little when their father was the one with the hollow holes. Thinking back now as a wife holding her husband this way, Jacks imagined that Kelly had learned this from their mother before she left and, as a little girl then, had absorbed it the same way she had absorbed other information—like putting ice on a bumped head, or a Band-Aid on a scraped knee. There were things that happened and the things that needed to be done to fix them.

From their mother to Kelly, from Kelly to Jacks, the procedures for managing a disturbed mind had been passed along like a pie recipe. And now, here she was again. Only this was not their father.

She felt him start to break, and she squeezed harder. He would cry now, releasing the energy that his body had manufactured to hold him so still, so silent in this place. He would cry for a long time and come back slowly to reality and the reasons that had started all of this. He would see them again and know that they were not the immediate threat his mind had woven them into, sending him into the state of mental shutdown. He would think about them again in a rational way, attempt to solve them and, undoubtedly, convince himself there was a way out that he could actually live with. And then he would return to normal. He would say things like *I don't know what got into me!* And they might even laugh about it as they enjoyed a meal together with the girls.

That was what was coming, and it was the only part about any of this that had Jacks terrified. Putting away the memories of her father, she was now remembering her own husband over the past two decades. There had never been anything like this. But there had been moments, small disconnects from the world that had sent him into milder forms of shutdown. Always following some event at work—a market downturn, a shake-up of management that threatened his job—these short-lived spells had altered him. He would withdraw from the family. His temper would flare, and this was so unlike him. He would decline social engagements, refuse calls from his parents, his sister. Jacks would say he was ill, some virus. The flu. A pulled muscle from a brutal squash match.

What did it matter? There was always a reason, and this was what had fooled her. She could see that now. It was the ability to identify a trigger that had made her blind to the truth. Her father's breakdowns had always seemed random. But then again, what did they know? As little children, they were not privy to the details of his life.

She felt David's tears on her arms, his body shaking with the release of the cry that was so intense it was silent but for the gasps of air that came and went. This was the worst he had ever been. This was the only time it had been this clear, and yet she could see now all those other spells and the pattern they formed. It was then she felt her own tears return. For all the convincing she had done over the years, all the efforts she made to stop history in its tracks, in the end, Kelly had been right. People do seek out their past.

She must have felt it radiating from deep within him, because the attraction to David Halstead had been instantaneous and powerful. And though nothing about him had given it away, the truth was here now in the broken man she held in her arms.

After all the steps she had taken to prevent this, she could not deny it for one second more. She had married her father.

THIRTY-FIVE

GRANDE CARAMEL MACHIATOS

"MAKE THAT TWO," AMANDA said over Cait's shoulder.

School was done, finished for eighteen days. They had faced final exams in four subjects, concluded the squash season with a second-place finish in the regional division, and endured the mandatory holiday concert in which they sang "holiday" songs about dreidels and Santa, with no mention of anyone's god. This was the night, the last night that they would all still be in town before the private jets fueled up and whisked them here and there for family reunions and vacations. Cait was staying put until the day after Christmas, but Amanda was leaving the next morning for Colorado and would not return until after the new year, making this Cait's last night to have a social life. With skillful precision, Amanda had remained Cait's gatekeeper to the rest of the circle of friends, and without her, Cait would be shut out entirely.

"Make mine skim," Amanda ordered to the Starbucks barista. Then she turned to Cait. "Fucking Colorado. Just shoot me now."

Cait grabbed the white paper cups loaded with sugar-free chocolate, sugar-free whipped cream, and the slightest hint of coffee and followed Amanda to the tables in the back, where a dozen of their peers had gathered. "No one's around anyway. It'll be dead. I already feel like a loser."

"I thought you were going to West Palm?"

They sat down on the arms of oversized chairs, which were already overflowing with plaid-kilted bodies.

"Not until after Christmas. I'm here for a week."

Amanda took a sip of her drink, then ran her tongue over her lips to remove the whipped cream that had gathered. "I know someone who'll be here," she said, winking.

"Who?" Cait could feel the energy just from the way Amanda had said those words, and her hopes were confirmed as she followed Amanda's eyes toward the long line of customers waiting to order their bar drinks. It was there she spotted Kyle Conrad.

"Kyle?"

Amanda leaned in and whispered. "I heard they're in town the *whole* vacation."

Cait raised her eyebrows. "All of it?"

Amanda nodded, and they shared a look of silent understanding. No one stayed in Wilshire for the whole break unless they were unable to afford a trip. That was a given, and it made sticking around somewhat humiliating. That the Conrads were in such a position meant they were in a tight spot. A very tight spot.

Maybe that's why he was here, alone and headed toward them. But Cait didn't care about reasons, only that he was, in fact, here and that her head was now spinning with the kind of euphoria she knew was going to get her into trouble.

"Hey," he said to the small crowd. It was mixed tonight, some ninth-graders, some tenth. Kyle was one of only three juniors, and his presence was instantly recognized.

"What's up?" he asked.

He took a seat across from them on one of the bar stools, and this seemed entirely appropriate to Cait, that he remain above them all. Whatever it was he had over her, it was determined, and she was not fighting it tonight. She pretended not to notice him as the conversations carried on. From one topic to the next, there were loud bursts of raucous teenage laughter, the occasional spattering of the word *fuck*, and exaggerated hand iterations—all of which were meant to draw attention and differentiate the young, irreverent free spirits from the older folks who came into Starbucks for a legitimate caffeine fix.

It lasted over an hour before small groups began to disperse. Some were walking down the street to catch a movie. Others were heading home to pack. Those who couldn't drive were at the whim of those who could, and so when Amanda's ride decided it was time to leave, Cait had no choice but to get up and follow.

But that was not the end of it.

"Hey, wait up." It was Kyle, and he was actually racing to catch them at the door.

Amanda smiled. "Hey."

Kyle ignored her. Turning to Cait, he gave her that look—the one she'd seen the night of the school dance. The one she'd seen since but never directed at her.

"I'm headed out your way. Need a ride?"

"Headed out to the backcountry?" Amanda was suspicious and not about to let Cait have her moment.

"Yeah. I am." And that was all he said. He didn't owe Amanda any explanations, and Cait didn't want one. There was no reason for him to be going near her estate except to drive her, and the thought of that felt like Christmas was coming early.

"That would be great. Thanks!" Cait said. She felt suddenly right, like everything she had done and said and thought for weeks was paying off. Every look, every word, even tonight, staying in her seat and avoiding him, it had all come together and *worked*! She had known all along. No, that was a lie. She had hoped and prayed and fought to convince herself that this part of her that believed was actually right. Now it seemed she hadn't been crazy after all.

She hugged Amanda quickly, saying the necessary good-byes as she trailed behind Kyle toward the car that was a frequent prop in her daydreams. Flipping her long blond hair, the smile stuck on her face, she climbed in and threw her backpack on the floor.

Kyle turned on the car. "It's fucking cold!" he said, shivering with a slight laugh as he adjusted the heat. Then he turned on some music. "Is that okay?" he asked.

Cait nodded. It was more than okay. It was perfect.

They pulled out of the Starbucks lot and began to drive north, away from town where the night seemed darker. Kyle asked about her exams, her vacation plans, and what they should do to kill the time. He asked like he cared, and he listened when she answered.

"You should totally have a party when they're away," he said.

Cait nodded and smiled. "Is anyone even around? It's right before Christmas."

He turned then and looked her dead in the eye. "I'm around."

Blood rushed into her cheeks as she smiled back. Had she stopped smiling this whole time? Fifteen minutes was a long time to smile, and her face was actually beginning to hurt.

"Well—think about it and send me a text. Do you have the number?"

Cait shook her head.

"Here," Kyle said, handing her his BlackBerry.

She got out her cell phone and entered his number. This was happening. It was *really* happening.

They got to her driveway and he drove in.

"Go left at the fork," Cait said, pointing ahead. "I go in through the service entrance." It was a lie, but there would be some privacy there. They could park for hours and no one would notice them.

"So, here we are," Kyle said. He put the car in park, but left it running with the music and the heat. Then he flicked off the lights. "You know—I never got to say sorry for that night. I kinda left you without a ride."

Cait blushed again. "It was fine. I got home."

Kyle shook his head. "No. Don't make excuses. It was a shit-head move, and Doug can be a prick."

Cait was suddenly grateful that he hadn't heard a thing about Doug and the ride home. "It was fine. He was pretty high, but we made it."

"Good. Okay. Anyway, I've been so stressed out. I've got Mr. Vointer for English. You know, *the Bear*? He's such a hard-ass, and this is the year . . . you know, for grades."

"Why do they call him the Bear?" Cait's face was shaking. They were having an actual conversation, and Kyle was letting her in—into his thoughts, his world. She was nervous and giddy and scared out of her mind.

"I guess he has a really hairy back. I've never seen it, but that's what they say. He's been a legend for, like, generations. Anyway," Kyle said before looking down awkwardly. It was an odd expression for his face, for his entire persona, but he managed to pull it off, and Cait found it endearing. When he looked up again, he reached for her the way he had that night, his hand running along the side of her face then through her hair. She leaned into it softly and closed her eyes. Nothing could feel this good. Nothing.

Moving his body closer to hers, he leaned over and kissed her, gently at first, then harder. She opened her mouth and felt his tongue sweep her lips, the roof of her mouth, and she did the same to him. They were breathing hard in and out of the kiss, both of his hands on her face now, stroking her hair. He moved his body back into his seat and pulled her over him, her legs straddling his body, her chest pressed to his—all the while kissing her with a hunger that she could not believe was finally meant for her. This was not the prelude to a favor. He wanted her, to be with her. It was *real*. She could feel the power of their attraction as his hands moved fluidly across her body, under her shirt, then the back of her thighs as they reached beneath the kilt. Through only the thin cotton panties, she could feel his erection and she moved against it, provoking him further. "Oh, God!" he whispered, grabbing her ass and pulling her against him.

Her mind was in a haze, and nothing could make her break away from him. She reached down and pulled at his buckle, and when he stopped kissing her to search her face, she smiled and leaned back into him, biting his lip. She wanted to consume him, every inch of him. This was not a moment that could last; it had to go forward to the end. She could feel it, the burning inside her, starting in her gut and running down her inner thighs. This was what they had warned her about—the teachers, the videos and books. Even her friend TF. What had she said? To think about what had happened to her, how it hurt, how it was over so quickly and then he never called. She didn't care. Kyle had taken her to a place that had just one exit.

As she pulled harder at the belt, he began gyrating against her. Then he moaned and leaned back, and her thighs felt wet. Her body was still moving against his, but his hands were now draped by his side. She tried to kiss him, but he was in another place. He moaned again, this time with a little laugh, and when he finally kissed her back, it was playful.

"Shit. Kinda made a mess."

Sensing that it was over, Cait climbed back to her seat. Her legs were shaking, her body still hungry, and she had no idea how to make it stop.

He wasn't embarrassed, though Cait imagined that another boy might have been. The crotch of his khakis now had a dark circle where he'd come, and it looked like he'd peed on himself. He reached into the backseat for a tissue and dried off what he could. Then he leaned over to kiss her one last time. "Look what you did to me. I'm a fucking mess, Cait Barlow."

She smiled at him as he pulled back, though every inch of her wanted more.

From the center console, he pulled out a cigarette. "Here. For later."

And Cait took it because she couldn't imagine getting out of this car without something to help her come down from this high. Not knowing what else to do, she reached for the door handle. This was all uncovered territory.

Kyle took her hand, and she stopped to look at him. "I had no idea you were . . ."

"What?" she asked.

"That you wanted to."

There were so many things she wanted. There was a list she kept in her head. She wanted to be with him, and not just in this car. She wanted to sit next to him at a party, feel his arm around her. She wanted to tell him things she hadn't told anyone else. She wanted to call him late at night and confess her sins. She wanted to love him, to be loved by him. *Yes*, she thought, she wanted to do all of those things. But tonight her body had shifted into overdrive, and what she wanted to do was finish the ride and fuck the consequences.

She had no words that would not make her sound like a porn star, so she just shrugged and smiled.

"You have the number. Text me when your parents leave."

He waited for her to get out, then waved and drove off. Thinking back on it later, she would remember him being polite. And as she walked to the back door, she felt high. She would wait until her parents left for Florida, their two-day jaunt to schmooze with the membership committee. Then she would text him, and he would return. She let the word float in her head. *Boyfriend*. That's what this might be. It sure as hell felt that way. And why not? That's what girls did—they had boyfriends, then fiancés, then husbands. Why was it so ridiculous to think it could happen to her, and with someone she actually wanted?

As she walked inside, quietly closing the door behind her, she refused to hear the evil voice inside that was playing over and over. *What about Victoria Lawson? What about the night of the party? What about the fact that you've never been on a date that didn't involve getting him off? And what about TF?*

When she got inside her room, she sat at her computer. She couldn't smoke the cigarette until her parents went to bed, and she needed something to settle her nerves. She could tell her, couldn't she? TF had never judged her before, and who better to understand? Maybe she would even see that this was different. That Kyle wasn't like her guy. Maybe she would see that Cait had played things just right, that Kyle really wanted her after all the doubting.

Making up her mind, she set the cigarette down on the desk, then pulled out the keyboard and began to type.

THIRTY-SIX

SARA IN SURREAL LIFE

"Cocktail, Mrs. Barlow?" A young woman in a neat blue uniform was leaning over Rosalyn with a small brown tray and a broad smile.

"No, thank you."

Barlow, who was sitting across from his wife, did not wait to be asked. "Scotch. Neat."

The woman left for the front of the plane and began to fix the drink.

Barlow leaned forward to see out the window one last time. "Where can they be? If we miss our time, we'll get bumped back an hour. Look at all those goddamned planes."

Rosalyn didn't bother to look up from her BlackBerry. "They'll be here. I sent a car for them."

"Uhh," Barlow moaned. What the hell were they doing anyway, jetting down to Florida for two days just to parade the Livingstons around in front of the admissions committee? This was their annual retreat, and they liked to be left alone. Rosalyn usually skipped the whole thing, feeling above the rest of them as a senior member and mother of young children. Most of the members were well into their sixties.

Of course, he knew the answer. Rosalyn was hell-bent on blackballing the Conrads, and this move would cement the deal. Still, she was pulling all of them away from home at the start of the holiday break—a time typically reserved for decorating, shopping, and being with family. At least, that was what he had observed from afar all these years. This was the first year he would not be working like a prison inmate, so he couldn't say for sure. But that was what he would like to be doing. Brett would be home tomorrow. Cait was already on break, and the little guys would have nothing to do but watch TV and wait for their parents to return. It was just wrong.

His wife, on the other hand, seemed to have no problem abandoning her children at Christmastime.

"Could you stop working for one second?" he asked finally, when his drink arrived.

Rosalyn looked up, annoyed by the interruption. "I only have a few more minutes before I'll have to stop, so no—I can't put it down for one second. This is a crazy time of year for me."

"How? How is it so crazy? What the hell are you doing?" Barlow took a long sip of the drink, then nodded a thank-you to the flight attendant, who was standing at attention by the front of the plane.

"Let's see—I'm checking the delivery status of the boys' iPods. They've been on back order for weeks, and if they don't ship by tomorrow, I'll have to bid for them on eBay. I'm checking our golf reservations for tomorrow. I'm scheduling a lunch with Dr. Wright, who's coming to town to discuss her presentation on blow jobs. I'm—"

"Enough!" Barlow raised his hand in a show of defeat. "Enough."

With her fingers moving quickly now across the tiny keypad, Rosalyn did not look up, but she kept speaking. "How many times have we had this discussion? When running the house becomes your job, you can tell me how I've done it all wrong for the past eighteen years. Until then—"

"Yes, I know—just shut up and do my job."

Only Barlow didn't have a job anymore, and Rosalyn was now convinced her husband's unemployment was at the heart of their recent marital freeze. He was bored and testy and needing to re-create himself. That he thought Sara Livingston could do that for him was laughable. Only it wasn't.

"There they are!" Barlow shouted, jumping from his seat.

Looking out the small window, Rosalyn saw the black town car pull up to the plane. She quickly finished her work and shut down her BlackBerry.

"Hello, welcome!" Barlow was standing at the top of the stairs, looking down at the Livingstons. "No, no—don't touch the luggage. Mitch will get it—Mitch! The bags!"

Rosalyn couldn't see them yet, but heard them as they climbed up to the plane's hull. *Sorry we're late . . . traffic . . . what a gorgeous plane . . . we've never been on a private jet.*

And there was Barlow, being the perfect host. "Welcome aboard," he said as they appeared through the door. They looked tired and disheveled, and mostly uneasy about having held up the plane.

"Come down here," Rosalyn said, grabbing their attention. "Let's sit together around the sofa."

Sara, with her hair pulled back in a baseball cap and a colorful knit scarf roped around her neck, looked like a kid as she walked back.

"Wow," she said, reaching Rosalyn. She leaned in to give her hostess a peck on the cheek. "This is incredible."

"Thanks. We've had it a few years. It makes much more sense when you've got five kids, three nannies, friends . . . and commercial flights these days . . . well, might as well stay home."

Sara smiled politely as she took a seat on a leather sofa in the center of the plane. It was like someone's living room, with end tables, reading lamps, and footrests, though everything was bolted to the floor. Toward the front were more traditional seats, which swiveled to face either direction and appeared to recline down into beds. There were little draperies for the windows, a wet bar, oven, and mini-fridge, and an attractive woman standing at attention, waiting to serve them. After a nice meal and a few drinks, they would walk off into the brilliant Florida sunshine. It was surreal. Too surreal for Sara, who didn't know what they were doing here and was already missing her little girl.

Nick, on the other hand, was in his bliss. Taking a seat beside his wife, he patted her gently on the knee and stole a look around while the Barlows took their seats in the plush chairs on the opposite side of the coffee table. When he caught her eye, he mouthed the word *wow*. Sara smiled and nodded. Why did she agree to do this? It was the start of the Christmas week, her favorite time of year. The smell of pine from the tree in the living room, the bright reds and greens, the cards from other families with the annual picture that the mothers pained themselves to acquire. Then, of course, there were cookies and more cookies, those cutout shapes that looked like blobs until the frosting was applied just so, Santa's red coat, an angel's white dress. She and her sisters would speculate about their gifts and watch the evening TV cartoons. Charlie Brown, Rudolph, and Frosty. Annie was just old enough to do these things with her, just old enough to start forging her own memories. And now, thanks to Nick, Annie would be making different memories with Nanna while her mother was golfing in Florida. And Sara didn't even play golf.

Sara in surreal life felt like bolting off the plane when she heard the door pulling shut. Her head was spinning as she felt her life being stolen out from under her by billionaires and private planes. By country clubs and golf. By her own husband, it seemed. And yet her husband was the only reason she remained in her seat—Nick, and her aversion to looking like a complete lunatic. Nothing had been the same between them. Even after she resumed taking her pills, in secret, they hadn't made love once. Not once in almost three weeks. That was a new record for them. Now he needed her to do this with him—to do this for him, if that was all she could manage it to be.

So she crossed her legs and ordered a drink. "I'll have whatever he's having," she said when the woman arrived, brown tray in hand.

Nick gave her another look, this one laced with disapproval. He hadn't exactly enjoyed her performance the last time she and Ernest Barlow had a few drinks together.

"Wonderful!" Barlow bellowed out. "And I'll have another."

"Champagne, thank you," Rosalyn said, her voice subdued by contrast. "Nick?"

"That sounds perfect for the occasion. Sara—how about champagne?"

"Fine." She didn't care. Not about the drink or the fact that her husband was treating her like a child. She had gone underground, to some bunker within herself, and she decided to pretend that nothing mattered for two days. Nothing mattered until she returned to Wilshire and her little girl and the cookie dough that was in the freezer.

"So. Are you ready to see the West Palm facility? It's really something. If you're not already sold on the club, this will certainly do the trick," Rosalyn said, smiling.

Nick jumped right in. "Oh, we are already sold! Truly, we're honored that you offered to sponsor us. I just hope we're able to meet enough people in time."

Barlow scowled. "Nonsense. You've met everyone you need to know right here. What my wife says goes."

Rosalyn pretended to take it as a compliment, though the sarcasm was hard to miss. "Thank you, darling. But I think it's wonderful they're coming with us. It is a good idea to meet the committee members."

When the drinks arrived, Barlow watched the faces of his guests. Nick was practically bursting out of his seat, his eyes were bright, his face on per-masmile.

"Well, we're glad for the company. But it must be hard to leave your little girl. Rosalyn had to pull me kicking and screaming away from Mellie."

Sara nodded, but she couldn't speak. Barlow's words had dragged her from her bunker right back to her reality, which was unbearable at the moment. Her eyes welled with tears as she got up from her seat. "Excuse me . . . ," she said.

"Sar—they've already pushed back . . . ," Nick called after her, but she was up and headed for the restroom. Spotting an unbuckled passenger, the flight attendant gave a knock on the pilot's door and the plane came to a smooth stop. Then the small phone on the wall buzzed softly.

"I'll get this, you get her," Rosalyn said, waving Barlow off to fetch Sara.

Nick sat there, helpless. He should have been the one to get his wife, but the orders had been issued and Rosalyn had her own agenda.

With the phone pressed to her ear, Rosalyn handled it seamlessly. "I know, Bob. We'll get her back in her seat. Don't take us out of rotation. . . . Okay . . . great." Rosalyn replaced the phone on its cradle, then smiled at Nick. "It's no problem. They'll hold our spot for a minute or two."

Nick shook his head. He was more than a little embarrassed. "I'm so sorry."

"Please. Don't worry about it."

Then they sat silently, watching the scene unfold at the back of the plane, where Barlow was now talking to Sara through a closed bathroom door. His face was serious at first, his head pressed to the wood paneling. Then he listened intently before speaking again. A smile broke out, then a slight laugh. Then he got that look—the one he always got when he was amusing someone and enjoying himself in the process. Nothing boosted Barlow's ego like making a woman laugh.

Nick shifted nervously in his seat. He checked his watch.

But Rosalyn had no worries. A few seconds later, the door opened. Sara stepped out, her eyes red, but a smile on her face. She gave Barlow a playful pat on his forearm, then followed him back to their seats.

"You see," Rosalyn said to Nick before they came within earshot, "Barlow has a way with women."

Nick looked at her, surprised by the comment, but whatever concern was born from it was quickly replaced with relief at the sight of his wife and, finally, the feel of the plane resuming its course to the runway.

"I'm sorry. I'm so sorry," Sara said, wiping her face one last time.

"It's my fault for bringing up those damned rugrats. No more mention of such things for the duration." Barlow raised his glass and the others followed, clinking glasses.

"To a wonderful trip," Nick said.

"Hear, hear," the others agreed. Then, as they were taking their first sips, Barlow winked at Sara, who managed to smile.

And Rosalyn, for the first time since boarding the plane, was unable to do the same.

THIRTY-SEVEN

THE ESCAPE

THE ROOM WAS DARK. It was nearly five and the sun had gone down, but neither of them had thought to turn on a light. They stood now, on opposite sides of the bed, passing things back and forth as they packed the bags that would carry the Christmas gifts to California for their annual family trip.

"We should just buy it all when we get there," Kelly said to her sister. "Every year it takes an entire day just to pack. Beth's the only one who still believes in Santa anyway."

Jacks tossed a wrapped box to Kelly. "Here—try this one in the duffel. I think it's clothing."

"Did you hear what I said?" Kelly asked, taking the box.

"I heard. It's just one more year. Maybe two."

Kelly shook her head. "I don't know about that. Andrea believed until she was ten."

"Well . . ." Jacks had more on her mind than the unruly amount of luggage they would be carting out west this year.

Kelly shoved the box in the duffel, then fought to zip it closed. "There. Is that it?"

"Yeah." Jacks pulled the duffel to her walk-in closet, where the other bags were piled up against her shoe rack. Then she closed the door. As she turned around, the light from the bathroom caught her eye, and she stood for a moment, just looking, and remembering.

Kelly was gathering the empty shopping bags when she saw her sister standing there in a daze. She folded the bags together and shoved them into a larger black one. Then she turned on the bedroom light, breaking the spell that had drawn Jacks in. "Hey," she said, walking up behind her. "It's over."

Jacks closed her eyes when she felt Kelly's arms around hers. "I just can't believe it. I can't believe it's over. It doesn't feel over."

Kelly gave her one last squeeze, then leaned against the wall beside her. "That's what Red's guy told him. The investigation is closed. It came right from the U.S. Attorney's office. Haven't there been any letters?"

Jacks shook her head. "Nothing. He just comes home, goes to work, comes home, goes to work, and the papers in that damned briefcase never change. It's like he's just carrying it around, for appearances or something."

Kelly shrugged. "And the calls?"

"They stopped last week. At least to the house. Maybe they call him at the office. I don't know."

Kelly watched her sister's face. There wasn't a trace of relief. "I know it doesn't seem like much with everything that's happened—with David's episode," she began, then pulled back for a moment, letting the memory return. "But, Jacks—think about it! He's not going to jail. You won't lose the house, or the rest of your savings. David can rebuild the business, get another job. He's always been resourceful that way."

Jacks turned now to face her sister. She should feel it, she knew. David had climbed out of that tub with excuses of work stress, a bad market—this, that, and the other thing. He had made light of it, saying he'd let himself unravel just to shock himself out of the self-pity that had taken hold inside him, and to make him think about Jacks and the girls and what was important. He'd confessed only the smallest piece of what had gone on, that some of his investments had taken a big hit and the investors were unhappy. That was how he had explained the phone calls and his odd behavior. He'd held her tight, told her not to worry, and when he'd turned from her to get on with the day and greet the girls, who had just walked through the door, he had not felt the wetness on his pants from the thin film of water that had remained in the tub after Beth's bath the night before. And that was how Jacks knew his mind was not right. That he had gone to a different place. And although it was a better place than the one that had driven him to crawl into that bathtub to begin with, it was still not a place that felt remotely safe to her.

"It's not right, Kelly. Not this time."

Jacks walked into the bathroom, where she had started to pack her cosmetics.

Kelly followed. "He *has* been under a lot of stress. Maybe he was crying out for help—for a way to tell you."

Jacks shook her head. "Remember that day you were here with the kids? We were sitting under the blankets, watching them in the leaves?"

"Yeah. I remember."

"Remember I asked you if there was something Red had found out, and you said something like 'Let's wait and see,' or 'Don't worry about that now'? Something like that?"

Kelly pretended to struggle with the recollection, but she knew exactly what Jacks what talking about. "Why?"

Setting her small makeup pouch on the vanity counter, Jacks looked Kelly in the eye. She needed an honest answer, and Kelly was already on that plane halfway to the California sun. "I need to know what that was."

Kelly waved it off. "Nothing—it was nothing."

But Jacks didn't move. "I need to know."

"Oh, shit, Jacks. Why? It was nothing." Kelly started to turn away, but Jacks grabbed her arm.

"Tell me."

With her sister's hand still holding on to her, Kelly stopped moving and looked up. "Fine. You want to know? Here it is. But don't overreact. He was wrong about it, okay?"

"Just tell me."

Kelly hesitated before confessing what she had been withholding for weeks. "When the investors started backing off the investigation, Red poked around to see where the money was coming from, to pay them. Remember I told you how he thought David might have had something squirreled away?"

Jacks nodded.

"Okay. Well, Red couldn't find anything, but that's a tall order for someone like Red. Private offshore banks don't exactly publish their clients' accounts in the *Post*."

"Right . . ."

Kelly took another long breath. "So he went to the city for a few days, used the money you gave him." She paused then, looking at her hands to avoid Jacks, and to figure out how to say what she was about to say. "He followed David."

"Followed him? Where? Where did he go?"

"He thought he could at least see what bank he was using. He figured David wouldn't risk doing anything online with the feds watching him."

Jacks felt the blood rush from her face. "So where did he go?"

"He went to a law office. . . ."

"Well, that's nothing. I already knew he had a lawyer."

Kelly grabbed hold of Jacks's hands. "No, Jacks. Not his lawyer. He went to see a man named Angelo Farrino."

"Farrino? Why do I know that name?"

"He represents organized crime families, that's why. He handled the Gianno appeal years ago—remember they aired it live? The man with the bald head, smooth-talker?"

Jacks remembered, but she couldn't speak. Of course it had crossed her mind that David had dug himself a deep hole and that he might have done something desperate to cling to the edges before falling to its depths. Of course it had crossed her mind when the phone calls came, when she felt compelled to start locking her doors and watching her kids like a hawk— when she found David curled up in the bathtub like a lost child. But her worst-case scenario involved some lunatic investor who wanted payback.

"Jacks?"

"I'm confused . . . hold on a sec." Jacks turned away as the images of that lawyer, Angelo Farrino, and her husband played in her head. Back and forth between the two, the lawyer on TV with his infamous client, her average Joe husband. It was inconceivable.

"Jacks—listen! He was wrong. The case went away. The phone calls stopped, and David hasn't pulled any more money out of your house or investments."

"Then why? Why would he go there?"

Kelly shrugged. "Maybe he wanted a higher-profile lawyer. Or maybe he needed someone to put pressure on the Vegas insurance company that wasn't paying out for the fire. Farrino would be the perfect guy for that job." Kelly was grasping at straws, but Jacks could see that she had already sold herself on a version of events that did not involve their lifeline owing money to a member of the Gianno crime family. And it would be easy for Jacks to join her.

"There was that man a few years back," Jacks said, her eyes widening as she recalled the story.

"What man?"

"This man—in Wilshire. He was murdered in his closet. Tied up, kneeling on the floor and shot in the back of the head. It turned out he was virtually bankrupt. His wife didn't even bother to sell the house, just let the bank have it. I remember now, there was an auction, but no one would touch it after what had happened. They tore it down."

Kelly pressed her hand into the white marble vanity, channeling her frustration. "Jacks, what the hell are you talking about?"

"I'm saying, it did happen here before. Here . . . in this town. I remember that story."

"And that story has nothing to do with David. You're not making any sense."

"No, it makes perfect sense. If David were Daddy, would you believe it then? Would you believe that he might have done something so desperate?"

Kelly shook her head and looked away. "Jacks—"

"No! Answer me. Would you believe it then?"

Kelly pulled her hands to her face and rubbed her palms over her eyelids. "Shit, Jacks . . ." This was the last place she wanted to go on the eve of their family trip, the trip that symbolized their escape from the hell Jacks was now wanting to delve back into.

"Fine. I would believe it, okay? Daddy could have found trouble in a bag of gumballs. But Daddy is not David. Daddy didn't go to Harvard. He didn't earn millions of dollars. And he didn't come home every night, have dinner, watch TV, and play with his kids. David is steady as a rock compared to Daddy."

Jacks was silent, and Kelly knew what she was thinking. David wasn't their father. But everything was about degrees—degrees of reality, degrees of love. Degrees of sanity.

"Jacks, everyone has cried in the bathroom with the faucet running. And if they haven't, they probably need to. It was *one time*."

But Kelly hadn't watched him walk away with soaked trousers as though nothing had happened. She hadn't seen the metamorphosis on his face, the stages he had gone through in a matter of minutes before her eyes. Kelly hadn't seen that for years. But if she had been there with Jacks, it would have played inside her like an old record. And she would have known.

"Okay," Kelly said, realizing she could not convince Jacks that David had not made such a colossal mistake. "What should we do? Right now. What should we do?"

Jacks stared out the window. The older three of their five children were in the yard, throwing snowballs at a tree; the younger two were building a snowman. She checked for the nanny, who was watching them as she had been told to do; she saw the gate closed and locked at the end of their driveway. And she thought about David with that briefcase full of papers that never changed. She had no idea what else to do. Ernest Barlow couldn't help her out of this one. *Please*, she thought. *Let me be wrong*.

"Jacks? Should we keep packing? Should we still take the trip?"

Turning from the window, Jacks looked at her sister. "I don't know. You tell me. Tell me what to do."

That had never been a difficult task for Kelly, and she did not hesitate with an answer. "I say we finish packing and get the hell out of here."

THIRTY-EIGHT

COLLARED SHIRTS

"EXCUSE ME."

It seemed as though those were the only words Sara had spoken since arriving in West Palm Beach. They had been deposited the night before in a small condo near the seventeenth tee with a golf cart and a basket of fruit. Having eaten on the plane (a ridiculously delicious meal of lobster and chopped romaine salad) and arrived in Florida after eleven, the Barlows and the Livingstons had parted ways until their planned meet-up on the first tee the next morning. The morning that was now here.

"Which way to the clubhouse?" Nick asked, calling out to a slightly frail man walking up the sixteenth fairway.

"The clubhouse? Of the Wilshire Country Club?" He asked the question rhetorically, though it somehow seemed he would never believe the answer.

"Yes. The Wilshire Country Club." Where else would it be? The small community was gated and guarded.

Sitting in their golf cart, dressed for golf but without any clubs because they didn't actually own any, Nick and Sara were sitting targets.

"Follow the cart path back to the tenth hole. You can pick up a scorecard in the little green box near the ball-washer. There's a map on the back." The man walked away, satisfied with his answer and eager to move on to see where his ball had landed up ahead, leaving Nick and Sara in the middle of the long, perfectly groomed stretch of grass.

"There . . . ," Sara said, pointing to a small paved path several yards in front of them.

Nick had started to drive, when he heard someone call out.

"Hello?" It was a woman, equal in age to the man but nowhere near as frail. She appeared from behind a small cluster of pine trees, and as she approached them, she wiped some mud from her ball then tossed it over her shoulder into the fairway.

Nick shrugged at Sara, who shrugged back. Not sure what to do, they drove over to the woman who had called out to them.

"Hello," Nick said, smiling.

The woman scrutinized them from behind a pair of oversized sunglasses. "Who *are* you?" she asked.

Through a look of utter bewilderment at such a question, and even more so the manner in which it was asked, Sara wondered if this was some kind of joke.

Nick elbowed her lightly in the ribs. "Nick and Sara Livingston," he answered cheerfully, hopping out of the cart. He extended his hand, but the gesture was not reciprocated.

"I don't understand," was all she said back.

"We're guests of the Barlows," Nick explained further. "We're staying just over there," he said, pointing at the condo. "We were trying to find our way to the clubhouse."

The woman maintained her quizzical expression as though everything he had just said was completely and utterly absurd. "The Barlows?" she asked.

"Yes," Nick answered.

The woman eyed Sara once more then turned back to Nick. "You're not supposed to take the carts on the fairway. It rained last night," she said as she looked at the ground and squished her gold cleats into the grass. "Can't you feel how spongy the grass is?"

Nick tried to look horrified. "Oh, we are so sorry. We'll get right over to the cart path."

But that was not enough. She looked over the situation again, searching for something.

"Gladys!" The man was yelling now from up ahead, but his wife ignored him completely.

Sighing with what appeared to be disappointment, she seemed ready to let them pass. Then she perked up a bit. "Your shirt!" she called over to Sara. "There's no collar!"

Sara squished her chin to her chest to get a better look at her shirt. Seeing nothing wrong with it, she pulled it out a bit at the waist and examined it further before looking back at the woman. "Excuse me? My shirt?" It was a V-neck tee with light-blue stripes, freshly ironed and tucked into her khaki shorts. It had taken her nearly an hour to dig the clothes from her summer things, and to her mind she looked about as appropriate as she knew how.

The woman shook her head with disgust as she looked at Nick. "Please tell your young friend that she must wear a *collared* shirt on the golf course."

"Actually, she's my wife. And we will be sure to get her a shirt at the pro shop. Thank you for informing us. We are so grateful—what an embarrassment it might have been!"

The woman tilted her head and sighed some more. "You're welcome."

Then she stood with her arms crossed until Nick realized this was his signal to pass. Taking advantage before the opportunity was lost over some other transgression against golf, he scurried back to the cart and drove it slowly toward the cart path.

When they were safely out of range, he burst out laughing.

But Sara couldn't find it in her to join him. "Who the hell does she think she is?"

"Oh, come on. She's just some old bat with nothing better to do. We probably made her day—she'll be talking about us to her friends at the West Palm Beach Assisted Living Mansion. *Those wretched youngsters tearing up the fairway—and without a collared shirt!*"

Looking out at the magnificent landscape, the bright green grass, palm trees, and blue ocean in the near distance, Sara felt exactly the same way she had at the Barlows' Halloween bash—immersed in luxury and unable to find in it the slightest bit of pleasure.

"Why would she treat us like that? Do we look like trash to her? Would she have done that to the Ridleys or the Halsteads? What the hell did we do to her?"

Reining himself in, Nick placed his hand on his wife's knee. "You're right. She had no business treating us that way. I'm sorry it upset you so much," he said. And then he drove to the tenth tee, where he found the small green box by the ball-washer with the scorecards inside with the map on the back. They were at the clubhouse five minutes later, where they found the Barlows, dressed to perfection in collared shirts.

"Good morning!" Barlow said as they drove up. "Park it right next to ours." Decked out in loud plaid shorts and an Arnold Palmer cap, he was smoking a cigar and smiling as he pointed toward a custom six-seater situated by the first tee.

"How was the condo? Everything okay?"

Nick parked the cart, then hopped out to shake Barlow's hand. "Perfect. What a place this is! I didn't appreciate it in the dark. The views are incredible."

"It's all right if you're into that sort of thing. You know, natural beauty, sunshine," he joked. But only he and Nick were smiling.

This had Barlow curious. "Sara—how are you feeling this morning?"

She smiled then, but it was not genuine.

And Barlow had to know why. "All right, let's have it."

Sara looked at him, then looked down, suddenly embarrassed that her mood was now infecting everyone around her. Nick jumped in to save her, or maybe to save both of them. "We ran into a very *informed* woman on the drive over who reminded us that Sara's shirt is lacking a collar."

Barlow's face became flushed with anger. "Don't tell me," he said, glancing up at his wife, who was schmoozing the second chair of the membership committee. "White sunhat—shaped like a bonnet. Enormous buglike sunglasses. Face like an alligator and mean as hell?"

Nick looked at Sara, and they both shrugged, neither of them willing to agree or disagree before they knew what they were dealing with. For all they knew, the woman could have been Barlow's mother.

Sensing their discomfort at being put on the spot, Barlow waved his hand like he was shooing a fly. "Mrs. Plevin. I'm so sorry. What a way to be introduced to the club. Christ! But tell me this—was she coming out of the woods?"

Nick nodded. "How did you know?"

Just then, Rosalyn walked over to join them, her tasseled golf shoes clicking against the pavement.

"Rosalyn," Barlow called out to her. "They had a little run-in with Mrs. Plevin. She was coming out of the woods."

"No—it was nothing, really," Nick interjected, trying to play down the whole incident. But Barlow seemed to be enjoying himself.

"Good God. Not again!" Rosalyn said, smiling appropriately. "That woman is shameless."

Nick was now confused. "I don't understand."

"You explain it to Nick, and I'll take Sara to the pro shop for a new shirt," Barlow said, and this seemed to please his wife in a perverse sort of way that made him uneasy. Still, the tee time was looming, and there was a shirt to hunt down.

Rosalyn took Nick's arm. "Come on. I'll explain it while we get the demos loaded up."

Doing as she was told, Sara followed Barlow's lead up a short hill to the pro shop. In spite of everything that had gone on—Mrs. Plevin, this whole trip, and the awkwardness that had inserted itself into her marriage—she was relieved to be alone with Ernest Barlow again. His humor had a way of reaching her, most likely because it came from the place she had been finding herself in lately, a cynical and unforgiving disdain for the world she inhabited. Of course, it was more Barlow's world than hers, and this made him all the more interesting to her.

When they reached the small patio near the snack bar, Barlow stopped and turned to face her. "The Plevins are in the early-bird tournament. See that scoreboard?"

Sara's eyes followed Barlow's to a large white posterboard propped upon an easel.

"I see it."

"The Plevins—" He paused then to take a long drag on the cigar. "—the Plevins like to win. And Mrs. Plevin likes to cheat. This isn't the first time someone's caught her tossing her ball out of the woods and onto the fairway."

Trying to understand what all of this meant, Sara watched Barlow's face as it took on a mischievous flair. "So this woman—Mrs. Plevin—was trying to humiliate us into keeping quiet? Are you serious?"

Barlow nodded, delighted that his new friend was seeing just how ridiculous country club culture could be. "Well," he said, his voice ominous. "You have to understand. There's a filet mignon dinner at stake here. The winning couple eats for free tonight, assuming they don't object to the slaughtering of cows."

Sara smiled, this time spontaneously. "Somehow I doubt Mrs. Plevin cares about cows. But, hey . . . a steak dinner. I guess that makes it all okay. Steak dinners are expensive."

"Yes," Barlow agreed. "And with a net worth of over three hundred mil . . . well, you can certainly understand how important it is that they win."

She laughed then as Barlow flicked a large ash to the ground, nodding his head with amusement. It had been a long time since someone had been able to read his dark thoughts so quickly, so silently. And he wondered if that's what it took, a person still young, still removed enough from their life to be able to see things with a modicum of objectivity.

He let out a long sigh as his eyes lingered on her face. "Come, madam," he said, already feeling sad that the moment had to be cut short by their approaching tee time. "Let's get you a collared shirt, and with it, a golden pass to do anything you please at the Wilshire Country Club."

Sara gave him a quizzical smile. "Even cheat on the golf course?"

"Yes. You could practically fornicate on the eighteenth green—as long as you left your shirt on. Your *collared* shirt."

Sara found this hysterical. "Okay, now *that* is not an image I wanted in my head."

They laughed then, like two little children making potty talk on the playground, and it was, for both of them, nothing short of liberating. Sara let it fill her up, let it replace the judgments she had begun to weigh against herself. And yet she knew there would be a price to pay for this moment of pleasure, like the hangover after a night of martinis. Somewhere inside her, she could feel that it was all wrong—her rapidly forming bond with Barlow, and Barlow himself. But she could also feel the smile across her face, the one Nick had not been able to inspire. And for now, a smile was what she needed most.

THIRTY-NINE

UNDER THE INFLUENCE

"TAKE IT EASY," BRETT said, grabbing the joint from Cait's fingertips. "I only have one." Placing it gently between his lips, he could feel the heat as he took a long drag.

"Shit." It was close to gone, burning his fingers, so he let it fall to the ground before squashing it into the frozen snow on the south side of the pool house. "What the fuck, Cait. You smoked the whole damned thing."

Brett's friend Reed, who had tagged along for another school break, was leaning against the glass wall, staring up at the sky.

"Whatever." Cait felt the buzz in her head as she exhaled. The air was cold, bone-chilling, and it held the smoke like a thick white cloud against the black sky surrounding them. She lifted her phone close to her face and hit a key to get it back to life. There were no new messages.

"What—expecting the president to call? Give it a rest."

This was torture. Her parents were in Florida, two of the three nannies had flown home to Poland for the holidays, and that left Cait and the guys to do as they pleased. There was a two-day window—that was it. She'd waited as long as she could, but maybe it hadn't been long enough. Maybe she seemed too anxious. Still, she had explained it all in the text message, the message he had asked her to send. Mommy and Daddy Dearest would be home in less than two days. It was now or never. She'd sent the text at four o'clock. It was already past seven.

"I'm going inside."

Brett sighed and looked her over. "Wait." He took a piece of gum from his back pocket and handed it to his little sister. Then he leaned in and smelled her hair. "You're good. Just don't get too close to Marta."

Cait took the gum and popped it in her mouth. "Thanks."

"No problem."

With her hands in her coat pockets, Cait turned toward the house. She didn't feel any better stoned than she had sober, and now her lungs ached from the cold air and hot smoke.

As her walk turned to a run to combat the freezing air, she heard her own thoughts about herself. *Pathetic. Idiot. Slut.* She had let these words into her head the night she'd climbed over that divide and into Kyle's lap. The night she'd felt his hands on her hips, against her skin, and his mouth on hers. But in the short time since that night, the heat inside her had become an omnipotent power, reducing her reservations to nothing more than theoretical exercises. *If I don't text him . . . if I don't meet him . . . if I don't . . .* The night she felt him want her for the first time, *really* want her, the decision was made.

Her chat with TF had given her pause, but that was all it had done. *Remember what happened to me*, TF had said again. *They can act like you are their lifeblood in those moments, then never need to see you again. They aren't like us, Cbow.* Cait had argued politely, told TF that there was no chance what she'd felt in the car that night wasn't real, that it would be nothing short of superhuman to fake that kind of passion. Maybe with words or token acts of affection like a hug or a small kiss. But how could a person lie with their entire body? At some point, it all seemed involuntary, like a sneeze or cough. The way he moaned so deeply, the way he pulled her into him, against him, all the while kissing her that way—it had been fluid, natural, like his body had just taken the reins and was riding off with both of them. How could that be faked? He would have to be a monster.

TF had taken a moment to respond. But then she did, saying simply, *He doesn't need to be a monster to do that. Just a guy.* The words had left Cait confounded because if she couldn't believe in this, in what happened between her and Kyle in that car, then she was certain she would be lost forever in an abyss of chaos. Wasn't that all the world was, if a person couldn't make sense of the most obvious things? If she couldn't trust her most primal instincts, about herself and the people around her? Utter chaos, and Cait could not believe that would be her fate.

Up the stairs she ran, straight to her room and into the shower to feel warm again, and to rid herself of the sickly sweet odor that had clung to her hair and clothing. She left the phone on the edge of the sink, and she focused on the silence, even through the pounding of the water against the shower walls, waiting for it to be broken by her ringtone. She dried off and checked the phone in case she'd missed the sound when the water had covered her ears while she rinsed the shampoo. Nothing.

She got dressed, blew out her hair, and finally plopped on her bed to hold herself in her own arms until she knew the answer to the question that was rising to the surface. *Will he call?* Eight o'clock came and went. Then eight thirty. She went downstairs and raided the liquor cabinet, pouring herself a glass of vodka, mixing it with a Diet Coke and some ice, then chugging it down. She could hear the guys down the hall in the game room on the Wii. The rest of the house was quiet, the little ones long since asleep, Marta probably in her room sneaking a call to her boyfriend—the one her parents didn't know about.

Even the nanny has a boyfriend. And by nine, there was still no message. Her head was spinning after the second vodka and Diet Coke, her self-restraint gone. But she still had her wits about her. She rushed to the game room, where the two stoned boneheads were battling some assassin with their strapped-on wrist wands, standing in front of the TV, swinging their arms about and yelling at each other. Cait stopped for a second to reconsider. They hated Kyle Conrad. But they were also stoned, and they were guys, which meant they would take everything she did and said at face value. They would be easy to manipulate.

"Hey," she said, standing behind them.

"Hey." They answered in unison but did not turn around from the TV.

"I need a favor. Can you pause it?"

Reed was on a roll. His guy was about to defeat the assassin in level five. Then, and only then, could they pause the game without losing the hour's worth of effort they had invested. It was the cornerstone of the addiction— the built-in penalties of stopping a game.

"One sec . . . Yeah! Yeah!" Brett was yelling, cheering on his buddy and ignoring his sister. "That's what I'm talking about! Die, you mother. . . ."

Cait focused her energy on standing without swaying, which was all her body wanted to do at the moment. When Brett finally turned around, she managed a sober stance.

"I need a favor," she said.

Brett pulled off the Wii controller strap and looked at his sister. He'd said there was only one joint, the one he'd shared with her by the pool house, but from his red, glassy eyes, she could see he'd been lying. No matter. His state of inebriation would only make things easier.

"Can you check around and see what's happening in town, parties and stuff?"

"You going out?" Reed asked, joining the conversation.

Cait shook her head. "No. Just checking for a friend. She hooked up with Kyle last week, and now he's blowing her off, too." Her face was steady and entirely believable. It was easy to lie when she needed to.

"Fuck! That guy is such a prick. Is that why you kept checking your phone?" Brett asked, fully sold on the story.

"Yeah. She said she'd let me know what happened. I just got a text. She hasn't heard from him."

"Prick!" Reed echoed the sentiment. "I'll find the little weenie."

Cait gave him half a smile. "Thanks."

He left then to get his phone, leaving Cait and Brett alone in the room.

"Wanna play?" Brett asked, still revved up from the assassination moments before.

Cait gave him her *as if* look and he nodded.

"TV?"

"Sure."

They moved to the couch that sat a few feet from the wall-sized high-def screen, and Brett switched off the Wii. "So . . . are you okay with your friend and Kyle and all that bullshit?"

Cait kept her eyes on the screen as Brett flipped channels. "Yeah, fine. He's a prick."

Brett paused for a moment, his fingers clicking on the remote. " 'Cause, you know, over Thanksgiving, you were still pretty hung up."

"Yeah." That was all she said, and Brett knew not to push it. No need to rub her face in the fact that he had been right about the guy she had blown in the school hallway.

They settled on an HBO rerun until Reed came bounding in a few minutes later, his face glowing with accomplishment, his eyes red from the pot.

"He's over on River Street. Victoria Lawson is having a party."

The room went quiet. Brett looked at Cait, who looked at Reed. Reed was watching the TV. "Maybe we should crash!"

No one answered. Cait held it in as long as she could, but the tears came on, violently and with the added force of the lingering pot and more recent vodka. She said nothing, but ran from the room.

"Cait!" Brett yelled after her. He was slow to respond, but his mind was quick to read what had just happened, and after a slight hesitation he was on his feet.

"What the fuck?" Reed was confused as he stood in the doorway, watching Brett chase his sister down the hallway toward the garage.

Cait was racing, her intent clear, her purpose driven by disbelief and despair. Her world was crashing in around her, and she had one impulse—to get the hell out of there, away from the words she'd just heard spoken, away from the guy who'd spoken them and the brother who now knew she was far too weak to be over a guy like Kyle. And, mostly, away from her life. She needed to fly, and fly fast, if there was any chance of outrunning herself.

The keys were hanging on the antique brass hook near the door, and she grabbed them.

"Cait!" She heard Brett yell from down the hall. He was gaining on her.

The garage door pulled open as he finally caught up, but she locked the doors to her father's Corvette.

"Cait! Stop!" He was pounding on the driver's-side window, watching tears stream down her face. Her eyes were on fire.

When the door cleared, Cait peeled out of the garage, spun the wheel, and kicked it into first, then shifted to second, third, and fourth before she was halfway down the driveway.

Running behind her because it was all he could think to do, Brett kept yelling, "*Cait!*" He couldn't see the car, and looking back on it when he was sober, he would remember that this was because she had forgotten the lights.

His lungs were wheezing, his legs burning as he ran into the cold night air, chasing after only a sound as the car cleared the lighting given off by the house.

Still, he kept running until he heard another sound, the distinctive screech of wheels on pavement, and then the hard, cold bang as the car crashed. Then came the worst sound of all.

The silence.

FORTY

INSIDE JOKES

ROSALYN BARLOW'S FACE CARRIED a light expression. Half a smile, soft eyes. A slight giggle here and there as they made dull jokes about Democrats and Northerners, though most of them were either transplants or seasonal residents who migrated like a flock of birds the moment the temperature dived below sixty. They were an older bunch, the members of the admissions committee, with Rosalyn being the sole exception. It had been no small undertaking joining their ranks, but her mother's untimely death had suspended their sense of reason. In a fit of uncharacteristic sentimentality, they had given Mrs. Eddings's seat to Rosalyn, and whatever regrets they came to have later were futile against Rosalyn's determination to stay put.

Now here she was, playing the fervent advocate of Nick Livingston and his young wife, who happened to be sleeping with her husband. And the two of them had been shameless. Like a couple of teenagers, they had laughed and snickered through an entire round of laborious amateur golf, then lunch and drinks. It was of her own making, she knew, having decided to throw them together under the microscope of their spouses. Still, she had expected misery to ensue—torturous, untenable misery—as they were made to be so close but untouchable. She had expected them to writhe in their own longing, obsess over the impossibility of sneaking off for a kiss, or more. But that had not been the case, at least not so far as she could see. Instead, they seemed downright giddy to be sharing this time together. And Rosalyn felt the sickness spreading inside her, right up to the impenetrable skin that was still holding a light expression when the main course arrived.

"Oh, how lovely!" one of the members said, eyeing the plate of filet, creamed spinach, and roasted fingerling potatoes.

The air was perfect. Warm, dry, and seventy-three degrees. They sat on the terrace under a starry sky, the Barlows, the Livingstons, and the two couples who were being courted.

"Did you know that Sara used to be a reporter?" Rosalyn said at an appropriate juncture in the conversation. There wasn't much time to shove Sara and Nick down their throats, and that was exactly what Rosalyn planned to do. Right along with the rare meat on their plates.

A collective *oh!* followed, making Sara blush.

"Almost. I finished journalism school, but then I met Nick and I never really got off the ground."

None of this mattered. As far as they were concerned, she was a reporter—not something they got to sink their teeth into every day—and the questions began to encircle her head.

"What do you think will happen with the medical reform bill?"

"Well, I'm not sure—"

"Did you ever go undercover?"

"No, I never got—"

"Yes, yes—and were you ever in bed with the soldiers?"

"That's *embedded*."

"Right. Embedded?"

"No. I never got to do—"

"And what about that teenage boy who's being charged as an adult? Has everyone heard about this case?" It was George Melman, senior member on the committee.

Rosalyn smiled politely as she cut into a soft potato. "No. What case is that, George?"

"Just awful," his wife, Betsy, answered. "Right here in Palm Beach. A sixteen-year-old boy had *relations* with his girlfriend, who was fourteen. Totally consensual," she added, waving her hand about dismissively. Her face took on a scrupulous expression, which perfectly conveyed her thoughts.

Obviously, the girl was trash. Then she sat back and sighed. "They charged this poor kid with rape and child endangerment."

"Yes," George added. "And they plan to try him as an adult."

Nick looked at Rosalyn, Sara at Barlow. Of all the things to come up.

Sensing Nick's eyes upon her, Rosalyn gave him a cool smile before motioning for a waiter to pour more wine. Barlow, on the other hand, did not let go of Sara's eyes as he swallowed hard against the jarring image that had returned to him. Would it ever leave him, this vision of his little girl on her knees?

He smiled at Sara in that way that told her he was about to be incredibly irreverent.

"Here's what I want to know. Was he, or was he not, wearing a collared shirt at the time?"

Sara let out a burst of uncontrollable laughter, leaving the rest of the table confused, but also acutely aware that they were not meant to understand, that this comment or joke or whatever it was had been meant for Sara and Sara alone. That it was something private between Barlow and the young woman sitting across the table.

Having had about all she could take, Rosalyn raised her fresh glass of wine and proposed a toast. "Before the evening winds down, I would like to thank everyone for coming." It was a bit out of the blue, and out of character for Rosalyn, who always found a clever segue before changing a conversation so abruptly. But something had shifted within her, just in that moment, as she watched the connection between her husband and another woman. There had been a time when *she* was the one on the other side of his inside jokes, when *she* was the one he turned to in a moment of discomfort like the one that had just passed. It was her daughter, *their* daughter, and instead of finding comfort with each other, she was guzzling wine and he was flirting shamelessly. This was more than jealousy, more than anger at her husband's midlife transgression. It felt like something was breathing its final breaths right before their eyes.

Everyone raised a glass. Clinks all around. *So glad to be here . . . great to meet you . . . what a beautiful evening.* Then they broke into the quiet paired-off chattering that was customary for main-course conversation at the club's Florida facility, where food was more important than God, and a close second to Republican politics.

Rosalyn was grateful for the respite, as she skillfully listened without engaging and picked at her food. Her mind was flooded with thoughts of Caitlin, the outrageous Conrad family, her husband and Sara Livingston, and the feeling that all the little balls she was juggling were about to come crashing down around her. She nodded once, smiled twice, all the while thinking quietly to herself, going over the list for the plans, the plans that would save her daughter and the family's reputation. And the plans that would punish the Conrads and her husband. She felt her blood slow as the thoughts calmed her mind and then her body. And after a few minutes, she began to believe that she would actually get through this dinner and whatever might follow.

But it was short-lived. Standing at the small desk by the club's exterior door, the dining manager gently set down the phone and began to walk to their table. Barlow was the first to notice.

"Mr. and Mrs. Barlow," he said after reaching them. Bent slightly at the waist and visibly uneasy with the task of delivering the message, he spoke softly to Rosalyn, though everyone at the table heard the words that are universally feared. "You have an urgent call. It's from home."

FORTY-ONE

THE JET-SETTERS

ROSALYN'S KNUCKLES WERE WHITE as she gripped the phone and rocked back and forth against the seat. Strapped in for takeoff, she had no other means of displacing the raw, bitter anguish.

Across the aisle, Barlow sat still and let the tears fall.

They heard the pilot's subdued voice over the speaker. "We're cleared. I'll have you home in no time."

They were so damned lucky their pilots had stayed in the area. The men were tired from a long day at the beach, but otherwise ready to fly. There'd been no time to find an attendant, but now, sitting alone in the dark cabin, both of the Barlows were thankful in their own way for the privacy.

"Why haven't they called?" Barlow asked through his sobbing, though he didn't expect an answer. The only thing either of them knew was that Caitlin had crashed the Corvette and was at the hospital.

"They'll call when they know something." Rosalyn's voice was steady as she braced herself like a piece of steel against the back of the chair. "That's what Eva said. She'll call when they know."

The plane took off, jolting them backwards and drowning out Barlow's sighs. Rosalyn closed her eyes as the sound of the engine filled her head, numbing her to her own silent cries. They had all been in a hurry. The boys,

Eva. And there were no cell phones allowed in the ER. Still, there hadn't been one call since the first one at the club over an hour ago.

They reached cruising altitude in a matter of minutes, the plane leveling off, the engines growing quieter.

"She was conscious. The whole time. She never blacked out." Barlow was talking again.

"Yes. That's what Eva said. They have to make sure now, that's all. Absolutely sure."

Barlow ran his hands over his cheeks, pushing aside the tears. "I need a drink."

He unbuckled his seat belt and walked to the front of the plane where he kept his scotch and the Waterford rocks glasses his wife had bought him when he'd purchased the jet. Pouring a tall one, he moved to the couch and sat down, just behind the row of chairs that held Rosalyn.

He took a long drink and calmed himself with the facts. The air bags had saved her from crashing through the windshield. She hadn't bothered with a seat belt—why would she? She was "under the influence," whatever that meant, chasing through the dark with no headlights after a boy who had thrown her out like trash. Who had time for a seat belt in the face of such exigent circumstances? She had no visible injuries, and that should have been enough. Knowing that should have settled the initial impact he'd felt upon hearing the words *car* and *crash* used in the same sentence with one of his children's names. But knowing she had escaped this one incident was close to insignificant in the face of everything else he knew, everything else that was happening to her inside her own head. He could lock her up and throw away the key, but he could not save her from that, from her own mind.

"Why?" It came out as a mumble, but it was heard.

Rosalyn got up and walked to the chair across from Barlow. She sat down, crossed her legs, and looked at him, at his red-streaked face and the drink that was again attached to his hand. "Why? Why what? Why has this happened?" Her face was hard, her tone sarcastic, almost mocking him.

"I'm sorry. Is that a stupid question to ask? Should I know why our daughter almost killed herself tonight?"

"No, Barlow," Rosalyn said with controlled hostility. "I wouldn't expect you to know with all of the things on your mind. All your little . . . what should we call them? Hobbies, I suppose."

Barlow looked at her curiously, wondering if she was referring to Jacks, if she somehow knew. It was true—he was guilty as sin. Even so, was he not entitled to even a shred of decency? To even the smallest hint of humanity in the face of this nightmare that they alone shared? Nothing he had done with Jacks was the cause of this horror.

He drained his drink, then got up to pour another. As he walked past his wife, he placed his hand on her shoulder, and for a split second she thought of placing her hand over his. Of touching him.

But then he spoke. "Just checking for a pulse."

His words cut through her, inciting a silent fury that took her breath away. "That's right. Get another drink. That should help."

In the front of the dimly lit cabin, she heard the ice against the glass, then the sound of the scotch poured.

"Actually, it does help. It's helped for years." He walked back to the couch, cradling the drink so it wouldn't spill. He settled into his seat and took a sip, studying her face for a long while.

She did not look away.

"I don't know when it happened. Do you remember?" Barlow asked. His voice echoed the defeat that he had accepted years before.

Rosalyn was annoyed. "What are you talking about now?"

"About us. I'm talking about when *this* happened to *us*."

Nodding her head sharply, Rosalyn felt ready for this battle because it was a battle she could actually fight. "Okay. Let's have it. Let's hear how I made you so miserable, you had to work all day and drink all night—and now just drink all day and night. Let's hear about that."

Barlow leaned forward and searched her eyes for some sign of comprehension. Had they even been living the same life all these years? "God, you don't even see it, do you? You can't even feel how cold you are."

"Cold?"

Sitting back, Barlow let the words fly. "Like fucking ice."

Rosalyn nodded again, acknowledging sentiments that he'd finally said aloud. They both knew he'd been thinking them for a long, long time. "Then why did you marry me? If I'm so cold, so cold like fucking ice . . . why did you drive to Wellesley every weekend, beg me to go out with you? There were plenty of cold bitches at Harvard, weren't there?" Her voice was hard, her face so constricted it was nearly trembling.

Barlow drank again, thinking back on those days, which he could barely remember anymore. God, how he had pursued Rosalyn Eddings. In spite of the inconvenience, the hassles of getting there, finding things to do in a small town, then driving home because she never let him stay over, and yes, in spite of the many women at Harvard who were smart and sophisticated—he had hunted her down. There had just been something about *her*.

"Maybe I didn't see it then."

"Oh. So I lured you in under false pretenses? Think about it. Have I really changed that much?"

The face before him was a mere shadow in the dark cabin, and when he let himself remember, he could see the woman he'd fallen so madly in love with twenty-five years before. The angular jawline, perfect cheekbones and soft hair that fell around them. Her almond eyes that were green like emeralds, and sharp as knives. But that was not all that he was now remembering.

"Maybe you're right," he said, lost in a revelation. "Maybe you haven't changed. This feeling I have now, like you're untouchable . . . or maybe impenetrable. I used to feel that with you. And then you would let me in, just for the smallest moment, and I would be hooked. Grateful, even."

Rosalyn listened, not because she had the slightest desire to tolerate his indulgent self-pity, but because she was there now, with him in their past, and it left her startled. And silent.

"I was a nobody from Minnesota," he continued. "Sure, I was at Harvard. But don't think a day went by when I wasn't reminded by some kid from places like Wilshire that I didn't belong. It's not that tough to stand out in Minnesota. Not a lot of kids from Minnesota set their sights on Harvard."

His tone became indignant as he reached deeper into wounds that still felt freshly inflicted. "And there you were—the very embodiment of this world I craved. And you wanted *me*. Of all the guys you could have had . . . and the guy you left behind in Wilshire, that guy you always threw in my face. You wanted *me*. I don't think I even cared for one minute who you really were. I couldn't see past the things you represented. You and your family."

Rosalyn's knuckles had gone white again, her hands clenched around her arms as she fought to contain herself. Was she meant to feel sorry for him? He was talking like this was somehow cathartic, like they were having an honest heart-to-heart conversation where he was finally able to see himself clearly, and wasn't that wonderful? Wasn't that just downright liberating?

"So you're saying our entire marriage, these twenty-five years, have been a lie? That they've been about you trying to prove yourself?" She steadied herself to hold back the rage, and the tears that she would not let him see. "Fuck you."

Barlow's face was burning as he thought about his wife, and her mother. Wilshire royalty. He was speaking the truth, finally, after all this time. He was trying to be honest now that he could see what existed in the ground that their lives were built upon.

"You know what, darling? Fuck you. You've spent a *lifetime* thinking you were better than I am, with your perfect breeding and your blond hair. But what have you ever done? You were born. You got the best-looking guy in high school to be your boyfriend by sleeping with him. Then you dumped him for a brief moment of liberation before latching on to your next meal ticket. Congratulations."

Rosalyn got up, turning her back to him. She braced herself against the walls of the plane, fighting to maintain her composure. He had stumbled on something he would never understand, something she had never and would never confide. And still he'd managed to cast a blade right into her heart. "You don't know a goddamned thing about my life. Not one goddamned thing!"

Barlow was up now, standing behind her. "You're wrong," he said, his voice stifled but defiant. "I know you never loved me. Hell—I don't think you've ever loved anyone."

Through sheer power of will, Rosalyn pulled herself back. Turning to face him, she looked into his eyes. "If I never loved you, then why did I marry you? Why did I marry some loser from Minnesota when I could have slept my way up the food chain? You had nothing back then."

Barlow grabbed her arms. He wanted to shake her and shake her until something fell out. No matter what he did or said, it would always be the same. Like beating his head into a brick wall. "I don't know. Why? Tell me why!" he demanded, and this time he wasn't looking for a response. He just needed to say it, to scream it at the top of his lungs.

Feeling the blood rush from her head, Rosalyn sighed. He was wrong. Dead wrong. She had loved him, truly loved him the only way she knew how. He had been her second chance at liberation, her chance to break the legacy of Wilshire wifedom, and all he'd done was bring her right back in. Full circle. He had not been her meal ticket. She had been his. And now, maybe it wasn't enough that she had really loved him. But it was still the truth, and having him stand there and not know it was close to unbearable.

She was about to push him off her, to retreat to the front of the plane and shut herself down until they landed in Connecticut or got the call from the hospital. But she didn't have to. The call came.

Reaching for the phone that was attached to the plane's inner wall, Rosalyn pulled it out. The question was already in the air when she held the phone to her mouth: "What happened?"

Barlow let go of her arms and stood before her, helplessly waiting. Then he saw the relief wash over her face.

"Thank God. Thank God . . . . Okay . . . we'll call as soon as we land." She hung up the phone and repeated the message, but Barlow was already smiling from ear to ear. "She's fine! She's really fine. They released her."

"Released her? She's home?"

Rosalyn nodded. Then, and only then, did it take her over. She drew a breath but could not feel the air reach her lungs. Barlow was before her, his head tilted upward as he swaggered from side to side, giddy with relief. Still, his smile had already faded. She heard his words as he repeated them over and over, *She's okay, she'll be okay*. And these were the same words Rosalyn whispered silently to herself as her body searched for air.

Her fists were clenched and she pushed them against Barlow's chest, forcing him to stand still before her. There was relief—*God*, was there relief. Their daughter was safe. But it was short-lived. This had been a minor miracle. Cait had plowed through two grown deer before swerving to miss the others and crashing into a tree. She could have died. But this was not just an accident. It was an accident that had been waiting to happen, and there were others in line behind this one, waiting, waiting. Cait was all right, but then, she wasn't really, was she?

Rosalyn's fists pounded against her husband, the husband who didn't believe she ever loved him, who thought she was incapable of love. She felt his hands upon hers, holding them in place. She pulled against them, but he was too strong, this man who married her for her social standing and—what else had he said?—her blond hair. Five children and a lifetime later, this had been his revelation. His confession.

The air rushed in again with a sudden gasp, forcing her to feel it, making her dizzy. She stopped struggling against him and laid her head against her forearms. He was crying, this time with desperation, with helplessness. And it was too much, these feelings that filled the plane and had become inescapable. Was this how Cait had felt last night? Is this what had drawn her into that car and down the driveway, stoned and drunk into the darkness? Rosalyn knew the answer.

"Caitie," she whispered, her face still pressed into the arms that Barlow had taken and would not release.

"I know," he said. "I know."

He let go then, but she didn't move. Instead, her body became limp, falling into him completely as she started to cry. With one hand on her back and the other gently stroking her hair, Barlow held his wife as she wept for their daughter, as they wept together for everything that had gone so wrong. But the tears were impotent against the anguish they held for their little girl, and they began to search for something more powerful. It started with the feel of their bodies against one another, then the touch of Barlow's hand against Rosalyn's face. She leaned into it, resting her head in his strong palm.

He said nothing. He didn't even look at her as he lifted her slight body and carried her back toward the couch. He laid her down, and only then did he dare see her face. There had been so many years of rejection, so much rejection that had come in so many insidious ways, and he expected to see it now. But all he saw was a drowning woman.

Falling down beside her, he grabbed her tear-streaked face and kissed her mouth. Then he felt her move, actually move with him, arms wrapped around his neck, body forming against his. She was kissing him back, and with a kind of sexual hunger he could barely remember.

"Barlow," she whispered as she pulled away, but that was the last thing she said. Instead, she kissed him harder, tearing at their clothing until she could feel his skin against hers, his body lying over her. He pulled away for a moment, and she searched his eyes. He kissed her gently before resting his head beside hers. She wrapped her legs around his back, closing her eyes as she felt him inside her, as they moved together to chase away the things that had happened, the things they'd said and done. To chase away the pain.

When it was over, they held each other silently for the remainder of the flight until the charges had died down. Until they were back in Wilshire, where their life was waiting for them.

FORTY-TWO

BLOOD IN THE SNOW

ROSALYN HEARD THE FOOTSTEPS approaching in the snow as she stared at the crash site. She did not turn around. Through the dim moonlight, she could just make out the patches of blood that appeared black against the white, frozen ground, seeping into a giant pool. The car had been towed, the muti-lated bodies of the deer removed along with other traces of the accident—scraps of metal and glass. That's what she imagined. Several yards away, the tree stood almost defiantly, without much more than a scrape against its bark, though some of the Christmas lights had broken and fallen around its trunk. But the blood—there was nothing to be done about the blood in the snow until morning, when a bulldozer could be brought in to carve it out of the otherwise pristine covering that had blanketed their property.

"Yuck." Rosalyn heard Eva Ridley from just behind her now. Then she felt the arm around her shoulders. "Come on. It's cold."

But Rosalyn didn't budge.

Eva sighed and pulled her mink coat tighter around her. "It is hunting season. Deer are being slaughtered all across the state. They'll get this cleaned up tomorrow."

Rosalyn nodded but said nothing. They both knew the deer were beside the point, except to stand as a symbol of the violence that had occurred in the place where they now stood.

"She fell asleep, finally. Barlow's sitting in there with her."

"Okay," Rosalyn said. Her friend's arm felt warm around her shivering body, and her voice was deeply comforting. Still, she could not take her eyes off the black pool of blood.

Eva gave her a long moment before pulling her out of her morbid indulgence. "Do you want to hear about it now?" she asked.

Rosalyn turned her head to see Eva's face. Did she want to hear about it, the story that led to this near miss, to her daughter's self-destruction? Was there a choice?

She looked away. "Why the hell not. No time like the present."

"It was Kyle Conrad. Ditched her for another girl. And the boys—well, I gave them a good talking-to."

"I know—the pot, the booze. That feels like amateur hour in light of Cait's little adventure. Where was she trying to go? To find Kyle?" For all her wisdom and savvy when it came to teenagers, she could not put this piece into place. "I get that she was pissed. Heartbroken. Whatever. And maybe she thought getting high would make her forget. Numb her somehow. But . . ." Rosalyn broke away, turning her back to the black pool and her face to Eva. "Why didn't she call her friends, plot revenge, obsess about other guys she could get? Isn't that what we did?"

Eva smiled. "Is that how you remember things?"

Rosalyn looked down and kicked up a scraping of snow. "Oh, you are such a bitch."

But Eva didn't hesitate. "And proud of it. I am also your memory at times like this. Times when you conveniently forget."

Rosalyn folded her arms and looked up at the night sky.

Eva watched Rosalyn. "Do you honestly not remember?"

Rosalyn looked back from the sky to her friend with a scowl. "I remember you with your perfect boyfriend who bought you diamonds and didn't expect more than your tongue in his mouth once in a while."

"Yeah, but then I had to marry him. You're not getting off that easy. You can beat me up later."

"Promise?"

Her feet were moving now, shuffling beneath her in lockstep with the discomfort that was rising to the surface.

Eva was steadfast before her, as she had always been.

"I thought I understood what she was feeling. I thought I could predict what she would do. But this . . ." Rosalyn looked back at the blood and shook her head.

Eva's voice was firm as she took Rosalyn's arms, forcing her to look at her again. "You do know what she's feeling. And the fact that she drove a car into a tree instead of sleeping with that little weenie is *because* you know . . . because she has you for a mother and not Mrs. Eddings."

"How can you say that?" Rosalyn looked at her with disbelief. "She could have been killed!"

"Yes, she could have been killed. But you're missing the point. She didn't go to her room to plot ways to get Kyle back. She ran from it, from everything she's feeling. She *ran*. She's crying out for help. Now it's up to you to give it to her."

Rosalyn shook her head. She felt too damned tired to help anyone, to do anything at all but stare at the blackened snow. Her thoughts were spinning, the sense she had made of her daughter and Kyle Conrad was all but gone. Eva was wrong. She remembered everything. Jeb Ashton had been her Kyle Conrad twenty-five years before, and she would never forget the things she did whenever he asked, the price she paid to be with him and how happy it made her mother. But it was not Jeb Ashton who filled her thoughts every day.

"I still think about him, you know."

Eva nodded. "I know."

"Every day. Every goddamned day."

"Be honest. Not *every* day. You probably didn't think about him the days you gave birth. All that yelling. All those drugs."

"Okay, every day but five. And I Google him once in a while."

"Ever find anything?"

Rosalyn shook her head. "He wasn't the Google type. Probably has a little farm somewhere. A perfect wife, three lovely kids."

Eva looked at her with empathy. "You were seventeen. It was one summer in Paris. It was doomed from the start."

Rosalyn's expression grew solemn, as though she were remembering the dead. "I wonder about that all the time. What if I had fought harder? What if

I hadn't caved in to my mother? I've never loved anyone like that again. Not ever. And now look at the life I have instead."

"Rosalyn Barlow! Is that a tear I see? Christ, woman, get ahold of yourself." Eva pulled her in and held her while she cried. It lasted a mere moment.

"This is the second time tonight," Rosalyn said, stepping away to wipe her eyes.

"That's a record, I think."

The two women smiled at each other.

"Can I ask you one more thing without having you fall to pieces?"

"Like it would matter anyway."

"Seriously."

"Seriously? Okay. You can ask one more question."

"Would you really have done anything differently if you'd had the choice?"

Rosalyn was taken by surprise. It had always been the story, the one they'd shared all these years, and the facts had never been disputed. Rosalyn had fallen in love in Paris, and her mother had forced her to return home to finish school, forced her to make amends with Jeb Ashton, to sell her soul for the good of the Eddings family reputation. They had threatened to disown her. She had been a victim, and later a survivor by moving away to college, dumping Jeb, and choosing Ernest Barlow. And as much as her love for Barlow had been real, her true love had been a casualty of her evil mother. Now Eva was questioning the bedrock of this history—a history that had become the core of her very being.

Had there been a choice? Not really. What could she have done at seventeen with no degree, no money? Still, to think she would have taken the same course of action on her own would change everything. She would no longer be a victim of her mother. She would be a product of her own making. Maybe she knew she could never live on a farm.

The answer was there, and despite its murky disposition, it was profoundly unsettling.

Rosalyn looked at Eva one last time before heading for the house. "I don't know," she said. And that was the truth.

They walked across the snow in silence, their thoughts lost in years long gone. Rosalyn hugged Eva, then watched her drive off. Inside, the house was quiet. Hoping to escape another lecture, the boys had gone to bed. Cait was in her room, the light was dim.

And Barlow was in the kitchen, leaning against the counter with a glass of scotch. "Are you all right?" he asked of his wife as she walked in the room.

They hadn't spoken since the plane ride, since making love for the first time in nearly six months. Still, they had been gentle with each other, kind and soft with their words.

"I'm fine. You?" Rosalyn did not stop walking until she was settled in at her desk.

Barlow followed with his drink. "What are you doing?" he asked, placing his hand on her shoulder.

But she did not feel the same beneath his touch as she had for that brief moment on the plane. Instead, she felt entirely too much like herself. "Just looking over the schedule."

She turned and smiled at him, though her hand reached for his and slowly removed it from her body. It was gone now, the need she'd felt on that plane that had been strong enough to overcome everything else that was still between them. His affair, the things he'd said to her, the worry for Cait and how to make this go away before the town returned from its vacation. She had things to do. Keep the Conrads out of the club, deal with her teenage son, and now rethink how to save her daughter. The wall was still there, and now the small window they had climbed through to reach each other had been closed.

Rosalyn looked at her screen, feeling Barlow beside her as he let the realization sink in. And when he did, he said nothing but instead retreated alone to their bedroom upstairs.

FORTY-THREE

PAST LIVES

JACKS HEARD THE BUZZING from her cell phone, but she let it be. They were on the porch that looked out at the Pacific, enjoying their morning coffee. The kids were playing on the beach with the nanny. The day was just beginning, and Jacks wanted to spend it like the others that had passed. Busy and distracted.

David sat beside her with the paper on his lap. It was his excuse not to talk, though she could tell he hadn't read a single word, because the page had not been turned for over twenty minutes. Still, he was there, he was present and, as always, playful with the children. He'd gone on the roller coasters at Disneyland, walked through the entire San Diego Zoo, and explored most of Legoland. Yesterday, he'd gone with the big kids for a surf lesson. Jeff the surfer with the lean, tan body and nipple piercings had found them waves and pushed them into shore, and David had crashed over and over, each time getting up with a smile on his face. It was so uncanny, this ability to fake life, that Jacks had begun to believe that he wasn't faking it at all—that everything was as fine as Kelly seemed to think. The case against him was over and that meeting with the Mafia lawyer was no longer of any consequence. There had been no phone calls, no ominous signs of doom that Jacks had begun to read into everything back home. So now, she had decided to sit back and try like hell to get on the same ride they all seemed to be on.

"I'll get more coffee," she said, smiling at her sister, who was watching the kids play. As she got up, she casually grabbed the phone from her purse and slipped inside.

Ducking into the bathroom when she saw the Barlows' number appear, she called for her messages. It was not like him to call like this, when he knew she was with David, but the voice she heard was not his. It was Rosalyn's. As she heard the news, she sank to the floor. Cait, the accident, the drugs. She thought about Barlow there, alone with his grief and worry. Rosalyn would be struggling in her own way, but Jacks knew them both too well to think they would find any lasting comfort in each other. This would have to be managed, and that would be Rosalyn's job. Barlow wouldn't have a job, and that was precisely why he would be such a mess. That, and the fact that he had been sleeping with his wife's best friend instead of tending to their daughter.

"We're all fine. I just wanted you to know so you wouldn't worry." Rosalyn's last words were painful to hear. There was not a chance that she was feeling as stoic as she sounded, but the affair with Barlow would now keep Jacks from reaching out to either of them.

She held the phone in her hands as she sat on the bathroom floor, thinking. Then she got up and headed for the porch. "I'm going for a walk on the beach. Can you watch the kids?"

David looked up and smiled. "Sure, honey. Go for a walk."

She leaned down and kissed him, catching his eyes as she pulled away. Something was in there, something alive that breathed air and spoke words. But it was not her husband. She was sure of it.

Kelly got up then, grabbing her sunglasses. "I'll come," she said.

"Great. You two have fun."

He was being too nice, too formal. It was eerie, and Jacks could tell that Kelly had sensed it as well. There was no other reason for her to come on the walk. Kelly didn't like exercise in any form, especially if it meant leaving her coffee behind.

They stopped to tell the nanny, say good-bye to the kids, then they were on their way.

"Was that Barlow?" It was the first thing Kelly said when the house disappeared from sight.

"Rosalyn, actually. Their daughter had an accident."

Kelly stopped and faced her sister. "Is she . . ."

"She's fine. Maybe I should I call him?" Jacks pulled out the phone, but Kelly grabbed her arm.

"Wait. Just wait a minute."

But Jacks didn't want to wait, she didn't want to stop or even slow down, for that matter. She needed to tend to one thing at a time, one crisis, one man, one day. And at the moment, that meant deciding what to do about the Barlows.

"Barlow can wait. He knows you're with your family. Besides, you said Rosalyn called."

"He's probably too afraid."

Kelly held her arm. "Just wait and see. See if he calls you."

Jacks put the phone away and started to walk again.

Kelly chased after her sister, who was moving fast. "Hold on!" she called.

Stopping suddenly, Jacks could no longer contain the anxiety that had been coming all week.

"Something's wrong. I know it," she said, almost pleading with Kelly to see what it was she was missing. Kelly had always been her beacon of reality. Kelly had seen far more.

"Can't you see how different he is? He's not himself, Kel. It's not my husband in that house."

Kelly sighed and looked out at the ocean. The view was indescribable compared with the decay she saw from every window of her own life. Real or not, she wanted to hold on to it for as long as she could. But Jacks was waiting for an answer.

"Please . . . tell me you see it."

Kelly closed her eyes, shutting out the surroundings that were tempting her to place reality on hold, even for a few more days.

"I see it," she said finally. "I see it."

It was their past that was now captured on David's face, in the pleasant but vacant expression it held and the absence of a human essence, the demarcations of a personality. He was in hiding within himself, and whether it was a conscious covering up of worry or a sign of a mental break mattered little to Kelly, because both scenarios pointed down the same road.

But it did matter to Jacks. This was her husband. "Tell me what it is, Kel. What has happened to him?"

"I don't know. I've told you everything I can about the investigation. Red is a little piece-of-shit drunk, and he could only do so much. There are no more letters, no more phone calls. Whatever is going on, we're not going to find it."

Jacks began to pace, running her hands through her hair, which was blowing wildly in the wind.

"He hasn't been the same since that day. But nothing has happened. If something happened, I could deal with it. This is like fighting with a ghost," she said, struggling now to keep her hair out of her face. "I'm really scared this time."

"Stop it!" Kelly's face was flushed as she grabbed her sister's arms. "Just stop it. I won't be scared with you, do you hear me?"

Jacks looked at her, surprised by her outburst. "It's getting to you, too, isn't it? It was one thing when he was just in financial trouble. But this is different, isn't it? I told you. Something is wrong."

Kelly closed her eyes again, this time to block out the face of her sister and to try to stop the thoughts that were once again in her mind. But it was not possible. It was all coming back, the past was now here, in the present in spite of everything they had done to keep it at bay. "I can see it, Jacks. I can see Daddy, the way he would disappear like that until he came back and then broke before our eyes. I can see it. Does that make you happy?"

Jacks reached out and grabbed Kelly, squeezing her tight. She had taken on the worst of it, holding their father like he were the child, letting him crawl into bed beside her and hold on to her through the night. Jacks had seen them in the mornings, their father asleep, wrapped up in the fetal position and clinging to a little girl who just lay there quietly and without expression. By the time Kelly finally left, Jacks had learned where to hide, and their father had learned how to drink to numb whatever it was he was feeling. Neither of them had forgotten.

Shaking it all off, Kelly pulled away. "Listen to me, now," she said. Her voice was unsteady. "You have to get away. Get the money from Barlow, take the kids, and leave."

Jacks thought about what she was asking. Taking the kids would destroy David.

"What if I can help him? I'm not a little girl anymore. I can get him help. Somewhere inside that man is my husband."

Kelly was shaking her head, her face determined as though she had just made a decision that would alter her forever. "I've been so selfish. I should have told you to leave that first day you came to my house with those letters. I didn't want it to end, I wanted the school for my kids and these trips together, and everything we've had all these years. I'm so sorry, Jacks. I should have told you then. I knew. . . ." She was off now, traveling down some one-way road, the only road she could see in the future.

But Jacks was not giving up. "Kelly, I can help him! Didn't you hear me?"

"No. Don't say that. Don't say you can help him. You can't. No one can."

They stood there, side by side, staring at each other as though they were the only two people in the world.

"I can help him," Jacks said again, and Kelly could see that she believed it. But there had been a time when she had believed things as well.

"You can't. And you have three daughters in that house."

Jacks had no response that would satisfy her sister. She would never abandon her girls with a sick man the way their mother had. Still, there were enough parallels.

The phone began to buzz again in Jacks's pocket. She pulled it out and checked the number calling. Then she looked up at Kelly.

"It's Barlow. What should I do?"

Kelly didn't hesitate. "Answer it."

FORTY-FOUR

THE BEAR

Cbow: Hi TF. You there?

Caitlin waited for a reply. It was a long shot on Christmas, but the day had come and gone for most people. Santa bullshit in the morning, the big meal at dusk. All that quality family time really wore people out. It was now half past eleven, and the rest of her house was asleep—except her mother, who would putter around until Cait finally turned out her light. As if she would do it again, take the car and slaughter two deer. The blood was gone, but her mother would never stop seeing it in the giant holes the bulldozer had removed from her perfect winter wonderland.

Totallyfkd: Hey Cbow. Merry Merry and all that crap.

Caitlin felt the smile stretch from ear to ear. For the past three days, TF was the only one who had kept her going. Her brother had steered clear. Apparently guilt could be added to the long list of things men couldn't deal with. Every time he saw her black-and-blue face, he turned on his heels and headed for the Wii. Then there was Daddy, with his constant tear-shedding, and Mother Dearest with that bitchy silence. No one seemed to know what to do with her. Except TF, who did the one thing she really needed. She listened.

Totallyfkd: How's the face? Still look like Darth Vader?

Cbow: Not as much. More like Hilary Swank in Million Dollar Baby.

Totallyfkd: Nice.

Cbow: Yeah. It's good for freaking out my little brothers. How was xmas?

Totallyfkd: Sucked.

Cbow: Mine too. Get any decent loot?

Totallyfkd: Lots of clothes. All too small. My mother can't admit to herself that I'm a size 10.

Cbow: Sucks. Can you return for cash?

Totallyfkd: I'm gonna try. What up with DH?

Cbow: Ugh. Finally got the text. Came at like eleven. He wanted to meet me after the party.

Totallyfkd: That would have been fun. Losing it in the hospital. Get any good drugs?

Cbow: I was high for two days. Still have five pills.

Totallyfkd: Nice. So what did he say?

Cbow: Didn't tell him.

Totallyfkd: No way.

Cbow: What was I gonna say? I was so desperate to see you I got stoned and crashed a car into a herd of innocent bambies? I told him I was sick.

Totallyfkd: So what's the new plan?

Cbow: I'm gonna lay low til my face heals. Then we're good to go. He keeps texting me. I think the playing hard to get thing is working. Not that I planned it. Still.

Totallyfkd: It's cool. Lay low and work it baby! What does he say?

Cbow: Just stuff about music, bitching about life.

Totallyfkd: Does he talk about the night in the car?

Cbow: Sometimes. He sounds embarrassed. Sounds like he wants to get it right next time.

Totallyfkd: I know I'm a drag, but are you sure you wanna go through with it? Seems like DH makes you a little loco.

Cbow: Ha. Funny. He's been really cool. And it was all in my head cause he did text me that night. I just didn't wait long enough.

Totallyfkd: I hate waiting for guys. Why don't they ever have to wait for us?

Cbow: My Dad says it all evens out after you get married.

Totallyfkd: Lovely. Can't wait.

Cbow: I gotta go cause ice queen's lurking. I can see the light from the kitchen. But thanks for everything. You saved me the last few days.

Totallyfkd: No prob. What are friends for?

Cbow: Are you OK?

Totallyfkd: Yeah fine. Got a bitch of a paper for this English teacher. We call him the bear cause he's really hairy and big. And cause he's a bear in general. Talk soon?

Cait paused for a second, staring at the screen. Wasn't that the nickname of the English teacher at the Academy? Kyle had told her that in the car. The Bear. She was certain of it.

Totallyfkd: You there cbow?

Cbow: Yeah, sorry. Talk soon. Luv ya.

Totallyfkd: You too babe. Hang in there. XO.

Cbow: XO.

Cait logged off the IM, but her eyes still could not leave the screen. What were the chances that there was another upper-school English teacher called the Bear? She started to think about everything she knew from TF. It was a private school. Had to be because they had the same vacation schedule. All the public schools went back right after New Year's Day. At least around here. Maybe she was from the Midwest, or Canada? Still, too many pieces were beginning to fit. She lived in a place where the seasons changed. She'd mentioned once that it was cold. She drove a car, so she probably didn't live in the city. Her family had gone to Smith, a traditional Northeastern school, and now she was going there as well. Had she mentioned playing squash, or was that just Cait? *Damn it!* She had to remember everything.

Her mind was racing now. Could TF live in Wilshire? Could she be a student at the Academy? She'd described herself as a nobody senior. Cait didn't know many seniors. She logged in to Google and searched for teachers nicknamed the Bear. All the relevant hits were from kids with My-Space pages, all from Wilshire. An hour went by, searching, thinking,

scanning last year's yearbook. It could be any of these girls, living this secret life on the Internet, being her friend. The boundaries of cyberfriends
had never bothered her before, but now she felt like she had to know this
girl, had to find out who she was. There was a chance to make it real, and
she was suddenly overcome with a new obsession. Finding the girl named
Totallyfkd.

FORTY-FIVE

A MERRY LITTLE CHRISTMAS

"WE PULLED IT OFF. One more year come and gone." Sara sat on the couch in the man cave, the only room that was finished and dust free. They had set up the tree there, even though the room was the coldest in the house, with its sleek black leather furniture and dark wood-paneled walls. It was not the Christmas Sara had hoped for, the one in the new family room with the soft yellow walls and fireplace, cushy sofas, and the smell of turkey pouring in from the kitchen. None of that had been possible, thanks to Roy and the construction delays. Still, it had been nice. Santa's arrival. Annie's glee at the pile of gifts. Now she was in bed, exhausted and fast asleep, and Nick and Sara were alone.

They had taken the first commercial flight back from West Palm Beach, and it had been nothing short of blissful. Long lines, overcrowded airport, and crammed seating on the plane. There was no food service, and they'd been too rushed to get anything in the terminal. Through the aggravation and hunger, the pushing and shoving as people struggled with their packages, Sara had been smiling. This was her world, one she understood, and the relief at the normalcy of it had almost made her forget the odd connection she'd forged with Ernest Barlow, and the horrific circumstances that had necessitated their hasty departure.

Nick sat beside her on the black leather love seat, bundling her in his arms as they watched the lights flicker on the tree.

"It was great. You did a nice job with everything. And . . . ," he said, kissing her on the back of her head. "You seem like yourself again."

"Thanks, sweetie. I feel like myself again. I'm sorry I was such a pain in the ass down there."

"No. Don't be sorry. You've always been a pain in the ass, and I love you anyway."

Sara nudged him as she leaned back farther against his body. "You really like the sweater?" she asked, noticing that he'd already put it on.

"What's not to like about cashmere?"

"True. It feels nice from where I'm sitting."

Nick felt warm against her. They'd placed so many things on hold until after the holidays. The construction problems, the talk of another baby and everything else that had come up around it, things that involved every corner of their lives. Sara had said nothing more about her unhappiness in Wilshire, and the possibility that she was unhappy with her life as a whole, their life that they had begun to build together. Now Christmas was taking its last gasp, and these things would soon be back on the table.

"I wish we could stay like this. Just like this."

"It does feel good."

"Why do you think it's so hard? When we wake up tomorrow and it all starts again. Work, Roy, Nanna, the club membership . . . ," Nick said, his thoughts rambling.

"And the baby." Sara knew it was on his mind, and probably a lot farther up on the list than the country club. He didn't respond. He didn't want to, not tonight. But he was right. Here she was, feeling about her husband the way she had the night they met, safe and warm and fiercely attracted. And yet, if she let herself, the memories of their trip to Florida could just as easily come back in, making her wonder if their marriage would survive the daily struggles of life. She had felt disdain for her husband at how much he seemed to enjoy the whole damned thing—the jet, the golf, the steak dinner. She had clung to Ernest Barlow as though he were the only air to breathe down there, simply because he was the only human being who seemed to share her X-ray vision of the place. And it had made her wonder if that was how easily it happened, affairs and divorces. A slipped connection with a spouse, replaced by a new connection with someone else. She had felt vulnerable to it, and it made her question everything, even now as she felt the strength of her love for Nick. Was it just them, or were all marriages that vulnerable? She was too damned young to know the answer.

"I remember your face," Nick said after a moment.

"I'm sitting right here."

"No. From that night. I remember your face. It killed me."

Sara smiled as she turned to kiss him. "It almost killed me."

"You were so pissed," he recalled; then he laughed at the thought of the night they met less than four years ago. "Pissed and distraught, crying, but mostly you were mad as hell and I thought *damn*—I have to know what that's about."

Sara closed her eyes and pictured him at the bar with one of his work buddies. They were downtown near their Wall Street office, and a few blocks from where Sara lived because it had been so cheap back then. She'd come in from the rain, drenched to the bone and reeling from events that seemed a lifetime ago.

"How he could have left you, I'll never understand."

"He was a coward. Or maybe just selfish. I should have known."

"His loss, my gain. You were hell-bent on finding revenge sex."

"Ah!" Sara elbowed him, then turned around to see his face. "Is that what you thought?"

"No question. You had that look in your eye like you weren't leaving that bar without a man to go home with."

Sara sighed. "Great. I'll have to remember not to have *that* look ever again. If I remember correctly, though, I went straight to the bathroom to clean the mascara from my face, then I ordered a beer and sat in the corner sulking."

"Yeah, but that's what made you so intriguing. You made this grand entrance, then played hard to get. It's classic."

Sara laughed with him. Maybe it was true. Maybe she had been hoping to pull someone in, to go home with him, screw all night, and the next day, until she could begin to forget the guy who'd left her standing in the rain as she begged and pleaded for him to stay. He was off to Afghanistan, where so many new journalists were flocking. She had not heard from him since. It had felt like divine intervention that Nick Livingston was the one who'd come to sit with her that night.

"I remember watching you walk over to me. You didn't have the slightest hint of insecurity."

"Oh, I was plenty nervous. But I had a hundred bucks riding on it."

"I still can't believe that's all I was worth. A hundred bucks to see if you could buy me a beer."

"But you didn't want to drink. Didn't want the one you'd bought, didn't want me to buy you another. I lost the hundred dollars on that technicality."

Sara laughed harder, then wrapped her arms around him. "You should have bet you could take me home if I looked so desperate for revenge sex."

"Yeah. But I wasn't exactly caring about the money when you stood up and headed for the door."

"But you just sat there."

"Until you turned around and looked at me like I was a total idiot."

"Did I?"

"Oh, yeah. Then you said 'Are you coming?' And I was gone in a shot, left my coat, my briefcase."

Sara kissed him on the neck and pulled him down around her on the sofa so they were lying together. She looked into his eyes the same way she had that night. "You never got any sex that night. After all that."

"But I got to hold you. All night, and into the next day."

"Yeah, and hear about another guy for hours and hours."

"That's 'cause I knew if I listened long enough, I'd eventually get sex."

"You did not!"

"Maybe not. But I hoped. And I was right."

Sara nodded. "You were right. How could I resist a man who would do all that for a complete stranger."

"You've never seemed like a stranger to me."

"And I don't ever want to."

She closed her eyes and drank in this feeling, this blissful tranquillity that all was as it should be. She loved her husband. They had a beautiful little girl, wealth, and comfort. She opened them again and kissed him, longer this time until he pulled away.

"Can we christen the couch? It's been weeks, and you drive me out of my mind, Sar."

Sara sat up and pulled off the silk pajama top he'd left in her stocking.

Nick grabbed her, kissing her neck, her breasts. "I don't want this to be a mistake for you," he said, breathless.

His words nearly killed her. Here she was, secretly back on her birth control pills, and he was concerned about making a baby. All because of her, because of her indecision and selfishness.

"Forget it. Forget everything, just for this one night. I've never wanted you more than I do right now."

Nick looked at her to make sure she knew what she was doing, but she couldn't meet his eyes. Instead, she tore off his sweater and shirt, the jeans and boxers until he was bare and against her on the sofa. They had so much waiting for them on the other side of this night, but she needed to be with him, to feel him the way she used to. Straddling his body, she grabbed his face in her hands and kissed him again and again, then whispered, "I love you." And when she pressed her face against his, their bodies touching head to toe, she could feel the tears on his cheek.

FORTY-SIX

THE DEEP FREEZE

By MID-JANUARY, THE WHOLE of Fairfield County was in a deep freeze.
The Christmas snowfall had melted down during two days of record highs,
only to reappear with near record lows the week following. A thick sheet of
ice was left in the wake of the erratic temperatures, and not even the rela-
tively mild forty-five degree days in early January seemed to be helping.
Roads had been cleared with salt and sand, but private drives, walkways,
pipes, and fragile trees had caused a multitude of hassles for homeowners.

Jacks sat in her car outside the Wee Ones nursery school waiting for Beth,
and watching Ernest Barlow. For the past few weeks, he had chosen to do the
pickup for Mellie, and Jacks was beginning to understand why. He was driving the Mercedes station wagon now, and it was not in the pickup line, but instead parked in the lot. And that wasn't all. Barlow was not in it, but instead
sitting in the red minivan with Sara Livingston. It was a daily routine that
Jacks had noticed of late, and it had her worried. She had been the one to set
Sara up, to make Rosalyn believe that Sara was Barlow's lover. And it had
seemed perfectly fortuitous that Rosalyn had reacted by drawing Sara in and
keeping her close with the trip to West Palm Beach. Now Jacks was beginning
to wonder if both their plans had backfired.

It was not jealousy that she felt as she watched them laughing through the window. In the fifteen years she'd known Barlow, she had never wanted him, never dreamed she would find herself making love to him in a hotel room on the outskirts of town. What she felt now was the same sense of helplessness and urgency that had propelled her down those stairs and into the wine cellar just a few months earlier, and it was back again after the trip to California. They had suffered through it, Kelly and Jacks, obsessively watching David, or the *absence* of David, all the while trying to stay up- lifted and fun for the kids. They had managed to do it, and they both left feeling relieved that none of this had yet touched their children. But since their return, Jacks had been on a frenetic daily search for anything that would tell her what was happening to her husband, and consequently, to her and the girls. There had been nothing. No papers, no letters or calls. Noth- ing but David coming and going on schedule with that vacant stare. It was maddening.

Barlow held something for her in all of this. It was twisted and dark, but having him want her, need her, had given her a sense of security. If every- thing fell apart, Barlow would save her because he wanted to, or—God help her for thinking it—because he had to. And now it had been weeks since her return, and they had done nothing but exchange a few phone calls, mostly about Cait and making plans that he kept breaking. She had assumed it was all Cait, the guilt of being away when she crashed the car being too much in itself to add the weight of the affair. But now she could see she was wrong. Something was happening in that red minivan.

She pulled at the handle and swung open her door. The line wasn't mov- ing yet, so she left the car in park and walked up to the van three cars ahead. As she stood by the driver's-side window, Barlow was the first to see her, and his face quickly lost its light expression.

Following Barlow's eyes, Sara turned her head to see Jacks standing there. She rolled down the window, smiling, and leaned her head out to give Jacks a Wilshire peck on the cheek. "Hi!" Sara said, honestly glad to see her friend. It had been nearly a month. "How was your trip? Christmas, New Year's, all of it?"

Jacks smiled broadly. "Wonderful. Everything was perfect. I love the warm weather. Can you believe this ice?"

"I know!" Sara responded, her tone genuine and friendly, making both

Barlow and Jacks uneasy. "Barlow and I were just saying that on top of all the hassles, the whole thing has brought out the climate-change naysayers who have just been *waiting* for a chance to plead their case."

"I guess it's fitting that Wilshire's two greatest cynics have found each other." Her voice was playful, but the message was delivered. And Barlow wasn't the only one who heard it.

"I should get in line," Barlow said. "The mothers will have my head if I hold it up. See you tomorrow?"

Sara smiled. "Sure."

"I'll walk you over. I want to hear how Cait is doing." Jacks stepped away from the window but did not turn yet. "Sara, great to see you. Let's have lunch."

"Great," Sara agreed.

The line started to move, and Sara drove up in search of her daughter. Barlow, on the other hand, remained in the parking lot with Jacks. Standing in the cold, shivering, they tried to have their own conversation, careful not to come close to the obvious bond that Barlow had forged with the young Mrs. Livingston.

"It's been a little crazy," Barlow said. "With Cait and everything. I'm sorry I haven't been able to see you."

Jacks looked at the ice beneath her feet, which was beginning to chill her toes. "I know. It's all right. Is Cait still a mess?"

Barlow thought about the answer. The truth was, she seemed better than before. Her face had healed, the blood was long gone from their lawn, and things seemed pretty normal. Still, he couldn't think of another excuse. "I'm just keeping a closer eye on her."

"And Mellie, I see. You've been doing a lot of pickups."

Barlow was the one to look away this time. No matter what he said, the friendship between him and Sara was obvious to everyone, and his picking up Mellie was nothing more than an excuse to see her in a gossip-proof setting. So he lied. "Yeah. I'm trying to let Rosalyn focus on the speaker. She's in town next week, and then the big event is what, that Friday night?"

"Friday. Is Cait okay with it? Rosalyn said she wanted her to attend, but I'm not sending Hailey. I think I'll just go and bring the messages home that seem appropriate."

"I don't know if she'll go or not. We haven't really discussed it. Rosalyn just spends all day going over the speech, figuring out the arrangements for the parking, and e-mailing the reminders to the parent body. It's a full-time job for her at the moment."

Jacks smiled sadly. "She probably needs that right now."

"Yeah. I guess. I'm not exactly the expert on what my wife needs."

Jacks felt like touching his arm, and not to draw him back in, but as an honest gesture between very old friends. Still, she kept her hands in her pockets.

"I should get back in the car. Beth hates it when I'm last."

Barlow let out a small chuckle. "Oh, I know. Mellie gives me an earful about it. They must talk about it while they're waiting. It's all about winning now. Who's first, who's last."

"And it only gets worse from here."

"True. Very true." Barlow seemed nervous, like he knew he should say more, but couldn't, or perhaps didn't want to.

He started to reach for the car door, and Jacks felt the panic return. Wicked or not, she needed to hold on to him. Just standing there with him now, she wanted to fall into his arms and beg for help. But that was not her way. And it was not part of the plan that Kelly had made her promise to execute. There was so much at stake.

"Barlow . . . ," she said, this time reaching for his arm. "I miss you."

Her words stopped him cold. They hadn't been together in weeks, and although he missed the comfort of feeling warm hands against his skin, so much had happened in between. The night on the jet with his wife, then watching her turn back to stone. And now this delightful, innocent friendship with Sara Livingston. There was a lot stirring around in the pot, and he had no idea what an encounter with Jacks would do to him right now.

He turned to face her, to look at her. He owed her that much. "I miss you, too, Jacks, I really do. Maybe next week?"

Jacks smiled. She could see everything he wasn't saying. But she held on to his words like they were a solemn promise.

"Next week. I'll call you."

Barlow smiled without answering, then got in his car and started the engine. Jacks walked slowly back to her own car and climbed inside, her mind and body reeling from the truth that was staring her down. And as the heat began to warm her, she could feel the desperation grabbing hold. She was sinking into a hole of uncertainty, and the rope that she had counted on to pull her out had just been yanked up. She hadn't held on tight enough. Or maybe it was inevitable. She didn't love him, and it was only a matter of time before he began to feel it. Either way, it was gone.

FORTY-SEVEN

NEW OBSESSIONS

CAIT WAITED OUTSIDE THE Bear's classroom. It was on the fourth floor, the junior/senior floor, where she had no business being as a ninth-grader. But she had to know. She had convinced herself that TF was someone in this school, and she had to know who. This new obsession was almost as bad as the first. Almost.

The bell rang, and she stood against the wall just down the hall. They shuffled out, talking and laughing, boys and girls, there were too many to take in. TF had said her ass was the size of Texas, but there wasn't a legitimately fat girl in the Academy. She'd mentioned being a size 10, but that could mean she was tall, or busty. Size 10 wasn't exactly the size of Texas. Hair color, length, breast size, shoe size—it was all a mystery. It could be any one of those girls.

Studying their faces, she looked for someone out of place, someone who felt like a nobody, because that was what TF had said. That she was a senior nobody. But no one fit that profile. They all seemed happy; they were all talking to someone. Even losers could fake it here, and Cait knew first-hand how easy it was to hide in a place like this. The second bell rang. *Shit!* She had to get to class. She started walking for the stairs when she felt a hand on her shoulder.

"Hey."

She knew that voice like her own. She could feel the energy from his body surging through the hand and into her core.

"Hey," she said casually, turning around.

He was as beautiful as ever, and her mind was instantly back in that car. She could not stop the flushing of blood through her cheeks.

"Heard there was some trouble at your place over break. You didn't say anything."

Cait waved it off. "Not really. My brother and I were partying and had a little mishap with my dad's car."

"The orange Corvette? No way." Kyle seemed impressed.

Cait went with it, shrugging her shoulder and smiling. "Yeah, afraid so. It's cool."

"Damn. Who would have thought. You're full of surprises."

Cait was silent. This was a good moment, and she was certain anything that came out of her mouth now would ruin it completely.

"Got a class to get to?"

Cait shrugged again. "It can wait. What's up?"

"So I've been thinking about our rain date. Got any plans next Friday?"

Her heart stopped pounding. It stopped altogether. "Nothing I can't break."

"Good, 'cause all the parents are coming to some school assembly. That leaves a lot of open houses."

Some assembly? Could he really not know? Was there a chance that he had not been told the assembly was her mother's brainchild, that they would all be discussing the hallway blow job she had given him in the fall? It seemed impossible, and yet his face was dead serious.

"Sounds great. Should I get a ride with someone?"

Kyle gave her a smile that she would remember forever. "No, silly. Just you and me. A rain date from before. We never got a chance to be alone over break. My bad, I know. I called so late that night."

"No, forget about it. I went out with my brother anyway."

"So Friday? I'll text you when I come up with a plan."

Cait nodded. "Sounds good."

"Okay. Later."

As he walked away, Cait turned for the stairs on shaky legs. This was it. There was no more doubt. He wanted her. She wanted him. She was ready.

She hurried down two flights to her history class. Amanda Jamison was already inside waiting for her along with the rest of the class. "You're late," she whispered.

Cait mouthed back *I know*, then looked up at the board, where their teacher was too busy scribbling out an assignment to notice her slip into her chair.

She tried to focus on the board, pulled out her notebook, and began to write. Soon there was a buzzing from her phone. It was a text from Amanda, which she read from beneath her desk.

Have you talked to Kyle?

Cait replied. *Why?*

The response came back a few seconds later: *Did you say yes to Friday?*

Cait looked at the phone, then back at Amanda, who was trying to seem happy for her but getting it all wrong.

Cait wrote back: *How do you know?*

Everyone knows.

Cait wanted to throw up, right then and there, but her stomach was empty. She took a deep breath and let it out slowly, all the while fighting to keep a steady expression as Amanda watched her. It was early payback, she imagined, for capturing Kyle's attention, for making him choose her over Amanda or Victoria Lawson—or any of them, for that matter. Still, it stung like a bitch.

Cait deleted the last entries. What was she, some kind of prisoner who was about to be subjected to scientific experimentation? The date had been set. All the parties had been notified. Caitlin Barlow would lose her virginity next Friday night. And although she would be alone somewhere with Kyle, the rest of them would be there with them in spirit, waiting for the full report.

Was it a conspiracy? Is that what it was? Was she a big fucking joke? It was back again, that feeling that life was nothing but chaos, cruel chaos where nothing was what it seemed, not words or feelings or the looks on people's faces. She wanted to run from this room right back home to her computer where she could IM TF. Only TF was probably two stories above her struggling through her class with the Bear. More deception.

She closed her eyes hard, then opened them again. Fuck it. This was high school. People talked. Surely not *everyone* knew. If everyone knew, then her mother would know, and then her father, and she would be wearing a metal chastity belt with the key locked in a vault at their Swiss bank. Maybe Kyle was as nervous as she was. Maybe he had confided in a few friends and they had told a few more and now Amanda knew and was making her feel like shit because that was what Amanda did. She hadn't called once over break, not even after returning from her trip. So screw her, and screw everyone who knew and couldn't keep a damned secret. She closed her eyes and saw Kyle's face. She remembered the smell of him, the way his hand had electrified her. And then she opened them again and talked herself back into the only version of the story she could stand to live with.

FORTY-EIGHT

_____

THE DELIVERYMAN

THE HOUSE WAS QUIET, leaving only thoughts to play in Jacks's head. Over and over they played, as they had been for weeks. It was merciless, this time when Beth was napping, the girls were at school, David was at work, and Jacks was alone with her memories, and her fear.

She straightened the covers around her daughter, gave her a kiss, then slipped out of the room. This would be the last year for these afternoon naps. Next year she would be in school all day, and Jacks was already beginning to feel the loss. She had planned on enjoying this time with her youngest, on taking her to lunch and the playground, on doing everything that she used to do with her older girls at this age. There were so many things she was eager to savor now, precious moments she would never get back and time was slipping away.

But none of that could concern her at the moment. There was too much to do. Tonight was the night, the assembly at the Wilshire Academy, and in many ways she was thankful for the distraction. Rosalyn had assigned her the RSVP list, which had created nearly two hundred e-mail responses and phone calls. People coming, then not coming, then maybe coming. Social lives were hard to manage, even at this dead time of year, and it was a Friday night. That was all part of the plan, placing the event on a night when husbands would be dragged along. Rosalyn wanted this to be more than the usual gathering of the hens to squawk on and on about the minutia of their children's many issues. There were several of those throughout the year, coming and going without the slightest impact. She wanted this to be an important event, and in Wilshire, that meant the inclusion of the husbands.

Jacks walked downstairs to the kitchen, poured the last of the coffee, got the milk from the fridge. She was at her computer when the doorbell rang.

Out of instinct, she got up and headed for the foyer. She was halfway there when she realized she hadn't buzzed anyone in through the gates. And where was Chester? Barking at strangers was what he lived for. She stopped suddenly, her head flushed with adrenaline. The doorbell rang a second time. She thought about Beth, asleep upstairs.

Struggling to steady her nerves, she backtracked through the living room. Then she slipped behind a curtain to shield herself from view as she looked out the window. It was just the deliveryman, dressed in a brown uniform. The package was in one hand, the clipboard in the other. *Thank God*.

Moving quickly now, because she felt like a complete idiot, she unlatched the door and opened it, letting in a burst of cold air.

"Mrs. Halstead?"

"Yes, sorry. I was upstairs," she lied.

She smiled and reached for the clipboard, but the man pulled it away. "Actually, it's for your husband. He needs to sign it himself."

Jacks looked up and studied his face. He was young, clean-cut, and wore a pleasant expression, not quite a smile but something close. Still, she saw no truck outside, only a small blue sedan.

"It's the middle of the day. He's at work in New York. I'll sign for it."

The man pushed past her and into the foyer, shivering and rubbing his arms. "Mind if I step inside? It's cold out there."

Jacks held her fears at bay. There were so many of them now, real and unreal, that she couldn't tell them apart. "Sure. Just for a minute. I was on my way out."

The man smiled. He knew she was lying, and he looked at her as though she was a complete amateur at it. "So, what should we do?" he asked, raising his eyebrows.

"Well, I suppose you can come back another day. I'll be sure to tell him."

Jacks reached for the door, but the man was walking now, toward the living room.

"Nice house," he said, and that was when Jacks knew. Her eyes went right for the stairs along with her thoughts of her sleeping child. There was no way to get Beth and get out. She was at the door. She could make it alone; he'd left it wide open for her. Which meant he knew. He knew that she had a child in the house.

But she still wasn't ready to believe any of this. "I really need you to leave. David will be home later. Can you come back?"

She followed him as far as the stairs, watching him as he took a seat on her sofa. She would not remove her body from the line between this man and her daughter.

"Actually, I think I'd rather wait. But if you want to call him, feel free." He was smug now, his expression polite but terrifying at the same time.

Jacks looked at the hallway that led to the kitchen, to the phone, but she could not leave the foot of the stairs.

The man smiled because he knew this, too. The offer had been little more than a joke.

Jacks felt the fear turn now to anger. This was her child, her house. "What are you going to do, wait here all day?" she said defiantly.

The man shrugged and settled deeper into the cushions. Then he pulled out a cell phone, dialed a number, and pressed the phone to his face. "David Halstead, please."

Jacks felt herself gasp. This was real, it was really happening. David had dug a grave for all of them.

"Mr. Halstead? . . . I'm here at your house, and I have a package for you. Unfortunately, I have instructions not to leave until I have delivered it in person."

Jacks could hear David yelling on the other end, but the man kept talking, his voice hushed. Then he issued an order.

The man listened for a moment, then held the phone into the air. "Could you please say hello to your husband?"

Jacks did not hesitate. "I'm here, David." Then she paused for moment. "With Beth."

The man ended the call and slipped the phone back in his pocket.

Minutes went by, or at least that was how long it seemed to Jacks as she stood there, waiting and thinking through her options. "Where's my dog?" she asked.

"He's taking a walk. Couldn't wait to get out of that collar."

Jacks drew a hand to her mouth as she thought about Chester out there on the main roads, and yet she was helpless. All over again, she was helpless. "He'll get run over!" she yelled.

"Not if he's smart."

They stayed that way for minutes more, until the anger turned to resignation. It was so familiar, the fear, rage, then finally, the acceptance that nothing could be done. That the situation was out of her hands. All these months, she had fought to avoid this. The search for answers, the affair with Barlow. But now it was too late.

The sound of the back door brought the man to his feet. He looked at Jacks.

"Jacks? Where the hell are you?"

It was Eva. She had the code for the gate, knew where the key was hidden. And she never knocked.

This was the only chance, and Jacks took it. "In here," she called out.

The man gathered his things, then walked toward the foyer. He seemed unsure of what to do, not having calculated on a nosy friend. The suburbs were generally places of complete isolation.

When Eva entered the foyer, she found them standing there in an eerie silence. Beads of sweat were falling from Jacks's face.

"Well, well. What do we have here?" Eva said whimsically, though she knew something was very wrong.

"Just a package for David. He's going to come back later." Jacks walked to the door and opened it. The man hesitated, but then followed.

Before he left, he looked Jacks in the eye. "Tell your husband I'll try another day."

Jacks pushed the door closed and locked it. Then she pressed her hands against the glass panels that flanked its sides and watched until the car disappeared down the driveway.

"Good Lord" was all Eva said as Jacks fell to the floor. She was gasping for air.

"Okay, sweetie, he's gone. He's gone. Go slow, sweetie. Slow."

Eva sat on the floor beside her friend and waited until Jacks caught her breath. Then she asked about Beth.

Jacks got up off the floor and raced for the stairs. Eva followed. They went to Beth's room and found her fast asleep.

"She's fine," Eva whispered. "Now tell me what the hell is happening here? Should we call the police?"

Jacks pulled the door closed. "No, please," she said.

Eva shook her head. "Then you're going to tell me everything. Right here, right now."

"I can't. Please, you don't want to get involved in this."

But Eva grabbed her, holding her so tight she couldn't break free. "I already know about Barlow, sweetie. Why don't we start with that?"

Jacks backed away and looked at Eva, studying her face. There was not a trace of judgment, only profound concern, and Jacks felt the tears stinging against her skin. "How long have you known?"

"Since the night of the party."

"That was the first night."

"Okay."

"There's a reason, Eva. Things I haven't told anyone."

Eva sighed. "That needs to change. Start from the beginning."

FORTY-NINE

HELLO, FRANK

SARA WAS IN THE kitchen, doing what she always seemed to be doing when her daughter was home from school—fighting with Roy.

"Nanna!" she called, though it killed her to do it. This was her time to spend with Annie, it was the good time. Lunch, a little snuggle by the TV. *Dora* was on, and Annie liked to doze off in her mother's arms. Now, it would be Nanna who would have the privilege of her child's sweet company while she haggled over the cost of tiles and wood stain. Not even her recent resignation that this would someday be over could help ease the hint of anguish as she handed Annie to Nanna and watched them disappear through the doorway.

"Okay, so what were you saying?" Sara asked, her hands on her hips and her blood pressure slowly rising.

But Roy didn't get a chance to answer.

"Hold on—someone's at the door." Sara left Roy in the kitchen while she ran to the back of the house. She was expecting nothing but more construction misery. Instead, she found Ernest Barlow.

"Hello, friend," he said, smiling broadly.

Sara accepted a peck on the cheek before stepping aside and letting him in.

"What are you doing here? Did we have a playdate?"

Barlow shook his head. "No. I let Marta get Mellie today. I have a surprise for you."

Sara smiled. Just the sight of Barlow almost made her forget the troubles that were waiting for her in the other room.

"I love surprises! What is it?"

Barlow waved his hand out the door and a short moment later a second man appeared. He was dressed in jeans and a leather jacket, neat but not exactly Barlow's type. Sara was curious.

"Meet Frank," Barlow said, stepping aside so they could shake hands.

"Hello, Frank. Good to meet you." Sara shook his hand, then looked quizzically at Barlow.

"Frank is an old buddy of mine. Worked on a few of our houses."

Frank smiled. "Just a few."

"I don't understand," Sara said, leading them into the mudroom and closing the door to keep out the frigid air.

"Frank is your surprise." Barlow was smiling now as he raised his eyebrows. It was clear he was enjoying this.

"Frank is my surprise?"

"Frank has a few months free, and he would love to take over your construction."

Sara stopped smiling. This was too much. "How? I mean, we've got all these contracts with the subs, and Roy has half our budget tied up."

Frank was the one smiling now. "Oh, nothing's impossible. Let me have a conversation with Roy. I'm sure there's something we can work out."

"I'll have to check with my husband, see what it's going to cost."

"We'll make it work. Is this Roy person in the house?"

Sara pointed toward the kitchen. "He's in there."

Frank bowed his head to excuse himself, then walked through the doorway, leaving Sara and Barlow alone in the mudroom.

"Barlow . . . ," Sara started to say.

"Shhh. Don't say it. I'm not paying for your house. I'm just loaning you a very scrupulous and savvy contractor who will bend over backwards for you and charge you something reasonable. He owes me after three houses that nearly wiped me out."

"You seem to be doing okay." Sara's tone was sarcastic and this made Barlow smile. She never let him get away with a damned thing.

"Well . . . maybe not. But I'm sure we got hosed on at least one of them. This is all a big game, and now you get to play it standing on two feet."

Sara thought about what he had just done, what he had given her. It wasn't money, but in many ways much more valuable. He'd lent her his name, his clout, and with it he was changing her life. She felt like crying.

"He will get this house finished in two months. Believe me. And you won't have to spend any more time dealing with it than you want to."

"Huh! That would be none! I don't know what to say," she said, the tears starting to form. No one had really understood what this house had been doing to her, how much she had come to hate every part of her days, except the moments with her child, and, lately, with Barlow.

Barlow was taken aback. "Sara, it's nothing. *Really*."

"It is something. You have no idea. It really is."

Not knowing what else to do, Barlow wrapped his arms around her, and she didn't stop him. He felt like a big lion, closing in around her, protecting her from the brutal world outside, and that was exactly what she needed, what she wanted, though it went against everything she believed about herself. Since moving to this town, she'd bitched plenty, cried plenty, but she got up every day ready to fight. She hadn't seen this rescue coming, hadn't known how much she'd wanted it. She would have survived Roy, and she never would have asked for help. Still, having someone give it to her anyway was powerful.

His hands were on her back, then on her face when she finally pulled away. He wiped away the tears with his soft fingers, but did not let go even after her cheeks were dry.

"I'm sorry," Sara said. "I guess I didn't realize how miserable I've been."

Barlow studied her, so honest and strong, but also vulnerable, and it moved him. As much as she had needed his help, he had needed this—this face she was letting him see in this very moment. It was one thing that was real, that he knew wouldn't suddenly morph into something else before his eyes, and he had nowhere to hide from the spell it was casting over him.

Sara saw it then, too, what had grown between them over the past several weeks, the friendship that had poured in to fill the gaping holes in both of their lives. It had happened so quickly, too quickly, and it scared her.

"Barlow . . . ," she started to say, but he couldn't let her finish. He didn't want to hear all the reasons. He leaned closer and kissed her gently on the lips and she did not pull away. Not until he did.

"Barlow," she started to say again, and this time he released his hands from her face.

"I know. Don't say it. It's why I feel the way I do right now. You're a good soul, Sara. I would only ruin that in you."

She smiled then, sweetly, as she took his hand and pressed it between hers. "No, you wouldn't. You are not the corrupt man you think you are. And I wanted you to kiss me. I just can't kiss you back. And not because you would ruin me, but because I love my husband."

Barlow nodded at her words, words he knew he would carry with him long after he left this room. He was a wretched old man to her unspoiled youth, and their connection had been grounded in a need to escape. He pulled his hand away and shoved it awkwardly into his pocket.

"I'm gonna go now. Why don't you find Annie and steal her from that despicable other woman."

Sara sighed. "Oh, that will be *so* nice. Thank you, Barlow. For your friendship, for Frank."

He was halfway out the door when he looked back at her. "Any time."

He heard the door close behind him. That was it, the one and only moment he would have with her. She was untouchable; through all her doubts and worries about her life and her marriage, she knew who she was. Not even Wilshire could change that.

His car was still warm when he climbed back inside. And as he turned on the ignition, he heard the phone beeping at him. There were two calls, both urgent, and they snapped him back into the mess he'd made of his own life.

The first was from Jacks. The second from Eva Ridley.

FIFTY

THE END OF THE ROAD

DAVID HALSTEAD ARRIVED HOME to a barking dog and an empty house. The gate had been left open, the back door as well. As he'd frantically raced home from the city, he had prepared himself for fear, for fighting, for despair. He hadn't known what he would find in this house, though he had followed the instructions carefully. No police, no private security. He'd emptied the firm's accounts, cashed out what was left on the home equity line. The mortgage deed was somewhere in the house and he would sign it over. Everything he could get his hands on was now in his briefcase, which he gripped tightly as he walked slowly through the house, room by room.

There were no cars in the driveway, no Jacks, no Beth. The other girls should have been home by now as well, and the nanny, the maid. The house always filled up after 3 P.M.

"Jacks?" he called out. There was no answer. He moved faster now, his mind spinning with thoughts too horrible to imagine. He thought about that execution years before, the husband facedown in a pool of blood on the closet floor, but when he raced through the remaining rooms of the house he found that they, too, were all empty.

Bounding back down the stairs, he retraced his steps in search of clues. It was then that he found the note on the counter. It was from his wife, and he scanned it quickly before reading each word. *The man left willingly. It was just a scare. Kids are fine, at a friend's house, but not sure if it's safe to say where. Tell you in person later. Everything is going to be OK. Please, just wait for me.*

David set the briefcase down, felt the charges settle inside him. They were safe for the moment, or so it seemed. Jacks was clever, she would have dropped some clue in the note if she'd been forced to write it. And her car was gone. No signs of struggle, which surely there would have been if they had taken Beth.

No, this wasn't like that. They just wanted the money, whoever they were; he didn't even know for sure. Everything had been arranged through that lawyer. It had all seemed so businesslike. Posh offices with secretaries. A Park Avenue address, fancy suits. He'd signed legal contracts, documents that had been notarized to obtain the loans, and he'd told himself they were nothing worse than junk bonds. Exorbitant interest, but that was to be expected given the level of risk he was asking them to take on. And now, one deadline come and gone and they were calling his house, his office. Sending a man to his home, scaring his wife, threatening his child. It was surreal, and yet the message had been delivered. This would never stop, would never end, because what he had in that briefcase was not even the first installment of what he now owed.

He looked out the window at the white, glistening snow. He saw the dog settling down, chasing after a squirrel. The tree swing swayed against the cold bursts of wind that the day had brought, along with the piercing sunshine and bitter cold temperatures. He took it all in, soaked it into his bones, then he grabbed the briefcase and went up the stairs.

In his study, he searched his files for the deed to the house. He pulled it out and signed it over to his wife, forging a notary's signature the best he could under the circumstances. Then he folded the deed and placed it inside the briefcase with the rest of the family's assets. He was on autopilot now, the fear gone, the panic subdued. What was left he couldn't recognize, but it propelled him forward and he didn't try to stop it. He didn't know how to begin to stop it after everything he'd done.

In the back of his closet, on the top shelf, was his hunting rifle, the one he'd been given as a gift by the Barlows years before and that had been put away soon after. David was not a hunter, though Barlow had dragged him along on a couple of his excursions. He knew how to use it. It wasn't that complicated.

His blood was moving faster now, though he had slowed his body, taking each step as it came, being careful. He walked inside the bathroom and closed the door, locking it shut. Then he laid the briefcase on the vanity counter, popping open the lid to expose the contents freely.

How had this happened? How had it come to this? Part of him was fighting it now, screaming that it couldn't be what it was. He thought back on his pleasant childhood, his years at Harvard and working on Wall Street. Then his own firm, and clients, the expensive lunches and golf conferences out west. Three children, a house in Wilshire, private schools, expensive cars. It couldn't all be gone after one mistake; it was not possible. But no, there had been more than one mistake. *Think about it!* He could not afford to have pity after what he'd done. He had not secured the insurance on the hotel; the most important detail had slipped right past him in his moment of arrogance, or forgetfulness. He'd jumped the gun; maybe he'd been too eager to get the investors on board, and in the end he had not done the due diligence. How and why, he could not say for sure. But the lapse occurred after the property transfer. It was on him and only him.

Still, is that all it took to ruin a man? One mistake? No, it was all that he had done after that, the covering up, raising a second fund to cover the first. It was fraud, and that was the moment he'd become more than a careless investor. He'd become a criminal. And the crime had been exposed, and then needed to be managed. It had seemed manageable that day in Angelo Ferrino's office. He had talked about it like any lawyer would, with a series of actions that could be taken to solve the problem. Only the solution relied upon David coming up with more money, more investors at a time when the market was taking a sudden dive and he was fresh off a criminal investigation. It was his own arrogance that had made the plan seem possible, and of course Ferrino had known that. He'd been banking on it.

David could see the road map now, the twists and turns he'd taken to get to this place. He had not been the victim of circumstance. There was no hand-wringing to be done. If he were on his own, he might find a way to disappear. Leave the money and the house and pray that it would be enough for them. But you can't hide a wife and three little girls. He had a two-million-dollar life insurance policy that Ferrino and his clients could never touch.

David Halstead was a lot of things, but he had never been a coward. He took the gun and headed outside to the woodshed.

FIFTY-ONE

A GOOD HEART

BARLOW WALKED IN THE room to find her standing by the window, watching the wind blow up the snow. The door was heavy as it closed behind him, but she did not turn around. Not yet. Still, he saw her take a heavy breath as he set his keys on the nightstand.

"Are you all right?" he asked, taking a few steps closer to her before stopping.

Jacks nodded. Then she twisted her neck to look at him. "I'm fine. Sorry about the message . . . if I worried you."

He smiled then, warmly, and she finally allowed herself to face him. "It's okay. No trouble. I'm sorry I never called."

He had promised last week in the parking lot, but Jacks had known then as she did now that the affair was over for him, that the promise had been a polite way of ending the conversation.

"Don't be sorry," Jacks said. If anyone needed to be sorry, it was she. And not only for drawing him into this sordid mess, but for what she was about to do. This was the moment that all of those stolen afternoons had been about. She'd gone over it with her sister, what she would say, how she would say it so he would understand what he had to do to save his marriage, his reputation. She would be as cold as she needed to be to make him believe she was serious, to make him feel the sting of her betrayal. He could not think for a moment that she would back down. It had to be all or nothing. The money for her silence.

She had the evidence—hotel receipts, text messages, and photos of him sleeping taken on her cell phone. It was textbook, cliché. But it was real. She had this all in her purse, which was next to her on the floor—the things that could destroy his life and that would surely destroy everything that remained of hers when she finished saving her husband.

Barlow walked closer to her, studied her face. "Eva called me just after you. Any idea what she wanted?" he asked.

Jacks shrugged, thankful he hadn't spoken to her yet. "Probably something about the speaker tonight."

Barlow nodded. "Of course."

It was awkward now, with both of them knowing it was over, but Jacks having called the meeting, having said she was desperate to see him.

With his eyes on hers, he pulled off his shoes, then his jacket. He reached for the buttons on his shirt, but Jacks walked quickly to where he stood, closing her hands around his.

"What is it?" he asked. "I thought . . ."

"Stop. Just stop. We both know it's over."

Barlow kissed her on the cheek, then buttoned the shirt. "Then why? Why am I here?"

She turned away, unable to think with all the voices screaming in her head. She could hear her sister pleading with her to get the money and run like hell. *Remember the past, nothing can change, not ever.* But then she heard David weeping in his sleep, her children laughing in the yard. She let the voices scream until she heard her own voice rising above all of them, though it sounded strange to her. Still, it was hers, and she knew she had to listen.

She turned back toward the window and grabbed her purse. Then she looked at Barlow for a long time, as though she might not ever see him quite the same way again, soft and loving.

"I have to go. This was a mistake." She walked past him quickly before she could change her mind. She had come so close, and that was something she would have to live with for the rest of her life. But that was all she could withstand. The degradation she almost inflicted upon her soul would have ripped out what was left of her humanity, leaving her with nothing but a shell. She could not do that to her children. Or to herself.

"Are you sure? You said you had something to tell me?" Barlow sounded confused.

"No. Please. Let me go." This was over for her. David would be coming home and they had an entire life to re-create. It would be drastic, devastating, but nothing could be worse than what she had almost done in this room.

As she turned away, Barlow grabbed her, pulling her back to him. With his strong arms, he held her tightly, then began to whisper in her ear.

"You have a good heart, Jacks. No matter what happens, I know you have a good heart, and I love you for it."

Taking in his words, Jacks pulled away and stood before him.

His face was serious now, serious and concerned.

"I've just made a call to my accountant. It seems there's a great deal on a hotel in Vegas that I simply can't pass up. The first owner lost it to a fire early on in the construction, and the insurance had lapsed."

Jacks was breathless, unable to speak or move. All she could do was listen as Barlow told his story.

"It's a shame because it has a lot of potential. Great piece of property. Just needs some cleaning up on the money end. Some debts and other things. But I've already gotten started on that."

Jacks shook her head, her hands pressed to her face trying to hold back the tears, but it was futile. He had lied about speaking with Eva, who now knew everything. Eva had insisted on it—names, dates, amounts. She'd written all of it down, and Jacks hadn't a clue what for, though her mind was reeling with possibilities of what might be done to them, and how having a witness might be useful. So she had complied with every request, then let Eva take Beth and the other girls to her house for the afternoon. Eva must have known she was coming right here, straight to this hotel room to ruin a man's life.

"It's going to be okay now" were the last words Barlow said before holding her, and she stayed there, crying for a long while, whispering over and over, "I'm sorry." Barlow stroked her hair and cried with her, for her. What had this life done to this woman? He'd have given her the money months ago if only she had asked. But that wasn't in the rulebook; there was no rulebook for what had happened to David Halstead.

"I have to go to him. He'll be worried sick about us," Jacks said. Then she kissed Barlow on his face and stared straight into his eyes.

"Will you ever forgive me?"

Barlow smiled in that disarming way of his. "What for? Some great sex?"

"Don't joke, please. I need to know. When I see you again—if I see you again—will you be able to look at me?"

"Of course. Go home to your family."

Jacks gathered her things, then faced Barlow one last time before leaving. He was a good man, generous and kind. For all his weaknesses and betrayals, he was still all of that. He'd told her she had a good heart, that he loved her. That all would be just as it was, but Jacks knew that would never be. She hadn't gone through with the blackmail, but she had seduced him to that end, and that was something that might be forgiven, but never forgotten. This was the last time she would share an intimate moment with this man, this man she'd known for fifteen years and who had become her dear friend. He was a casualty in all of this, along with the piece of her she would never, ever be able to get back.

FIFTY-TWO

MAKING PLANS

Cbow: TF?

Totallyfkd: Here. What up?

Cbow: It's Friday. Duh.

Totallyfkd: Shit!

Cbow: I know.

Totallyfkd: What's the plan?

Cbow: He's meeting me at the end of the service driveway at eight. That's
      less than three hours from now.

Totallyfkd: Service driveway? How rich are you?

Cbow: You don't want to know. As if it mattered anyway.

Totallyfkd: True. So three hours! Are you freaking?

Cbow: Totally.

Totallyfkd: Where will you go?

Cbow: His house.

Totallyfkd: Parents out?

Cbow: Yep. Mine, too.

Totallyfkd: Weren't you supposed to do something with them?

Cbow: I'm just not going to go. I'll use the accident if I have to, make a scene. Whatever. I'm just not going and they can't make me. My dad will back me up.

Totallyfkd: Good old pop.

Cbow: Yeah.

Totallyfkd: So . . . can I be a bitch again and ask if you're sure?

Cbow: No. I'm going. I know you want to help, but my guy isn't your guy. Does that sound harsh? I'm sorry if it does, but my guy's been really sweet.

Totallyfkd: OK.

Cbow: OK? That's it? No lecture?

Totallyfkd: Nope. The thing is, I knew in my gut that it wasn't right. I just knew. DH might be different. Sounds like he's into you.

Cbow: Fuck you, now I am confused!

Totallyfkd: Why?

Cbow: What is a boyfriend anyway? I think I had one last year, but it was so lame. It never made me feel like this. Not once, even when we were doing shit. I don't want to lie and say my new guy is like sending me flowers and calling every day, and sometimes he still walks past me. He did it today, but then he turned and smiled.

Totallyfkd: God, cbow, I know what you're feeling. You're describing me a few months ago. And now he's chasing after some girl for some social climbing bullshit. He has no soul, and I swear to you, if he knocked on my door, I'd probably let him in.

Cbow: Don't say that! After what he did! I don't believe you. You're going to college. Get over this prick! I command you . . .

Totallyfkd: Easy to say, harder to do. It's unbelievable. His parents want to get into some fucking country club to save their reputation. Everyone thinks they're secretly broke so this prick is all over their daughter.

Cbow: You think his parents told him to do it?

Totallyfkd: No. I think he just knows. Like some slimy little scavenger.

Cbow: A slimy scavenger you would open your door for?

Totallyfkd: Pathetic. I suck. So do you need any advice? Are you "prepared"?

Cbow: He said he would be, or at least he hinted. How could he not? Duh.

Totallyfkd: Well, believe me—it happens. Make sure. Write first thing when you get home. Please. I'll be waiting.

Cbow: I'll try. Hey, it just started to snow. Are you freezing your ass off like me?

Totallyfkd: Gotta go—late! Promise you'll write first thing.

Cbow: Promise.

Totallyfkd: OK. Good luck. XO.

Cbow: Thanks. Good bye. XO.

FIFTY-THREE

FINDING DAVID

SHE SAW HIS CAR as she pulled up the drive. It was parked at an angle just at the back walkway, its front end turned sharply toward the house as though he'd considered driving right up the steps and through the door, and this brought an unexpected surge of relief. He was back, living with her in this crisis. The trance or spell or whatever it was he'd been in these past weeks must be over. The deliveryman must have shocked it right out of him.

Parking behind his car, she reached for her purse and set it on her lap. One after the other, she removed the traces of her affair that she had collected to use against Barlow. She wouldn't think of that now. The receipts, the photos. She didn't look at them as she placed them carefully into the plastic bag from the morning paper. It was over, and she wanted to erase it, all of it. She felt the exhaustion deep in her bones, replacing the anxious waiting and wondering about what she would do, what would happen. She still didn't have the answers, but the devil had shown himself and now she could fight him out in the open, in the daylight.

She tied a knot at the top of the bag, then stepped out of the car. Her movements were sluggish as she closed the door and walked with a steady pace to the garage, where she tossed the plastic bag containing her crimes into the trash. A smile came across her face when she saw Chester waiting patiently for her at the foot of the door that led to the house.

"Ches!" she called, and he came to her and let her pet him. She bent down and rubbed his ears, checking him head to toe. Except for the missing collar, he was perfect.

"Come on," she said, leading the way to the door. She pushed it open and Chester ran inside to his bowl of food that Jacks had put out earlier that morning, before that ring at her front door. Before this day had washed over her.

She set her purse on the counter, then her keys. She stopped and took in the silence. With her mind so burdened with all that had happened and all that still lay ahead, she had forgotten what she had expected to find when she walked into the house. David.

She called his name, but there was no answer. Just the panting from the dog, the ticking from the clock that hung on the wall. She called out again.

Sweeping away everything in her thoughts but the relevant facts, she walked herself through her husband's day. He'd left that morning with that vacant expression, coffee mug in one hand, briefcase in the other. He'd kissed the girls, said good-bye, though she had ignored him because her tolerance for his denial had been depleted days before. She'd watched the car roll down the driveway, and that was the last she'd seen of him.

Fast-forward to the man in her house, sitting on her sofa with his implied threats and eerily pleasant smile. He'd called David, and Jacks had heard her husband's voice yelling through from miles away. David had snapped back, there was no question. The anger, the fear—she had heard it even though she had not been able to make out his words. There had been hushed instructions given, along with the orders to come home, and now here he was, home somewhere in this house, but it was quiet and seemingly empty. She'd left the note, told him not to worry. Still, would he not be waiting anxiously for her return? Would he not have tried to call her cell? What human being could really sit and wait when the things he loved most in this world were in danger?

"Chester, come," she said, fully alert now, back on the rush. She patted the side of her leg and the dog obeyed, walking with her slowly through each room.

"David?" she called out, and suddenly she knew. It was happening all over again.

Bounding up the stairs, the dog at her side, she didn't bother to check his study or the bedroom. She didn't stop until she was at the bathroom door.

"David!" she screamed as she pushed through it. But David wasn't there and she was strangely relieved. Catching her breath, she noticed the briefcase and the signed deed that lay on the very top of the papers inside. She lifted it up and studied the signature, the date. Then she reached inside the briefcase, finding a stack of bearer bonds and other bank documents that he had signed on behalf of his firm. He had done all of it, everything they had instructed him to do. And he had come home to save them.

She heard the wind slam against the window and her eyes turned to it by reflex. Through the window she saw the woodshed in the yard, the one with the broken door hinge that always got pulled open on days like this, when the wind barreled across the lawn. But today its broken door somehow remained closed.

Dropping the papers on the floor, she ran out of the room, down the stairs, and through the back of the house. She ran to the garage and out the open door, then around to the backyard through the snow until she reached the shed.

"David!" Her voice was more urgent now as she laid her hands against the rough wood door and pushed hard. She grabbed the handle and turned it up, then down, not remembering which way opened it. It didn't budge.

"David!" Her voice echoed across the yard and into the brisk, blue sky.

She pushed again and again until the obstruction gave way, a piece of wood that had been jammed into the handle from the inside. Stumbling into the room, she braced herself for what she would find, pulling from her memory the images of her father, and of David that day in their bathroom. But nothing could have prepared her for the way she found him now.

"Oh, God!" she screamed, kneeling at his side. Her hands were shaking as she stared at the rifle. Still, she managed to reach in and pry it from his hands.

"David?" she said, softer this time. His eyes were blank as they stared back at her. The switch had been turned off and he was gone.

Not knowing if the rifle was loaded, she held it by the barrel and placed it on the floor, out of reach.

Watching him, alive but so close to being dead, everything she had thought in her darkest hours, the things she had imagined that he had done, the mistakes he'd made and the risks he'd taken that she had wanted to believe were not true—none of it mattered anymore. An innocent man would not have come home with his life's possessions in a case. An innocent man would not have placed a gun in his hands. Looking at him as he sat there, exactly as he had been weeks before, she felt no urge to crawl inside his world and hold him. What had that done anyway? Nothing had changed.

She sat beside him, but did not touch him as her face streamed with tears. "It's over, David. If you can even hear me, it's over." She spoke without looking at his face.

"Listen to me now. I have taken care of everything. A very generous investor has stepped forward. Your debts are paid, the hotel is off your hands."

She looked at him then for a sign of recognition.

"David? Are you hearing me? It's over." She wiped her face with her jacket sleeve and pulled in the tears. "We will be indebted for the rest of our lives, and if it takes that long, we will find a way to repay this man. But for now, it's over. Our house, our life here. Everything is going to be all right." With the fear subsiding, her voice was now laced with anger, because that was how she felt. Throughout her childhood, her entire life, she had been forced to swallow it down. It seemed inhuman to hold anger for a sick man, and her father had been sick. Still, things had been done, to her and her sister, that were unforgivable and she could not forgive. Somehow the anger had not come, not until this very moment, and she felt it like an enormous wave that had been slowly building for decades and had finally made its way to shore.

Jacks studied her husband. He was sick, just like her father, maybe different, but still the same. She knew this. *God*, how she knew this. But what she had not realized was how contagious his sickness had been. Looking within herself, she could see the infection, the deadness that had begun to take hold of her. It was in her soul because she had let it in. She had taken it on as her own, the way her sister had done for their father. She saw in herself what she had always seen in Kelly and it left her in a state of quiet devastation.

David began to weep. He had heard what she'd said, and now maybe he was coming back to reality, to relief that it was over, or perhaps the fear at knowing what he had come so close to doing to himself in this dark place.

She took one short moment before reaching for him. "It will be all right now, David."

He looked up, his face strewn with tears, his mouth gaping. All of this left her cold. She handed him a towel and gave him a moment to dry his face and pull himself together. Then she spoke to him one last time before taking his arm and pulling him to his feet.

"You need to get up, get dressed. We have to be somewhere."

FIFTY-FOUR

DEAFENING INDIFFERENCE

ROSALYN WAS DRESSED TO the nines when Barlow walked in the door. He could smell the perfume, the fine cosmetics, the hair spray. They were subtle, always so subtle, the way the expensive products tended to be, but he knew them like he knew the smell of his own skin, and smelling them had always made him feel he was home. Tonight, he felt like a stranger.

He heard the clicking of the keyboard. She was at the computer, where she had been every second of every day as this damned assembly barreled toward them. Now it was here and she was still more concerned with her precious plans than the myriad catastrophes that filled every corner of this house.

"Still working?" he asked as he poured a glass of scotch.

"Having a drink?" Rosalyn retorted.

Barlow didn't answer. Instead, he asked a question.

"Where is Cait?"

Rosalyn tried to swallow but her throat was dry. "She's upstairs."

"She's not coming?"

"No."

Barlow smiled to himself with amusement. After all the work, the schmoozing and planning and manipulating to make this sex-speaker assembly grander than the damned Oscars, and Cait had won the battle after all.

"What happened? I thought you were going to make her come?" He couldn't help but rub it in her face. Just one time. Just a little.

But Rosalyn was unfazed. "She doesn't want to come. She asked very nicely, the first nice thing she's said to me in months. After the accident and everything . . . just let it go."

Christ, there was so much he wanted to say right now, ways he could needle her. She had lost the battle, why couldn't she just admit it? Instead, she was acting as though she could care less, as though not dragging Cait there had all been part of her plan. After the day he'd had, he felt entitled to a little satisfaction, but denying him satisfaction was what his wife seemed to be best at. *Fuck*. He poured another drink.

"What time?" he asked, relenting.

"I'd like to leave the house in fifteen minutes." She was still typing as she spoke.

"And we're leaving Cait here, by herself?"

Rosalyn typed and typed, then lifted her hands when the printer clicked on. "Marta's here."

"Marta?" he looked at her, incredulous. "She did a fantastic job last time, didn't she?"

Rosalyn turned to face him. "That's hardly fair. No one could have stopped Cait that night."

"We'll never know, will we?"

It was a low blow, even for Barlow. Even in the face of his wife's maddening, deafening indifference to the reality that surrounded them. She had planned the trip to West Palm Beach, but he had gone willingly and had been, if he was remembering correctly through the blissful buzz of the alcohol, shamelessly flirting with Sara Livingston the moment his daughter took out two deer and one Corvette, nearly killing herself.

Rosalyn ignored the barb. Instead, she turned her head and watched the letter as it emerged from the printer. Then she signed it and placed it out on the counter next to her desk.

"What's that?" Barlow asked, picking up the sheet of stationery.

"A letter."

"A letter? You're writing a letter now?"

"Yes."

Barlow scanned the contents. "You amaze me," he said. It wasn't a compliment.

"Fifteen minutes," Rosalyn said as she waited for him to return the letter to the counter.

Barlow looked at his wife. The back of her head, that gorgeous blond hair. The drop-dead burgundy dress, black boots that hugged her calves. He wanted to hold her, kill her, fuck her, something. Just standing there watching her was driving him out of his skin.

He closed his eyes, blocking out the sight of her. Then he left her to her work.

FIFTY-FIVE

NO WAY TO SAVE A MARRIAGE

SARA KISSED ANNIE ONE last time before heading to her room to change. The poor thing was almost asleep by six, having skipped her nap and run around outside for most of the afternoon.

"I stay?" Nanna asked, but Sara shook her head. They'd had a great afternoon together, Sara and her daughter, even with Ernest Barlow's kiss playing in her mind.

"She'll fall asleep. Let her snuggle with her blanket. There's some laundry if you don't mind."

Nanna shrugged, clearly disapproving, but she obeyed.

Nick was just coming out of the shower. "When do we have to leave?" he asked from behind the door. His voice drifted out with the steam and the smell of his soap.

Sara sat on the bed, just watching, smelling him. And thinking. "We have a few minutes. I'm not even dressed yet."

Popping his head out, Nick was smiling and drying his hair with a towel. "Are we going to have a fashion crisis?"

Sara tried to join him in his laughter, but she couldn't. She couldn't laugh or smile or do anything at the moment because she had kissed another man, felt attracted to another man, and keeping it quiet was no way to save a marriage. "Nick," she said, catching him before he disappeared again.

"Yeah?"

Sara patted the space next to her on the bed. "Come here a sec."

She could tell by his face that he was considering a come-on of some kind, but her mood trumped his. He walked out slowly, almost afraid to join her.

"What? What is it?"

Sara looked at her bare toes as she dug them into the carpet. How could she do this? He had been wonderful that afternoon, accepting Barlow's "gift," not threatened or intimidated. He'd let her manage the finances, trusted her when she told him it would work out. He'd done all that and for weeks said nothing about the baby he so desperately wanted.

"I have to tell you something."

"Okay." Now he was nervous, but she still couldn't look at him.

"Okay. Here goes." She felt him sit down beside her, put his arm around her. He had no idea what was coming.

"When Barlow was here this afternoon, when he brought Frank and everything, I was a little emotional. I guess I didn't realize how much all of this has gotten to me."

She stopped for a moment to give him a chance to respond, but he was quiet. Still, she felt his arm drop from her shoulders to the side of the bed.

"I started to cry and Barlow was comforting me. Oh, shit." She got up then, standing firmly before him, and said it, just said it. "He kissed me, Nick, and I let him. Right there in our mudroom, with Annie upstairs and the workers here. He kissed me. And I let him."

She exhaled, letting out a day's worth of guilt and fear and sadness. Then she looked at her husband, who was staring at her with an intensity she had never seen before.

"What?" he asked. "What are you telling me?"

"I don't know. . . ."

"That you love Ernest Barlow? That you're leaving me?"

Sara reached out for his hand, but he moved away quickly, to the other side of the room. "No, no—"

"Has this happened before, in Florida? God, why didn't I see it? You two were so friendly—"

"Nick!" Sara shouted at him to stop his runaway thoughts. "Listen to me! I don't love Barlow. I love you. That's why I'm telling you what happened. Can't you see that? That's why I'm telling you!"

Nick ran his hand across his face, pulling at his skin as though he might somehow erase the past three minutes. He heard what she was saying. She loved him, not Barlow. The old son of a bitch kissed his wife in a moment of vulnerability, and she was so miserable with the life he'd tried to give her that she'd let him, maybe kissed him back, though she wasn't fessing up to that. Not yet. Maybe that was coming. Still, it was about so much more than this one kiss. In her confession, he heard everything they had been avoiding for months.

"Why is this happening to us? Is this because of Wilshire? Is it because I want another baby?"

Sara shook her head as the tears came down. "I don't know. I wish I knew. I've been telling you for months that something is wrong."

"So it's my fault? I haven't been listening?"

"No. I didn't say that."

He was pacing now, his face red with anguish, and Sara was powerless to help him. She didn't know how to stop any of this. "We knew this might happen, didn't we?" he said, standing still to look at her.

"What are you talking about?"

"The day we decided what to do about Annie. We hardly knew each other, but we decided anyway because we thought we could do it. Maybe we were wrong."

Sara walked to where he was standing, but she didn't reach for him, didn't dare touch him for fear he might ignite. "No. It's not about Annie. We did the right thing."

But Nick was shaking his head, lost now in the memory of their past. "I loved you so much, so fast. And there you were, coming into my life as a package. You and Annie, already three months along. There was no choice for me. It didn't matter whose child she was. I wanted you, I wanted her. Maybe this is my punishment for wanting more."

Sara buried her head in her hands. How could he think such a thing? How could he think wanting to have a child with her was so wrong? She had never thought for a second that he would love her daughter more if she had been his. Not for one second. In her mind, he was as much Annie's father as any man could ever be.

She let out a long sigh, then took his face in her hands, drawing his eyes back to hers. "This is not about Annie. Don't ever say that again. I loved you that first night we met, and I never expected you to want me with another man's child. But you did, and you have loved her with your whole heart and soul. This is not about her. It's about me."

"Then I don't understand. Not even a little."

"Oh, shit. I don't understand it either. Please, just believe that I love you."

Nick was shaking his head, studying her face, and she could see that he couldn't believe anything right now.

A voice came from downstairs. It was Nanna. "Miss Sara! You be late!"

Sara looked at the clock on the wall. It was half past seven. Nanna was right. "We have to go," she said. Then she yelled down the stairs, "We're coming!"

"We're going to go? Now, in the middle of all this?" Nick asked.

But Sara looked at him and said, simply, "It's Rosalyn Barlow." And though she could tell he wanted to say *Fuck it, fuck the Barlows!* he never would.

"How can we go? How can I look at Barlow?"

"I don't know. But somehow, you will, won't you?"

Yes, he would. They both knew it. He was attached to this life, the one he'd had as a child but not quite. Not fully. The roots were planted, with their marriage and Annie, his job and this house. He wanted it, all of it. And Sara, in spite of her deep ambivalence, would never bring herself to burn it to the ground.

She reached out and touched his face.

"I'll get dressed."

FIFTY-SIX

THE PSYCHOLOGY OF
SELF-DESTRUCTION

THE LIGHTS WERE DIMMED in the auditorium of the Wilshire Academy as Marcia Preston stepped up to the podium. Seated in the third row, Rosalyn caught a glimpse of her husband still standing in the aisle, apparently not wanting to be near her. She had saved a seat for him, and his childish defiance was not amusing her in the least. But nothing could be done about that. Not now anyway.

"Thank you all for coming," Ms. Preston said, drawing down the chatter that had transferred from the atrium.

Standing on the stage in her customary black, flat shoes and glasses, she seemed almost giddy that the parent body was taking such an interest.

"We are all aware of the issues that brought us here tonight. It's in the news, it's on the Internet. It's in our homes. Like it or not, our children are increasingly exposed to sexual content in their music and films, and of course through millions of Web sites."

Blah, blah, blah. Rosalyn was tuned out. It was the same watered-down bullshit they got every day, and she braced herself for the hourlong speech that was approaching as the crowd applauded and Dr. Wright took to the podium. But that was soon to change.

"Thank you. It's very nice to be here." Dr. Wright was beaming. She was an attractive woman, just into her fifties and sensual in her demeanor. With long auburn hair flowing, and her suit jacket showing just a hint of cleavage, she had instantly captured the interest of the audience. "I must say," she continued, "I'm looking out at all of you and it's so clear to me that you are probably the most educated and sophisticated crowd I've been fortunate enough to address. So how about this? Why don't we skip the part where I tell you what you already know. Teenagers have sex. Been happening since the beginning of time, I imagine. Is there anyone here who feels incapable or unwilling to talk to their kids about birth control and STDs? Condoms, pills, over-the-counter Plan B?"

Rosalyn felt her face blush as she glanced casually from side to side, unsure whether to smile and laugh, or be insulted. Thankfully, not one person was looking at her for a reaction. They were all captivated now by the commanding tone that resonated from the doctor. And not a hand was raised.

"Okay," Dr. Wright continued. "Is there anyone here tonight who feels incapable or unwilling to talk to their kids about their family's values and expectations about sex? About gaining consent, giving consent, respecting other human beings?"

Again, not a hand.

"Pretty simple stuff, right? Not fun, maybe, but simple. Straightforward."

She nodded, then flipped over half of the pages that she'd laid before her on the podium.

"Let's talk then about something else. I want to talk about what drives a kid to do something that makes her—or him—feel bad inside. And I think we all agree that some of the casual sex, the sex happening between two kids who don't even like, or know, each other probably makes that kid feel bad. Maybe not in the moment, but soon after. And maybe they need to have a drink to feel better, or smoke a joint, pop a pill. But then that doesn't really work either, does it, because it's bad for you, gets you in trouble. Makes you feel deviant. It's a cycle. What I'm talking about is sex and the psychology of self-destruction. What I'm talking about is an entire generation that may become so damaged that they will never know what real love is, what real physical love is. Imagine that. An entire generation that will never know self-respect, and the bliss of making love."

Rosalyn stared at Dr. Wright. She hadn't mentioned any of this, not one word, during their multitude of e-mail exchanges, or at the lunch meeting the day before. But even as she was taken aback by the bait and switch that was taking place before her eyes, she was mesmerized as the doctor spoke of low self-esteem. How it was the seed that, when planted, was like a weed, fighting for room to grow and multiply. Her voice was firm, passionate. Verging, even, on anger.

"Ever heard of the expression that history repeats itself? Want to know why? It seems antithetical, but once a child grows accustomed to a feeling, even a bad feeling, *that* becomes the feeling that the child seeks again and again because it's familiar, and familiar is what we all crave, isn't it? We like to sleep in the same bed, with the same pillow—maybe even with the same person beside us—" She paused then for a burst of laughter. "We want the chef to make our dinner the same way every time we order it. Feelings have the same hold on us. That's why I have a job."

The questions kept coming, rhetorical questions that were shocking just the same. *Do you think your daughter really believed he would call? The guy who treated her like dirt at school and made out with another girl five minutes earlier at the party? Ever wonder what it was she wanted from him?*

Rosalyn listened to them, these questions and answers—so obvious but evasive at the same time. *What does Cait want with Kyle Conrad?* The same thing Rosalyn had wanted from Jeb Ashton twenty-five years before? She closed her eyes for a second to chase it away, but it was there, the feeling she would get with him and the things she would do. It wasn't until Paris, until she felt what love was, that she understood the difference, and still, she had returned. Damn her mother. She could hear the words, the lecture over the phone. *You have to end things and come home. What are you going to do, throw away a boy like Jeb, a boy who has everything?* She had obeyed, and when she returned there had been a penance to pay, one she would never forget.

What had he told her that night in his basement? Through the musty smell that came from the old couch, the dampness in the air—what was it? That she owed it to him. Everyone was talking about how he'd been humiliated the summer before his senior year. The feelings she'd had for him, the way she had coveted him so desperately, had all turned to hatred the moment she returned from Paris, but still, that night, she had a job to do and she'd done it well. To this day, Jeb Ashton believed he'd been her first, and his stupidity was the only thing about that night that she could tolerate remembering.

Ever wonder what your daughter wants from a boy like that? What had she wanted? To please her mother? Rosalyn fought to remember as she sat there with everything in the world, and yet this one night, this stupid teenage night that was decades old still gripped her insides like it had just happened.

. What had she wanted? She thought then about Barlow and his confession on the plane. How he never loved her, how she was his token rich girl with blond hair and good breeding. She had felt love for him, hadn't she? She'd told herself Barlow was her second chance to escape, but how had she not seen his burning need to conquer Wilshire? Had her entire life been about repeating history? Finding ways to feel as bad about herself as she did every time her mother looked at her? Was everything she had ever done part of this formula that was now being laid out by Dr. Wright—this deadly cocktail of childhood dysfunction and low self-esteem?

She felt a tear roll down her face and it shocked her back from the past. She could not afford this self-indulgence. Not in front of all these people. Not with Barlow watching her. This was not about her.

With the slightest movement, she brushed a strand of hair from her face, and with it the tear that had found its way out. Then she tilted her head in a subtle, curious way. She would sit there for the hour, remember to smile at the comic breaks that would surely come because that was the rough-and-tumble tone the doctor had chosen. She would do all of that. But that was all. She would not, could not, continue to listen. The night was far from over.

She discreetly pulled her BlackBerry from her coat pocket and read the screen. Then she caught Eva's attention. Eva nodded, her expression solemn, and it settled Rosalyn's nerves as she leaned back against her seat. After a few moments, Eva whispered something to her husband, then excused herself and headed for the door.

FIFTY-SEVEN

THE LETTER

CAIT RUSHED DOWN THE stairs. She'd spent close to an hour getting ready. The shower, shaving, plucking, blow-drying and curling. Then the body spray, the choosing of clothing, the dressing and makeup. Her hands hadn't stopped shaking.

Marta was upstairs with the little ones. Her parents were gone. She carried her shoes in her hands so she wouldn't make a sound.

There was only one way out that would be silent and dark, and that was through the kitchen. If she went anywhere near the backyard, the floodlights would come on. In the front, the dog would bark.

She walked across the marble floor, past the island with the stools, the massive black cooktop and refrigerator drawers. She reached the back end where her mother kept her computer and desk. The mudroom was just beyond it and she needed a coat. She was almost past it when she saw a paper on the ground.

Looking back first to make sure she was still alone, she picked it up and began to place it back on her mother's desk. But then she saw the name on the letter.

Dear George and Betsy,

It was so nice to see you in Florida. Hope you are continuing to enjoy the warm weather. We're freezing up north!

I'm writing about the consideration of the Conrad family for membership. As you know, I am in favor of supporting the Livingstons, who are a lovely couple. I have been informed that the committee is leaning towards the Conrads, but I would like to discuss the matter upon your return next week for your granddaughter's christening. I still have my concerns, as you know. Call at your convenience.

Yours truly,
Rosalyn Barlow

Cait read it again until she realized why it had captured her interest. As she set it down on the desk, the pieces fell like dominoes. *TF. The Bear. The guy who screwed her then never called. The guy from the junior class. And now that guy was hitting on a girl who belonged to a club—the club his parents wanted to belong to because they were losing ground in Wilshire.*

She wanted to scream. How could this be? She fought to deny it, to deny the evidence, but it was all there in front of her. She saw the headlights through the trees. They were not moving; the car was parked at the edge of her property.

She had been consumed by a torturous wanting whose antidote was waiting for her in that car, and now the choice was no longer a hazy pool of maybe's. *Maybe he likes me. Maybe this will be it, the one thing that will make him mine.* She knew the answer now. It was undeniable. She meant nothing. And still the wanting remained.

Moving even faster than before, Cait grabbed her coat and headed outside.

FIFTY-EIGHT

THE HALSTEADS

JACKS SET HER KEYS down on the counter. The house was still.

"Are the girls asleep?" she asked the nanny, who was ready to leave for her weekend. It was her time off and she had already stayed later than she'd wanted to.

"They're quiet. Sleeping? I couldn't say."

Jacks nodded and said good-bye. As the woman's car receded down the driveway, Jacks locked the door, turned out the lights.

"Are you coming up?" David's voice startled her.

"God," she said. "Don't do that. Not tonight."

Standing on the other side of the darkened room, she could barely make out the shape of his face. He'd taken off his jacket, loosened his tie, and was now leaning casually against the doorframe as if they had just come home from a fabulous dinner party, or a play in the city. But the night's events had been far from any of that.

"Are you coming up?" he asked again, and she could tell by the tone of his voice that he had returned from that other place, not completely, but as much as he could. She stared at his body, let his voice settle inside her, this man she'd lived with for seventeen years. The man she'd loved, and still did after everything. Beside him, she could see the phone that she'd answered that day after Thanksgiving. Beyond him, she could see the hallway and the foyer, the front door where the intruder had entered. And yet, turning her eyes back to him, hearing his voice, she could almost believe that none of this had really happened.

She smiled and walked to where he stood. "I'm tired," she said. Then she walked past him toward the stairs and he followed, silently. On the second floor, she let him pass and retreat to the bedroom. He looked back at her for a brief moment, but she waved him on. She needed to see her children. Opening the door to Beth's room, Jacks found her sleeping, her little body all curled up beneath an overstuffed quilt. She walked to the bed and pressed her face against her daughter's, letting the warm breath touch her skin, and it felt like life itself, pure and untouched. There had been so much talk about undoing damage, damage that had been done to children unknowingly, innocently, by the most loving but ignorant parents. It had gone on for nearly two hours, the lecture then questions and answers, this talk about degradation and self-destruction, the corruption of young bodies, young souls.

She kissed Beth, then left her with her sweet dreams. She went next to Andrea's room. Her middle child was growing up so fast that she now appeared more like Hailey, a teenager, than a little girl. Still, she was just a child, and Jacks kissed her and tucked her in like a child, then moved on down the hall. Hailey's light was on, so Jacks knocked softly on the outside of the door.

"Yeah?" was the response. Her teenager was on the computer and not in the mood for distractions. Jacks walked in anyway and sat on the edge of her bed.

"What's up?" her daughter asked, turning her head for a brief second, then back again. "What's wrong with you?" she asked.

Jacks seemed surprised, then realized she'd been crying. She wiped her face and smiled. "Nothing. Don't worry about it."

"What! What did they fill your mind with at that assembly?"

"Nothing, really."

Hailey seemed angry. "Mom, I'm *fine*! Are you gonna cut back my curfew? Just tell me. What did they tell you to do?"

Jacks got up from the bed and stood beside her daughter. Then she leaned down and took her child's face in her hands, meeting her eyes. It was, she knew, one of the worst things a mother could do to her daughter, so she made it quick.

"I love you, you know that, don't you?"

Hailey looked away, squirming out of her mother's embrace. "Okay, yeah," she said, and Jacks didn't make her give more. Instead, she kissed the top of her head and left her to her life.

In the hall outside, she took a moment to feel it. They were okay. These children were, somehow, still okay. She placed a hand across her chest as she walked to her room. David was waiting, still dressed and sitting on the bed, his head hanging low. He looked up when he heard her come in and shut the door. His face was anguished.

"Will you ever tell me?" he asked, and Jacks knew exactly what he meant. She had no more doubts about what was real or not real. And the reasons she had been unable to see this before no longer mattered, though she would remember them always. Her husband was sick. He'd been sick for years though she had no diagnosis, no name for the affliction that had spun him out of control, distracted him and made him careless, reckless with their lives. But that was not her job, to find the answers, to cure him. He needed help, and she would stand by him through it because losing the hope that he would return to her was not an option.

Would she ever tell him? No, she never would. What she had done to save their family was something she would carry alone and forever and it would exact a heavy toll. She would always wonder what might have happened if she'd confronted him the day she found that first letter. What had she been so afraid of? Facing the fact that he was ill, or that they might lose this life that they had come to covet? Or maybe the realization that everything she had become over the past seventeen years, the highly skilled professional wife and mother, only held value in the world if she was attached to a man. And so she had turned to Barlow as the only means of escape. She had held on to her conviction that everything, anything she did to save them was justified. But that was a lie. Now she had one job, and this time she knew her motives were pure. History would end here, in this room, tonight.

She looked at David, her mind swimming in all that had to be done. There was still a mess to be straightened out at the firm, with the investors. And David needed to get well. It would take most of the night to convince him of that. So she started with one word, an answer to his question.

Looking at him from the doorway, she shook her head.

"No," she said. And he never asked her again.

FIFTY-NINE

CAITLIN

EVA FOUND HER EXACTLY where Rosalyn said she'd be. Shivering from the cold because her skirt was too short and she had no hat or gloves, Caitlin looked right past Eva's car. *Teenagers*, Eva thought to herself as she parked.

The air was biting cold, whipping across the Starbucks patio like a swarm of ice pellets. The things she did for her friends. First Jacks, then Barlow. There was still the matter of poor Sara Livingston—she would handle that somehow, and in some way that would shield the truth. Rosalyn didn't need to know *everything*. Now this . . .

Sighing with dismay at what the world was coming to, Eva got out of the car and walked to the bench where Caitlin was huddled. Eva knew the sight of her would at first shock the girl then piss her off when she realized this could not be a coincidence.

"Don't say it," Eva announced before Cait had even looked up.

Cait stood, her hands dropped from her pockets and her face in a state of shock. She started to speak, but Eva held her hand to her mouth. "Don't say it. I know."

After the shock came anger, and Eva knew she'd have to let Cait say something now. Still, it was too damned cold.

"Can we get in the car first?"

Cait huffed as she followed Eva to the car. Eva had taken the Porsche because it would be harder for Cait to hate her in a Porsche, and because the seats were heated.

"Okay," Eva said, closing her door and turning on the ignition. "*Now* you may speak."

But Cait didn't speak. She just started to cry.

"Oh, shit. Here we go." Eva handed her a tissue from her purse, then placed a hand on Cait's shoulder.

"Are you okay?" she asked.

Cait nodded. She was okay. Cold, but okay.

"I hate her," she said when the tears subsided.

Eva nodded. "I know."

"How did she know I'd be here?" The question was straightforward, but they both knew that Cait's worries went much deeper.

Eva groaned. It wasn't her place to give Rosalyn's teen-spying techniques away, but Cait was on to her now.

"Your iPhone has a GPS tracker."

Cait shook her head. "Oh my God. How long?"

Eva could see her trying to remember everything she'd done, every place she'd gone without telling her mother.

"Your mother can be a real pain in the ass when she wants to be. But now, that she's spoiled everything, can I drive you home?"

"No."

"I wasn't really asking."

The tears started again. "I hate her. I'll hate her for the rest of my life!"

Eva put the car in reverse, then turned on the seat warmers. "I know. But in a few seconds your butt's gonna be really warm. That's something, right?"

Cait wasn't amused, but it hadn't really been for Cait. Someday, if she was lucky, Cait would have a life where she could find pleasure in something so small. When all of this angst and pain would be gone and life would roll along the way it was meant to—not with trauma and crises and the continuous loop of drama that played like a top-forty hit, over and over until it was stuck in your head. If she was lucky, and Eva believed she was, she would fall into bed with her best friend and whisper that her butt had been nice and warm in the car. And that it had been a good day.

SIXTY

THE LIVINGSTONS

It was there, though neither of them knew how to face it. Through the assembly, the casual chatter that followed, the drive home. Through saying good night to Nanna, discussing the schedule for the next week, locking up, hanging keys and coats. Through the climb up the stairs to Annie's room, where they took turns saying good night, kissing her and tucking her in though she hardly needed it after Nanna's close supervision.

It was there, right where they'd left it hours before, sitting in their bedroom waiting for one of them to acknowledge it. At the very least, it was screaming out for that.

Nick hesitated at the door, looking at his wife. But she turned away and he shook his head and carried on toward his closet on the other side of the room.

It had been building inside her all night, listening to Dr. Wright talk about mistakes that could change a life forever. Yes, the hallway blow jobs were red flags that something was wrong, but they were also, in and of themselves, events that would live on—transgressions against one's own self that would remain like little scars. She had thought then not of Caitlin Barlow, but of her own little scars and how they had resulted in that little girl who was asleep in the next room. *God*, how she loved Annie, but it was not what she had planned for her life. And the truth was, had it not been for Annie, Nick Livingston would have left that bar alone four years ago.

She went to her closet and began to undress. It felt evil to think what she was now thinking—had she used him? Was that why she resented this life so much, this wonderful fairy-tale life? There was no doubt in her mind that she would have found another man like the one who'd left her alone and pregnant in the rain. Then another, and another. Annie was a godsend that way, changing her insides so she would want a man that could love her, really love her the way Nick did. Still, she had not asked to be changed that way. It had all been the result of a mistake, a misstep, and knowing this left her floating in a whirlwind of chaos. What was left to hold on to if you didn't even know your own mind?

She stopped undressing and walked across the room. Nick was hanging up his jacket. His back was to her and as she waited for him to turn around, she chased from her thoughts everything but this moment, this man, this feeling. When he finally saw her in front of him, searching his face for answers, he knew he couldn't give them to her. He only knew what he felt.

"I love you," he said.

Sara walked to him and slid her arms around his waist.

"I know," she said. "I love you back." It was the truth. It was what she was feeling, and yet there was so much else. It had been so easy to stop loving him, those little hiccups when she saw his eyes light up at the Barlows' estate, on that golf course in Florida. How could love survive a lifetime when it could be chased away so easily by another man simply because he made her laugh?

Still, it was here now and it was real—Nick's arms around her back, his body pressed to hers and the way the smell of him made her feel safe and good. She wanted to create a wall around it, an invisible shield that would keep it inside. How could love be something that had to be constantly recreated, reinvented? Why had no one told her?

"We can move. We can change. Whatever it takes." Nick was making promises now, and she was grateful. But she couldn't stop herself from wondering if he would stop loving her somewhere along the way if he gave up his dream just to keep her.

"We'll figure it out. Somehow, we'll figure it out."

She made this promise to her husband, and to herself. Because, at the end of a day like this one, what else was there to do?

SIXTY-ONE

———————

TOTALLYFKD

Cbow: TF?

Totallyfkd: Here. What happened? Did you make it home?

Cbow: Yeah, but it's all fucked up. My mom put a fucking tracker in my
    phone. She sent someone to get me.

Pause.

Totallyfkd: Shit! How do you know?

Cbow: She knew where I'd be. And then her friend told me.

Totallyfkd: God.

Cbow: I know.

Totallyfkd: Does she know you were at DH's house?

Cbow: Yeah. I guess. Unless his house is somehow blocked by satellite inter-
    ference.

Totallyfkd: Well, it could be worse.

Cbow: I know. If I hadn't run out of there like an idiot. I didn't even know how
    I was gonna get home.

Totallyfkd: Yeah—at least you got a ride.

Cbow: I'd rather have frozen to death.

Totallyfkd: Ugh. I hate your mother. Hate mine too. I would never do that to
  my kid.

Cbow: No shit.

Totallyfkd: And DH? Do you think he'll tell everyone you came to your
  senses and bailed?

Cbow: More like chickened out. And does it matter? If he doesn't, I'm a slut.
  If he does, then everyone will know how I chickened out. I'm such a
  loser.

Totallyfkd: It is kind of funny. I keep picturing him lying there. . . .

Cbow: Doesn't feel funny. Feels like shit.

Totallyfkd: I know. Sorry. You know how I feel about DH.

Cait sat back at her desk and read the last entry. TF had no idea how well
she knew about all of this, and Cait wanted so much to tell her—that they
shared a school, a town, a guy. They shared an entire life. But there was some
divine comfort in this anonymity and what it had allowed them to have. For
now, it was enough that they had this. A friendship.

Cbow: What do I do about my insides? Can't even get a drink til they go
  to bed.

Totallyfkd: When will that be?

Cbow: An hour I guess.

Totallyfkd: Wanna keep talking? You haven't told me every detail.

Cbow: OK. I went outside and got in his car. . . .

Barlow walked through the kitchen. He stopped to pour a drink, took the
glass from the cabinet, reached for the bottle he kept up high. As he loosened
the cap, a sound stopped him, made him turn. It was his wife, and she was
laughing.

Curious now, he put the glass down and walked toward the back of the
large room, turned the corner, and saw her at her desk. She was reading the
screen, then typing. But she wasn't laughing. She was crying.

He watched her, still undetected, thinking through all the things he was
going to say to her tonight. Over and over, he had rehearsed them in his
mind, quietly and calmly to himself. They had suffered for so long, forcing

life into something that was already dead. He had been cruel on that plane, telling her that he never loved her, that she had been nothing more to him than an admission ticket. It was weak and self-indulgent. And it wasn't entirely accurate. It was one thing to feel the truth twenty years later, in hindsight. It was quite another to believe that the feelings he'd had for her had been nothing more than calculations. Love couldn't be sorted out that easily. Especially not now, after all these years. He had wanted her, chased her, made love to her honestly and with his whole heart believing in what they had. Then he'd married her, had five children with her. They had a history together that demanded his respect, regardless of where they now stood.

He drew a breath and thought about the drink. He could have it after, when the fallout began. He would need it then, surely more than he did in this moment.

Rosalyn felt him approaching, so she typed quickly.

Totallyfkd: Cbow, gotta go. Will you be OK?

Then came the response.

Cbow: Yeah. I feel better. Maybe just go to sleep. Thanks a mil. You're a
    good friend.

Rosalyn wiped the tears from her face.

Totallyfkd: So are you. Write tomorrow. XO, TF.

She shut down the screen. Barlow pulled up a chair. She looked at him, studied him for a brief moment. And she knew.

"Are you okay? You've been crying," he said. The conflict was evident, written all over his face. *Maybe she wasn't that person he couldn't love. Maybe she was soft and vulnerable and he could hold her and feel like a man. Maybe he shouldn't say what he so wanted to say to her right now, to put an end to this long chapter in their lives.*

Rosalyn smiled. "I'm fine." And she was, without his pity or sympathy or whatever feeling her tears had always provoked in him. She couldn't spend a lifetime crying just to make her husband love her.

"I think we should talk. We haven't really, since the plane."

Rosalyn crossed her arms.

"I know what you think about Sara. About me and Sara." Barlow lowered his eyes as he spoke, forcing the words out in an awkward way. "But you're wrong. Dead wrong."

Rosalyn knew the way anyone would after so many years that he was telling the truth. And although it changed many things, in this moment it didn't matter at all.

"Stop. Just stop," she said, meeting his eyes. "We do need to talk. But not about the identity of your lover. We need to talk about what happened on the plane."

Barlow nodded several times, garnering the courage to face that night and the reconnection that had been so fleeting, and yet still do what had to be done. For him, for her. For all of them.

"I know. I've been thinking a lot about it—," he began, but Rosalyn cut him off.

"Barlow, I'm pregnant."

The words may as well have lifted him from his seat and thrown him to the ground, leaving him bleeding as she continued.

"The plane. I'm six weeks."

From that place where he lay, completely and totally decimated, he looked at her for a sign, something that would help him understand this. But all he saw was resignation.

She said nothing else, but waited, patiently, for him to climb back into that chair, sit up straight, and face what they now had to face. Together. And when she saw that he was coming around, she got up and went to the kitchen to pour him that drink, a big one, in the glass he liked with lots of cold ice and warm scotch. She walked back to her chair and placed the drink on the desk beside him. But he did not take it. He just let it sit there.

Instead, he took her hand. And within her open palm, he gently laid his head.

The lives of four wives and mothers intertwine and collide in this brilliant tale of suburban angst

On the outside, it appears as though Love Welsh, Marie Passetti, Gayle Beck, and Janie Kirk lead enviable lives—but in the wealthy suburb of Hunting Ridge, appearances mask a deeper truth. As they try to maintain a façade of bliss, behind closed doors they must reconcile their innermost desires with the lives they have chosen.

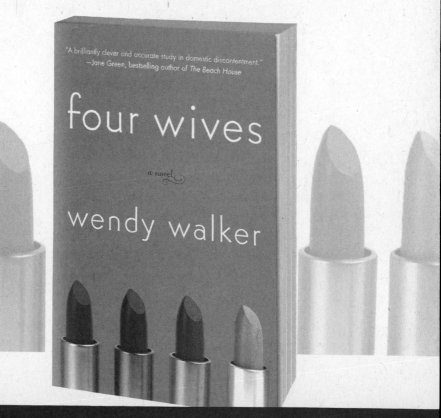

"A brilliantly clever and accurate study in domestic discontentment."
—Jane Green, bestselling author of *The Beach House*

four wives

a novel

wendy walker